Amaranth

Mandy Jo

To Lisa & Lauren,
Happy Reading
Mandy Jo

Amaranth

The Evil Witch's Daughter

Mandy Jo

mandyjo@mandyjo.us
mandyjo.live

1. Edition, 2022
ISBN # 978-1-6781-0692-8

Mandy Jo - Wixom
mandyjo@mandyjo.us

Dedication

I have a lot of people to thank:

Rick Squires, my boyfriend and my rock for being there and being supportive

Vickie Hohauser, my friend and editor

My boys, Bryan Rindhage & Bradley Suwienski

My parents, Fred & Mary Lou Rindhage, for being supportive

Aspiring Writers Association of America (AWAOA), so many friends and wonderful insights for my writing

All of my supportive friends and family

Emily–fantasynamegenerators.com for character and place names

Table of Contents

Chapter 1

Dark ominous clouds followed Evatius, the centaur, out of the forest as he galloped toward Oldirrim, the white barn owl, and Zyrsit, the miniature bright green dragon.

They sat on a boulder overlooking the grassland from outside the Rissingshire Castle. The clouds swirled around the three creatures. As the clouds cleared, Oizu, the black dragon, was standing before them.

With a deep and raspy voice he says to the three, "I have come to give you warning of things to come. The days of the Maerith Kingdom are coming to a close. Dark days are ahead." He flapped his wings and was gone, along with the dark clouds.

Oldirrim looked at Zyrsit with wide eyes and shook his head. They both sat there for a few minutes in bewilderment. Neither knew what to think or do.

Evatius broke the silence when he stomped his hoof into the log, splitting it in two and said, "These dragons are always trying to stir up trouble. There's no way the Maerith Kingdom is coming to a close. It's too big to fall."

They were quickly joined by dozens of mystical forest creatures. All the creatures, including Evatius, Oldirrim and Zyrsit were gathered in silence when the drawbridge slammed down as it opened. A white carriage sped out being led by six Pegasuses. The carriage flew into the sky above the forest and disappeared.

Zyrsit looked at Evatius and said, "Well, Amaranth is certainly in a hurry," while raising his eyebrows and smirking.

The sky grew dark as the black clouds rolled in darkening the skies over the castle, grassland and forest. A mist formed and brought thunder and lightning. The forest creatures scurried back into the trees to seek shelter. Howling through the branches, the wind kept getting stronger and faster. Soon it was encircling the castle.

Above the castle rose Odulore the wizard in his purple and gold robe. With his arms outstretched he shouted, "Alterenim Serpenerous!" Amber dust flew from his hands covering the dark clouds until they disappeared.

In the far distance you could faintly hear Crumazz, the evil wizard, threaten, "I will be back and you will be sorry." His evil laugh filled the shadows.

Odulore went back inside the castle to his study, where there were countless shelves of books of all shapes and sizes. He sat at his desk with his writing book open and quill in hand and began writing furiously.

Oldirrim flew in and sat on his desk, rotating his head back and forth while blinking his dark eyes. A short time later Ash, a brown barn owl, joined him. The two sat there quietly when Narella came prancing in and up onto the desk. Narella sat down on the book right under Odulore's nose.

"What are you doing Narella, you crazy cat?" he questioned.

She looked up at him with her bright orange eyes, rubbed the side of her head on his arm, laid down on his book and started purring as she closed her eyes. He picked her up and put Narella in her four-poster bed, adorned with a wood carved headboard with her name engraved on it.

"Now stay there while I get some work done," he said to her, and he sat back down at his desk to write.

Not even five minutes later the chandelier in the entryway started to sway back and forth before falling to the floor two stories below it. The crash startled Odulore and the owls. They all took off out of the study to the entryway. There was no one there. A broken chandelier lay on the floor along with pictures and paintings hanging in skewed positions on the wall.

Amaranth flew into the outer courtyard with the carriage and Pegasuses. "I am back!" She exclaimed.

Ash flew out to greet her and landed on the back of the first Pegasus. She walked up to him, petted him on the head and floated into the entryway, "What happened?"

He looked up at her, "I have no idea."

"Glurx! Glurx! Come here! Where is that goblin?" she yelled.

Glurx came sauntering in with his eyes fixed on the floor, "Yes?"

"You need to clean this up immediately," Amaranth told him firmly.

He proceeded to go back into the other room to get a broom. His feet slowly shuffled along at a snail's pace.

Amaranth stood there with her arms crossed and brow furrowed. With her blue eyes blazing, she turned her head to the wooden front door. Moments later there was a loud bang on it.

The dragons, Pymmut, Gairrulit, and Irreineot, flew up and circled over the castle. Pymmut, the dark green dragon, landed next to Amaranth. Putting his wing around her, he said in a deep voice, "The darkness has come to the door. If you let it in, no one is safe. If you go out to it, the castle will be safe but you will not."

She looked into his dark eyes, a tear ran down her cheek, "Why me?"

"Your mother had caused great distress throughout the Calegan Forest. She left behind a legacy which can no longer be allowed to continue. The darkness has come to take you back," he explained.

Irreineot continued for him, "You will no longer reign in Rissingshire Castle, but you will go to the Crystal Crypt. This is your destiny. You will go with Gairrulit, and he will take you there."

She looked at Irreineot, shook her head and stomped her foot, "I will not go! I belong here." She flipped her hair back and glared ahead.

"You can make that choice, but remember that your choices have consequences. The consequence for this choice will be that the darkness will come in here and take you away. It will also destroy anything or anyone that gets in it's way. So, you can choose that, but you are choosing destruction for your friends," Pymmut whispers in her ear.

Jumping away from him, she squinted her eyes, raised her hands and shouted, "Alterenim Serpenerous!" However, nothing happened for her, like it did for Odulore. She yells it again, "Alterenim Serpenerous!" Nothing happened again. Spinning around she glared at Odulore, "Why is it not working?"

He shrugged his shoulders and said, "Well, it worked for me. However, you are causing all this chaos. It must not work if you are the cause. Go with Gairrulit. See what needs to be done."

Her eyes widened and her jaw dropped, "Are you insane? They want to take me to the Crystal Crypt. I'll never get out of there. My mother went there and never returned."

The dragons took to the air once again circling overhead. The owls joined them. Soon there were other birds and winged creatures circling above the castle. Gairrulit swooped down, grabbed Amaranth with his wing and took off into the darkness.

The birds and winged creatures followed him. Oizu flew over the wall and into the castle. He landed close to Odulore, "You have done well. She will be far away and her evil will not transcend this castle."

His eyes widened and eyebrows lifted up, "I did not realize how evil she was. She was devious at times, but never truly evil."

The dragon shook his head, flapped his wings and off he went over the castle wall and left behind Odulore. The owls landed at his feet and looked up at him, and tilted their heads to the side.

He walked back to his study and sat down at his desk. This time he didn't start writing. He just sat there thinking, "How could I be so wrong? She said that her mother had left her many years ago, but never said why. I figured she didn't want to talk about it."

Oldirrim and Ash flew in and sat on his desk. Both were blinking their eyes and tilting their heads side to side in unison. Odulore looked up at them and shook his head.

"She comes from a long line of evil. There is no good to come from her. We know you love her, but you are going to have to let her go," Oldirrim told him while Ash sat there and nodded his head no and then yes.

Glurx strolled in and stood in front of his desk, "The castle will be much better without her. She was never nice to me."

Odulore nodded and grimaced. He picked up his pen and wrote down his thoughts in his notebook.

The mystical forest creatures slowly gathered in Odulore's study and out in the hall. Zyrsit flew above them and landed on his desk, an advantage of being miniature he could get through the crowd easily. Although the room was now crowded, not one spoke, but just watched him write.

Chapter 2

Amaranth sat on a wooden bench behind iron bars in the basement level of the Crystal Crypt. Crumazz came down the stairs glaring at her. With his eyes squinted and brow furrowed he asked her, “Are you ready for your destiny?”

She lifted up her head, bit her bottom lip and glared back at him. Standing up she asked him, “Do I get the whole kingdom of Maerith? Is it truly all mine?”

“You will rule with me, but only if you are truly with me,” he replied and gave her a smirk. “That means that you have to give up Odulore. You have to stay here, but, of course, in a better room. Think of what all we can do. Think of how the mystical creatures of the forest will be at your command.”

With her hands on her hips, she flung her hair back and walked up to the bars. Amaranth grabbed the bars and leaned into them, “Well, I think we can work something out.”

He unlocked the door and she pushed it open, “Show me to my room. I want to make sure this is somewhere that I approve of. At Rissingshire Castle I had a fabulous room. Plus, I had Narella. Will I have a cat? I would like a black one.”

Puggaald, the goblin, stood at the top of the stairs. “Are you going to show me my room?” Amaranth asked him.

He waited for her to get to the top of the stairs. He didn’t say a word, but reached for her hand. She pulled back, “I don’t think so. You don’t touch me, you just lead the way.”

Shaking his head, he continued walking to her room. On occasion he would trip over his own feet, as they were slightly too big and made him clumsy. When they arrived at her room, he lifted his hand and pointed into the room.

"Yes, finally a room for me. You are awfully quiet. What is up with that? Do you not speak?" She asked.

Puggaald shook his head no in response. He had been in a fight when he was younger with a wizard that took his voice away from him.

"Oh you poor thing. We'll have to see what we can do about that. Although it is nice that you can't talk back."

Crumazz walked up to her, "Well, does this suit you? Are you pleased with your room?"

"I am. I think we will get along just fine. Now, I need a black cat. I can't go without a pet and we didn't bring Narella with me."

He pointed into the room, and she turned to see what he was pointing at. A sleek black cat walked across the bed. Amaranth looked back at Crumazz, gave him a devilish smile, and went over to the cat. Petting her, she sat down on the bed, and motioned for them to go away.

Outside the crypt the dragons sat guarding the entry. Pymmut looked at Oizu, "I thought we were putting her away. I thought she was evil and this was going to get rid of her."

"Obviously we were tricked. Sounds like she is going to be ruling with Crumazz instead of being a prisoner. He certainly changed his tune quickly once she got here."

"You were inquiring about my motives?" Crumazz said to them as he walked out of the crypt.

They both sat silently and lowered their heads in shame. "I don't believe I answer to you, but that you answer to me." He pointed to them and then himself. "You don't worry about what is going on inside the Crystal Crypt, you just guard the entry. Although, I do not believe you will have to worry about Odulore coming to her rescue once I send Gairrulit back with a note telling him that she is staying and no longer wants to be with him."

He handed him the note and off he flew through the Calegan Forest. The mystical creatures watched him as he sped past them. Within minutes he reached the castle, which was being guarded by Turmodoir and Fraevie. He dropped the note by their feet and flew off back into the forest.

Back at the Crystal Crypt, Amaranth sat with her new cat, "I am going to call you Valora." She rubbed up against her, purred and meowed. "Oh, how disappointing, I was hoping that you could have a real conversation. I'd love for you to go spy on Crumazz and let me know what he's really up to. Why would he bring me here the way he did, just to get me to a nice room. He's up to something. I just don't know what yet."

Valora got down off the bed and scampered out the doorway. "Really? I hope she comes back. Plus, where is the door? No privacy in here and it's really dark," she says out loud to herself.

She looked around and found some candles to light. Although once the room was more well lit, and she could see more than just the path to and from the doorway she was a little uneasy. All around her were black books, dark bottles and pots. *I think I know where he's going with this. He wants me to do black magic for him. What happens if I don't? I bet he'll put me back in the dungeon. Although, it's not like this is a huge improvement.* She went up to the books and grabbed one, placed it on the table and began to read it. *If he expects me to do something I should probably read up on what he wants done.* She bit her lower lip again as she was reading.

Gairrulit retuned to the crypt entrance where the other dragons sat. "All delivered. I did not stick around for a return note. He can get his own dragons to do that."

"Very good, I believe I wrote a very convincing note." He turned and walked back into the crypt. As he walked past Amaranth's room he noticed she had lit some candles. He walked right in and up to where she was reading. "So, how do the books look? Does it look like something that you'll be able to help with?"

"Exactly what are you expecting me to do?"

"I expect you to create potions that will make all the mystical and grassland creatures obedient to only my demands. Next, we will be taking over Rissingshire Castle. You will get your castle back, but Odulore will not be in charge. I will be. This is the ultimate goal. Are you in or do you prefer these accommodations?"

She looked at him, took a deep breath, bit her lip and answered, "It doesn't look like I have much of a choice. It's either do this or be locked up. Not really good options. However, being that this will help me, than I will help you."

"Excellent choice, no matter how you came up with it." He turned and walked away.

Amaranth sat there staring at her book. *What a choice? I will do what I have to, but he wants me to get rid of Odulore? Seriously, I don't think I can do that*, she thought to herself. Amaranth did not dare to speak her thought out loud.

Hours went by, and she didn't hear from him or that mute goblin. She got up from her desk and walked out of her room. Before she got too far she noticed a bunch of tunnels, which way should she go?

Crumazz popped around the corner, "Where are you going?"

"I figured I'd go for a walk and see where I am. I know that it's the Crystal Crypt, but I have never been here."

"You have been here. Your mother brought you here when you were younger. For those that are not a part of Rissingshire Castle this is where we live. We rule from here. You got spoiled over in the castle."

Glaring at him, she tossed back her black hair, spun around and walked away. *I am not dealing with him right now. I will figure this place out on my own. He and that goblin can stay out of my way*, she thought to herself.

Amaranth started down a tunnel. Valora walked up next to her and stayed by her side. The cat continued to stay with her wherever she went.

Down the one tunnel it got darker and darker, and then she spotted glowing eyes looking back at her. She stopped in her tracks. Valora also stopped. The dampness started to creep upon her. The eyes started to move towards them, and they got closer and closer. They got close enough so that Amaranth was able to see that they were bats. She rolled her eyes, turned around and headed back to the start of the tunnel.

This is crazy. These tunnels don't lead anywhere, I am not going to be walking in the dark. I'll have to bring some light with me. At least, I have Valora with me though.

They arrived at the tunnel entrance and this time the dragons were there guarding it. "I think you made a wrong turn. You'll have to go back before Crumazz finds you out here," Pymmut told them.

Amaranth let out a big huff, turned around and went back into the tunnel. *I can't believe this. I don't remember passing any other way out of this crazy tunnel system.*

Valora scampered ahead of her, she had to run to keep up with her. An opening appeared to her right, and they both entered into it. She looked ahead and saw more light. Puggaald strolled out from an entryway and stood in the middle of the tunnel. She heard something behind her, so she looked over her shoulder to the left and saw a bunch of eyes following her. This time she knew they were the bats. They had followed them.

She walked up to Puggaald, "Ok, so how do I get back to my room?"

He looked up at her and put his hand out. She took it and followed him as he led her back to her room. Crumazz was in her room waiting for her, "You just couldn't resist andering around."

"What did you think I was going to do? Just sit around?"

"I expected that you would get reading and figuring out what your mother was working on when she was here. That is what you need to be doing."

She rolled her eyes at him, "I have no idea what she was working on and exactly how do you think I can figure it out?"

"Try reading the book that belonged to her. This was her room. The only thing I know is that she was working on something that would ultimately help her to rule the Maerith Kingdom."

Chapter 3

Back at Rissingshire Castle, Odulore was sitting at his desk when Oldirrim flew in and landed on his desk. "What do you want?" he snapped at him.

Oldirrim sat up straight and shook his head, "Do you want us to go check on Amaranth? We can fly over there."

"No, I do not want you to go check on her. We need to figure out what they are up to."

He flew out of the room. Odulore sat there just staring into space. *How am I going to figure this one out? I will need to enlist the mystic creatures of the forest. They can do this.* "Hey, Narella, you need to go get Zyrsit."

Narella got up out of her comfy bed, stretched her front legs and then her back legs. She walked out of the room and went off to find Zyrsit.

Ash and Oldirrim both flew into the room. "You need to come quick," Ash told Odulore while he flew in circles.

He got up and followed them out into the courtyard area where a group of the mystical forest creatures were all gathered together.

Evatius stepped forward, "We need to go rescue Amaranth."

"I don't know if she wants to be rescued or not. Her mother ruled the Crystal Crypt as an evil witch. We don't know if she is following in her footsteps or not."

"How are we going to know if we don't go find out?" asked Tamon the pixie.

They all stood there just looking at each other. Glurx came strolling out into the courtyard. "Isn't there some magical ball or something that you could use?"

"My father had one. I have not used it. He would use it in all kinds of ways. It's still in his study. We'll have to see how that thing works."

They all nodded, he turned around and followed Glurx to his father's study. He hadn't been in the room since his father was killed by an evil dragon.

As he walked into the room, he felt this presence, as though someone was in the room. He looked around and there was no one but him and Glurx. They stopped and looked at his father's crystal ball as it sat on the pedestal in the opposite end of the room. Slowly he proceeded closer to the ball and there were little electrical pulses he could see flashing inside of it.

Standing at the crystal ball he looked at Glurx. "What should I do now?" he asked him.

"Well, your father used to ask it all kinds of questions. I never heard it speak back to him though. He just kept looking at it."

He looked back at the ball, "Where is Amaranth?"

The electrical pulses turned into lightning bolts and a picture appeared of Amaranth in her room at her desk in the Crystal Crypt.

"Well now, that's interesting. She looks pretty cozy and not in any danger," he said to Glurx.

"Ah, so that thing shows you pictures. That explains why your father would stare into it."

"I would say that she is looking like she is going to be picking up where her evil mother left off. Let's go talk to the others." They left the room and went back out into the courtyard where everyone was still waiting for them.

"The crystal ball was very helpful. I asked it where Amaranth was at and it showed me that she is at a desk in a room. She does not look as though she needs to be rescued. On the contrary, she looks like she is working towards taking up where her evil mother left off," he told them.

Evatius stomped his hoof and said, "Are you sure? I can't believe she had us all fooled. I thought that she didn't want to be anything like her mother."

"I know, that's what she said, but I saw it. She was sitting there reading at a desk in a nice room. It didn't look like she was being kept against her will. It looked more like she was studying. If they have her studying what her mother was up to, we could all be in for a lot of trouble. Her mother was trying to take over the entire Maerith Kingdom."

Glurx spoke up, "Hey, how about everyone go into the dining hall. It's lunch time and we can figure this out." He walked towards the dining hall and looked over his shoulder. Then he motioned for everyone to follow him.

They sat down in the dining hall with Odulore at the head of the table. The seat at the other end was empty, as that is where Amaranth used to sit.

Zizor the ogre entered the dining hall from the kitchen door. He was followed by goblins that brought out the food on carts. They placed the platters of food in the middle of the table, as the places were already set for the meal. Zizor was always ready to serve a meal.

He walked up to Odulore, “We are missing one. Where is she?”

“She will not be joining us. The dragons came and took her to Crystal Crypt. I checked and it looks like she is very comfortable there. So, don’t expect her any time soon,” he replied as he looked up at him.

As soon as the platters were set down, everyone dug in and got their stomachs filled. The only thing you could hear was every-one eating.

A dark whirlwind encircled the chandeliers, and Crumazz appeared at the front of the dining hall. “I have Amaranth and she will pick up where her mother left off. You have been warned,” he thundered. The dark whirlwind appeared again and he was gone.

“He’s a bit late. We already figured that out,” Odulore remarked.

The goblins picked up all the dirty dishes and returned to the kitchen. Zizor sat down next to Odulore, “Don’t you think he is wrong? I can’t believe she is going to take up where her mother left off. Her mother was so evil. What happened to her mother? How was she killed?”

“I’m not quite sure. We just got word through the forest that she was dead. I don’t think anyone said how. I do know that my father, her mother and Crumazz’s father are all gone.”

“Ok, so where is your mother, her father and Crumazz’s mother?”

“My mother died when I was little. I don’t even remember her. As for the other two, I have no idea who they are or were. I only know that I haven’t heard mention of them.”

"I wonder if the answer to what will happen next lies with the ones you knew or the ones you didn't know?"

"All right, you are being philosophical now. Although that is a good question, which one will lead to our answers? There is so much uncertainty right now. Normally I would talk to Amaranth. She was always good for talking things out. I guess I will be using the magical ball. Hopefully it will provide some good answers."

He got up from the table and walked out into the courtyard, to his surprise there were quite a few mystical woodland creatures gathered around. They were all watching him. He sat down on a wooden bench. Tamon came up in front of him. She looked at him and asked, "What is troubling you? Can we help?"

Odulore just sat there and looked at her. He wasn't sure what to say. Plus, he had never confided in a pixie. He wasn't sure he could trust her. Taking a deep breath, he told her, "Nothing you can do anything about." He got up and went into his father's study.

He looked around the room and saw many books on the shelves. One caught his eye. It had a bright blue binding with gold trim. He took it off the shelf and laid it on his father's desk. When he opened it, the front page said, "Trodus' Book of Spells" in gold calligraphy. Odulore thought to himself, *Well, this is going to be interesting. I didn't even know he had this book. I hope it will provide answers to what's going on with Amaranth. I still cannot believe that she so easily went over to the dark side. How could she? Why?*

Narella jumped up on the desk and laid down on the book. After being startled, he started to pet her. His mind raced again to Amaranth and what was going on. Then the magical ball caught his eye. He walked over to it and said, "What do I do now? I have this book but do I use it?"

The electrical pulses raced around the magical ball. They slowed down and the word, "patience" appeared. He chuckled and walked away. Ash and Oldirrim flew in and landed on the desk by Narella. "Do you want us to go check on her anyway?" Ash asked.

"Sure, why not? It can't hurt anything. I know what Crumazz said, but can we really believe him? I know what I saw, but was it the whole picture?"

The owls flew out from the room and stopped in the courtyard. The mystical forest creatures gathered around them. "We are going to go find Amaranth and see if she really is going to the dark side of things. Who wants to help us?" Oldirrim asked.

Evatius answered, "I can go with you and I can bring along a couple of friends to help out."

"Ok, you do that. We'll have to do this closer to dusk. We will meet at the edge of the forest where the Demack grasslands end," Ash informed him. They all went their separate ways.

Chapter 4

Amaranth sat at her desk with Valora laying next to the book she was trying to read. She thought to herself, *I guess I will start with this one. It looks like my mother's journal. There are no dates entered in this journal, and I have no idea when she wrote it.*

The first page had the name, Zaleria, written in large calligraphy style letters. She turned the page and began to read about a portion of her mother's life. This is what was written.

The days are getting shorter, so winter is coming soon, with colder weather as well. Crumazz is doing a fine job of keeping the dragons and goblins inline. He is so much like his father, but lacks the resourcefulness of his father, Qrizor. This one is not very creative. He is leaving the thinking and creativity up to me.

This book will contain all my spells, stories, thoughts, and ideas. I hope that it does not land in the wrong hands. Crumazz will probably not be able to figure these out on his own. My only hope is that Amaranth will be able to follow and pick up wherever I leave off. I do not trust Qrizor to return. He has been gone way too long.

Let's catch up on what has been going on in the kingdom before moving forward. Qrizor went to take over a new castle for the kingdom. He went to Miserth. This is on the opposite side of the Calegan Forest from Rissingshire. We want this castle so that we have both sides of the forest covered. The Crystal Crypt is a great hideaway, but we need something that will give us more room and ability to take over the entire Maerith Kingdom.

Crumazz was going to go with Qrizor, but he did not because we wanted to make sure that there was at least one of them left behind to help me take over. I'm not sure that Crumazz totally agreed with this decision. It appears that he felt slighted. I have felt a strange aura about him ever since his father left.

This is why I am writing this all down. I have a feeling that if Qrizor does not come back soon I will not be around much longer.

Amaranth, if you are reading this, and I am no longer around, please be careful with Crumazz. DO NOT TRUST HIM!

She paused and thought to herself, *Wow! She did not trust him. I wonder what happened to her?* Amaranth continued on reading what Zaleria wrote to her.

As you read through these pages, remember that some of this is written so that only you will know what it says. This is for a reason and that reason is Crumazz. Now, if Qrizor has returned, you can rest assured that he knew what our plans were and how to include you in them.

The first thing that you are going to need to do is to organize all my herbs, crystals, and potions. There should be nothing in my cauldron, if there is, dump it out outside. I will draw you a diagram of how I have my table setup. This will help you to maximize your time and be able to follow my spells easier.

She turned the page and there was the diagram. Amaranth held up the book and looked at the cauldron and table. The two did not match up. She shook her head.

Crumazz appeared in the doorway, "Hey, have you figured it out yet?"

"No, I am only a few pages in. This is going to take a few days or longer just to get things set up the way I need them."

"You better hurry up. We have things to do and a kingdom to take over."

"I am reading as fast as I can. The more you interrupt me, the longer it is going to take. Plus, this isn't the best room. Do you know if she had a place that she was going to set up her laboratory?"

"You mean, like a castle? Well, we will have to take over Rissingshire first."

Amaranth did not answer but turned around, put the book down, and started to organize the herbs. Crumazz shook his head and left.

She thought to herself, *He obviously has no clue what is going on with the other castle. Either that or he is trying to see what I will tell him. I will listen to my mother and not trust him. Although, it's not like she was the nicest person either.*

Hours went by and all was quiet. She was enjoying the solitude. Although, she did miss some of the hustle and bustle of the castle. Suddenly there was a lot of commotion outside. She went to see what was going on.

The dragons were circling outside the crypt and making all kinds of noise. As she got closer to the entrance she could hear other creatures. It sounded like owls and something that she couldn't quite recognize.

The owls were flying amongst the dragons. She could see that it was Ash and Oldirrim. They were making it difficult for the dragons to catch them. She watched them and then yelled out, “Ash. Oldirrim. Go away!”

Crumazz appeared outside. “Isn’t this nice? They have come to check on you,” he said sarcastically.

“Oh shut up Crumazz. Just because no one would miss you if you disappeared.” She turned and walked back inside.

Crumazz let out a loud evil laugh and then tried to throw lightning bolts at the owls. He didn’t have very good aim, and they flew back into the forest.

Returning to her mother’s book, she continued reading.

I will assume that you took the time to organize everything according to the chart before moving forward. It is actually very important to be organized. You want to make sure that you don’t mess anything up.

Amaranth rolled her eyes and went back to the diagram and tried to figure out if she could get everything organized. *Mother always knew that I would take shortcuts.*

Valora sat on the desk and watched her put things together. She walked up and moved a few things with her paw. *Seriously, this cat knows where everything goes?* She thought to herself.

She opened an armoire cabinet. It was filled with candles: black, red, and white. Some were new, others were well-used and very short. *I have never seen this many candles. This is crazy. I hope she explains why she has so many.* Amaranth thought to herself. She grabbed a few and put them on the desk.

The cat had jumped down off the desk and was walking around the room when Frally flew in and startled her. "What the hell?" She spun around. "Who are you?"

"I am Frally. What do you need?"

"I really don't need any help. I just need time to get things together."

"I think you need help. You need to get things moving. You are wasting time. We need to get things back on track."

"So, you were helping my mother and Qrizor?"

"Yes, you need to read her journal. There is so much that you don't know."

Frally flew away just as quickly as she came in. Amaranth sat down to the desk and started reading.

Have you met Frally? I hope so. She will help you to know and hear things that you won't be able to without her. She can be places that you cannot. Frally is a mini dragon that will be invaluable. You be sure to treat her right. You can trust her.

Next you need to know what all is in the Maerith Kingdom and what we were planning on adding to it. You will now be against Odulore and Trodus. I know that you spent too much time with them They are not your friends anymore. You will be over them.

She thought to herself, *Wait, she doesn't know that Trodus was killed by a dragon. How does she not know this? Who really killed him? I was told that she sent the dragon to kill him. This does not appear to be so.*

Amaranth went back to reading.

The first thing you need to do is to take over the Crystal Crypt. Yes, it means what you think it means. You will need to get the dragons all on your side first. This may not be easy. Gairrulit is his favorite and the feeling is mutual. The other dragons will be easier to get on your side. I do not think that the goblins like him, so that won't be a problem.

Your first potion will be Philter of Immobilizing.

To brew, gather the following ingredients and follow the steps closely and with great attention to detail.

- 5 teaspoons of Sour Basil
- 3 teaspoons of Mountain Garlic
- 1 sprinkle of Fire Quassia
- 2 heaps of Water Petal
- 4 bits of Dream Parsley

Squeeze the Sour Basil by summoning Puggaald and having him do the work for you and put the result in a cup. Add some ice, let it melt to turn it into a smooth emulsion, then add the Mountain Garlic, a quarter first, then a half and then a third of it.

Fill a pan with unsalted seawater, add the mixture and let it steep while you make friends with the dragons, then come back and bring it to a boil. Let it simmer and steep while you take a power nap before adding the Fire Quassia and Water Petal, a half at a time, alternating between the two.

Bring everything back to a boil, turn off the heat, mix in the Dream Parsley and let everything rest over night.

Stir the mixture a final time, if it sticks you know it's right. Your potion is ready to be used.

How do you get him to drink it? This is where you get Puggaald to add it to his next meal. However, he has to be careful with it and make sure that only Crumazz gets it.

Now go get Puggaald and have him help you. Come back to read more once you have this taken care of.

Amaranth left her room to go find Puggaald. The tunnels were confusing her. She continued walking until coming upon him. "Puggaald, I have something I need you to do."

"Let me guess, you were reading your mother's journal."

"Yes, of course, I am. I had to figure out why I am here."

"Ok, let's go to your room and work on what needs to be worked on."

Chapter 5

Odulore walked out into the courtyard and sat down on a bench. Zyrsit the mini dragon flew in and sat next to him. Tilting his head he looked up at him and said, "Whatcha thinking?"

"What our next move is. Do we go rescue her or do we stay here and just move on?"

"I vote to rescue her."

Ash flew up and sat on the ground in front of them. "What's up?"

"We are contemplating whether or not to go rescue Amaranth," Ash told him.

Shortly there was a small group of mystical forest creatures surrounding them. Glurx walked out and joined them. "You guys keep repeating the same thing over and over. Either go after her or forget about it. The sooner, the better," he told them and walked away.

Odulore got up and went back into his father's room. He went up to the crystal ball and asked, "Should I go after Amaranth?"

The thunderbolts and electrical pulses went wild all around the ball. A message came up facing him, "No! Be prepared!"

Wait? What? I need to prepare. That must mean that she is picking up where her mother left off. Great, this is going to get real interesting. I wonder if Crumazz is working with her or against her.

Narella ran in and rubbed up against his legs. She looked up at him and said, "What's the verdict?"

"We need to prepare and not go after her. I am betting that it means that she is taking over for her mother. The thing we don't know is if Crumazz is working with her or against her."

Oldirrim flew in and landed on the desk, "So, it's a no go for the rescue. What do we do next to prepare?"

He sat down at the desk and opened the book he found earlier. He began to read the paper that was stuffed in the front of it.

Odulore, I assume that you are reading this and that I am gone. This book will help you with what to do and when to do it. This letter will give you some background that I always wanted to tell you, but didn't know how.

Let me help you with the family tree that is going on in the area. This will help you understand things very well. Also, it will help with why you cannot be with Amaranth.

Amaranth's mother is Zaleria and Qrizor is Crumazz's father. The part that you didn't know before was that Zaleria and Qrizor were married and Crumazz's mother is also Zaleria. So, yes, Amaranth and Crumazz are siblings. This makes them very dangerous. I do not believe that they know. They raised them separately and did not speak of their marriage. They are full siblings and very close in age.

Qrizor wanted to rule the kingdom by himself and did not want the hassle of being married. He took Crumazz to live in Miserth Castle, and he left Zaleria in the Crystal Crypt to raise Amaranth on her own. However, she decided that she did not want Amaranth and dropped her off here for us to raise her.

Why would she leave her here? She knew that your mother would never turn away an abandoned child, no matter whose it was. We never would have thought that you two would be attracted to each other. We tried to raise you as siblings.

Zaleria was an evil witch and has descended from a long line of evil witches. Just as Qrizor has descended from a long line of evil warlocks. You put the two together and you end up with children that will be evil as well.

When Zaleria was in the Crystal Crypt the only thing she couldn't do was leave because Qrizor had put a spell on it that kept her there. When Zaleria or Qrizor pass, the spell will be lifted from the crypt.

If the dragons have come for Amaranth, then one or the other or both has happened. When they come for her, they will make it appear that she is kidnapped. However, they will be putting her in place to take over where her mother left off, especially if Qrizor is gone. Please do not go after her. I hope that you have already asked this of the crystal ball.

I have known Zaleria for a long time, and I am sure that she has written up what Amaranth is to do next. This is where things are going to be very interesting. I am sure that they are written to have her take over the kingdom. This was their plan, but they waited for Amaranth and Crumazz to become adults.

You will need to prepare for this! You will need to defend Rissingshire Castle, Demack Grassland, Bredenrath Pond, and the Calegan Forest. This is the only way to keep them from over taking Maerith Kingdom. There are more castles in the kingdom. You will need to seek them out to get them to help you defend our section from Crumazz and Amaranth. If either Qrizor or Zaleria is still alive, that will complicate things.

If you are reading this, I assume that I am gone. This means that you will also have to figure out who is responsible for my death.

Good luck on all of this. Pay close attention to the spells. These will help you.

Father

Wow! This is crazy! Odulore thought to himself. He got up and walked out into the courtyard. The mystical forest creatures were still there.

"You are not going to believe this. I just read a letter from my father. To sum things up, Crumazz and Amaranth are siblings. They are gearing up to try to take over Maerith Kingdom. We need to communicate with the other castles about defending our areas including the forest, grassland and pond. We cannot let them take over," he shared with them.

Evatius stepped forward, "That is messed up! We need to make sure that does not happen. Although, it does explain the strange feelings I have gotten while out in the forest."

"Does anyone know what other castles are out there?" Ash asked.

"Yes, I know which ones we need to contact. There's a master list in my father's room. Let's go get the list," Odulore answered and motioned for them to follow him.

He left again and this time Evatius, Tamon, Ash, Oldirrim and Narella follow him. Standing in front of his father's bookshelf, he reads all the titles, "Book of Crystals, Book of Potions, Maerith Kingdom. Here it is." Odulore took the book off the shelf and laid it on the desk.

The owls and mini dragon sat on the desk looking at the book as he opened it to the map of the kingdom. Tamon sat on the back of Evatius next to the desk. "Alright, here's a map and out here are the castles. There's a few ponds with some of the castles in them. How do we want to break this up? Let's go over the map.

We have Grimtol Castle within the Glassy Lagoon. We have Xodius and Zabine. This one is the furthest away. They normally just stay to themselves.

In the far west is Staedan and Shelyn who are in Glottenham Castle. They have the Bordshall Cove that they overlook.

Closer to us we have Avras and Arietta that are up in Eagleview Castle that overlooks Tortoise Lake.

Finally, we have Langdale Castle that is at the top of Lavalbourg Gorge. Drozan and Zolya are not the most friendly. They may be the difficult ones for us to approach.

Does anyone have a preference?" Odulore asked them.

Tamon spoke up, "I think the pixies can help with Zolya. She's always really nice to us. We will go talk to them."

"I will head out to Xodius and take a couple others with me," Evatius offered.

Ash added, "Oldirrim and I can fly out to Staedan. He has Chrono and that will help us."

"Who is Chrono?"

"He's an owl."

"Ok, then I will go talk to Avras. We need to do this now. I don't know how quick of a learner Amaranth is going to be."

They all exited and headed off in their own directions.

Zyrsit flew up to Odulore, “Where are you headed?”

“You can come with me. I am going to see Avras.”

Zyrsit replied, “Yes. I will.”

Odulore walked out to the livery. He went up to Magnus, a black Percheron stallion that stands 19 hands high. “Ok, we are going to see Avras. You know the way.” They walked into the courtyard where Odulore got on the back of Magnus. Zyrsit flew up and joined him.

They rode out of the castle on Magnus, at first trotting then changing to a canter and finally into a run with its black mane and tail blowing in the wind.

Chapter 6

They arrived at Tortoise Lake and Magnus slows to a trot along the tall grassy banks. Two tigers are seated on the outer shore of the Tortoise Lake by the drawbridge gate of Eagleview Castle. Raja walked out to greet them as Aslan sat watching the area.

“How may we help you?” Raja asked.

“We are here to talk to Avras about the state of the kingdom.”

“He is not expecting you.”

“Yes, I know. We just discovered something that may need his attention.”

“Follow me,” Raja motioned for them to follow behind him.

They went into the castle. “Stay here,” Raja told them, and he disappeared down a hallway.

A few minutes later Raja returns with Avras. “What do you think needs my attention Odulore?”

“Did you know that Amaranth and Crumazz are working to take over the kingdom?”

“No, I did not. We stay to ourselves. How and when did this all happen?”

“Just a couple of days ago. Crumazz had the dragons come get Amaranth. My father left me a letter telling me all about what’s going on including that they are siblings, even though they were not raised together and no one knew about it."

Avras looked puzzled at them. He took a few minutes to think to himself, *Are these guys right? I cannot have this happen. If this happens, then my peace and quiet will be gone. Plus, Crumazz will be cruel to my felines.*

"Ok, so what do you want me to do?" He asked Odulore.

"I am thinking that they will be coming for me first. We are going to have extra powers at the Rissingshire Castle. We are talking with everyone at all the castles in Maerith Kingdom. What we don't know is if they are going to recruit from other kingdoms."

At this point a dozen tigers and panthers had gathered around them. They all sat and listened to what was going on. Soon the parapets and battlements of the castle and its courtyard were filled with winged lions.

"As you can see I have quite a large tribe of felines. We will help with what we can spare. I will need to have some felines here guarding this castle while we are helping you. I will let Arietta know what's going on when she gets back with some of the snow leopards."

"Thank you. I will send Ash and Oldirrim when we need your assistance."

Odulore got back on Magnus and left the castle. Raja followed them out to the front and joined Aslan.

In the middle of the Calegan Forest they met up with a group of pixies. "Odulore, we met up with Zolya. She said that we can have some of their elves help us. She will send them when she gets word from us," Tamon told them.

"Great! Now we need to gather everyone together. I told Avras the owls would bring him notification of our need for his felines."

Evatius came galloping to them. "We have help from Xodius and their hares. We need to let them know when to come."

"I told Avras that we would send out the owls. We will have the owls notify everyone. That will work. Let's go talk in the dining hall."

They all headed out of the forest and through the Demack Grassland when there were lightning bolts that flashed over the forest that came from the direction of the Miserth Castle. Everyone picked up the pace.

When they arrived inside the castle they were greeted by Ash and Oldirrim. "We are getting help from Staedan and the owls," Ash blurted out.

"Great, let's go into the dining hall," Odulore replied.

Zizor greeted them as they entered the room, "Welcome everyone! I haven't prepared dinner prepared yet."

"That's ok, we are just here to discuss our strategy," Odulore informed him.

They sat down at the table and Odulore rolled out a map of the castle. "Ok, here's what we have to work with. We'll line the winged lions on the right. Then along the left we'll have the owls. The hares and elves will be lined up around the outside right by the base of the castle. We have the Pegasuses that can help with covering the middle air of the castle area. I will also go out of the kingdom to Azohr, he has griffins and gargoyles that can assist."

Zizor spoke up, "Don't forget that you have goblins here. They can help as well."

"This is perfect. I now need to go read up on the spells and potions that I need for this fight."

Odulore got up and headed off to his father's room. He sat down at the desk with his father's book of spells. At first, he just sat there staring at the pages and not reading them. His thoughts wandered off, *How could I be so wrong about Amaranth? How could she so easily go to the other side? We could have ruled the kingdom together. I do not like going up against her. Although with her evil mother, maybe it was just inevitable. Plus, her evil brother is not going to make this easy.*

Zyrsit flew in and landed on the book right in front of him, "Hey, what are you thinking?"

"What? Oh, yeah, what am I thinking? I don't know. I am just confused by this whole thing. I don't understand why she went so easily."

Glurx came in and stood in front of the desk, "Look, you have to get her out of your brain. She's gone to the evil side and there's nothing you can do about it. The dragons tricked you into thinking she was not willing, but obviously, that was wrong. Get your head into the present and figure out how you are going to keep her in her place. Do you have a spell you use to keep her and Crumazz in the Crystal Crypt and they can't get out?"

He looked at the book, moved Zyrsit to the side, and what was on that page? Flarello Viralerous, it's a spell that creates a spell blocking barrier. "Hey, I can use this to protect our castle. Father was right, I need to look through this book."

He turned the page and the next spell was Ignitim Serpite and this one would cause those to be trapped in wherever they are at. "I found it!" He hollered out.

"What did you find?" Zyrsit asked him after almost falling off the desk from being startled.

"I found the spell that I could use to trap them in the Crystal Crypt. I need to figure out how to trap them both in there though. That will be difficult. I need to read up more on this spell."

He turned the pages and read what was on the page.

Ignitim Serpite–Trap someone in an object such as a castle or crypt. This is to be used sparingly. This spell cannot be undone until those trapped die or the caster of the spell dies. There is no exit. There is no visible blockage that can be removed. This is an invisible wall that keeps those inside in and outside out.

You will need to be within 25 feet of the object. It will take effect immediately.

There is no way to dig under the force field either. As they dig down, the force field goes with it. If there is water, it will trap the water way in the trapped zone. At the edge of the force field, it will go to the bottom of the water.

Odulore thought to himself, *This is what Qrizor used on Zaleria. She lived for many years in the Crystal Crypt. So, this should work on Amaranth. Will this work? I hope so. I need it to. Although, I'd love to just trap Crumazz and try to get her over to my side of things. Maybe I can trap him at Miserth Castle.*

Narella came prancing in and jumped up on the desk. "Well, what are we doing? I heard about how to protect the castle, but you know that will not deter them for long and you can't keep all those guards forever," She told him.

"That's what I am trying to figure out. The part that has me torn though is that Amaranth went to the evil side. I just cannot comprehend it.

Glurx offered his opinion, "I don't think you should worry about trying to turn her from evil. Just worry about them not taking over this castle. You are over the Maerith Kingdom right now, and we do not want that to change, especially by them. They come from two evil parents. You cannot honestly expect that either of them won't become evil. Crumazz has already proved that he is evil. Good grief, he had the dragons do his dirty work. He kidnapped his own sister or at least he made it appear that way."

"Yeah, yeah, I know. It's just that we spent so much time together. I just can't imagine her being evil enough to want to take over the kingdom without me."

"My boy, you are thinking with your heart instead of your head. Quit it! You won't be any good if you don't," Glurx ordered him and walked out of the room.

Chapter 7

Amaranth stood in the entry to Crystal Crypt. She looked out at the Calegan Forest. There was no movement. There was no noise. It was eerily quiet. She thought to herself, *What is going on? This is too quiet. I wonder what Odulore is up to. Does he know what's happening over here? How would he? I miss Narella, but I have Valora. I miss the Pegasuses and taking them for a flight around the kingdom. However, I can get it all back if I help Crumazz take over the kingdom. Do I want that? Do I want to deal with Crumazz?*

Valora came up and rubbed up against her leg. "What do you want?" She asked.

The cat sat down and looked up at her, "We need to get back to work. Have you figured out which way you are going to go?"

Crumazz appeared behind her, she spun around and glared at him, "What do you want?"

"Have you figured out what's next? What do we do? Come on, what's the plan?"

"How do I know I can trust you?" She asked him.

"You don't. Does it matter?"

"Yes. Yes, it does matter. How can I work with you if I don't know if I can trust you?"

He rolled his eyes, turned around and stomped off. Crumazz almost stepped on Puggaald. He looked down and huffed off.

"What's his problem?" Puggaald asked.

"I didn't give him the answer he wanted."

"Ah, well, he'll get over it."

They stood looking out into the forest. "Why is it so silent today?" He asked her.

"Wait, what? You speak? You didn't speak just a few days ago."

"Yes, I speak, but only once I determine if you are trustworthy."

The skies started growing dark over the forest. A dark cloud filled the upper branches. It grew more and more ominous. The forest was still silent. Amaranth thought to herself,

What is going on? This is strange. I will have to see what my mother's journal has to say.

She turned and walked to her mother's room. Puggaald followed her. When she sat down at the desk Valora jumped on the desk and laid down in the corner.

Amaranth opened her mother's journal to where she had left off.

Now go get Puggaald and have him help you. Come back to read more once you have this taken care of.

Oh yeah, that's where I was at, Amaranth thought to herself. She looked at Puggaald and said, "Now you need to squeeze the sour basil. Then once we get this made, place it into Crumazz's meal. Make sure it is only his meal. This is very important. He also cannot know that you have it. If he knows, then it could be used against us."

Puggaald nodded and proceeded to squeeze the sour basil. Amaranth added some ice, let it melt to turn it into a smooth emulsion, then added the Mountain Garlic, a quarter first, then a half and then a third of it.

She filled a pan with unsalted seawater, added the mixture and let it steep. Amaranth did just as her mother wrote and made friends with the dragons, then came back and brought the sour basil emulsion to a boil. She then let it simmer and steep while she took a power nap. She awoke refreshed from her nap and continued to cook the compound, adding the Fire Quassia and Water Petal, a half at a time, alternating between the two.

Everything returned to a boil. Amaranth turned off the heat, mixed in the Dream Parsley and let everything rest overnight.

Puggaald wandered back into the room, "Is it ready?"

"Yes. So, you need to take it and make sure it gets put into the correct meal. Don't screw this up!"

He took the potion in a container, put it in his pocket, and walked out of the room.

Amaranth cleaned everything up and got it all put away quickly. She did not want Crumazz to come in and find out what she had done.

Once everything was put away she sat back down to the table and began to read more of the journal.

I hope that you got the potion done correctly and that Puggaald does not screw it up. You want to be rid of Crumazz. You do not need him to rule the kingdom.

The next thing you will have to worry about is what to do with Odulore. I know that you and him were raised together as if your were siblings, but I have a feeling that the two of you don't think of each other as siblings. I think that there's more there. Now, do you want to have him at your side or do you want to go without him? The only one that figures that one out is you.

Is Trodus still alive? If so, then you will have another one that will back you. Is Qrizor still alive? Then he will also help you. However, you cannot have them all. It will either be Trodus and Odulore or it will be Qrizor.

One thing to consider is that Trodus and Odulore do have the rest of the kingdom with them. If you go with Qrizor, then you will have to take over all the castles that are not for you. The only castle that Qrizor has is Miserth Castle. It's a nice castle, much better than this crypt, but it's not as nice as the other castles. They also have animal back-up. So, you will be pretty much on your own and will only have potions to help you.

Amaranth thought to herself, *Gee, what a choice. I have to go it myself or go with Odulore. The thing is, if I go that route I have to get word to him that I am with him before he uses Trodus' Book of Spells against me. I don't believe Qrizor is still alive. He hasn't been around in forever. Plus, he just has one castle and no backup. If he is alive, it's just him.*

"Puggaald!" She yelled, in hopes that he could hear her.

He came running in, "Yes, I was on my way back. What do you want?"

"How can I get word to Odulore? I want him to be aware of my plans without letting Crumazz know."

"If you are patient you won't have to worry about it."

"I don't want to be too late though. There is a dark cloud coming and I have no idea what it is. Mother hasn't said in her journal."

"Well, get reading. I will have dinner ready in a couple of hours."

Crumazz walked in, "Still a couple of hours until dinner?"

"Yes, I can fix you something earlier if you like."

"I would like that. I am starving and don't want to wait a couple of more hours."

Puggaald walked out of the room and headed to the kitchen. Crumazz stayed behind. "So, are you any further along? You certainly do read slowly."

"Well, I do read, which is more than I can say for you. Don't make fun of how slow I read when you don't read at all."

"Good point. I am going to go see what Puggaald has come up with for an early dinner for me." He turned and exited.

Oh, thank God that he finally left. I hope this takes place quickly. I need to get word to Odulore, she contemplated. I should focus my energies on reading. There is so much I need to know. I must do this for myself, not Crumazz.

Down the tunnel to the dining room Crumazz quickly walked. Once there he yelled out, "Puggaald, do you have my dinner ready?"

Puggaald appeared from the kitchen with a pot of stew. "Yes, yes, Crumazz, I have your dinner ready. I made this pot of stew just for you."

He sat down at the table and waited for his meal. The moment Puggaald sat it down in front of him. He picked it up and drank down half the broth. Then he started picking out the large pieces of meat. Suddenly, with his hand help up to his mouth, Crumazz's movements froze. He was immobile. His body became very stiff. Not a single movement was possible. His ability to speak or make any sound was suppressed, too.

Puggaald ran out of the room and went to Amaranth. "It worked! He is frozen. What do you want to do next?"

"Let me scan this journal to the next potion." She scanned down multiple pages and came to the next potion. "Yes, here it is. It's a death potion! Get me the following ingredients:

- 1 teaspoon of Angel Galangal
- 4 tablespoons of Dream Blossom
- 2 heaps of Autumn Leaves
- 1 dash of Cave Oregano
- 6 bits of Devil Curry Leaf

Crush the Angel Galangal and put it in a container. Add some ice, let it melt to turn it into a lumpy cream, then add the Dream Blossom, careful to add a tiny amount at first, and then everything else.

Fill a pan with water, add the mixture, and bring the mixture to a boil. Let it steam for a short while before adding the Autumn Leaves and Cave Oregano, a quarter at a time of a mixture of both.

Reduce the cooking temperature and gently warm the disgusting mixture. Mix in the Devil Curry Leaf and let everything rest for a few minutes.

Whisk the mixture gently to break up any potential clumps. Your potion is ready to be used."

"All right, everything is ready for you to use. He is immobile at the moment. Thankfully he was in the middle of eating the meat, so his mouth is open," Puggaald said.

They take the potion and quickly go to the dining room. Crumazz is still seated right where Puggaald left him and in the same pose. The previous potion is still working. Amaranth took the potion bottle, placing it at his lips, she tilted it up and poured the potion into his mouth. She stood watching him. Crumazz's eyes went blank and a black smokey spirit came out of his mouth and evaporated right in front of him.

"Yes!!" Amaranth exclaimed. "We are now rid of Crumazz. You'll need to get him out of the dining room. . I need to go get Oizu. He will fly me back to Rissingshire Castle. Odulore must know that I am not against him."

Puggaald snapped his fingers and a few minutes later Oizu was there at the entry to the dining room. "You called?"

"Yes, you need to take Amaranth to Rissingshire Castle and make it quick. Time is of the essence."

"Get on my back and we'll be off." She climbed on his back and off they flew to Rissingshire Castle.

Chapter 8

Glurx was walking through the courtyard when Oizu landed with Amaranth on his back.

"What are you doing here?" He asked her.

"I need to speak with Odulore immediately."

Ash and Oldirrim flew out from a room to greet her. "You are here?" Ash asked with a confused tone.

"Yes, I just told Glurx that I need to speak with Odulore right now."

A few moments later Odulore appeared in the courtyard. "Well here I am," he said to her. Standing with his arms folded and an inquiring look on his face, he asked. What do you need to speak to me about so urgently?"

"I know you may not believe me, but let me finish before you say anything. Crumazz had Gairrulit capture me. My mother is dead. He knew that there was a plan for her and Qrizor to take over the kingdom by force. So, he had me sit in her room and read through her journal. What he did not know was that she did not trust him, and she made that very clear to me in her journal. Then she told me that I had to make a decision. I had to choose Crumazz and Qrizor or you and Trodus. She did not know that your father was gone. With making this decision she gave me a couple of potions that helped me to get here safely. I do not know if Qrizor is alive or not. I have not seen or heard from him. I can tell you that Crumazz is now dead. We took care of that right before coming here. My decision is to not be against you. I would love to rule the kingdom, but with you. I think with your father's spells and my mother's potions we can make a great pair that can protect Maerith Kingdom for many years to come. What do you think?"

He did not immediately answer her. He looked at her, then at Oizu, and then over to the owls and Glurx. "Why should I believe you? We used the crystal ball and it looked like you were pretty comfortable."

"I am not surprised that you don't believe me. I can explain. You most likely saw me when I was reading her journal. I was caged most of the time and Crumazz never let me leave or explore on my own. I went to the entrance, and he'd be there checking to see what I was doing.

Mother gave me a potion to immobilize him and then one for his death. They both worked very well," She explained.

"So, you want me to believe that your mother had you kill Crumazz and she told you in her journal?" He looked at her with confusion. "Why would she have you kill him? Did she explain to you about the family tree? Your family tree?"

Amaranth shook her head no, "No she did not explain anything about the family tree. All I know is that she was my mother, but I was raised by your family."

"Let's go into the dining hall. There we can all sit and I can explain some things." He motioned for them to follow him.

On their way to the dining hall Odulore stopped, went into his father's room and grabbed his book of spells with the letter inside.

When they got into the dining hall Zizor was waiting for them. He ran up to Amaranth and gave her a huge hug. "I knew you would be back!" He kept saying excitedly.

"Put her down Zizor," Glurx told him.

They all sat down at the dining table with Odulore across the table from Amaranth. He placed his father's book of spells in between them. "You see, my father left me a letter in addition to his book of spells. In his letter he explained to me your family tree. Let me first assure you that we are not related." He laughed and smiled at her. She smiled back, but didn't say anything.

He took the letter out of the book and read part of it to her. "I will read to you a part of the letter I think you will find interesting.

Amaranth's mother is Zaleria and Qrizor is Crumazz's father. The part that you didn't know before was that Zaleria and Qrizor were married and Crumazz's mother is also Zaleria. So, yes, they are siblings, Amaranth and Crumazz. This makes them dangerous. I do not believe that they know. They raised them separately and did not speak of their marriage. They are full siblings and very close in age.

Qrizor wanted to rule the kingdom by himself and did not want the hassle of being married. He took Crumazz to live in Miserth Castle, and he left Zaleria in the Crystal Crypt to raise Amaranth on her own. However, she decided that she did not want Amaranth and dropped her off here for us to raise her.

Why would she leave her here? She knew that your mother would never turn away an abandoned child, no matter whose it was. We never would have thought that you two would be attracted to each other. We tried to raise you as siblings.

Zaleria was an evil witch and has descended from a long line of evil witches. Just as Qrizor has descended from a long line of evil warlocks. You put the two of them together and you end up with children that will be evil as well.

When Zaleria was in the Crystal Crypt the only thing she couldn't do was leave because Qrizor had put a spell on it that kept her there. When Zaleria or Qrizor pass, the spell will be lifted from the crypt.

If the dragons have come for Amaranth, then one or the other or both has happened. When they come for her, they will make it appear that she is kidnapped. However, they will be putting her in place to take over where her mother left off, especially if Qrizor is gone. Please do not go after her. I hope that you have already asked this of the crystal ball.

So, with that knowledge. What do you want me to believe?"

Amaranth sat there taking it all in. She looked up at him. Her eyes looked hurt. They were not her normal brightness. They had tears in the corners. One tear escaped and fell down beside her nose, and landed on the top of her lip. She gave a big sigh. She remained silent and motionless. Her mind began to wander, *My mother gave me up. My father is Qrizor? My brother was Crumazz? So, she had me kill my brother, her son and did not bother to tell me who he was. How can I trust what she has to say? What about Qrizor? Is he dead? Is he alive? Why didn't he want me? What do I say? What do I do? Where do I go?*

She opened her mouth but nothing came out for a few moments. "I don't know what to say. I had no idea. Your parents did not tell me who both of my parents were. I only knew of my mother. My mother did not tell me who my father was nor who my brother was. Why would she want him killed? I just thought that he was evil and I did it for my own survival. Now what?"

They all sat there for a few more moments. Evatius came trotting in. He looked around the room and shook his head. "Ok, what in the world is going on here? Why is SHE here?"

He stood at the end of the table waiting for an answer. Everyone looked up at him, but it was still silent. "Well?"

Finally the silence broke, "I just read the letter from my father to Amaranth after she told us that her mother left her a letter that told her to kill Crumazz. So, Crumazz is dead. She appears to feel totally betrayed and doesn't know what to think or do."

Slowly more animals and creatures joined them in the dining hall. As they came in, they did not make a noise. It was eerily silent. The hall was filled. Every seat was occupied by an animal, witch, wizard or creature.

In the doorway Avras appeared and immediately went to be next to Odulore. "No need to explain. I have it figured out. The two of you have a lot to figure out. The good news is that we are less one evil wizard. The next question that we need to answer is, is Qrizor still alive? Then which side will Amaranth choose? Will she go with Qrizor, who is her father or will she stay with us and live in peace and harmony?"

Amaranth looked up him as she stood up, "I have been betrayed by my biological family. I can forgive Trodus for not telling me about my father. It was not his place. He did much more for me than my own family. I cannot go against him and his wishes. If we find that Qrizor is alive, I will not go with him. I will be against him. I like the life of peace and harmony. How can I go with him? He abandoned me. My mother abandoned me and then set me up to kill my own brother. Although, that's not exactly a bad thing. The only one that we may have trouble with is Gairrulit the black dragon. He was loyal to Crumazz. We have not seen him and don't know if he knows that Crumazz is dead." She sat back down.

"I am glad to hear this. We can work with this. Now we have to visit Miserth Castle to see if Qrizor is alive or not. Also, we need to purge all the evil from Crystal Crypt. There are many tunnels and rooms in that place. We may be better off getting the good ones out and then trapping the rest of it." Avras told them.

There was a great eruption of cheers in the dining hall. Odulore spoke up, “Now I know everyone is happy that Crumazz is gone. This does take care of one of the evil wizards. However, we need to make sure that his father is gone. Then Maerith Kingdom will be rid of evil.”

Zizor disappeared into the kitchen and then returned with goblins pushing carts laden with food for all. Soon the only sounds were of everyone eating. The goblins took the plates to the kitchen where they cleaned the dishes and the food areas.

Everyone exited the dining hall and went their own ways. She followed Odulore back to his father’s room. They sat down in chairs placed to enjoy the glow of the fireplace. Zyrsit lit the fireplace for them.

There was a calm throughout the castle and the kingdom.

Chapter 9

In Miserth Castle, Dax and Darca, the Great Danes, were lying on the floor in front of the fireplace. Qbaris came in and flopped in the chair near them. He let out a deep sigh and closed his eyes.

Outside there was a loud bang and the Great Danes jumped up and went out to see what was going on. They found Ash and Oldirrim had flown into the hanging cymbal. Dax went over to them, "You guys ok?"

They shook it off, stood up and nodded yes.

"What are you doing here?"

"We are here to see who is living here," Ash replied.

Qbaris walked out when he heard voices. "Hey, who are you?"

"I am Ash and this is Oldirrim. We are from Rissingshire Castle. Who are you?"

He chuckled and said, "I am Qbaris. I took over this castle after my father was killed by a dragon."

"Who was your father?" Oldirrim questioned.

"Qrizor. He was killed by a dragon a few months ago. This black dragon came in and attacked him. Amazingly, he did not know the dragon was in the area. Then it killed him. Just snapped him in half and then took off with him." He explained.

"Come in. I don't get visitors. My father left me his journal, which of course, is incomplete. I have enjoyed the peace and quiet. I really didn't want to go wandering around. Right after my father died, Crumazz also disappeared. I have no idea where he went. Although, I am not going to bother going looking for him. For me, the longer he stays away, the better."

The owls looked at each, to the Great Danes and back to Qbaris. Ash shook his head, cleared his throat and then told him, "I am going to share with you what we just learned. I don't know what all you know about your family tree. So, I am not going to fill in all the blanks. I will just give you the highlights. Zaleria is dead. Amaranth was kidnapped and then killed Crumazz so that she could escape. We came out here to see who is occupying the castle."

"Seriously?! Crumazz is dead! This is great news. I don't have to worry about him coming back here. I do ask that you let Odulore know that I just want to live here in peace."

Ash and Oldirrim both nodded and then flew off out of the castle. The Great Danes walked back inside and laid down next to the fireplace. Qbaris walked around the courtyard. He thought to himself, *I am so glad to hear about Crumazz. It takes a load off my mind. He won't be bothering me anymore. Although, let me get this straight. Qrizor is dead along with Zaleria and Crumazz. Pretty good, a bunch of evil is gone. The owls did not know who I was. Word must not have gotten to Rissingshire Castle about me. No surprise. I never saw my mother. I think father liked that he had her captive. It gave him that sense of power. He never spoke of her. I do know that he went to see her. The question is, how many more siblings are there? Are there more than myself and Crumazz? Does this crazy family end with me?*

The owls returned to Rissingshire Castle. They landed in the courtyard where Odulore and Amaranth were sitting outside by the bonfire.

“Ok, so what did you find out?” Odulore asked them.

“Did you know that there is another sibling? There’s a wizard that is living in Miserth Castle by the name of Qbaris. He claims to be Qrizor’s son, however, we don’t know if he knows that Amaranth is a sibling. We did not go into detail but gave him the highlights that Zaleria and Crumazz were both dead. He was excited to hear that Crumazz is gone. He says that he just wants to be left to live in peace.”

“What? Another brother? Oh, good grief! How many siblings do I have? Are there only the three of us? Do we have any siblings outside of Maerith Kingdom? This is just crazy!” Amaranth was greatly agitated.

“The good news is that he appears to want to live in peace and won’t be trying to take over. How many kids did Qrizor have?”

They sat there enjoying the moment of peace and then it hit him, “Owls, you need to go to the other castles and let them know what has happened. Make sure they know that Amaranth is here now, Crumazz is dead along with both his parents and that his sibling, Qbaris, wishes to live in peace at Miserth Castle.”

The owls took off and headed out to the other castles. This trip would take them much longer with four castles to notify of the news.

Amaranth looked at Odulore and then watched the owls as they flew out of sight. She sighed and then sat back. Her mind raced and then she felt exhausted, just from thinking about everything. Odulore could see that she was stressed and breathing heavily. He motioned for Glurx to come over, “Can you get her some water?” Off he went to get some water for her.

Glurx returned shortly with a glass of water and some lemons floating in it. Those were her favorites. “Thanks. Hey, you remembered I love lemons." She smiled at him and drank her water.

Tamon appeared next to Amaranth. She flitted around her and landed on the ground in front of her. "Are you friends of pixies?"

"What?"

"Do you like pixies?"

"Oh, yes, of course. The only one I wasn't a friend of was that Crumazz. He was evil and did not want me to be friends with anyone. Now that he is gone, I can be friends with whoever I want to."

Tamon flew up and stood on Amaranth's lap. She smiled and then blew kisses at her.

Narella came up to her and curled up by her feet. "OH! That reminds me. I had a cat at the Crystal Crypt. It was a black one named Valora. I think you'd like her. We'll have to go get her and the other good ones. I want them here, but I do not want to go back there."

Odulore sat watching her. He didn't say anything but just watched. His mind was working. *I am glad she is back. I knew she couldn't be evil. I don't care who her parents are. This will work. She doesn't want anything to do with evil. Although, now it appears that she has a new sibling; he chooses to live in peace and rejects evil. This is going to be interesting. Plus, how do we figure out if there are more siblings out there?*

As they sat there more and more of the mystical forest creatures came in and surrounded them. The birds were singing, creating a peaceful setting. Amaranth was able to sit back in her chair and close her eyes. She had nothing to worry about. For the time being there was no evil around her.

Irreineot and Frally flew in and landed in the courtyard. They stood in front of Amaranth. She opened her eyes and smiled. "What are you guys doing here?"

Frally stepped forward, "We came here to check on you. Plus..." He spun around to reveal that Valora was on his back. "Plus, we brought you a little friend."

Amaranth got up and grabbed Valora, "Oh, I am so glad to see you. You really helped me when I was at the Crystal Crypt."

"I am glad you are ok. We were worried when we figured out that Crumazz was dead," Irreineot told her. "Plus, Gairrulit is not happy. He's the one that found Crumazz. We grabbed Valora and took off. I don't know how Puggaald is doing. We did not see him."

"You guys need to go back for Puggaald. He helped me get rid of Crumazz. Crumazz wanted to take over the kingdom and destroy it," She told them.

They took off out of the castle.

Chapter 10

Ash and Oldirrim flew into Glottenham Castle. Staedan was nowhere to be seen. However, Chrono saw them land in the courtyard. He greeted them, "Greetings friends! When do you need assistance?"

"We are here to tell you that at this time, we won't be needing any assistance. Amaranth is now at Rissingshire Castle. She was able to escape by killing Crumazz. We were also informed that Qrizor is also dead."

"Great! I will let Staedan and Shelyn know."

They flew out of the castle and on to the next one. They landed at Grimtol Castle where Xodius was in the garden area of the castle and were greeted by the rabbits, Nesquix and Periwinkle.

"How are..." Nesquix asked while Periwinkle interrupted him, "Who are you?"

Ash answered them, "We are Ash and Oldirrim. We come from Rissingshire Castle. Our message is for Xodius. It is good news. We do not need assistance and Crumazz and Qrizor are both dead."

Xodius got up and walked quickly over to the owls. "What is this you say?" He questioned.

"Your assistance is no longer needed. Amaranth is not looking to take over the kingdom. She is now at Rissingshire Castle with Odulore. Both Crumazz and Qrizor are dead. So the kingdom will be in peace for a while longer."

"I am so grateful. Can you imagine trying to get these two to pay attention? Nesquix and Periwinkle are great companions, but easily distracted."

"We need to continue spreading the word," Oldirrim told him.

They flew up and out of the castle. The last castle that they had to visit was Langdale Castle where Drozan and Zolya live with the elves. This castle sits a top the Lavalbourg Gorge.

Head elf, Fenian, greeted them, "Hello my fair owls. How are you? Where do you come from?"

Ash landed next to him and told him, "I am Ash and this is Oldirrim. We come from Rissingshire Castle. Is Drozan here?"

Zolya came out from her sitting room when she heard the voices. "Hi Ash! Hi Oldirrim! How are things at Rissingshire?"

"They are wonderful. We require no assistance. Amaranth is back at Rissingshire and things are good. Plus, Crumazz and his father Qrizor are both dead."

Drozan joined them in the courtyard, "This is good news. We will have a peaceful kingdom for a while."

Both owls nod yes and then flew away from the castle and back to Rissingshire.

When they get to Rissingshire there is still a great gathering of animals and mystical forest creatures. Odulore and Amaranth are seated by the fireplace. The owls land next to them. Odulore looked up and asked, "Did you notify everyone?" Both of the owls nodded yes. "Thank you."

Amaranth turned her head and looked at Odulore, "We should compare journals. See what they say and how their information can both help us. We need to keep the peace of the kingdom."

"Yes, I agree. However, you don't look like you want to go anywhere that is not in that chair." He smiled at her.

"True."

The dragons returned and this time it was three of them and Puggaald. Gairrulit went up to Amaranth, wiping away any creature in his way with his wings. He glared at her, "Did you kill Crumazz?" He demanded.

She stood up and looked him directly in the eyes, "Yes, I did. I had a choice of killing him or turning into my mother. I have no desire to be that evil and trapped in a crypt for a lifetime. No thank you! So, in order to escape, I had to kill Crumazz. I know you won't agree with me, but I did what I had to do." They stood there staring at each other.

Gairrulit turned and walked away. Then he turned back to her and said, "You are right. I do not agree with you. Crumazz was a great wizard. There was no reason to kill him. You weren't there long enough to come to that conclusion. I hope you are happy."

"I am!" She sat back down. Her energy was draining out of her. She had to get re-energized. "I need to get some rest. This is draining."

"I didn't do anything with your room. So, you can go back to your own room. I was not completely convinced that you were not coming back. I did take precautions and planned, just in case you were going to the dark side. I'm not stupid."

She nodded, "I understand and I appreciate that. I will head off to my room. I will see you in the morning." She got up and walked off to her room.

Avras appeared in the courtyard next to Odulore, "Hey, do you know what you are doing?"

"Can you just enter like everyone else? Do you have to just appear? Sit down and take a load off your feet that you didn't use."

"You did not answer my question." He said as he sat down.

"I know. Yes, I know what I am doing. She may have had the most evil parents in the kingdom, but she is nothing like them. She was raised in my household with good parents. Also, now she knows that they abandoned her and her mother got her to kill her brother when she did not know it was her brother. I believe that she still would have killed him, but it would have been more difficult."

"Ok, as long as you realize what you are getting yourself into. I think you are thinking with your heart and not your head."

"That's your opinion, and we all have one. I just don't agree with you."

He shook his head back and forth in disagreement.

A griffin landed in the courtyard with Azohr holding on to his back. Azohr walked over to Odulore, "I hear there has been some excitement over here in Maerith Kingdom. What kind of trouble have you been up to?"

"No trouble here friend. Excitement, well, that very well could be. Amaranth was kidnapped by Crumazz or at least the dragon that Crumazz sent to get her. She ended up killing him so that she could escape. We found out that she and Crumazz were siblings and that they had another sibling, Qbaris. No one had heard of him at all. We will try to figure out who all the siblings are. We believe that Qrizor populated more than Maerith Kingdom with his kids.The amazing part is that so far only Crumazz was evil."

"You all are crazy busy over here. I heard correctly. So, where is Amaranth?"

"She is here, in her room. She has made her allegiance known."

Azohr looked at Avras and Avras shook his head back and forth. "I see we have some disagreement here," Azohr laughed.

"Yes, I disagree with him. He's not thinking with his head."

"Well, the sun is setting. So, it's time to retire for the evening. I will disagree with you another day," Odulore said, getting up and walking out to his room.

Azohr took off with his griffin and Avras disappeared. The rest of the animals and mystical forest creatures left the castle.

Chapter 11

The sun was peeking through the treetops of the forest as Amaranth stood out front of the Rissingshire Castle and watched the pixies as they flew around the grassland. There were colored sparkles as they flew back and forth. It put a smile on her face until her mind went wandering, *What a mixed up life I have. I cannot believe that Qrizor was my father and Crumazz was my brother. No one told me. My mother should have been the one to tell me. Why did she hide it from me? Who is Qbaris? I know she says he is my brother, but it sounds like he doesn't know the family tree either. I know I need to get this out of my head, but how?*

Odulore walked up to her and handed her a hot mug of coffee, "What's on your mind?"

"Same ole, same ole that has been on my mind lately. I think I'll go back to my room and read my mother's journal. There has to be some answers in there. She addressed it to me. I hope she will tell me why she did what she did. Why did I not know about my brothers? Are there any others out there? Half-siblings? So, if you need me, I'll be in my room," she told him and walked away to her room.

A group of pixies flew up and surrounded him. Tamon said to him, "How is she doing? Can we help?"

"She'll be ok. She just has a lot on her mind. I can't say as though I blame her. She just found out that a large portion of her life is a lie."

Tamon smiled and said, "We will send her positive energy." They flew off into the grassland. Odulore stood and watched them fly away. He leaned back against the castle and slid down to sit on the ground.

Evatius trotted up to Odulore. He stopped in front of him. “I tell you there is going to be trouble.”

“Why do you say this?”

“This whole situation with Amaranth and Qbaris. Their parents were both very evil. How can we trust them?”

“Well, I guess we’ll see about that. I trust her. I don’t know Qbaris to say not to trust him. What do you know about him?”

“I know that he doesn’t come in to the forest. I had never heard of him. How do we have someone at a castle in the kingdom, and we do not know about him?”

Odulore shrugged his shoulders, “I don’t know. We stayed away from that castle because Qrizor was there.”

Back in her room, Amaranth sat at her table. She had her mother’s journal in front of her. She thought to herself, *Time to get reading and see if she has anything to tell me about my father and brothers. I need answers.*

She opened the journal and found the spot where she had stopped reading. She scanned the page to get past the death potion. She began reading again.

Did you use the potions on Crumazz? Is he now gone? That is a good thing. He was pure evil. Now the question is, did you go back to Odulore? Don’t be surprised if he does not believe you. By now his father has probably told him about your family tree. The question is, did he tell you? If he did, then I am sure that you are mad at me. I did not tell you who your father and siblings were. If not, then let me explain to you who your father is along with who you siblings are.

Your father is Qrizor. Yes, this means that Crumazz was your brother. Also, there is another brother, Qbaris. Both of them were raised at Miserth Castle. Also, Qrizor has a habit of going off for long periods of time to other kingdoms. I would not be surprised if there are more half-siblings out there. I just do not know who they are.

I am sure that your next question is why were you not raised at Miserth? I did not want you raised with them. I had to give you to someone else to raise because Qrizor would not allow me to have you at the Crystal Crypt. I knew that Trodus and his wife, Tatiana, would take great care of, as if you were their own.

Qrizor let me out of the Crystal Crypt long enough to take you to Rissingshire Castle and drop you off. I left a note for them to keep my secret and take care of you.

Your last question would be, why did I have you kill Crumazz? The answer to that is that he was pure evil. I overheard his plans with Qrizor of taking over the kingdom. It was beyond evil. Then one day Crumazz came to the crypt and told me that his father was dead. He said that there was a fight between Qrizor and a dragon Qrizor lost the battle and perished. Crumazz laughed as he told me the story I knew that it was his dragon and that he had set the whole thing up. It wouldn't be just dark days with him but dark years.

I want you to know that all the evil that I did was because I had no choice. You have a choice of either good or evil. I hope that you chose to go back to Rissingshire Castle.

If you are in the Crystal Crypt and Crumazz is dead, you need to get out. This crypt will bring nothing but evil.

I was a good witch prior to being with Qrizor. He was the ultimate bad boy. I could not resist him. I fell into his trance and my life was changed. He promised me the kingdom.

I told you earlier that Qrizor would help you rule the kingdom. That was to get you to go against Crumazz. I also did not tell you about Qbaris because if you knew that you may have someone on your side with Qrizor, you may not go against Crumazz.

I knew that you would weigh having only 1 wizard backing you versus the whole rest of the kingdom backing you. I hope that you made the decision that I thought you would.

If you did not kill Crumazz, you now know that there is no escape. He will hold you hostage. His unbridled anger and the fact you are siblings could put your life at risk. When he takes a wife, you will also be expendable, and he will kill you if you hadn't already done it.

Amaranth sat there at the table and looked up from the journal. Both the cats came in and jumped up in front of her. She petted them both. Narella looked up at her, "Is everything ok?"

She shook her head and tears ran down her cheeks while she stroked the backs of both cats. Nothing was spoken by her.

Zyrsit flew in and sat between the cats. He tilted his head back and forth as he looked at her. Glurx walked in, "It's almost time for breakfast. Are you coming? I made your favorite breakfast."

"Thanks Glurx, I will be there shortly," she answered him as she wiped away her tears.

Glurx left and went to the dining hall. Amaranth sat for a few more moments. Zyrsit said, "Let's go! I'm hungry." The felines both nodded, and they jumped down from the table. She got up from her table and followed them to the dining hall.

On the way Odulore came up beside her, "Did the journal tell you anything more?"

"She confirmed my family tree. Plus, she supposedly does not know if Qrizor had any more children. I'm not sure if I believe her or not. I mean, I didn't know about Crumazz and Qbaris. What other facts and family remain unknown to me? Oh yeah, she also claims that she was a good witch and it's all Qrizor's fault that she turned evil," Amaranth told him and let out a big sigh. They walked in silence to the dining hall and sat down in their usual spots.

Zizor and the goblins came out with the trays of breakfast. "I hope you like your breakfast. I made your favorites: deep-fried French toast with pineapple and lots of powdered sugar., bacon done to the crispiness you like and a bowl of fruit. I also made your special morning beverage of orange-pineapple and green tea," he said to Amaranth with his hands on her shoulders.

Amaranth placed her hand on his and said, "Thank you. I really do appreciate it. They are my favorites." She then went on to eat her breakfast.

Odulore looked up at her and asked, "Are you going to want to compare journals?"

"So far, there is nothing to compare. She basically fessed up to everything that your father told you in his. Give me some more time to read further and see if there is anything in there. I am sure that at some point I am going to have to verify what she says it true," she answered him.

Dax, the Great Dane walked into the dining hall and directly next to Odulore. He looked at him and said, "Qbaris has sent me here. He wants to know your plan for the Maerith Kingdom. Does it include Miserth Castle and if so, what are your plans?"

"Well, first of all, we are having breakfast. Secondly, why doesn't he come here and ask for himself?" Odulore answered him.

"I will let him know," Dax replied and left.

Odulore shook his head and said, "If he wants to know our plans, he should come ask and not send his dog."

"You could have been a bit nicer though. It's not the dog's fault," Amaranth told him.

Zizor and the goblins came back out from the kitchen and cleaned up the trays while everyone else left the dining hall.

Amaranth returned to her room to read more of her mother's journal. She turned the page and this is what was written.

Now what? You have a book of potions. These are all the potions that you will ever need and some that you will never use.

Know that I will forever be known as the evil witch. You get to choose which you will be.

Her mother's signature was at the bottom of the letter.

She looked up and shook her head. Odulore walked in and asked, "What are you shaking your head about?"

"Basically, she didn't tell me anything except what I already told you and that the book is full of all the potions I could ever need. I was really hoping that there was more she could tell me. It's a huge disappointment," she explained.

"We have your book of potions and my book of spells. I am sure that we will be able to keep things under control in the Maerith Kingdom together."

In flew the owls and dragons while the felines pranced in. They gathered around them and listened intently.

"What are you suggesting?" She asked him.

"You'll find out soon enough. Although, it looks like we have quite the audience."

She smiled and looked directly into his eyes, "Do you have something in mind and are not sharing?"

"Of course, but you will find out later. Trust me, you'll like it." He stood there smiling at her. The animals all exited the room.

Chapter 12

Dax returned to Miserth Castle and sat down next to Qbaris, "He told me to tell you that if you want to know what the plan is that you need to come ask for yourself."

Qbaris shook his head, "Why am I not surprised? I really do not want to leave the castle, yet he wants me to go over there."

Darca walked in to Qbaris' room, "I see Odulore on his horse, Magnus coming through the forest."

Qbaris got up and walked out to the courtyard as Odulore and Magnus enter. "Greetings, friends!" he says to them.

"Greetings!" Odulore replied. "I know that you wanted to know about my plans for the Maerith Kingdom. I figured I would come out here to let you know. Where would you like to talk?"

"Let's sit by the fireplace. It's the best place." He motions for him to follow him.

They sat down in the chairs and Odulore assured him, "I want the Maerith Kingdom to be one of peace and quiet. I want everyone to be able to go about their own business. I understand that you are wanting the same."

"Yes, I want peace and to be left alone. I don't need to be a part of the Maerith Kingdom social club. I have done just fine by myself here at Miserth Castle. Now that Crumazz is gone. I don't even have to worry about him coming home. I will be cleaning out his room. I want nothing evil here. Where should I dispose of all of his things?"

"What did he have?"

"He had quite the collection of crystals."

"The crystals will be fine and you don't need to get rid of them. They are not inherently evil."

"Ok, that works for me. Although, I do want his room cleared out. I don't know what I will use that room for, but having him out of there is a great start," He smiled.

Odulore smiled and replied, "Understood. I will be off and leave you alone. The only time we will contact you is if there is something you need to know in order to protect the castle." He got up and left on Magnus.

Qbaris sat there. Dax and Darca came up with one on each side of his so that he could pet them both on their heads at the same time. He laid his head back and closed his eyes.

Suddenly there was a loud crash that opened his eyes. He looked up and there stood a wizard with two winged lions next to him. Qbaris stood up and asked, "Who are you and what do you want?"

"I am Avras. These are my companions Axe and Artimas. I am here to find out what you are up to. I know that your parents were Qrizor and Zaleria and that your siblings are Crumazz and Amaranth. Only you and Amaranth remain. I know that Amaranth took care of Crumazz. What happened to Qrizor and Zaleria? Did you have anything to do with those?" He asked him.

"Ok, so you think I had something to do with their demise? I did not. I was told of their deaths. All of my knowledge is second hand. What am I up to? I was relaxing until you got here. I just had Odulore here that was telling me that his plans for the Maerith Kingdom are peace and quiet."

They both stood there with their companions by their sides in silence for a few moments. Avras spoke up, "I am glad to hear all of this. I have wanted the kingdom to be peaceful and quiet for some time. I hope that we are entering this time of peace and quiet for a long while. I will leave you and your dogs be in peace." He turned, got on Axe, and they flew out of the castle.

Qbaris sat back down and thought to himself, *Good grief, these guys need to get together and leave me alone. I haven't done a thing, and they all are up in arms about my parents and brother dying. I have no idea who killed my parents. Honestly, with how evil they both were, I really don't care to know. They did me a favor.* Then he closed his eyes and went off to sleep with Dax and Darca by his side.

Back at the Rissingshire Castle Odulore and Magnus return with Oizu and Irreineot out front of the castle keeping watch. They entered the courtyard and Amaranth walked out of her room. "Where did you go?"

"I went to let Qbaris know our plans of keeping Maerith Kingdom peaceful and quiet," Odulore told her.

"Good. I am sure he appreciated knowing that. It would be nice if this all goes peacefully. I have had enough excitement for a while."

Avras appeared in the courtyard with his winged lions. He looked at them and announced, "I went to see Qbaris. I wanted to let him know that peace and quiet is the plan and asked him what his plans were. He says it's for peace and quiet. I hope he is truthful."

Odulore shook his head and said to him, "Really? I was just there. You didn't need to go there. He probably feels ambushed."

"Yeah, well, I went anyway. We need this to be clear to anyone associated with Qrizor and Zaleria. They need to know that we will not permit evil in Maerith Kingdom." Avras said as he looked right at Amaranth.

"Yeah, I get the hint. I know you are talking directly to me. I am all for peace and quiet. If you remember, I grew up here and not with all the evil. They were my parents, but I never knew them. I did not have their influence at all. No worries," Amaranth said to him with a snarkiness in her voice and shook her head at him in disbelief.

Odulore shook his head also, rolled his eyes, and looked at him. Avras shrugged his shoulders, turned around, and took off with his winged lions.

They went into Trodus' room and sat at the table. Odulore laid out the book of spells and the letter from his father. "I think we need to keep this book and yours close together. What are your thoughts?"

"I think you are right. I will add it to your bookshelf. I have never been in this room. He would never allow me in here. This is a great room. I love all the candles and the crystal ball. Have you used the crystal ball yet?"

He smiled at her, "Yes, I have. It's pretty accurate. Although, for pictures, it doesn't give a full picture. For example, I asked where you were and it showed you at a table reading."

"So, you did spy on me. It is reassuring and creepy all at the same time. I wish it would have given you context along with the picture." She told him and smiled back at him.

The felines walked in and jumped up on the table in between them. Then the owls flew in sat on the table also. Odulore looked at all of them and then back to Amaranth. "Isn't this crazy? They all want to be in here with us. Like this castle isn't big enough."

"Yeah, it's nice to have them close by. They are comforting. This whole thing is getting more and more comfortable. I feel safe and secure here now. Although, Avras is a bit disturbing."

Zyrsit flew in and landed on the table, "I saw Gairrulit is on his way here. I don't know what kind of trouble he is going to cause, but you needed to know."

"Thank you Zyrsit. I will go greet him," said Odulore. "You don't need to deal with him." He got up and walked outside to the courtyard.

Gairrulit landed in the courtyard in front of Odulore. Soon there were many mystical forest creatures in the courtyard with them. Evatius galloped in and stood next to him.

"What do you want Gairrulit?"

"I am here to warn you that even though you think the Maerith Kingdom is rid of evil, it is not too far away and in a form that will surprise you. Your peace and quiet will not last long."

"What are you talking about?"

"Exactly what I said. You will be in for a surprise and the day will happen when you least expect it to. Keep a watch out for it."

Gairrulit turned and flew out of the castle. Odulore looked at Evatius and shook his head. He turned and walked back into Trodus' room where Amaranth was still sitting.

"What did he want?" She asked him.

He looked at her, paused for a moment and then told her, "He said that evil is coming, and we will be surprised. He did not say how we will be surprised. He also did not say when."

She sat there and looked at him. Amaranth put her face in her hands with her elbows on the table. She shook her head and looked up at him again. Narella rubbed up against her arm. She scratched her on her chin.

“What do you want to do?” She questioned.

“I think that we can only be prepared, but there’s really not much to do. We will need to have some spells and potions ready for anything. The problem is we have no idea what or who the evil is.”

Chapter 13

At the Crystal Crypt there was a dark cloud of smoke that was slowly creeping along the floor. It entered all the tunnels and rooms and found no one there.

Simultaneously Amaranth got an eerie feeling run through her body. It was as if she could feel the dark cloud. She went to Odulore and asked him, "Did you have a spell that my father used on my mother to keep her in the Crystal Crypt? I have this feeling that there is an evil presence there."

"Yes, I did. I can have one of the Peagsuses take me there and call out the spell at a safe distance. We have no evil ones here." He left his room and went out to the livery. Ranios was waiting for him. Odulore got on his back, and they flew off to a spot in the forest where no one could see them.

Odulore stood there, raised up his arms towards the Crystal Crypt, and commanded, "Ignitim Serpite to the Crystal Crypt, all entrances and exits from the greatest heights and the deepest depths. Ignitim Serpite for all enternity."

They stood there for a few moments when they saw the smoke rise in the entrance to the Crystal Crypt, but it could not come out. "Let's return home," he said to Ranios.

Evatius followed them back to Rissingshire Castle. "What were you up to?" He asked him.

"We went to the Crystal Crypt to put a spell on it and trap whatever and whoever is in it so that we don't have to deal with any more evil from the crypt," Odulore told him. "I am positive that this spell will do the trick. I used one that was out of my father's spell book."

Amaranth came out to the courtyard and sat down next to the fireplace. Narella and Valora followed her and laid down at her feet. The mystical forest creatures came in and gathered around them.

Odulore went up to her, ran his fingers through her thick black hair, and then walked to the kitchen. He met up with Zizor. "What do you need?" He questioned.

"I need you to fix all of Amaranth's dinner favorites for tonight. I want it served right at sunset."

"Ok, I will have it ready at sunset." Zizor turned to the goblins and told them, "You heard him. We need to get moving so that everything is ready for sunset."

Odulore went back out to the courtyard. "Would you like to go for a nice walk? How about we walk over to Bredenrath Pond?" He held out his hand to Amaranth. She took his hand and stood up, "Why I would love to." They walked out of the castle and out into the Demack Grassland.

The pixies encircled them as they walked to the pond. When they got to the dock, there were fish jumping in the pond along with fireflies dancing above the water. Odulore took her hand, got down on one knee, and pulled a ring out of his pocket. He looked up at her and said, "Amaranth, we have known each other our entire lives. There has been this connection between us that I have never felt with anyone else. I want you by my side. I want you to rule the Maerith Kingdom with me. Will you marry me? Will you be my wife?"

She smiled from ear to ear and a tear rolled down her cheek. It took her a few moments that to Odulore felt like forever. She stared into his eyes, still holding his hand, she said, "Yes, of course. Yes, I will marry you. I will be your wife."

He put the gold and amethyst ring on her finger, got up, gave her a big hug and twirled her around. The pixies all cheered.

Hand in hand, they walked back to Rissingshire Castle. When they entered the courtyard they were greeted by Zizor and the goblins including Glurx and Puggaald. "She said yes!" Odulore exclaimed. The courtyard erupted with cheers.

Avras and Arietta landed in the courtyard with Axe and Artimas. "Did we hear cheering?" Arietta asked.

"Yes, yes, you did," Amaranth excitedly answered her. She ran over to her and showed off her ring.

"I like it. Good job Odulore. Nice ring," Arietta smiled at him.

"Seriously, you popped the question already?"

"Avras! Shut up! They are happy. You don't need to be so mean," his wife snapped at him.

"Don't worry about Arietta. He's fine. Yes, I already popped the question. Hey, if anything this week has shown me that we can take nothing for granted. We need to maximize every day's potential. Plus, to tell you the truth, I have had the ring for a while. I was waiting for the right moment. I found the right moment." Odulore explained.

The sun just started to set and Zizor said, "Dinner is ready in the dining hall. Let's all head down there." He and the goblins walked off to the kitchen.

"Come on, let's go eat." Odulore waved everyone to go to the dining hall.

Amaranth sat down at the table and Zizor brought out her tray first. As he placed it in front of her, he said, "I hope it's all to your liking."

She looked at the tray, smiled, looked up at him, and said, "Yes, everything looks perfect. They are all my dinner favorites."
Amaranth enjoyed her dinner of dry rub ribs, smashed potatoes and honey carrots.

Odulore sat across from her, and he kept looking up at her while he was eating. He enjoyed watching her enjoy your dinner.

Zizor and the goblins came out and cleared the empty trays. Everyone else went out to the courtyard. The sun had set while they were eating. The courtyard was lined with torches. Everyone gathered around the fireplace. Zyrsit flew up to the castle wall and yelled, "Ready!"

The sky filled with fireworks. The mystical forest creatures entered the courtyard and surrounded them. The goblins came out from the kitchen and also joined in. There were lots of "ooo's" and "ahhh's."

Amaranth moved her chair closer to Odulore and held his hand while they watched the giant display. Periodically she looked over at him and smiled. He returned her smile with a smile. She thought to herself, *I cannot believe how this week has gone from tragedy to happiness. I would have never thought that I was going to escape that horrible crypt and now I am engaged to the love of my life. I cannot wait to get married.*

The fireworks display ended and Avras said, "Congratulations to you both. We are going to head back to Eagleview Castle. See you soon." Arietta and Avras flew out of the castle on Axe and Artimas.

The mystical forest creatures exited the castle leaving Amaranth and Odulore in the courtyard. "What's on your mind?" He asked her.

"I am completely enjoying how this day has gone. Also, I can't believe how this week has gone. It's been a whirlwind. I went from being kidnapped to killing a guy that ended up being my brother, finding out that I had another brother, and now I am engaged to the love of my life."

"Well, you can't say that life has been dull then," he chuckled.

She smiled at him, "That's for sure. It has not been dull. I am looking forward to the wedding. I can also do without some of that excitement. I do not want to be kidnapped ever again."

Odulore smiled at her, stood up, motioned for her hand, and walked her to her room. He gave her a kiss on the cheek and went to his own room.

Chapter 14

Zyrsit sat on the wall of the castle as he watched the Demack Grassland and the edge of the Calegan Forest. Evatius ran out of the forest to the castle entrance. He flew down to greet him. "Why are you in a hurry?"

"I was by the edge of the forest near the Crystal Crypt and there was black smoke encircling it but only right above it. I have to let Odulore know this."

Ash and Oldirrim flew into the courtyard from the livery. They landed on the chairs by the fireplace. Zyrsit joined them and Evatius stood close by. Soon they were joined by Narella and Valora.

Odulore walked out into the courtyard, "What's the gathering about?"

"There's black smoke encircling the Crystal Crypt, but it isn't going anywhere. It's just right over top of it," Evatius informs him.

"Yes, I am not surprised. This means that my spell is working and that we were right that there was still evil in the crypt. No worries."

Amaranth walked out into the courtyard and heard what Odulore said. She smiled and nodded, "I am glad that I got out of the Crystal Crypt when I did."

Puggaald and Glurx ran into the courtyard. "Come quick, something is wrong with Zizor," They yelled. Everyone ran to the kitchen. Zizor was lying on the floor with a spoon still in his hand.

Odulore sprinted to get the book of spells. He grabbed it off the table and ran back to the kitchen. When he opened the book the spell of healing was there. He raised his arms toward Zizor and said, "Augior Intimius, Augior Intimius."

Zizor woke up and sat up on the floor. He blinked his round green eyes multiple times, focused on Odulore, and said, "What happened?"

"That's what we want to know."

"I was stirring the morning oatmeal and the next thing I knew is that I woke up on the floor."

"No one, go near the oatmeal. Where's the lid to the pot?"

Puggaald handed it to him. Odulore took the lid, looked away from the pot but side-eyed it to put the lid on the pot. He looked into the book of spells, turned the page and saw one to dismiss other spells. He raised his arms towards the pot of oatmeal and said, "Repium Demones, Repium Demones."

Odulore turned around and instructed the goblins, "Take that pot outside of the castle and bury it." Puggaald and Glurx each took one handle and scurried out of the kitchen and then out of the castle with the pot. Zezerm followed closely behind them with a shovel. He dug the hole, and they placed the pot down into it. The three of them threw the dirt over the pot and returned to the castle.

Zizor got up off the floor and sat in a chair. "How are you feeling now?" Amaranth asked him.

"Fine, I guess. I am fine."

The goblins ran in and announced, "It's buried!"

Odulore looked at them and said, "Good. Thank you. Now the question is, what happened to the oatmeal and who messed with it?"

Zizor raised his hand, pointed toward the side door of the kitchen, and said, "I saw a shadowy figure in the doorway this morning, but it didn't stay long. I thought I had just imagined it, but maybe not."

"Great, now we have an evil being here in the castle," Amaranth shook her head in dismay. "I thought we would get some peace with the crypt being sealed."

They all looked at each other for a moment and a shadowy figure went past the entry to the dining hall. The figure entered into the dining hall and just floated in one spot. Odulore asked it, "What is your name?"

"I am Kezrin from the dark underworld," it answered.

"What do you want?"

"I have come to warn you that entrance to the dark underworld is opening once again and there is great evil coming to the Maerith Kingdom. The day is coming soon when it will be dark. You have been warned," it informed them.

Then as quickly as it appeared, it disappeared. They looked around for it, but it was gone. Odulore ran out of the dining hall and back to his father's room. He read through the titles on the shelf and came upon one that was titled, Tales of the Dark Underworld. He grabbed the book and ran back to the dining hall.

"I remembered seeing this book on the shelf. It is titled, Tales of the Dark Underworld. The questions are, what does it tell us and is it accurate or just tales?"

"What will happen next? I thought that there was going to be peace. Now we've had this creature and Gairrulit that both gave us a warning about evil coming soon. Anyone want to guess what will happen?" Amaranth pondered out loud.

All she had for a response was a bunch of shoulder shrugs from everyone. They all exited the dining hall and went their separate ways.

Odulore went back to his father's room and scanned the bookshelves for more books about the dark underworld. He removed a few books from the book shelves and set them down on the table. Within a few moments Amaranth joined him, "I can help you read through those to see what could potentially happen."

"Great! Pick one and start reading. I will start with the book of tales. It should be interesting to say the least."

He began to read the intro to himself.

This book will take you into take you into the dark underworld. Be careful that you do not read it out loud. Some things may be conjured up if said out loud.

"Oh this encouraging and scary all at the same time. There's a disclaimer at the front saying not to read the book out loud because of things that may be conjured up."

"Yikes, that is scary. This book is titled, The Great Dark Underworld. I wonder what is so great about it. I do see the same disclaimer on the intro page."

They continued reading to themselves. Periodically they looked up at each other. A few hours went by and they were still reading.

Avras appeared in the doorway. “Hey! What are we reading so intently?”

Amaranth looked up. “Fun stuff. We are reading about the great Dark Underworld. Want to join in?” She remarked in a snarky voice.

“We were visited by Kezrin this morning. He tried to poison Zizor and we are not sure if he was the intended target or not. We were able to help Zizor, but Kezrin told us that the evil from the Dark Underworld was going to escape soon and the kingdom would become dark.”

He nodded his head and replied, “Great! I thought that Kezrin was banished permanently ages ago. This is not a good thing. If he was able to escape it’s hard telling who else will be returning. This could be disastrous. Do you know who else was sent there?”

They both held up their books and pointed to the other books that were on the table. Odulore spoke up, “No, that’s why we are reading these books. They are all on the Dark Underworld. What do you know?”

“I know that when anyone evil in this world dies, their spirit goes to the dark underworld to continue their life. They do not actually die. So, yes, as you are imagining Qrizor, Zaleria, and Crumazz would be included in this. If the Dark Underworld spirits and demons are escaping it is going to include the three of them. I don’t know where the escape portal is, but obviously Kezrin was able to escape. I would anticipate visits from those three and who knows who else. There were so many that went there in the early years of when Trodus was cleaning up Maerith Kingdom. You better start reading faster. You not only need to know who was banished to the Dark Underworld, but you also need to know your spells and potions in order to send them back to where they belong and seal up the portal.”

The owls and Zyrsit flew in and landed on top of the books. The looked around the room at each of them. No words were said at the moment. The room was silent.

Amaranth interrupted the silence, "Wow! This is going to get crazier than crazy. So, what you are saying is that when they die, they don't really die. This means that Crumazz will come back and most likely take revenge on me because I sent him to the Dark Underworld. Although, I did not know that was even a thing. It's never been spoken about."

"I had heard of it, but I thought it was just an imaginary place that parents told their children about to make them behave. I didn't think it was real. I remember my dad telling us about a few of them. They were some really scary creatures. He never said their names, but just gave descriptions of them and what they did that got them banished," Odulore told them.

Avras disappeared, and they went back to reading the books about the Dark Underworld. The cats came in and sat at their feet. Hours of silence slipped by as they emerged themselves in the books' content.

Chapter 15

The dark underworld was brimming with evil spirits and demons. Kezrin floated up to Crumazz, Qrizor and Zaleria and told them, "I have warned them. I don't know if they believed me or not. Zizor survived because Odulore came to his rescue. When will we all return? Who are you taking with you?"

Qrizor gave him a twisted smirky smile, "I cannot wait to see what has happened with them. They think they are going to live happily ever after. That is not going to happen if I can help it. No daughter of mine will be with a son of Trodus'. We will rule the kingdom, NOT them!"

"Oh come on, he makes her happy. What harm can come from it?" Zaleria questioned him.

"Do NOT question me, witch. Remember I had you banished to the Crystal Crypt for a lifetime. I can make you disappear for ever, even from here." Qrizor snapped at her.

Crumazz smiled and said, "I will get back at her. She didn't think twice about sending me here. I will get my revenge!"

"No, you don't need to do that. You don't need revenge on her. She's your sister," Zaleria pleaded with him.

"You need to stop defending her. She has gone to the other side. If I hear you defend her just one more time, you will be banished forever! You will never see her nor anyone else ever again. Don't think that I can't do it," Qrizor glared at Zaleria.

Zaleria backed away from him. She thought to herself, *Man this is ridiculous. She is my daughter. She is his daughter. He has turned into a level of mean that I have never seen before. I really hope that Odulore figures out how to not let us return. If only there was a way for me to return without him.*

"What are you thinking witch?" Qrizor yelled at her.

"Nothing. I am thinking nothing."

"Father, do we really need her? She is the reason Amaranth sent me here. I bet she didn't even tell her where I was going. It's all HER fault. These witches are nothing but trouble and in the way," Crumazz said.

The dark smoke enveloped them and Ozrig appeared in front of them. "You three need to stop fighting amongst yourselves. You need to band together and use the witches to your advantage. Do not dismiss how you can use them to take over the Maerith Kingdom. However, before we take over Maerith Kingdom we need to take over Zodel Kingdom. We will take it over and then attack Maerith Kingdom from the east. The first castle to take over is Corlach Castle, home of Azohr. Be ready to escape through the portal tonight."

They all nodded in agreement. Ozrig disappeared from them. He reappeared over at the portal entrance that was being guarded by Gairrulit and Frally. "Be prepared for a great exiting tonight. We are heading out to take over Corlach Castle. We need those griffins and gargoyles to help us." They nodded to him.

Korzath appeared in Ozrig's cove and questioned him, "Are they going to leave Zaleria behind? I think she needs to be taught a lesson. I can put her in the cove with the Tarantulas. She has been disrespectful of Qrizor, and she turned her daughter on her son."

"She will be dealt with in time, but first we will use her and get the most that we can out of her. She is expendable, but can be quite useful. I think that Amaranth will trust her. She will want to trust her so much that she will make a mistake, and we should end up with both witches. It will be better to do away with both of them at the same time. They need to know who the ruler is and what the consequences are for disloyalty. Now leave me."

Ozrig sat at his table and thought to himself, *These demons, witches, and wizards are troublesome. They are going to drive me crazy. However, once we take over the kingdoms I will use them to continue my quest to take over both worlds. Now to get my evil partner in on the whole scheme. She will not be surprised but she will be thrilled. We will rule the worlds together!* He creepily laughed out loud.

Annamaaz appeared in his cove. She went up to Ozrig and ran her fingers through his pitch black hair. "You were thinking about me. I know it. Please tell me more."

"Oh my evilness, we are going to take over both worlds. You will be my goddess. I will be a god. We will convert all the good to evil. It is going to be so evil!" He told her as he held her tight to him.

"This will be exciting. Can I watch it unfold? I want to watch you take over the other world. You are already a god here," she implored him.

He stood up and took her over to a crystal ball. "Here, when we are out tonight, you can come over here and tell it to show you the take over. The ball will light up and show you everything going on. You can cheer for us from here."

Zaleria walked to her cove and sat down on a boulder. She stared out into the tunnel. She thought to herself, *This is horrible. This is beyond evil. I do not trust them. I have never trusted them. What in the world is going to happen tonight? Are they going to capture my daughter again? What will they do to me? What will they do to her? Was I not evil enough?*

Crumazz entered his mother's cove. He glared at her, "You always loved her more than me. You favored her. She was your favorite. You hated me. Now we will get back at you and at her. I don't care what you think anymore."

"If you don't care what I think, then why did you come in here and tell me all of this?"

"I wanted you to know."

"I didn't favor her. I didn't see her either. Qrizor kept all of you from me."

"Sure, blame him. It's never your fault. It's all his fault. I don't believe you. I think you went away on your own. I think you did sneak off to see her and that's why he put a spell on the crypt to keep you in your place." He turned and left.

Zaleria sat there and shook her head. *When is this going to end? When will he quit blaming me? He thinks his father is perfect. That is so not true. I need to figure out how to escape the Dark Underworld for good. I don't care if it means that I am dead. That would be better than dealing with all of this.*

Ozrig appeared in the middle of the Dark Underworld and summoned everyone to be in his presence. "We are going to escape this world tonight and enter our previous world. This is where they believe that evil is gone. They are wrong. We will be taking over both worlds. I will be the god and Annamaaz will be the goddess. You all will do as you are told. If not, I will let Korzath take care of you. Our first castle that we are taking over will be Corlach Castle in the Zodel Kingdom. We will go about taking over one castle at a time. We will do it swiftly and quietly. This way the other castles do not suspect anything is going on. You can all go to your caves until such time I summon you again."

Immediately they left his presence so as to avoid angering him.

Chapter 16

Odulore sat reading the book of spells with Amaranth across the table reading the tales of the Dark Underworld. He looked up at her and excitedly said, “I have it figured out. I will do a spell that will protect us and the surrounding kingdoms. This will make it to where any of the evil will have to go to a different island. They will leave Parrcaster Island alone. They won’t be happy about it, but we have to protect the island. What do you think?”

“Great idea! You better get working on it and fast. If I had to guess, I would bet that they are coming this evening. Everything in these tales tells of them moving at night,” She told him.

“I will get this spell put together, and then we’ll take Ranios and Raithy out for a flight where we chant the spell together while encircling the island.”

He picked up a pen and a blank journal. In the journal he wrote out the spell.

Incenecto Vexenus for all of Parrcaster Island above and below–to lock magic portals

Flarello Viralerous for all of Parrcaster Island above and below–to block evil spells

Proticum Banio for all of Parrcaster Island above and below–to strength the magical barrier

Immolortia Feliatis send your protection to Parrcaster Island above and below–magical guardian spirit

"Are you ready for this? We will repeat these four spells as we fly a mile out from the shore line all the way around the island. Incenecto Vexenus for all of Parrcaster Island above and below, Flarello Viralerous for all of Parrcaster Island above and below, Proticum Banio for all of Parrcaster Island above and below, Immolortia Feliatis send your protection to Parrcaster Island above and below. I have written it down, but it's better if we can memorize it and repeat it incessantly."

Amaranth looked at him, "I completely agree and will work with you."

"Let's go now. We have a few hours until sundown, so we are ahead of them." They got up from the table and walked out to the livery to get Ranios and Raithy out of their stable to fly.

They flew out of the castle, went over Zodel Kingdom, and went to a mile out from the shoreline. They both chanted the spell, "Incenecto Vexenus for all of Parrcaster Island above and below, Flarello Viralerous for all of Parrcaster Island above and below, Proticum Banio for all of Parrcaster Island above and below, Immolortia Feliatis send your protection to Parrcaster Island above and below," over and over as they flew around Parrcaster Island. Odulore and Amaranth did not stop or even pause until they had completely circumvented the island. The spells were complete and protected the island. Ranios and Raithy flew them back to the castle and stopped in the courtyard. They got off them and sat by the fireplace. Casting the spells for that long took a lot of energy out of both of them. Narella and Valora came up and laid between them on the ground.

Avras appeared before them, "What happened to you two?"

Odulore opened his eyes and told him, "We just got back from casting a spell of protection around the whole island. It has exhausted us both. However, the island is protected both above and below. This will protect from those that may try to come to the island from the Dark Underworld."

"Wow, is there anything the rest of us can do?"

"Yes, if I give you the spell, can you do the same thing we did? We need this reinforced from all the kingdoms," he asked him.

"I will get the word to all the kingdoms, and we'll all cast the same spells." Avras disappeared to the other kingdoms around Parrcaster Island.

Odulore and Amaranth relaxed once again. The goblins came out from the kitchen and encircled them. Then the pixies came from the grassland and encircled them. Next came the mystical forest creatures. There was a calm the filled the courtyard.

Zizor stood in the doorway to the dining hall, "Everybody, Lunch is ready! Come on in."

Oizu and Irreineot flew in and assisted Odulore and Amaranth to get them to the dining hall to eat and restore their energy. They sat them down in their chairs at the dining table. The goblins brought their trays and steadily their energy returned to them. Slowly they sat upright in their chairs.

"Thanks everyone. We were out and cast a spell of protection over the whole island," Odulore told them.

Zyrsit flew in and announced, "Drozan and Zolya are headed this way with some elves. They look to be in a hurry."

They all got up from the table and walked to the courtyard. The goblins and Zizor cleaned up the trays and joined them later. As they entered the courtyard Drozan walked in a few steps ahead of Zolya and the elves. "Hi! How can we help you?" Odulore asked him.

"We heard that you were out casting a spell to keep us safe. Do you really think the portal to the Dark Underworld is opening?"

"We were told that it was opening and that we should expect a bunch of visitors including Qrizor, Zaleria, and Crumazz. We went out early to get the spell cast. We are assuming that they are going out at night fall. This is what we read in the various books of tales of the Dark Underworld," Odulore explained.

"Did you cover the entire island or just Maerith Kingdom?"

"We encircled the island and had it covered both above and below. We also told Avras about it and he volunteered to go to the other kingdoms and have them all cast the same spell so that it is well covered before night fall."

"There is a portal that is over by Lavalbourg Gorge. Did you close all the portals?"

"Yes, we did include that in the spells."

"Night fall is coming soon. Everyone should still be on alert. I am very confident in the spells, but I don't know how strong Ozrig is and if we are going to need anything more. This is why the head wizards of each kingdom are casting the same spell to cover the island in multitude."

They all got up and left the courtyard and the castle. They went to shores of the island. They kept repeating the spell–all the witches, wizards, warlocks, animals and mystic creatures of the forest. Each kingdom was lined side by side and connecting kingdom to kingdom. The spell was repeated until five minutes after night fall.

Chapter 17

Nightfall came and Ozrig summoned all the evil spirits, demons, witches, warlocks, and wizards that were in the Dark Underworld to the center. “We are going out through a different portal. The ones we wanted to use have been blocked. The island that we are targeting is Parrcaster Island. When we return we shall have the island as a vacation spot.” He let out a loud menacing laugh.

Three miles out from the Parrcaster Island in the Kiniriden Sea a dark water spout appeared with evil spirits, demons, witches, warlocks, and wizards pouring out of it and the sky became dark. They went toward the island but came upon a force field that they could not penetrate.

Ozrig kept repeating the spell, “Corentus Miserula” over and over. Nothing happened. He screamed out in anger, making 3-foot waves that crashed into the force field that surrounded the island.

He summoned everyone back to the portal and to the center of the Dark Underworld. His anger was pulsing. Ozrig glared around the room and yelled out while gritting his teeth, “Qrizor, Zaleria, and Crumazz front and center!”

“What is going on with this island? We could not get to it. It didn’t matter what we did. This was to be an easy takeover.”

“I don’t know. There was never a force field there before. That’s something new,” Qrizor answered.

“The three of you are being sent to Korzath for an undetermined amount of time. You lied to me. No one lies to me and gets away with it.”

Korzath came and took them away to his cave of tarantulas. Back in the center Ozrig commands the rest of them, "Let this be a lesson to all of you that no one lies to me. I will find out. If we cannot take over the island that you suggest, you will be going to Korzath's cave of tarantulas. I will go back to figuring out where our next island will be. You may all go to your caves."

Everyone quickly exited from his presence. There was not a word said among them. The only noise that you could hear were the screams coming from Korzath's cave of tarantulas.

Back in Rissingshire Castle Odulore and Amaranth were in the courtyard with Xodius, Zabine, Staedan, Shelyn, Avras, Arietta, Drozan, Zolya and Azohr. They were gathered together watching the lightning bolts cross over above the force field.

All of the Pegasuses, horses, goblins, owls, dragons, pixies, mystical forest creatures and Zizor gathered around them to listen in.

"I want to thank everyone for their assistance. I do not know if they will be back. The force field will hold up against anything. The spell that was cast does not have a time frame. That being said, I am going to repeat it once a week. Feel free to join me in doing this. I have also not seen Gairrulit and Frally. Please let me know if you see them.," Odulore told them.

Amaranth stood up, "I just want to say thank you as well. Plus, I wanted to announce that I said yes to his marriage proposal. We have not yet set a date because of all that happened yesterday and today. Witches, we will be planning something great and grand!"

Qbaris walked into the courtyard, "Hi everyone. I know that something happened today. Anyone care to share?"

"I thought you knew about the evil portal opening up today," Amaranth told him.

"Well, I didn't. Did that evil portal have anything to do with our parents?"

"Yes, yes, it did. It was reported that they were coming back here to try to take over the island and give it to Ozrig, the god of the Dark Underworld. I don't know if it was just one of their ideas or if it was all three of them. The force field protected us from whatever they had planned."

"So, now it's just you and I with none of them?"

"The only thing we don't know is how many children Qrizor fathered in any of the other kingdoms. I just found out about him after mother was gone. She never told me about him. She only referred to him as my father, but no name. Now, if you have something that tells of his other kingdom adventures, it could help us."

"I have not been in his room since he left. I will have to go through his bookshelves and see what he left behind. I will leave you all to enjoy the rest of your evening," Qbaris said, turned around and exited the castle.

Zizor whispered into the ear of Puggaald, and he took off quickly to the kitchen. Puggaald returned with a basket of marshmallows and sticks. He passed them out to everyone that wanted one. Oizu breathed fire into the bonfire pit.

The evening went on for hours with melted marshmallows and conversations. Amaranth sat down in her chair, looked around the courtyard, and thought to herself, *I cannot believe how awesome this day and evening turned out. We cast a spell together and protected the island. We didn't just protect our kingdom, but the whole island. I look forward to our life together. Here's to never hearing from the parents or Crumazz ever again.*

As the night wore on, everyone left, it was just Odulore and Amaranth sitting by the fire. The animals went back to their stables. They could see the stars on the other side of the transparent force field. He reached his hand out and took hers. They took a collective sigh, looked at each other, and closed their eyes.

Chapter 18

Evatius was in the middle of the Calegan Forest with Chrysonia. They galloped over to Bredenrath Pond. Axe and Artimas joined them.

“Hey, what do you think about yesterday?” Evatius asked them.

Axe looked at them and said, “I was glad to see that the force field worked. The Dark Underworld is no joke. They are beyond evil. I would not want to be the one that suggested they come to the island. I am sure that did not turn out well for them.”

“I think it was suggested by Qrizor, Zaleria, and Crumazz. So, being that it was a complete bust, I don’t think we’ll be bothered by them anymore. I am sure that Ozrig took care of them.”

Chrysonia spoke up, “Well, I can’t wait for the wedding. That has my vote for the next thing to focus on. How beautiful of a bride will she make? Plus, that castle courtyard will be all decorated. I am sure there will be a great variety of flowers all over the place.”

“I am with you on that. This is exciting. What a great event to plan. This is going to bring the kingdom together,” Artimas chimed in.

They were joined by hares, owls, elves, more felines, and canines. The pond was encircled with the animals. Garnet and Dewdrop jumped up out the water multiple times and swam over to Evatius.

The crowd of animals cheered for the fish. Evatius told them, “Great job! Thanks for the entertainment.”

As the sun got higher in the sky the animals dispersed back to where they came from. Evatius and Chrysonia galloped up to Rissingshire Castle. In the courtyard they were greeted by Glurx, "Hi! What do you need?"

"We are here for Odulore and Amaranth. Who did you think we wanted?" Evatius said sarcastically.

Glurx rolled his eyes and walked away to Odulore's room. "Evatius and Chrysonia are here to see you and Amaranth," he told him.

"Ok, I will go get Amaranth. Thanks." Odulore closed his book and walked over to her room. "Evatius and Chrysonia are here. Are you available?"

Amaranth looked up from her book, "Yeah, hold on." She closed her book and joined him. They walked out to the courtyard hand in hand.

"Hi!" They both greeted them. Amaranth went up and gave Chrysonia a big hug.

"Are you ready to plan a great party? We need to plan a girls night."

"I guess, they don't need our help," Odulore chuckled.

"Yeah, let's go talk elsewhere." Evatius and Odulore walked off to the dining hall.

The girls sat down and discussed their plans for the girls night. "I want tons of purple everywhere. I want purple flowers of all kinds and amethyst crystals all around. For the food, I want to have snack-size food. I don't want to use any utensils. For beverages, I want Zizor to mix my favorites, he does such a great job." She told her.

Zolya walked in, "Hey, do you need help planning anything?"

"Yes! I can always use help. I just mentioned what food and drinks I want plus the decorations for the girls party. I figure we'll do that the night before the wedding. Then we'll have the great wedding with another party, but everyone is invited to that."

Chrysonia asks Amaranth, "What do you think about having the wedding ceremony out at Lavalbourg Gorge? There's a great waterfall there. Plus, the deck that overlooks it will be great for a small ceremony."

"That would be so awesome! We want the ceremony to be small. I don't know who will be performing the ceremony though. With neither of us having our parents here. I certainly would not want mine, but I am bummed that his are not around." Amaranth told her and a small tear ran down her cheek.

Zolya gave her a big hug, "Girl, I know this is going to be rough emotionally. What about Qbaris? Would he do the ceremony? If not, I am sure Azohr would come over and do it for you."

She broke down in tears, her emotions just overflowed. "Can you believe what all has happened? Can you believe that my father turned out to be Qrizor? I knew of my mother, but didn't know her. I also just found out that I have two brothers, one of which is now gone. The thing that we don't know is if there are any other half-siblings in any of the other kingdoms. Evidently, Qrizor was quite the player."

"Just get it all off your chest. Talk it out and it'll help you. Anytime you need to talk, just let me know," Zolya said as she had her arm around her shoulder.

A few moments later Shelyn, Zabine, and Arietta walked into the courtyard to join them. "Hey witches!" Amaranth hollered to them.

It was a witch's rally in the courtyard. Zizor walked up and asked, "Would anyone want something to drink? I brought some beverages."

They all nodded yes to him while they continued to talk. He handed out the glasses of beverages and returned to the kitchen.

The pixies flew in and sat among the witches. Tamon spoke up, "What can we do?"

Amaranth told her, "I would love some purple pixie dust all around. A variety of shades of purple would be great."

"Done! We will provide it for you. I am picturing throwing of the purple pixie dust as you walk down the flowered aisle."

"Perfect! This is getting so exciting. Now I have to figure out a dress."

Shelyn spoke up, "I can help you with that. Do you want it in black with your burgundy cloak?"

"Yes! Yes! Do your magic with a black dress. I want the top to be tight-fitting. Make these babies look good," she said holding up her breasts.

"You got it! We will make you look hot! He won't know what hit him."

The wedding talk went on for hours when Puggaald came out and asked them, "Are you ready for dinner?"

Amaranth looked at him, "Oh yeah. I am hungry. Come on witches, let's go to the dining hall." They all got up and walked to the dining hall where Odulore was already waiting with the guys. They got up and helped to seat their witches.

"I want to say how thankful I am for all of you. Thank you for helping us plan this awesome event.," Odulore announced.

Zizor and the goblins brought out the trays for dinner. The only noise in the room was the sound of everyone eating. Zyrsit flew in and landed next to Odulore. "I saw Frally. I saw Frally," he frantically told them.

"Where did you see him?" Odulore asked him.

"He was outside of the force field. It was like he was scouting it out and looking for a way in."

"No worries. We are out there reinforcing the force field. He won't find a way in."

Zyrsit flew out of the dining hall. Zizor and the goblins walked around, picked up the empty trays, and returned to the kitchen.

Everyone walked out of the dining hall. They gathered around the fireplace and kept talking about the wedding. It dominated the conversation.

Azohr appeared in the courtyard, "I thought I heard my name mentioned today. Did I?"

"Yes, you did. I believe it was mentioned a few times. We would like you to perform our wedding ceremony. Would you?" Odulore questioned.

"Man, that would be my honor. Where is the ceremony?"

"We will be on the deck overlooking the Alacana Falls in the Lavalbourg Gorge," Amaranth informed him.

"I will be there for you guys. Just let know when it will be."

Azohr disappeared as quickly as he had appeared. Leaving just a poof of smoke behind for a moment.

They returned to talking amongst themselves. As the sun was setting, multiple colors spread across the sky as it got darker and darker.

Everyone got up and left the castle. Amaranth and Odulore sat by the fireplace. They looked into each other's eyes and could hear the pixies singing in the distance. He reached for her hand, lifted it up, and gave it a gentle kiss. "It's time to turn in for the night." They got up, he walked her to her room, and returned to his own.

Chapter 19

Qbaris walked into his father's room. He had never been in there. His father never allowed anyone in there. Crumazz never entered because he couldn't read and there were too many books. He stood there looking at the bookshelves. There were so many books, probably hundreds. Qbaris thought to himself, *Wow, there are a lot of books. Where to begin? A lot of them look handwritten. Will any of them explain what happened around the kingdom? What happened to my mother? Why does Crumazz not know how to read? Why was Amaranth over at Rissingshire Castle this whole time?*

He ran his fingers along the spines of the books and stopped on the one titled Taking Over the Kingdom/Family Tree. *This one should be interesting reading at least*, he chuckled and thought to himself.

Qbaris couldn't shake the eerie feeling in his father's room, so he took the book and went into his own room to read it. He still had a strange feeling he could not shake, so he went out into the courtyard and sat down by the fireplace. Dax and Darca laid down by his feet. He opened the book and started reading.

This is my reference book so that after I take over the Maerith Kingdom I can continue on to all of the other kingdoms on Parrcaster Island. I will rule the island! I will rule the island! No one will stop me! I will take over every castle! Yes, even in Rissingshire Castle where that goodie wizard, Trodus lives with his perfect family including my daughter, Amaranth. She will learn where she really comes from and what should be hers. If she does not accept it, then I will do away with her like I did her mother. The only thing that Zaleria was good for was giving me children. Although, the one is beyond stupid. Thankfully, I have one that has hope. Which is which? Just talk to them for a moment and it will be self-explanatory.

Crumazz will come to his own demise by doing something stupid. Yes, he is the stupid one. I have zero hope for him. The only good thing about him is that he is evil. The things he has told me that he wants to do to the kingdom. They do make me proud. However, he has no desire to read, so he won't be able to carry any of it out. He'll end up poisoning himself by accident.

Qbaris is the smart one and the one I put my hope in. Although, he seems like he isn't really my son. He is way too good. He is nice to all the animals. He is gentle with the pixies. I don't think he has an evil bone in his body. This is so disappointing. I will get rid of him at some point, because he will be difficult to deal with as he gets older. I certainly do not want him to have good children.

Amaranth is being raised at that good castle of Rissingshire. That family is too nice. They want everyone to get along. They want peace and harmony. It's enough to make me sick. I can't imagine this kingdom being good forever. They placed good values in her. It makes my skin crawl just thinking what they have turned her into.

I have two children that are good. How does that happen? I will have to rid the kingdom of all the good. Then I have one that is just plain stupid. I had some really bad luck here in the Maerith Kingdom. It's a good thing that I went into the other kingdoms on the island to have more children. You can just tell when they are little whether they will do you any good or not. The three in Maerith Kingdom will do me no good.

Zaleria was good for sex and that was about it. She gave me worthless children. This is why I stopped at three for her and banished her to the Crystal Crypt.

I have written this for any of my children that read this after I have moved onto the Dark Underworld or for my own reading pleasure. I love to read and remind myself of how great I am and what I accomplished.

Now I am going to leave a family tree so that all of my children can find each other. Hopefully the evil ones will take out the good ones. I will make sure that I have enough children that somewhere I should have a smart evil one.

Let's start in the Zodel Kingdom. This kingdom had a few evil witches that I was able to have children with. This was a fun kingdom to visit. Well, they weren't really evil, but they were cooperative, even if it wasn't always completely consensual. They were fun to play with and create more children. Sometimes I had to do some really smooth talking to get them to do what I wanted them to.

This first one I went to right after Amaranth was born. I was done with Zaleria. Her name was so pretty. I couldn't resist her. I mean, really, to take over a witch named Azalea? I had to pluck that flower for myself.

The first child we had did not survive to term. That was greatly disappointing, but we went for number two. This is a boy. I was so happy to have a boy. His name is Rhixon. This one is smarter than Crumazz, but he ended up being a good wizard also. What a disappointment. He loves going to the water and swimming. Who does that? He talks to the fish, like they are going to answer back. Just a complete disappointment.

We tried again and this time we got a girl. This one's name is Antha. Oh, I had such high hopes. She loved playing with the crystals when she was little. Then she grew to play with fairies. Of course, the good fairies. Another disappointment.

I wasn't about to have another one with Azalea. She was just as disappointing as Zaleria. Can I get an evil child? Is it too much to ask?

I moved on to Onyx. I mean, come on, her name is a black stone. She should be evil. Her parents named her wrong or had high hopes and those were dashed. She was at least fun to have sex with. She was the adventurous type. The first one I could get to do whatever I felt like doing and whenever I felt like doing it. She was a very willing accomplice.

We decided that we would name all the children after crystals. They are all girls. I don't know how I got all girls, but I did. They were all good girls too. Yes, for some reason I haven't been able to get any evil children with the exception of Crumazz, and he was too stupid.

Jade is the oldest. She loves all the flowers and the pixies. She's always humming happy tunes. It's sickening and disappointing.

Next was Rhodonite. This one wasn't any better. She was always found with the rabbits and squirrels. Her favorite place to visit was the Wargon Forest. I really hope she falls in a hole and never returns some day. To play with animals–just disgusting.

The third one wasn't any better either. Sapphire was supposed to be the one that would make me proud. She is always reading. I would give her a book of evil spells, and she would tell me how to make them good.

So far, three witches and what do I get? I get nine children and only one that is evil, and he's too stupid to be reliable for anything.

No time to rest, gotta keep trying for that evil child, preferably I would like to have a whole bunch of evil children. I will then continue on to all of the kingdoms for as long as I have to. The Maerith Kingdom and the Zodel Kingdom gave me nothing but disappointments.

Qbaris looked up, shook his head and said to the canines, " You would not believe how evil Qrizor was. He was also a player. He was playing in all the kingdoms with multiple women. So far I am up to eight siblings, and he didn't like any of us. I knew that he was disappointed in me, but I didn't realize there were all of these children and he didn't like any of them."

Odulore and Amaranth got off their horses and walked into the castle to see Qbaris.

"Hi! What are you guys doing here?" He asked them.

"We figured we'd stop by and see what you were up to. We don't really know you. We figured we would come and talk," Odulore told him.

"Well, Amaranth, we have a whole bunch of siblings out there in what sounds like it will be all the other kingdoms. So far, I am only to Zodel Kingdom. He had six children with two witches. The very first one didn't survive, but then he had one boy and then four girls in a row. None of them are evil. I never knew he was this mean. He doesn't like any of us."

"You said that it sounds like ALL the other kingdoms?" She asked him.

"Yes, and I will read right from his journal here: I had some really bad luck in Maerith Kingdom. It's a good thing that I went into the other kingdoms on the island to have more children."

"WOW! So, you are the oldest surviving sibling then. Crumazz was older than you?"

"Again, you are correct. He went from here after you were born and went over to Zodel Kingdom. He wasn't even happy with Crumazz. He keeps calling him stupid. This man was pure evil. He wanted to take over the island and do so by populating it with evil children. However, nine children in and so far he only got one that was evil. He has had nothing good to say about the three witches either. From what I have read. He got them to do what he wanted one way or another. Qrizor was not even a good father to any of them that I had read about thus far."

"I want to read this after you get done with it. I want to have a sibling reunion, especially being that you said that they are all good."

Qbaris nodded and said, "I can't wait to finish reading it. We have three more kingdoms to get through. So far, everyone sounds great. Well, with the exception of Crumazz. Who would have thought that we would have so many siblings?"

Odulore held Amaranth closer, "I think we'll leave you to read and head back to the castle. Come on by for dinner anytime. There will always be a chair ready for you. Good luck reading."

They walked back to their horses and rode off into the Calegan Forest.

He looked into the fire and thought, *WOW! I think that Qrizor did do something good. He may not have gotten his evil group of kids, but I think he gave us a great family to carry on and do the opposite of what he would have wanted. How many of us are out there?*

Qbaris looked down at the book, found the spot he left off at and continued to read.

The Maerith Kingdom and the Zodel Kingdom gave me nothing but disappointments. It's time to go on to the next kingdom or should I try with one more here? There is that sexy witch by the name of Cyrena in Zodel Kingdom. I love the name Cyrena. It sounds like siren. Will she make me scream like a siren? I will stay here before moving on.

I was able to convince Cyrena that I would be fun to have sex with. Of course, she got pregnant right away. I am good that way or is it evil that way? Anyway, I am glad that all it takes is one time with each of these witches to get them pregnant. I want as many children as I can possibly have. Oh yeah, for someone else that is reading this. All the children are only nine months apart. These witches need to give me as many children as possible. If they are not evil children, I need to move on. So, yes, there are only nine months between the youngest of one and the oldest of the next. The only thing I am thinking of changing up is maybe I need to get more than one pregnant at the same time. I could do this between different kingdoms. This would get the ages closer together. Anyway, back to my Cyrena. She also gave me three children. This time all boys, but once again, none were evil. What am I doing wrong?

Okius is the oldest one with Cyrena. He loves to read, but not potions or spells. He wants to read books of tales and good tales. This was greatly disappointing. So, we went on to the next one.

Thaxeor, the middle one, loves animals. How do I get so many animal lovers? These kids drive me crazy. I need an evil child.

The last one with Cyrena was Zinaxx. I was so hopeful. This one disappointed as well. He made friends with Rhixon, and they swam and talked with the fish. It's just crazy. This is going to drive me insane. I wish that these kids would become evil.

I wasn't about to stick around with all these good kids. So, I moved on to Dravocia Kingdom. I also decided that I would sleep with two witches at a time. I need to maximize my off-spring.

If the one reading this is one of my children, you are definitely getting to know more than you would want to know about your father. However, I am holding no punches and telling it exactly like it is. I want this to be an accurate accounting of what I thought was going to be my great evil island. I wanted to take over all the kingdoms and make them one great kingdom. MY great kingdom. The Kingdom of Qrizor.

Qbaris looked up from the journal and thought to himself, *I have to put this down. I want to read on, but WOW! He is beyond evil and such a player. We do need to get the family tree out to the entire island so that siblings don't end up with siblings. What a mess. I will sit this down and continue tomorrow.*

He returned the journal to his father's room and then went to sleep in his own room.

Chapter 20

The sun rose over the side of Miserth Castle. Qbaris thought to himself, *I have to get through this journal. I have to know who all my siblings are. I am going to have to keep my own journal with just the names to keep them all straight. How many children can this wizard have? Well, time to find out!*

He walked down to Qrizor's room and grabbed the journal. On his way to the fireplace he grabbed a mug of orange juice, pineapple juice, and green tea. The canines joined him and laid at his feet. Qbaris told the canines, "I am going to finish this book. It is down right scary how many children my father had. So far we are at a dozen. Thankfully only one was evil, and he's gone now. Thanks for being here you two."

Qbaris opened the book to where he left off last night.

MY great kingdom. The Kingdom of Qrizor.

He thought to himself, *Of course he wants his own kingdom.*

Continuing on...

I have found two very willing witches in Dravocia Kingdom. They are not evil, but at least they are willing. They are even willing to be with me at the same time. It's much more efficient this way. Their names are Cordelia and Circe. They are lovely. Both of them are beautiful blonds with piercing blue eyes. They are twins! Yes! I hope I can get twins out of this deal. Having multiple sets of twin is awesome. I can get even more chances at evil children.

They both got pregnant at the same time. This is perfect. I could not have planned this any better if I had tried.

They both just found out that they are having twins. YES! I will have four more children at the same time. I have told them what the names will be if they are boys or girls. This is, of course, all about me and my kingdom. So, do I name it the kingdom or the island. I know, The Island of the Kingdom of Qrizor. Oh that has a great sound to it.

The two sets of twins have arrived. I got all girls. Are you kidding me? This has to be a joke! Not one is evil. The four of them love to play together in the Cardminster Fields. Oh yeah, their names.

Tia was born first of the four and her mother is Cordelia. Then Circe had Shyla and Raven came super quick behind her. Finally Cedonia came. They all look like their mothers with their blond hair and blue eyes. It's sickeningly sweet.

We had to get to work right away. I need some evil children! Thankfully they both got pregnant just two weeks later. They said they wanted to wait, but I am not having any of that. I need to get this island populated. I am making my own kingdom.

They just told me that they are both pregnant with twins again. This is great! I thought getting twins pregnant was awesome, but this is just making it much easier to populate this island with MY children.

Yes! These twins are coming early as well. I named them all as well. I am in charge here. This time Circe had the first one and I named her Topaz. The second one came right away and her name is Arabella. Finally Cordelia had hers. I thought she was going to be late. She had more girls as well. These two are Artemis and Samara.

Once again I am disappointed. These are all good girls. This is making me more and more determined. I am done with these twins. All they give me is good girls. I have a bunch of animal loving girls. This is terrible.

I went to Dravocia Kingdom again. This time I found a couple of witches that aren't evil, but they are not goodies either. They are a lot of fun, and they are not twins!

I got them both pregnant, and they are only having one child each. I am done with these twins. That's just too much of a hassle.

The witches are Acacia and Phoenix. I am loving the curly brown hair with deep, dark brown eyes. They at least look evil, even if they aren't.

Acacia had her girl and I named her Mardella. I was hoping for an evil one. This one is a flower girl. Once again, sickening sweet. Later that day Phoenix had her girl. I don't know what it is about all these girls. Yikes. This one I named Marigold. Being that she was good and sweet, I am disappointed. Why can I not have an evil one. The very first one was evil and nothing but good ones since then.

The three of us decided to try once again for more children. They know I am trying to get an evil one.

Yes! They both got pregnant. I am so evil. I love that they get pregnant so quickly. Now if I could speed up the process.

I was there when they both went into labor. Of course, more girls. This is getting old. I am done with this kingdom. I have two more kingdoms on this island. Hopefully I can get some evil boys.

Phoenix had her girl first and I named her Serafina. Then Acacia had her girl and I named her Serafine. Yes, I know the names are similar. These girls may as well be twins. They look like twins and act like twins. Once again they are good.

I am moving on to Zallesian Kingdom.

Qbaris put the journal down and said to the canines, "This is pure insanity. Let me go back and count the number of siblings that he added in just one kingdom. One, two, three, four, five, six, seven, eight, nine, ten, eleven, and twelve. Yes, you heard me right–twelve siblings added to the previous dozen. I am only three kingdoms in, and he has had twenty-four children. I am one of twenty-four. Amaranth is not going to believe this."

"What am I not going to believe?" Amaranth asked him.

"Hey, where did you come from?"

"I rode over here. I really want to know what you have found out. I am really curious. I have a wedding coming up and I would love to invite all of our siblings."

"Well, you better be prepared for a big wedding. I do not suggest putting them all in the wedding party."

"What are you talking about?"

"Let me explain that I believe our father reproduces like a rabbit. He is determined to have a whole island that is dedicated to him and his children. I have only made it through Maerith Kingdom, Zodel Kingdom and Dravocia Kingdom. With that being said, there are a total of twenty-four children so far. There are eight mothers."

"That is insane! There are two more kingdoms on this island. Should I be writing just the names of our siblings and mothers down? It might help so that no one gets together with a sibling," she chuckled.

"I can read you the next two kingdoms. I do have to warn you that unfortunately he does get rather crude," Qbaris told her.

"Sure, I'd love to know. Although, you could always just skim it and give me the names. I don't need the details."

"Ok, that sounds good. I am at the point where he is going into Zallesian Kingdom. I will skim it for you. Let's see....Here it is, Lia is the next witch. She had all boys. The first one is Draxeor, then a set of twins–Shabras and Shudore Then she had another boy, Ubus. So, twenty-four plus four. We are up to twenty-eight."

"Insane! Continue please."

"Yes, next is Blossom and she had three girls, Willow, Venus and Mystia. Oh yeah, I almost forgot to mention. He explicitly says that these are all nine months apart or less."

"Nice, like we really needed that detail."

"Oh, trust me, you don't want to read the details. This man was crude, rude, and very much into himself. I will continue on to witch number three in the Zallesian Kingdom. This one's name is Akiye, and she had a set of twin girls named Evanora and Euphenia. Then she had another girl named Electra."

Amaranth interrupted him, "So, who came up with all the names? He's at more than a couple dozen. I need paper and a pencil to figure out ages too. This man was busy."

"I know. Some of these were born at the same time. He was glad that he had twins. He said that it was efficient," Qbaris chuckled and Amaranth laughed with him.

"Next up we have twin witches, Coral and Calla. Coral had two sets of twin girls, Opal and Oceana and then Meadow and Clover. Her twin had twin girls Zena and Agate and then twin boys Odapix and Ezohr."

"At least he got his wish of twins. Are any of them evil?"

"No, none of them thus far, other than Crumazz. Oh, he was super proud of this one. He moved on to Xoba Kingdom. This witch's name was Astrid. She gave him a set of triplet boys. Their names are Odius, Odaprix, and Odileus. Then while she was pregnant he moved on to Xantha and she gave him three boys, but not triplets. She got pregnant three times while he got another witch by the name of Raina pregnant at the same times. However, Raina gave him three sets of twins. The boys from Xantha was Zijamar, Izalener, and Oruzohr. The twins of Raina are Rhaharis and Rowix, then Azosior and Azutora and finally Enzatrix and Elzaviar."

"WOW! I hope he gets done soon. This is beyond a crazy amount of siblings. He just kept going from one to the next to the next. He just left behind more and more kids. We didn't know about each other. Does it say if any of the others knew of each other?"

"I think the only ones that knew of each other were the ones that he got the mother's pregnant at the same time. He said that he slept with some of them at the same time even. Gross!" Qbaris made a disgusted face.

"How many siblings are we at? I think, I think I counted fifty-four. Yes, fifty-four children. There are fifty-four people on this island that are siblings. Well, it sounds like all but two are still alive."

"Amaranth, we just have to think about it in a positive light. He did give us a great family. We have a large amount of siblings. We have a huge family. There are sixteen mothers with these fifty-four children. I am not sure if they are going to want to meet us. We were the disappointments that started him on his mission to seek women to bear his evil children in the other kingdoms," Qbaris told her.

She looked at him and shook her head, "I know, but I want to know who they are. I want to meet all of them. We have a large enough dining hall for them all to come for dinner. Or we can gather in the Demack Grassland. That's big enough."

Odulore appeared in the castle entry, "Hey! How's it going? What have we learned?"

Both of them laughed and Qbaris told him, "Let me summarize it for you. There is a total of sixteen mothers and fifty-four children. The man lived to reproduce. He actually wanted to have his own kingdom. He wanted the island to be all one kingdom. He wanted to call it The Island of the Kingdom of Qrizor. Also, you definitely do NOT want to read this journal. He gets into way too much detail. Maybe it wouldn't be so bad if I was his child."

Odulore cringed, "OH, one of THOSE journals. I am sorry. I am glad that you got the names of your siblings and their mothers. Amaranth, ready to go home?"

"Yeah, thanks for the information Qbaris," she told him, gave him a hug, and went home with Odulore.

Chapter 21

It was a witch's gathering at Rissingshire Castle. Amaranth was meeting with her witches to talk about her father, siblings, and the wedding preparations.

"Witches, you are not going to believe what I found out over the last couple of days. My father was quite the player. He went into all of the kingdoms that surround us and had children. In fact, there is a total of fifty-four children with fifty-two of them that are still living. What I found almost more horrifying is that there were only sixteen witches that he used. To my knowledge he was only married to my mother," Amaranth told them.

They all stared at her and their mouths dropped open with wide eyes. Zolya spoke up, "That is one seriously busy wizard. Have you figured out the approximate ages of everyone? What was his goal?"

"From what Qbaris told me, he wanted to take over the entire island by populating it with evil. However, it backfired, and he only got one evil child and that Crumazz. He wanted to combine all the kingdoms into one, his. Qbaris said that he was very vocal about how disappointing everyone was because no one turned out evil like him. To me, it sounded like he went from kingdom to kingdom getting witches pregnant. Sometimes he was getting them pregnant at the same time. He was really excited when he got twins or triplets, because it was more efficient. I don't know what to do with this knowledge. It does give me some relief in knowing that it wasn't me, but it was definitely him.," Amaranth said to the witches.

They sat there around the fireplace and shook their heads in complete disbelief. “What do we do with the information?” Shelyn asked.

“I want to know who they are. I want them to know there are a lot of us, and they are not alone. Although, I think some of them know about each other, because he had a couple of twin witches that had twins. There were some witches that were not related but he had relations with them, simultaneously. So, some of them knew what was going on. My mother had some idea that something was going on, but didn’t know any of the details. I think I will plan multiple dinners with each kingdom, and then have one big dinner with all of them.”

Arietta questioned, “Amaranth, do you know how much work that’s going to be? That’s going to be crazy! Plus, when are you and Odulore getting married? Does he know your new plans?”

“Yes, he knows all about it. He went with me over to Qbaris’ place and heard parts of it. Then I filled him in with what I was told when he wasn’t there. I know it’s going to be a lot of work. I still want to do it. As far as a date, we haven’t nailed that down yet. I will let you know when that’s going to happen.”

Odulore walked into the courtyard and up to Amaranth, “Qbaris is going to get us a list of everyone according to the kingdom’s census. Then we can send out invites and have the owls deliver them. However, before that all happens, Zizor has lunch ready in the dining hall. Are you witches hungry?”

They all answered with a yes and walked to the dining hall. When they entered they were greeted with a table full of trays and there was no waiting for the goblins to bring it out.

Zizor came out from the kitchen and ran up to Amaranth, “When do I get to make dinner for all of your siblings?”

"I don't know yet. I will let you know. It will be multiple meals," she told him.

The witches voraciously, leaving their trays clean. Following lunch, they returned to the courtyard and sat around the fire-place.

Qbaris entered the courtyard, "Hi! I have brought the list. I have it organized by kingdom and then by mother. I also wrote out approximate ages. It's seriously crazy! I hope it helps. The thing is, I did some more reading and found that these witches were young witches. He had a certain criteria, which was that they were all eighteen when he first got with them. I figured out the age range for all the siblings. From the oldest to the youngest is twenty years. So, that means that the youngest ones are only a few months old!"

"Crumazz and I are only eightteen months apart. So, there's nineteen years between me and the youngest ones, which are..." Amaranth looked down at the bottom of the list, "Oruzohr, Enzatrix and Elzaviar. They were all born in the Xoba Kingdom," Amaranth added.

Zolya said, "That was a busy wizard and what did he get from it? Basically nothing. When did he die?"

"He died only a few months ago. This journal went right up to the point of hours before he was killed. It looks like he got back from the last births, wrote in his journal, and then he headed back out to Xoba to check on another witch that he wasn't sure if she was pregnant or not. I do have her name. He was killed by the dragon between the Miserth Castle and Xoba Kingdom," Qbaris told them.

Amaranth shook her head, "You mean to tell me there could be more?"

"Yes, because towards the end, he was trying to get as many witches pregnant as possible. I think he knew that he was going to be killed soon," Qbaris shook his and smirked.

Zabine said, "The only thing I can say is that at least there weren't too many children per witch. It's only about three to four children per witch. Still, that's a lot of witches that he was with. Plus, there may be more?!"

"This will be interesting. Do we want to figure out who the others are? Do we want to go to Xoba Kingdom and see who they are? How many more can there be?" Amaranth questioned.

Odulore put his hands on Amaranth's shoulders, leaned down, and kissed her on the cheek. She closed her eyes for a moment and pictured a whole bunch of witches around the dining hall table. *I have a huge family. How awesome! I thought it was just me and that I was abandoned. Granted, he meant it for evil, but I think it will be good. I will make it for good.* Amaranth thought to herself.

"I want to thank everyone for being here for me and for Qbaris. I had always known that my mother abandoned me. I had no idea why or where she went. I also had no idea who my father was and if I had any siblings. Now I know that I have two brothers and fifty-two half siblings, fifty of which are alive. What I don't know is if there are any more and if there are, how many more are there? It sounds like he thought very highly of himself and so much so that he wanted a whole island of his own offspring. My mother was only eighteen when she had Crumazz, which means that she was only thirty-nine when she died. My father was just shy of his fortieth birthday when he died. This is what you get when you are evil," Amaranth said.

All the witches got up and gave her a group hug. The positive energy that was flowing from the group was overwhelming for Amaranth, who had happy tears rolling down her cheeks. The energy went out of the castle and into the grassland where the pixies were, and they instantly flew into the courtyard of the castle. They were pulled by the energy, and surrounded the group hug. Zizor could not resist either and joined in the group hug.

Avras entered the courtyard, “What an awesome sight to behold! The positive energy that has surrounded this castle is amazing. I could feel it as I approached, and now I can see it.”

“Come join in!” Arietta motioned for him to come to her. He ran over to her.

As the sun went down, the positive energy remained in and around the castle. The group hug broke up, but they stayed together at the fireplace. Zizor went to the kitchen for a quick moment to bring back beverages for all.

A streak of energy bolted across the sky, far above the castle. “What was that?” Amaranth questioned.

“No worries that was above the force field,” Odulore assured her as he hugged her tight.

Chapter 22

Qbaris arose to loud noises. He wasn't completely sure what he was hearing. When he walked outside he could see many streaks of dark energy and clouds above the force field. The clouds cleared, and he could very clearly see Kezrin and Korzath flying back and forth across the sky. They stopped and made eye contact. He could feel the eerie chill go down his spine. They disappeared and the chill left him.

He thought to himself. *This is going to be an interesting day. Two from the Dark Underworld are here to visit this early?*

Dax and Darca were still in their beds in his room. Qbaris went back into his room, nudged them, and then left to fix himself some breakfast.

Zyrsit flew into the kitchen and sat on the edge of the counter, "I have come with a message from Odulore. The Dark Underworld is starting to cause some trouble again. He would like you to come to Rissingshire Castle to help with plans to get rid of them."

"Tell him that I will be over shortly after breakfast."

He nodded and flew off into the forest. Ash joined him and they flew together to Rissingshire Castle.

Odulore and Amaranth were in the dining hall. The owl and mini-dragon flew in and landed on the chair at the end of the table. "He will be over shortly after breakfast," Zyrsit told them.

"Oh good. There's just too much dark energy hovering over the force field. Now it's in the morning as well as at night. Something is brewing," Odulore said.

Zizor and the goblins came into the dining hall and cleared away the trays. Odulore and Amaranth went to Trodus' room and sat at his table reading some more books on the Dark Underworld.

"We refer to the room as Trodus' room or my father's room. Do you think we should rename it? We are in here a lot and I want it to be more of our room, even though all of his stuff is still in here. What do you think?"

Amaranth looked up at him and said, "I know what you mean, but what were you thinking?"

"Nothing has come to mind yet, but just thought we could give it some thought."

"Yeah, I understand, but I think we have bigger issues at hand and that was just your mind distracting you."

They continued to read through the journals about the Dark Underworld when Qbaris walked in. "So, what are we going to do about the Dark Underworld. This morning I saw Kezrin and Korzath above my castle. I mean, I made eye contact with them through the force field. I got an eerie chill down my spine."

Odulore and Amaranth looked up from their journals. Amaranth spoke first, "That's what we are reading right now. What to do with them." "This is exactly why I wanted you to come here. Last night is when it started up again."

Qbaris pulled up a chair to the table, "I wonder if there's a big stirring going on because of the force field. I bet Ozrig is not happy with not being able to get to the island. I am sure that our parents and brother got into some trouble for that. He was not a nice guy before he went to the Dark Underworld. Annamaaz always has to have her way too. So, Ozrig isn't really in charge all the time. He bows to her every whim."

Zizor brought in some beverages, sat them on the table, and left. The three drank them while they were reading the journals.

A few hours went by, and they hadn't moved, but they were still reading. The owls flew in and landed on the table. "There are dark clouds moving in over the water. We were out to the beach and saw it slowly moving in. It was going wider as it came closer," Ash told them.

"Ok, now what we need to do is get a spell, crystals, and a potion together that will banish them all to the Dark Underworld so that they cannot exit it once they enter it. This will take a bit, but we will have to have it done before sun down today," Odulore explained.

Qbaris looked at him and responded, "I think we need to gather the half-siblings and their mothers. With all of their powers and ours, we should be able to hold back that evil and banish it. There is power in numbers. We will have to send out the owls with notes to all the mothers and older siblings to come here to Rissingshire Castle. This will be where we gather for all the meetings. Hopefully there is only one for this issue."

"Yes, but you have to figure out who the last ones are that are pregnant. They may not be able to participate in much, with how far along they are in their pregnancies," Amaranth added.

"I have the name of one, but the way he wrote it, it sounded like she wasn't the only one. Almost like he went to a coven and had sex with every eligible witch in hopes that all of them would get pregnant. It was written really weird. It almost sounded like there was someone that went with him to this witch's coven. I wrote the name down, along with where it's located. We could go there right away."

"What's her name?" Odulore asked.

Qbaris told them, "Her name is Moira and her coven's name is Coven of the Sacred Flame. Here's what Qrizor had to say:

We went to see Moira and her witch sisters at Coven of the Sacred Flame. It was the most magical time we have ever had together. They were so willing and able. They made us feel like we were in charge of their whole being. We will return to see if she and any of the other sister witches are pregnant. My hope is that they all are and that this time it's not a bunch of goodies. I am tired of these goodies. I need some more evil on this island!"

Odulore shook his head, "This is going to be interesting. I would say that we have a whole coven of pregnant witches. I have never heard of this one though, so it must be a fairly small one. Was this his last entry in the journal?"

"Yes it was, unfortunately, because I'd like to know more about who these witches are before we go over there. We don't even have a number, which after reading his journal is just down right scary," Qbaris chuckled.

Amaranth stood up and said, "Let's head on over there. The coven is over in Xoba Kingdom. It shouldn't be too hard to find."

"I am just trying to picture the three of us walking up to a coven to see if Qrizor had been there and if anyone is pregnant. To me, it's just comical," Odulore laughed.

They got up from the table and went to the livery. They rode three Pegasuses to Xoba Kingdom. The first area they came upon was a small group of thatched huts. Amaranth got down off of Raithy and walked towards the first hut. There was a witch that was just walking out. She did not look pregnant. Amaranth asked her, "Are you Moira?"

"No, she is in Coven of the Sacred Flame. That is closer to the beach."

“Thank you. We’ll head there then.” Amaranth got on Raithy, and they took off for the beach.

When they got within sight of Coven of the Sacred Flame, they could see quite a few witches gathered in a circle. Amaranth went ahead of Odulore and Qbaris to reach them first. She got down and walked up to the circle. The guys followed close behind.

“May I help you?” Moira asked as Amaranth approached.

“Yes, I am looking for Moira.”

“I am her. Who are you?”

“I am Amaranth.”

“Ok, so how can I help you?”

“Do you know Qrizor?”

“Yes. Why do you ask?”

“Well, he’s my father, and we found his journal. He revealed all my siblings and half-siblings. However, at the end of the journal his last entry was that he came here and was hoping to get all the witches he slept with pregnant.”

“Well, I haven’t seen him since he and his son were here. His son did come back once, but I haven’t seen him either. Do you know what happened to them?”

“Yes, they are both banished to the Dark Underworld. So, as I can see, it looks like they were rather successful in getting witches pregnant. Are all those pregnant in this circle because of them?”

Moira hollered, "Flickwe, can you bring three chairs?"

The gnome quickly brought over the chairs and added them to the circle. Then left the group alone.

"I don't think you understand what all went on here. Let me explain that to you. All eight of us are sisters, and we did not just have sex with Qrizor, but we also all had sex with Crumazz. The goal was to make sure that all of us were pregnant. This goal was achieved, but we do not know which one got us pregnant. We do know that three are pregnant with single girls, three are pregnant with twin girls, one is pregnant with twin boys, and the last one is pregnant with triplet girls. We are only three months along, so we will have quite the population increase shortly. I would say the triplet girls will be born first at six months, then the twins at seven months and finally the single ones will be here at nine months. They were supposed to come back when they were born. I don't know what we'll do now."

"Let me tell you that you are not alone. In fact, in Xoba Kingdom he has gotten three other witches pregnant with twelve children. We have all their names and it may help you with the children. Can I ask you what all of your names are and what you plan to name your children?"

"Yes, let me introduce everyone. I will start with myself. I am Moira and I am pregnant with Adonia. This is Starla and she is pregnant with Melusina. Next we have Nissa who is pregnant with Nimue and Echo is pregnant with Fawn and Feba. There is Piper who is pregnant with Peony and Paige. Next to her is Ember who is pregnant with Crenorim and Qrornas. Then we have Rose who is pregnant with Lilac, Lilura and Lydia."

"Hello everyone. Ember, I noticed that you have named your boys with the same first two letters of Crumazz and Qrizor. What made you do that?" Amaranth questioned.

Ember smiled at her with a crooked smile, "I don't know which one got me pregnant. So, I will use both their names. Also, I want them to be like their fathers. I will tell them about both of them. They are both so gentle and kind to me. They made me feel special, like I was the only one. I know that they had sex with all eight of us, but when I was with them, it wasn't like that. I keep focusing all my energy on them and asking for them to be like their fathers."

Amaranth, Odulore and Qbaris looked at each other in surprise. Qbaris spoke up, "I am Qbaris. Qrizor is my father and Crumazz is my brother. I grew up in the same castle with them. I had no idea that Amaranth existed and nor that he was populating the island. Plus, this is new news that he brought Crumazz with him. There was a mention of we in the journal, but he did not say who the we was. On the entire island Qrizor already had fifty-four children including one that was a still born. Now we have another dozen children that we don't if they are Qrizor's or Crumazz's. Now you are putting all your energy in hopes that your boys are like them?"

"So what is wrong with Crumazz? What is wrong with Qrizor wanting to have a lot of children?" Ember snapped back.

He replied to her, "Well, Qrizor sent away Amaranth and locked away our mother. Then he goes to populate the island and his goal was to have evil children. He wanted to rule the island for himself. In fact, he even wanted to rename it after himself.

Qrizor kept going from kingdom to kingdom trying to have evil children. He only got one and he was disappointed in Crumazz because he couldn't read. Multiple times in his journal he has mentioned how stupid he was.

Qrizor then died, and got banished to the Dark Underworld. We do not know what happened there. Somehow our mother died, actually banished to the dark Underworld.

She left instructions that led to Amaranth killing, well she thought he was killed, but Crumazz was also banished to the Dark Underworld. That is after he had kidnapped Amaranth.

I didn't know Amaranth existed. So, Qrizor and Crumazz are not good wizards. They are both evil."

Her face grew angry and she glared at him. Ember stood up and walked right up to Qbaris and said to him, "I don't care what you say. They were very good to me. They made me feel special. I want my boys to be as gentle as them. If they were still here, I would do it all over again and again, as many times as they would want me to. I am here, ready and available for them." She walked away and went to her hut.

Moira followed after her to make sure she was ok. Odulore, Qbaris, and Amaranth shook their heads, and they looked around at the other witches.

Rosa adjusted in her chair and then spoke up, "I understand what you guys are saying. However, when they were here with us, they treated us all like royalty. We each felt like we were the only one. They worked so well together with each of us. It was a beautiful thing when the three of us were together. Yes, it was always a three-some. They insisted on it because that way they would be completely focused on who they were with. So, all of us here would do it over and over again with them. It's not just Ember. When they were here, they were not evil."

Amaranth looked at her and listened intently at what she was saying. She thought to herself, *Seriously, these witches all think Crumazz and Qrizor are great wizards. They would help them populate the island? This is not good. They will not help us nor are they capable of keeping them in the Dark Underworld.*

Odulore nodded at Rose and said, “I can see that you all think they are great wizards. We will not disrupt your pregnancies. We will add your names and your children’s names to the ever expanding family tree. Thank you for the information. We will leave now.”

The three got on their Pegasuses and flew back to Rissingshire Castle.

Chapter 23

Ozrig entered the center of the Dark Underworld. Annamaaz was right by his side. He yells out, "Kezrin! Korzath!"

They immediately appeared in front of them. "What did you find out on your journey around the island?" He asked them.

"We were able to listen in on conversations that included Qbaris, Odulore and Amaranth. They have found a journal that Qrizor wrote. He has many, many children throughout the island. The only evil child he had out over fifty so far, was Crumazz. There are some witches that are currently pregnant. It is good news in that area. They all want their children to be Crumazz and Qrizor. They don't know who the father is because they both had sex with these witches at the same time. From the sounds of it, they are all happy that they are pregnant with Crumazz's and Qrizor's children and that if given the opportunity, they would do it over and over again."

Ozrig had an evil smile that appeared on his face. "I am glad to hear this. We will use Crumazz and Qrizor. Now we just have to get that portion of the island outside the force field. The only question would be, will their children be good or evil. Hopefully Crumazz was able to assist with getting them to be evil. It appears that Qrizor failed miserably at that." He paused for a moment and then yelled, "Crumazz! Qrizor!"

The two were let out of the tarantula's cave to go to Ozrig. They stood before them.

"I want to give you some good news. There is a group of witches that are currently pregnant and they do not know which of the two of you got them pregnant because they had sex with both of you at the same time. Is that correct? You both had sex with these witches at the same time?"

They both nodded in agreement.

"Wonderful! That is truly evil! I am pleased to hear that you at least tried to populate the island with evil. Then when that didn't work, you brought in your son. That's brilliant. What's even more wonderful is that not only are they all pregnant, but they are happy about it and if they could, they would do it over and over again, as many times as the two of you would want them. Next we need to figure out how to get that part of the island outside the force field. We need to make sure that these children become evil. We can then take over the island by that small cove." He looked at Kezrin and Korzath, "Do you two know how many witches and potential evil children there are?"

Korzath spoke up, "Yes, there are eight witches and a total of twelve children. They are all girls, except for one set of twin boys. The witch that is pregnant with the twin boys and is even naming them with the same first two letters of their names."

"Oh good. I will now keep the two of you out of the tarantula cave. You may go back to your previous caves."

Qrizor spoke up, "What about Zaleria?"

"Do you think she will be of any help in our plan?"

"Yes, once we get this section of the island outside the force field, we can send her there to help take care of the children. She is evil. She was able to trick Amaranth into killing her brother, even though she didn't tell her that it was her brother."

Ozrig smiled and nodded, "I agree, she will be helpful. You can get her out of the tarantula cave as well. You two are dismissed."

"Now, you two. You need to go back to the island and get more information. I want lots of details. Now go!"

Kezrin and Korzath left and flew off to the island. Crumazz and Qrizor went into the tarantula cave for Zaleria. Qrizor took her hand and led her out. They all arrived at the cave that they were in previously.

"What happened? I am thankful to be out of there."

"Ozrig is figuring out how to get a certain section of the island out from under the force field. We are expecting a dozen children from eight witches. They all want to help us. When those children are born, you are going to go to the coven and help them take care of the children."

Zaleria stared at him, blinking her eyes multiple times, and said, "What?! So, because you were going around like a rabbit, I get out to help them with YOUR children?!"

"Well, they don't know if they are mine or Crumazz's children."

"Are you kidding me? You took him with you? Are you insane? How could you?"

"Well, hopefully, these children will be evil. I kept having good children. It was disgusting. So, I had to do something. He is the oldest. He's twenty. He is certainly old enough to have children. Why not?"

She shook her head and looked at him and then at Crumazz, "You went along with this?"

"Of course, it was a great time. What else was I supposed to do? He even made sure that I did it right."

She rolled her eyes, glared at them, and shook her head, "You two are unbelievable! I will help their children, but only because it keeps me out of that other cave. Where on the island is this?"

Qrizor smiled and told her, "It's in Xoba Kingdom at Coven of the Sacred Flame. So, it's near the beach. It'll be a great place to live."

"I am NOT going there because it is a great place. I am going because it is better than the cave. You are beyond evil and I want nothing to do with you."

"No worries, you are too old for me," Qrizor snapped at her.

She glared at him, "What!?"

"Yeah, I made a requirement that any witch that I would have sex with could only be eighteen years old. I don't want them any older for the first child. I need them young so that if I can get evil children, we can keep having more and more. Then I had to make sure that Crumazz would have lots of evil children. It looks like we may have finally succeeded," Qrizor boasted.

Zaleria shook her head, rolled her eyes and responded, "You are impossible. That is just beyond evil. Because I only gave you one evil child, you went around the entire island? How many do you have? Do you even know? Do you know their names? Their ages? What are they like? I mean more than just writing once in your sick journal? I saw you writing, and the smile on your face while you wrote said it all."

"Mother, you just don't understand. Father needed to do this. There are too many goodies on the island. How could he deal with all those good witches and wizards? He needed more evil. I was more than happy to help him populate the island. I will gladly continue what he started. However, YOU decided to get in the way! YOU don't understand! So, you better help when we get to

Xoba Kingdom. Those children need to be evil!" Crumazz yelled at her.

She turned and walked away to a dark corner of the cave. *Wow! I can't believe what is going on. This is beyond evil, which, I guess, is the whole point they are getting at. They want evil and are willing to do absolutely anything to get it. I really hope that the other two have turned out good. Their goodness will be my revenge. He banished me to the Crystal Crypt, took MY children away, and now he wants me to take care of HIS children?! He's not even sure WHO got them pregnant. He had sex with them along with his own son at the same time. I just can't accept this. Care for his children in the coven, no way! I didn't know this was going on. He would brag about how evil Crumazz was and that he was doing a much better job than I could ever do.*

I want out of this, but not in the tarantula cave. I should have never gotten taken in by Qrizor. I should have gone for a good wizard, but it was so much fun in the beginning. My mother, her mother, and her mother's mother were all evil. They made it sound like it was the only way to live. Qrizor was so smooth and cunning when we first got together. I can imagine he was the same with all those other witches.

So, let me see if I can wrap my brain around this. The latest conquests of Qrizor and Crumazz, what else would you call it, is a group of EIGHT witches that are pregnant with over a DOZEN children. That means multiples for the same witch. Yikes! It's no wonder they need help, but it sounds like this may happen over and over. I just can't. I just can't.

Qrizor walked back to her, smiled, and laughed, "Did you think I would stop with just three children and only one was evil? We were raised by evil witches. I had to continue the line. Otherwise, our line of evil would not continue. You know where things would have gone if I had been banished and not gotten any more evil children, right?!"

His evil smile made her cringe. She shook her head, "You mean, you would have continued what our parents did? You would put your own daughter through that?"

"Yes, I would have. That was my last resort. I would have put Crumazz with Amaranth. YES! That would have been been the most evil plot of all. I may not have even waited for my last resort!" He smiled even larger and rubbed his hands together. Zaleria shook her head again.

Crumazz walked up, "What are you guys talking about now?"

"Oh, I was just telling her that if we didn't get any evil children that would I do with you what our parents did with us."

"What's that?"

"You would have gotten together with Amaranth. Yes, your mother and I are siblings."

Crumazz looked at him, then at Zaleria, back at him, smiled, and replied, "Well, that explains a lot. Plus, that would have been the ultimate in evil. I must say though, I don't think she'd be much fun. Oh, but how evil it would have been to turn her evil. I am glad that didn't happen, because I had way more fun at the coven. Having eight witches in a day is much better than just one. Plus, you were there to make sure everything went right." He smiled and nodded.

Zaleria sighed greatly and thought to herself, *I am a failure, my son would have thought that was great and fun. Although, my mother and father would have loved it. They were siblings as well.*

Annamaaz entered their cave, "Where is Zaleria? I must talk with Zaleria."

“I am here in the back. What do you want?” She responded in a defeated voice.

She walked back to her and informed her, “We need to work together to get that force field to move off of Xoba Kingdom. Ultimately, it needs to move off the entire island, but we will take Xoba Kingdom for now. We need those pregnant witches to make sure they have evil children.”

“So I have heard. You want me to help with the potion?”

Annamaaz sat down next to Zaleria, “Witch, you are not only going to do the potion, but you are going to help raise these children to make sure that they are evil. If you are lucky, you will even have more children of your own.” She had the most evil smile and laugh that Zaleria had ever heard.

“What does that mean, if I am lucky? I already had three children and only one was evil. It was the first one and he’s here. Qrizor already said that I am too old for him. Plus, I haven’t had any children in over eighteen years. Who would I have children with? I am here.”

“Oh my dear, Ozrig can make any witch pregnant. It’s his gift. If we don’t get any evil children out of Xoba Kingdom, then we will use other means. We could get your daughter, but I think it would be better if after eighteen years, you started having children again. What fun! Oh yeah, if Ozrig doesn’t find you appealing, he will use one of his sons.”

“How many sons does he have? Why is everyone wanting to populate this island so much? What is so special about this island?” Zaleria questioned.

“Oh, we lost count ages ago. He’s been with all the female demons and witches in the Dark Underworld. He chooses who he gets pregnant.

Now to answer why this island. Ozrig was raised on this island back when it was only one kingdom. The good wizards came in, divided it up, and got rid of the evil as soon as they found it there.

It is a special island to Ozrig. He won't leave it alone. He wants it back. He will get it back. It will be his."

Zaleria sat there and shook her head. She couldn't speak. She couldn't think. Her mind went blank. Annamaaz left the cave. Zaleria sat there in the dark for many hours. She was completely empty of all energy, emotion and ideas.

Chapter 24

The white puffy clouds were all around and only a few feet off the ground. Jaril stood in front of Trodus and spoke, "Parrcaster Island is in grave danger. The Dark Underworld is trying to take it back. Your son and his soon-to-be wife will need your assistance more than ever. We cannot allow this to happen. Your father, his father, and his brothers worked hard to take over the island and return it to good."

"What do you need me to do? Can Tatiana help?"

"We need you to go back to the island, to your son, and make sure that he has stronger spells to keep Qrizor's evil contained. You know, the ones that have no time limit. She may go with you. We will make it so that first you appear in his dreams and then you will appear in person. We will return you to your former glory and you will be there for their wedding. That must go off as as planned."

Trodus smiled, took a great sigh of relief, and replied, "We will gladly help them with their wedding and securing the island. Do we know if they have any evil that is brewing on the island or is it only in the Dark Underworld?"

"They have a great number of children that are about to be born. These children have the greatest chance of being evil as they were conceived by not one but two evil wizards. You will need to rid the whole kingdom of these witches and children. This is where their focus will be. I have information that says that they will send Amaranth's mother to help the children become evil. Although, I am not sure why they are using her, she had two out of three children that are good."

"How is it possible that they were conceived by two evil wizards? That doesn't seem like it could even happen. Zaleria has no clue how to raise children. We raised Amaranth. She lucked out and Qbaris was good."

"I will spare you the details, but basically Qrizor took Crumazz with him to impregnate the witches. They shared the pleasure as a threesome to increase the odds of the children being evil. It is one of the most evil things they have done, other than what they have planned for Amaranth. This is why you must make sure that she marries Odulore and that the island is safe from their evil."

"What is planned for Amaranth?"

"First, did you know that Qrizor and Zaleria are actually siblings and not just husband and wife?"

"No! I did not know that, but it certainly explains some things that were going on."

"Yes, their plan is to follow the tradition in their family line of siblings marrying and conceiving. They are convinced that this is the best way to assure there is more evil. Both their parents and their parents' parents are all siblings. We need to break this cycle," Jaril explained with great passion.

Trodus with a surprised look on his face said, "That is absolutely crazy, sick, and disgusting. I knew there was something off about their family, but this, this I could not guess. What do we do with the witches and children that they are going after?"

"First, go get Tatiana and have her come here. I will then explain things to both of you."

He left and went to her, as Jaril told him to do. Trodus gave her his hand and implored her, "Tatiana, please come with me. Jaril must give us instructions. We must leave the Holy Dimension and return to Parrcaster Island to help Odulore and Amaranth save the island and get married."

"Get married!" She squealed with glee, jumped up, and took his hand. They quickly went to Jaril.

In front of Jaril, they stood waiting anxiously for his instructions. "You will return to the island in the morning. I will give Odulore a dream about both of you. This way he will be excited to see you. I have already given you the spells that he will need to help them. Now, this is not a permanent return. You will come back to the Holy Dimension when your mission is complete. Do you both understand? In the meantime, you can send prayers on their and your behalf."

They both nodded with happy smiles from ear to ear on their faces. As they held hands, Jaril disappeared as a white cloud enveloped him. Trodus led his wife in prayer, "God, please be with Odulore and Amaranth as they plan their marriage. Give us your guidance as we assist them to protect the island and start them off on a faithful and forever marriage." They both repeated this prayer over and over through the night.

The night came on Parrcaster Island, Odulore laid down for rest. He had a dream, which was not normal for him. An angel came to him and told him, "You will need angelic help in order to defeat the Dark Underworld. God is sending you two of his angels. You will recognize them as your parents. They will stay through the evening after your wedding. Use their assistance both securing the island and in planning your wedding." Just as quickly as he appeared in his dream, he left.

Odulore woke up, *What was that? Are my parents able to come back for Amaranth & my wedding? Oh, she is going to love this. This is going to be such a happy day. Although, he talked about securing the island. So, it's not going to be all happiness between now and the wedding. We don't even have a date set or do we? I can't remember. Amaranth knows these things. I have to go to her and let her know about my dream.* He got up and ran out of his room to hers.

"Amaranth, Amaranth, wake up! My good witch, wake up. I have great news to share with you."

She opened her eyes, rubbed them, and sat up, "What? What are you talking about and why so early?"

"I had a dream. I never have dreams, but tonight I did. An angel came to me and told me that my parents are returning to help us secure the island and plan our wedding. They will be here for our wedding," he excitedly explained to her.

Her eyes blinked multiple times, "That is great news! I wonder when they will be here and how they are going to help us secure the island? It will be great to have them back, even if it's just for a short time."

"I will meet you in the dining hall for breakfast." Odulore left her room, returned to his, and got dressed in day clothes. He ran to the dining hall in excitement.

Amaranth got dressed and walked to the dining hall, *This is so exciting. How will they assist us with securing the island? Does Trodus have new and improved powers? The Dark Underworld looks really scary above the force field. The best part is that they will be here for the planning and the wedding. Yes! Yes!* She arrived at the dining hall and went to her seat.

Zizor and the goblins came out of the kitchen with the trays of French toast with pineapple and whipped cream, bacon and fresh made orange juice, pineapple juice, and green tea mixture. He placed a tray in front of Amaranth. She looked up at him and smiled, "Thank you," she mouthed. Her voice was silent.

"What's wrong with your voice?" Odulore asked her.

She took a drink and then replied, "I think it was just a dry throat. I'm good now."

"Oh good, I was worried for a moment there. I am still excited about my dream."

Zizor placed the tray in front of Odulore, "You had a dream? Please share."

"I had an angel appear in my dream and tell me that my parents are returning to help secure the island and with planning our wedding."

"Oh, that is awesome news! I look forward to their return." Zizor continued on with the goblins and placed trays in front of everyone. They disappeared into the kitchen.

Trodus and Tatiana appeared in the courtyard. They waited for them to come out of the dining hall.

The goblins and Zizor entered the dining hall and picked up the emptied trays. "Let's go to the courtyard and wait for Qbaris. We need to talk about my parents returning and what we need to do about the pregnant witches."

"Sounds like a plan to me," Amaranth agreed with him. They got up and walked hand in hand to the courtyard. Within a few yards of the courtyard they saw a bright light. They slowly approached it.

Tatiana spoke with excitement, "Odulore! Amaranth! It is so good to see you both!"

They ran to greet each other with a group hug. The positive energy filled the castle and spilled out into Demack Grassland and Calegan Forest. Qbaris saw the bright light beaming through the trees. He took off through the forest to follow the light. As he ran through the forest, the mystical forest creatures joined him and then the animals from the Demack Grassland. By the time he arrived at the castle he had quite the following.

"Hi Qbaris!" Trodus and Tatiana greeted him.

He stopped in his tracks and his jaw dropped open, "Wait! What? How is this possible? Don't get me wrong, it's great to see you two, but how?"

"We have returned from the Holy Dimension to help secure the island and plan their wedding. We are unable to stay long, but will be here through the evening of their wedding," Trodus explained to him.

Amaranth ran up to him and gave him a hug, "Isn't this great? We will have assistance from the Holy Dimension to secure the island."

"That is one thing we definitely need help with. Let's get down to business. I assume you know all about the Coven of the Sacred Flame. That is where we need the most help. They do look at Qrizor and Crumazz as evil. However, I have a hard time doing anything to a group of pregnant witches, especially with some of them being pregnant with multiple children. Yet, I know something needs to be done because of how they view these wizards. I am happy to help in any way that you need me," Qbaris told them.

Trodus smiled and looked around at all those that had joined in. He took a small journal out his robe pocket, held it up, and said, "This book will assist us. It has our answers. The spell that I am to cast with all of your help is here. It is also in my brain. I have this memorized. You will need to memorize it as well."

He opened the book and read to them, "First we will surround the coven from beach to beach. Then we will repeat With the Power of the Holy Dimension - Purifenis Dragate–Away with the Coven of the Sacred Flame! Purifenis Dragate–Away with the witches from the Coven of the Sacred Flame! Purifenis Dragate–Away with the children of the witches from the Coven of the Sacred Flame! This will cause the ground to shake and deep gorge will be made to where the coven will now be their own island. Once that has separated from Parrcaster Island, then we will repeat these four spells as we walk forward into the water. With the Power of the Holy Dimension - Incenecto Vexenus for all of Parrcaster Island above and below, Flarello Viralerous for all of Parrcaster Island above and below, Proticum Banio for all of Parrcaster Island above and below, Immolortia Feliatis send your protection to Parrcaster Island above and below. Do not say these outloud, but repeat them over and over in your minds."

"We will go out and be there an hour before sundown. This has to be completed before the sun sets. The Dark Underworld is coming to get them. Remember each set of spells must include the Power of the Holy Dimension. This is the most powerful part of the whole spell. It will hold back the Dark Underworld from the island, forever!" Tatiana explained to them.

The mystical creatures from the forest and the grasslands all exited the castle to work on memorizing the spells.

Chapter 25

Odulore, Amaranth, Qbaris, Trodus, and Tatiana sat in the dining hall. They shared tortilla chips and cherry salsa that Zizor had made.

Trodus sat at the head of the table, "I am so happy to see you all again. I know our visit will be short, but fruitful. I assure you that the witches and their children will not be harmed. They are just getting their own island. This is to appease Ozrig for the moment. He will have control over the new island. Ultimately he wants to be the ruler of this island. We will not allow it to happen. It won't be easy, but it will all turn out good in the end."

"I do not understand the witches in the coven. How can they believe that these two are anything but evil?" Qbaris asked.

Tatiana answered, "Because they are all alone, and they want to see that hero. They want them to be good. It didn't take much convincing. They were shown attention, and they didn't care what kind of attention. It was all seen as good. When witches are so starved for attention, they will take whatever kindness they can get. They will see it as good. Did you three go and see them? Did you talk to them?"

"Yes we did. The only one with boys was really defensive. She got right in Qbaris' face about it. She is pregnant with twin boys and even chose names with the first two letters of their fathers' names. It was just bizarre. She kept saying that they were gentle with her and good to her. I don't understand how she could even think that," Amaranth said.

She nodded in agreement, "Yes, it is really hard to understand. You were given to us by your mother. So, you were raised in a loving home. These witches did not have that. They were raised in a coven. My understanding of them is that their mother got pregnant from a son of Ozrig. Then she was taken away when they were young. They had to fend for themselves. Slowly each sister was taken away until there was just one. Then another son of Ozrig impregnated the remaining witch and the cycle began again."

There was a moment of silence until Odulore spoke, "It really is hard to understand. I cannot imagine growing up in such an environment. Do we know if there are any issues with the other kingdoms where Qrizor went around fathering children? Are there any others that we will have to deal with like this?"

"I have not heard of any. So, I would assume not at this time. Our only focus right now is to split of the coven and then plan your wedding. We need to put the Power of the Holy Dimension around the two of you as one. So, the sooner the better," Trodus told them.

They left the dining hall, walked out to the livery where they all got on Pegasuses, and flew out to a few yards back from the Coven of the Sacred Flame where they were joined by mystical forest creatures and the creatures of the Demack Grassland.

Trodus commanded, "Let's begin! With the Power of the Holy Dimension - Purifenis Dragate–Away with the Coven of the Sacred Flame! Purifenis Dragate–Away with the witches from the Coven of the Sacred Flame! Purifenis Dragate–Away with the children of the witches from the Coven of the Sacred Flame!" They all repeated it over and over. The ground began to shake, it cracked, and the crack widened more and more as they kept repeating it.

Finally, the crack split the coven off onto their own island. The pregnant witches came out to the edge and watched as their own island was created. Water spilled into the gorge and the island went further and further from the shore line.

"Now for the second part. With the Power of the Holy Dimension - Incenecto Vexenus for all of Parrcaster Island above and below, Flarello Viralerous for all of Parrcaster Island above and below, Proticum Banio for all of Parrcaster Island above and below, Immolortia Feliatis send your protection to Parrcaster Island above and below." This was repeated over and over as they walked into the water. The force field was complete and the Coven of the Sacred Flame was their own island.

Tatiana instructed, "We have completed both spells. You all may return to your homes." They got on their Pegasuses again and returned to the Rissingshire Castle.

When they arrived back at the castle, they put the Pegasuses in their stalls. Then they sat by the fireplace. Puggaald walked out to join them with marshmallows and sticks. He placed them on the hearth.

Avras and Arietta appeared in the courtyard, "Hi everyone! I heard that Trodus and Tatiana were back. Welcome back! How did this afternoon go? Plus, what in the world was that about?"

"You remember all the witches and children throughout these kingdoms?" Odulore asked him.

"Yeah!"

"Well, we found some more. This time it was a coven of eight witches, and they all got pregnant from not only Qrizor but also Crumazz. Evidently, it was a father/son outing. These witches thought they were the greatest thing. So, Trodus and Tatiana came back to help separate the coven from the rest of the Xoba Kingdom. Then we resealed the force field. Well, I say we, but these spells included calling on the Holy Dimension," Odulore explained.

Trodus added, "We are also here to help them plan their wedding. That will be the best part. Plus, I can do the ceremony if they like."

"Yes! I would love that!" Amaranth exclaimed.

They sat and enjoyed the quiet evening. The pixies and fairies lit up the Demack Grassland, and flew into the courtyard. They then surrounded the seven of them. Positive energy emanated from them producing a great light. It lit up the entire castle and then the kingdom. The other kingdoms could see it and bask in the light.

Within fifteen minutes there were witches and wizards of all ages who started to enter the castle courtyard. It wasn't long and the castle was filled, every hallway with witches and wizards, grassland and forest creatures.

"Are you Amaranth?"

"Yes, yes, I am. Who are you?"

"I am Jade. My mother is Onyx, and she told me recently that my father was Qrizor. I understand that your father is also Qrizor."

Amaranth smiled, gave her a hug, and said, "Yes, my father is Qrizor. My mother is Zaleria. My brother Qbaris is right here. We share the same parents, but we were not raised together. Do you have other siblings?"

"Yes, I do. I am the oldest of three of us. The others are over here. Their names are Rhodonite and Sapphire. There are also others in our kingdom of Zodel. There are five others that are still living. However, they have different mothers. Had you heard of any of us?"

Amaranth smiled at her, nodded, and said, "Well, how do I say this? I have heard of you. In fact, there are many of us. We are a part of a very, very large family. Qrizor was a bit of a player. He went from kingdom to kingdom creating more children."

Jade pursed her lips and then asked, "Do I want to know how many? I guess the first question to ask when dating is what is your father's name," she chuckled. With so many siblings throughout the kingdom an embarrassing relationship could occur.

"Have a seat before I tell you this. When I said that he was a player, I mean that seriously. He was driven to create an island of his children and in hopes that they would be evil, like him. There were fifty-four of us. There was one still-born and then one that got banished to the Dark Underworld. Just before Qrizor and Crumazz got banished, they went to the Coven of the Sacred Flame, and they proceeded to get all eight witches pregnant. There are another dozen children that have not been born yet. This coven was smitten by them, and we had to cut the coven off from the island," Amaranth explained.

She closed her eyes and asked, "You said THEY got the eight witches pregnant. What do you mean by they?"

"Qrizor and Crumazz went to the coven and together they both got all the witches pregnant. These witches do not know which one or if both of them got them pregnant. Evidently, they were all done in threesomes. I know, it's disgusting," she shivered.

Qbaris walked over and asked, "Everything ok over here?"

"Yes, Qbaris, this is Jade. Her mother is Onyx and her father is Qrizor. Onyx, this is my brother, Qbaris."

Jade sat there shaking her head, and looking from Amaranth to Qbaris and back. “I have to go. I will be back, later.” She walked away from the castle. *What in the world? What am I a part of? How are there so many siblings? That last part is beyond disturbing. How am I a part of that wizard?* Jade thought to herself, over and over on her way back home in Zodel Kingdom.

Chapter 26

It was just before sun down in the Dark Underworld. Ozrig and Annamaaz stood at the portal exit. Evil Witches, wizards, and demons stood before them. "Now is the time that we are going to the Coven of the Sacred Flame. We are going to leave Qrizor, Crumazz, and Zaleria there. This area is important to us. We need all these witches to have evil children. If they do, that means we have a dozen children and their eight mothers that are ours! Some may recognize the coven because you yourself were raised there. Some of you even became pregnant there. The only ones staying are Qrizor, Crumazz, and Zaleria. This is in Xoba Kingdom. We have to work at getting to it. Everybody–To Xoba!" Ozrig commanded.

The darkness left through the portal and filled the sky. A deep dark cloud with streaks of lightning all around sped out from the portal to envelop the Coven of the Sacred Flame. Qrizor, Crumazz, and Zaleria are dropped onto the beach of the newly formed island.

Moira came out to greet them, "Hi Qrizor and Crumazz! Who is with you?"

"This is Zaleria. We are here to help you witches through the rest of your pregnancies and so is she. I understand that all of you are pregnant and some with multiples Is this correct?"

Ember ran up and hugged Crumazz, "Oh, I knew you guys would be back! They said you guys wouldn't, but I knew better. I am pregnant with twin boys. I am going to name them Crenorim and Qrornas."

“Twin boys! I love it! Where are the others? I want all the details!” Qrizor announced.

The remaining witches came out of their huts and sat down in their chairs on the beach. Moira said, “I will go through who everyone is. This is Rose and she is pregnant with triplet girls: Lilac, Lilura, and Lydia. Next is Piper, she is happily carrying twin girls: Peony and Paige. Then there is Echo. Another happy mama of twin girls: Fawn and Feba. Nissa is expecting one girl, Nimue. Starla is also expecting one girl, Melusina. Then you have myself, Moira, and I am having a girl named Adonia. You have eight witches that are all happily pregnant with twelve of your children.”

“Ï am extremely happy that all of you pregnant. As soon as we can, we will get you all pregnant again. I understand that you are all willing to do that as well,” Qrizor smiled.

Crumazz spoke up, “I am very pleased with this. I will now have a dozen children. I am helping to build the empire!” He was so pleased with himself.

“What happened that this is now an island? It was not an island previously,” Qrizor asked.

Moira looked at him, “I don’t understand what happened. We were just minding our own business and then there was a great earthquake and our coven broke off from the island. Slowly it has been moving further and further from the island. It has also grown. There’s more land than at first.”

“Where do we sleep? Where are our rooms?” Crumazz asked.

Ember spoke up first, “You can stay in my hut. You both can.”

Rose answered next, “I will take Qrizor. You can’t have them both for this first night.”

Zaleria rolled her eyes and thought to herself, *This is ridiculous. I hope I get my own hut. The last thing I want is to see them with anyone. These two are just disgusting. This whole thing is disgusting. I guess that's what I get for choosing the evil one.*

She questioned, "Where will I sleep? Is there an empty hut?"

Moira chuckled and looked at her, "We all have our own huts. Yes, there is an empty one. How do you fit into this? I know your name, but that's it."

"I am Zaleria. I am married to Qrizor and Crumazz is my oldest child of three."

"I must say, you did a great job with Crumazz. He is a perfect wizard and so gentle with myself and my sister witches. Then Qrizor, thank you for sharing him with us. He worked so well with Crumazz and us. I am very thankful. We all are," Moira told her.

"I am glad you are so happy," She smiled and then thought to herself, *I did not create this. I want nothing to do with this. I will help the children with the basics. I will not teach them evil. I am sure that Qrizor and Crumazz will take care of that. Plus, these witches practically worship them. I need to get this out of my brain. Can I scrub my brain? This is truly torture. I am not sure what's worse, a life of this or putting up with tarantulas.*

Piper got up from her chair, "I am going back to my hut. I am tired. I will show her to her hut."

They both walked off to the huts. The rest of them stayed in their chairs that encircled the bonfire on the beach.

Crumazz got up, walked over to Ember, held out his hand, and said, "Are you ready to go to your hut? I am." She got up and took his hand. They walked off to her hut.

"Well, witches, you have me all to yourselves. What would you like out of this wizard? I am here to please you," Qrizor said with an evil laugh.

Rose stood up, "I am ready to go to my hut. Qrizor, would you join me?" He got up, put his arm around her, and escorted her to her hut.

The rest of the witches went to their huts for the night.

A few hours later the sun rose across the water and the witches and wizards came out of the huts. They went to the hut where they had all their meals. Moira was the cook for the day. She made them breakfast burritos with salsa.

Crumazz appeared with Ember and made an announcement, "I know these boys are mine. I know that all of these children are mine. I don't want to be married to just one witch, like my father. I want to be married to all of them. I will go from hut to hut each day."

An evil laugh came from across the hut, it was Qrizor, "I love this! I will join you. They will all be married to both of us. We will be one big evil family. What do you think Zaleria?

"I think I have lost my appetite," She responded and walked out of the hut.

Qrizor laughed and laughed at her. He said to the remaining witches, "She just doesn't like sharing me."

Chapter 27

Amaranth sat at the table in her room. A blank journal laid open in front of her with a pen in her hand. Tatiana walked in, "How are you this morning?"

"I am doing great. Just going to get started on writing out what I want for the wedding. I know that I need to figure out who all is standing up with me, what my dress will look like, what flowers I will hold, and the most important, when is the wedding." She laughed.

Tatiana sat down across from her, "I can help you with those. Which do you want to start with?"

"Let's start with who is in the wedding. I found all kinds of half-siblings and a brother. I don't want all of the half-siblings, some are just too young, actually, most of them are too young for a wedding. So, there's only a few I want to invite, but not have them IN the wedding. My brother will definitely be in my wedding. He has been awesome ever since we found out about each other."

"That sounds like a great start. For the actual wedding party, which witches do you want? I know you have connected with the witches around the various kingdoms. I love that," she tells her.

Narella and Valora walked in and jumped up on the table between them. They each went up and rubbed on Amaranth. "Yes! We need all kinds of creatures and animals at the wedding!"

"Of course, they are very important and have to be there. That is without question. Which witches?"

Amaranth grinned, pushed the felines off her journal, and wrote down some names, “My best witch is Arietta. Then we will have Shelyn, Zabine and Zolya. It’s so hard to put them in an order, so I went with alphabetical.”

“I like that,” Tatiana smiled at her.

Zyrsit, Ash, and Oldirrim flew in and landed on the table. “Happy day is coming soon,” Zyrsit commented.

They both laughed. “Yes, happy day is coming soon. You will be there,” Amaranth told him.

Odulore walked in, gave her a hug and kiss on the cheek, “Hey how’s it going?”

“We have to determine when the wedding is. Right now we are getting the wedding guest & party lists together.”

“I will go get my father and see what kind of time frame we are talking about.” He exited the room.

The two witches continued adding names to the lists. The felines, owls, and dragon sat watching and turning their heads back and forth as each witch spoke. A few hours later they had the lists wrapped up, along with a menu for the celebration after the ceremony.

“Let’s take a break and get a bite to eat. I bet that Zizor and the goblins have some great food,” Tatiana suggested.

“Great idea. Let’s go!” They all get up and walk to the dining hall.

They are greeted by Zizor, “Are you ready for lunch? I have some great cheese sandwiches and tomato soup ready.”

“That sounds great!” Amaranth told him.

The goblins brought out the trays of sandwiches and soup and placed them in front of them.

A few minutes later they were joined by Odulore and Trodus. "This is perfect, after we get done with lunch we can talk about wedding timing," Odulore let them know, and then he sat down to eat.

Zizor and the goblins came out and cleared away the empty trays. With the table cleared Odulore asked, "So, father, what kind of timing do we have to do our wedding?"

"I would recommend, the sooner, the better. There are a couple of reasons for this. The first is that you two belong together and I can't wait for that to happen. The second is that we need that protective hedge around Amaranth. There is a rumor coming from the Dark Underworld that Qrizor wants to send Crumazz to be with Amaranth. Why? You ask. Qrizor and Zaleria are actually siblings. Their parents set them up and that's because their parents were also siblings and set them up. So, you are looking at a minimum of three generations where the parents are siblings as well. We need to make sure that it is broken."

Amaranth and Odulore looked at each other, then she looked at Trodus, and asked, "Are you kidding me? My parents are brother and sister? Their parents matched them up, on purpose!? They did that because their own parents did the same to them. This is a generational thing? Ugh! I cannot. I just cannot believe these people. Can they get any more evil?"

"This is exactly why we want to get you married and have the Power of the Holy Dimension surround you with a protective hedge," Tatiana assured them.

Odulore looked at his mother, then his father, and finally he took Amaranth's hands, looked her in her eyes, and then said, "I want you to be my wife and as soon as possible. Let's get married tomorrow afternoon. I want it small, intimate, and full of love."

"I completely agree with you. We do not want to risk the Dark Underworld getting near us without the protective hedge from the Power of the Holy Dimension."

He gave her a kiss on the forehead, and turned to the owls, "You owls need to get the word out to the witches that normally come to the castle. We will all meet at the deck by the waterfall over in Lavalbourg Gorge. Father will officiate." The owls flew off to spread the message accordingly.

Qbaris walked into the dining hall, "Good afternoon all!"

"Good afternoon!" They all greeted him.

Odulore shared with him, "We decided to have the wedding tomorrow afternoon by the waterfall in the Lavalbourg Gorge."

"That's great. Why so quickly?"

Amaranth looked at Qbaris, "Have you come across anymore interesting family tree information in any of the journals?"

"No, I have not been reading any of his journals. I was disgusted with the one that I did read. I am not sure that I want to read about any of his adventures. He's really crude."

"Well, we have something new to share with you. Did you know that Qrizor and Zaleria are actually siblings?"

"No, that's not one I knew and definitely would not have guessed. You mean, they are brother and sister, like us?"

"Exactly, but they got married. Plus, their parents were siblings and their parents' parents were also siblings."

Trodus chimed in, "This came up due to a rumor coming out of the Dark Underworld that they want to send Crumazz to be with Amaranth. However, we are going to get Odulore and Amaranth married so that they will have the protective hedge of the Power of the Holy Dimension over them."

"You know, every time I hear something new with Qrizor, it just gets more and more evil. How is this wizard MY father? We are nothing alike. I mean, like worlds a part. So, let me summarize what I have found out about my father. He did not die, but was banished to the Dark Underworld. He was a complete rabbit and went around populating the island. Then just before he was banished, he took his evil son to help him populate a witch's coven. Now we can add to that, that he is actually the brother of his own wife and it's because it's a three generation tradition. Oh yeah and let's not forget that he wants to carry on that tradition. Yuck. This is just beyond evil."

Odulore spoke up, "Yeah, this guy is very evil. However, once we get married, we will have an extra protective hedge around us. I look at that as a bonus to getting a fabulous wife."

"Awe, thank you my love," Amaranth smiled and gave him a hug.

Tatiana said to her, "Now, let's go get your dress together. We don't have much time, but it will be beautiful." They got up and went to Amaranth's room.

The wizards stayed in the dining room and enjoyed a variety of beverages and snacks that took them late into evening. They were joined by some of the mystical forest creatures.

In Amaranth's room, Tatiana and Amaranth worked on her dress. With Amaranth's favorite color being purple, Tatiana created a deep dark rich purple lace mermaid shaped dress. The plunging neckline was trimmed in black scallops that buttoned just above the waist. Under the lace was a black silky skirt. The back was an open v-shape. This dress was sexy and comfortable. She loved the way it was custom fit to her shape. It took them quite a while to finish the dress, but it had to be perfect and ready for tomorrow.

The witches walked into her room. Tatiana made sure that they all had form fitted dresses in various shades of purple. Every dress had a plunging neckline, but there was a thin lace that went across bridesmaids dresses. Their dresses also had a thin lace back.

When all the dresses were completed the sun had been set for a few hours. The witches all left and Amaranth laid down for a final sleep as a single witch. Both Narella and Valora snuggled up with her. She petted them both, while she thought to herself, *This is my last night as a single witch. I cannot believe that I get to marry the love of my life. The wizard that will be by next to me forever.* With a smile on her face, she closed her eyes.

Chapter 28

Annamaaz swirled around the Dark Underworld. She went to Ozrig and asked, “Can I go out and see how things are going on the island? I want to make sure it is perfectly evil?”

“Which island?”

“The new one, the Coven of the Sacred Flame. I want to make sure that Zaleria is miserable. This island should be way worse. We let her out of the cave of tarantulas.”

“I love the way you think, perfectly evil. Yes, you can. Make sure that those witches are going to have evil children.”

She flew off through the portal and floated above the water to the Coven of the Sacred Flame. When she arrived on the island, she was not happy at what she found. Annamaaz appeared next to Zaleria, who was in her hut. “What are you doing in here? You are supposed to be helping the pregnant witches. Get out there and help them. You do whatever any of them needs. I mean, whatever and whenever they need it.”

Zaleria looked at her, glared, shook her head, and replied, “Oh boy, how lucky for me. I get to help the witches impregnated by my husband and son at the same time. Oh joy is me.”

“This wasn’t meant to be a picnic. You were banished to the Dark Underworld because you were evil. Did you think you were going to have a good time here? The only reason Qrizor and Crumazz are having a good time is because they can provide us with evil children. Now, if you want to get pregnant, we can arrange that. The thing is though, because you only gave Qrizor one evil child, you will have to have sex with both of them, like the other witches. It's the only way to make sure you have an evil one. Your choice."

"I will help the pregnant witches with that choice." Zaleria walked out of her hut. Annamaaz floated close behind her.

The witches were all in their chairs by the bonfire. Crumazz and Qrizor were also there. They were massaging the witches' feet, going from one to another right around the circle. "Hey, we could use some help here, start with Ember and massage her feet," Qrizor ordered.

Zaleria went to Ember and started massaging her feet. "You are doing it wrong. Can you do anything right? We know you couldn't give him more than one evil child," she said to Zaleria.

"Sorry, I will massage harder," Zaleria pressed harder, "There, is that better?"

"Yes, yes it is. I demand you make sure to massage all of me, except my belly. The only ones allowed to touch me there are Qrizor and Crumazz. Make sure you get ALL spots and holes too."

Annamaaz saw enough and flew back to the Dark Underworld. When she arrived Ozrig asked, "Well, what did you find?"

"I will have to make quite a few returns to make sure she is doing as she is told. However, she is definitely miserable. Right now they have her giving a FULL body massage to the pregnant witches. Trust me on this, she is not enjoying herself."

"Very good. We don't want anyone to have a good time, unless it benefits us. How are Crumazz and Qrizor doing?"

"They were also giving massages to the pregnant witches. At the moment they were working on their feet. So, not completely an enjoyment. I imagine that it will become enjoyable, but they can give us more children. Oh yeah, I did give Zaleria a choice of helping with the pregnant witches or getting pregnant by both Qrizor and Crumazz. She chose helping the pregnant witches," Annamaaz laughed.

Ozrig broke out in a loud thunderous laugh, "That is perfectly evil. You can also give her a couple of other options. She can get pregnant by me or by Zaras and Qrizor. She got pregnant the last time she had sex with both of them. For some reason, she only gave us an evil child with both her husband and father. It's been very convenient for her to forget that fact. I don't think she told anyone and pushed it out of her own memory. You may have to remind her that Qrizor is unable to produce an evil child by himself."

"Oh yes! But why are we bothering with Qrizor if he has to have someone with him? The only evil he has provided is with Zaras or Crumazz. Can we get rid of him?" she questioned.

"No, we will keep him. He does a good job of keeping Zaleria in line. She will do anything he tells her. I don't think she'll listen to Crumazz. He does serve a purpose."

They transported to the dining cavern. Witches, wizards, and demons were all eating foods that they didn't like. Ozrig was pleased to see so many miserable faces. "Oh, seeing misery makes me happy. I hope that you do not enjoy your meal." He let out another thunderous evil laugh.

Annamaaz floated among them, in and out, around, over the top of the tables, under them, up close to some of them, and even took bites out of their food. Just as quickly as she had appeared, she disappeared to her cave.

Ozrig appeared in her cave, "I want you to go to the island multiple times a day. Then see if there are any holes in that force field around Parrcaster Island. Make sure that Qrizor is making his wife, Zaleria miserable. The only ones that should be having a really good time on that island are the witches of the coven and Crumazz. Zaleria will make Qrizor miserable or at the very least, irritated. This is perfect. That island will be the most evil island on the planet. I might, that is a might, leave Parrcaster Island alone and focus solely on the other island, which I need to name. What's a perfectly evil name for it?" He said while pulling at chin.

"I know, how about the Sanctum Island? It sounds like it could be good, but it has that evil feel."

"I want it to be even more evil."

"The Fertilized Flame Island," she suggested.

"That is awesome! I think the Permeated Flame Island would be a touch better. I like your thinking though. We will populate this island and then spread them throughout the world. Yes, you need to go let them know we have renamed the island. Also, we will be increasing the size of the island and sending all witches there that are able to get pregnant, and any wizards that are able to get witches pregnant with evil children."

Annamaaz flew out of the portal and zoomed to the island. She appeared amongst the pregnant witches. Three of them were getting thoroughly massaged in their chairs around the bonfire. "I have an announcement!"

They all immediately paid attention to her and stopped what they were doing. "I have come to announce the new name of the island. Ozrig has named it the Permeated Flame Island. He chose permeated because we will have you witches pregnant over and over and over again. You better provide us with evil children. Flame is because it is a part of the Dark Underworld. We will be increasing the size of the island and sending all witches here that are able to get pregnant and any wizards that are able to get witches pregnant with evil children."

Zaleria thought to herself, *WOW! How did I end up on an island forever where I am pleasuring witches? Not just any witches, but witches that are pregnant because of MY husband and son. Now there are going to be more witches and wizards. This island is going to be nothing but an evil breeding ground.*

"I heard what you thought! You ended up here because of a choice that you made to be with Qrizor. Oh wait, it wasn't really your choice. It was made for you, but made to look like you made the choice. Also, I wanted to remind you of another tidbit that you have conveniently forgotten. Do you remember who got you pregnant with Crumazz?" Annamaaz teased her.

She defended herself, "Qrizor. I was not with anyone else."

"Ah, yes, you have forgotten so well. You have convinced yourself that it was ONLY Qrizor. You got pregnant in the same way that these witches got pregnant. Yes, it was you, Qrizor and Zaras. For those of you here that don't know, Zaras is Zaleria's father. So, it's a family tradition to marry your sibling and have sex with your father and sibling. Ozrig thought it was so evil that he will continue this lovely tradition on for this island. I need to get back. Enjoy!" She disappeared as quickly as she appeared.

Wait? What?! Crumazz was conceived with MY father AND Qrizor!? I knew I blocked that out for a reason. So nice of her to remind me. Although, it does make sense why Qrizor brought Crumazz with him and upped the evilness. She can hear my thoughts when she is here, so I have to be careful. Maybe, I can get lucky and if they do get me pregnant it will be a different father/son combination. I would volunteer to get pregnant then.

Qrizor glared at her, "What are you thinking? You went from glaring to smiling. YOU should NOT be smiling. YOU need to get back to massaging Ember or as I like to refer to it as pleasuring her. It just sounds more accurate and evil for you."

Zaleria shook her head, rolled her eyes, and went back to what she was doing. "Don't roll your eyes at me! I will make you pay for that!" He yelled at her.

"What is worse that you could do to me? This is already the most evil thing you have EVER done! Yes, I find this worse than getting pregnant with Crumazz. That was a one-time event, this is every day, over and over from one witch to the next and now I hear we will get more witches. Oh joy!"

"Keep it up and I will ask Ozrig what would be worse for you. Annamaaz is able to hear your thoughts, so I am sure she could fill me in."

Crumazz interrupted, "Stop it! These witches are not going to be pleasured or massaged in comfort if you two keep arguing. I don't know about you father, but I am completely enjoying myself and it would be even better if I didn't hear HER voice while I am doing this."

"You are correct. Zaleria, no more noise out of you. The only noise I want to hear from you is actually from the witch you are massaging and pleasuring," Qrizor gave her an evil grin.

Annamaaz returned to Ozrig's presence, "It has been told for you. Zaleria is having an absolutely miserable time. I heard her think that she would be willing to get pregnant if by another father/son combination other than Qrizor and Crumazz. I think we could arrange that. I don't think she will think it is all that great when she gets pregnant over and over and over again. We will wear her out and then return her to helping to keep the other witches pleasured."

"My evil demon, I knew there was a reason that we go together so well. You are just as evil as me. I will send more witches and wizards to that island. We are getting some Petrobiens Reef. It is another island that is only partially evil. Too many good witches and wizards on there. So, when the evil ones join us, we will send them off to the Permeated Flame Island. The first father/son pair will take Zaleria and get her pregnant with an evil child, hopefully more than one. Oh, wouldn't that be just the most evil if she had multiple children per pregnancy?"

"Oh yes, my favorite demon, that would be absolutely evil. She thinks she would enjoy it, but that will be short-lived." They both let out an evil laugh that filled all the caverns and caves of the Dark Underworld.

Chapter 29

Amaranth smiled as she sat on her bed. *I am marrying Odulore shortly. I am so excited.* Her thoughts were interrupted by witches coming into her room.

"Are you ready for this awesome day?" Arietta excitedly asked her.

"YES! Are all of you ready? Your dresses are all right here. Let's get changed. We'll be taking the carriage and Pegasuses."

Shelyn answered, "I am ready. I believe we all are."

All of them nodded in agreement, and then went about putting on their dresses. Amaranth got into her dress and Arietta fastened it at the waist in the back for her. Dressed and ready to go, they all walked out to the courtyard where Qbaris had the carriage and Pegasuses waiting for them. He assisted them into the carriage, jumped into the front, and took off over to Lavalbourg Gorge.

They landed a few yards from the deck. All the witches got out of the carriage. Her bridesmaids walked down the aisle to wait for her at the front. Amaranth took Qbaris' arm, and they walked down the aisle to where Trodus was at the front with Odulore.

"Who gives this witch away?" Trodus asked.

Qbaris smiled and said, "I do." He took her hand and placed it in Odulore's.

They looked into each other's eyes as they held hands. Trodus said, "We are gathered here today to join Odulore and Amaranth together in holy matrimony. Today is a day of celebration. The celebration of the love between Odulore and Amaranth. They have written their own vows, so I will let them share those with you now. Odulore."

"Amaranth, you have always been there for me. You are the witch that I want by my side through everything. I will be there for you through the good and the bad, in sickness and in health, for richer and poorer, even through kidnapping, which we hope never happens again. I will be your wizard, your king, your best friend, your lover, the father of your children, and the one to grow old with you. I will be with you every day until we both enter the Holy Dimension together. Amaranth, you are my forever."

"Odulore, we have been friends forever. You are the wizard that I want by my side in any and all occasions. I will be with you always, whether we are rich or poor, if you are sick or healthy, whether there is good or bad going on around us. I will be your witch, your queen, your best friend, your lover, the mother of your children, and the one to grow old with. I will be with you every day and night until we both enter the Holy Dimension together. Odulore, you are my forever."

Trodus smiled and looked at them, "What wonderful vows. I hope you have many children. Now for a display from the pixies and fairies. Watch over by the waterfall."

The pixies and fairies flew up and made a heart, they encircled them, flew back out above the water and made another heart.

"Thank you pixies and fairies. We are to my favorite part of the ceremony. Odulore, do you take Amaranth to be your wife?"

"I do," he smiled at her.

"Amaranth, do you take Odulore to be your husband?"

"I do," she smiled at him.

"The Power given to me from the Holy Dimension now spreads an extra hedge of protection over the two of you from now until the day you enter the Holy Dimension. What the Holy Dimension has blessed, no evil will ever be able to separate. The two of you now have everlasting life either in this world or in the Holy Dimension. No evil will be able to touch either of you. The Holy Dimension will protect you. Your children will also be protected by your hedge of protection until they are of age to marry. Are you ready for the last step?"

"YES!" They both said with excited voices.

"I now pronounce you, husband and wife. Odulore and Amaranth, you are now married. You may kiss the bride."

Odulore pulled Amaranth close and gave her a long, passionate kiss. She had never felt a kiss like this one. Butterflies were in her stomach, and she tingled all over from her toes to the top of her head.

They turned and walked down the aisle to the carriage. Everyone returned to the carriage or the way they arrived. Magnus ran through the forest to meet them back at the castle. Odulore and Amaranth got out of the carriage last when they returned to the castle. They enjoyed some private kissing, while everyone else went into the dining hall for the party.

He helped her out of the carriage. Then he picked her up, cradling her in his arms, and carried her into the castle. They got in the middle of the doorway he planted another kiss on her. Odulore and Amaranth walked into the dining hall hand in hand. Everyone erupted with cheers.

They sat down in their chairs at the table in the front of the hall. Zizor and the goblins came out from the kitchen, and placed trays of food in front Odulore and Amaranth first. They placed them in front of all the guests. After which they returned to the kitchen.

Odulore and Amaranth stood up at their table. He spoke first, "I want to thank everyone for celebrating with us. Today has been such a special day. First, I got to marry this fine witch. She will be with me forever, both here and in the Holy Dimension. Secondly, my parents were able to come and join us. Not only that, but my father was able to perform our wedding ceremony. Thirdly, we are able to celebrate with all of you. Finally and most importantly, we now have the protective hedge around us through the Power of the Holy Dimension. I wish that all of you would get married and have this protective hedge be around you. This hedge goes out to your children until they marry. You can protect yourselves and your families for all eternity both here and into the Holy Dimension."

"I want to also thank everyone, including all my witches that have been there for me. You are the best witches anyone could ask for. You have the best wizards that are by your side. I, too, implore all of you to officially be married in the presence of the Holy Dimension. We can protect the entire kingdom this way. We can witness to the other kingdoms how we are protected. Next, let us continue to celebrate this evening. Follow us out to the courtyard. We will dance and laugh into the late evening."

With that, Odulore and Amaranth walked out of the dining hall and into the courtyard. Their guests followed them and the party continued into the late night.

Trodus and Tatiana walked up to Odulore and Amaranth. "We must return to the Holy Dimension now. We are pleased that we could be here to welcome you as a couple into the protection of the Holy Dimension. We will see you again," Trodus said. They all hugged. Then Trodus and Tatiana disappeared in a white cloud.

Odulore hugged Amaranth tight and whispered into her ear, "I love you, my wife." Then they had a very passionate kiss and returned to dancing with their guests.

The sun started to peak through the forest and barely over the castle wall. “Attention everyone! Thanks for joining us. We ask that everyone leave now so that we can enjoy our honeymoon.”

Everyone came up to them, gave them hugs and kisses, and left out of the castle.

Once they were all gone, Odulore and Amaranth went hand in hand and walked to their new room. This room was one that was set aside for once they were married.

Chapter 30

Rhixon walked into the castle courtyard. Amaranth sat in a chair by the fireplace with her journal and a pen. She looked up at him, "Hi! Can I help you?"

"Yeah, are you Amaranth?" He asked.

"Yes, who are you?"

"I am Rhixon. I am Azalea's oldest surviving child. I wanted to come meet you. I understand that we are half-siblings."

Amaranth stood up and shook his hand, "Glad to meet you. Have a seat."

"Thanks. I will," he sat down near her. "I have one sister, her name is Antha. She is nine months younger than I am. We had another sibling that was older than me, but they were a stillborn. They were only nine months older than myself. I found a journal that my mother wrote. The stillborn was only 3 months along."

"Oh wow! When's your birthday? Mine is August thirtieth and I am eighteen."

"Mine is September twenty-sixth and I am seventeen."

"Yes, I heard that we are all nine months apart. The only thing that changed there was the stillborn. Otherwise, you would have been eighteen months younger than me instead of only thirteen. Do you know how many there are?"

"I know that there was a total of nine of us in Zodel Kingdom with eight of us surviving. Are there more?"

Amaranth chuckled and told him, “Oh my, yes. There are many more. In fact, there are a total of fifty-four of us. I know one of them, my oldest brother was banished to the Dark Underworld. So, we have fifty-two still on the island. Now the next part is a bit more bizarre. There is a section of Xoba Kingdom that got torn off the island. It is where the Coven of the Sacred Flame is located. That was where the most bizarre part of this tale took place. My father and oldest brother together got all of the witches pregnant. Because of the witches’ attitudes towards them, we could not risk them being about this island. The witches thought they were the greatest wizards and would get pregnant by them again, if given the opportunity. Crumazz, my oldest brother, is the only one that is evil. In that coven, there are eight witches, and they are expecting a dozen children. So, Trodus and Tatiana came back from the Holy Dimension to secure this island and sever off the coven.”

“WOW! This is crazy. I had no idea. Do you know how many mothers there are? In Zodel Kingdom we have three mothers with nine children, eight living,” he asked.

“Sixteen mothers in total on this island. Plus the eight in the coven.”

He shook his head, “This is just so hard to believe. I mean, I know that you are telling the truth. It’s just crazy to think that our father got so many witches pregnant. Then the last ones he added in his oldest son. I don’t understand.”

Odulore walked up and sat down, “Hi! What’s your name?”

“My name is Rhixon and you must be Odulore, Amaranth’s new husband.”

“Yes, I am. We just got married yesterday. Glad to meet you. You must be one of the half-siblings,” He said.

Rhixon replied, "You are correct. I am one of many half-siblings. Sounds like there are quite a few of us."

"There are a lot of your family. Would you like to join us for lunch? Zizor has prepared more than enough," Odulore asked him.

"I would love to join you."

They all got up and walked to the dining hall. When they entered Zizor came out of the kitchen with a couple of goblins, all of them carrying a tray for lunch. "I love when we have guests," he said as he laid the tray down in front of Rhixon.

It didn't take long, and they all finished the meatball, pepperoni, and provolone cheese sandwiches on hard rolls. Zizor returned to clear the trays. They went back out to the courtyard. Qbaris walked in with Dax and Darca by his side, "Hey everyone!"

"Hello!" They all replied.

"Who are you? I am Qbaris."

"I am Rhixon."

"Ah, yes, one of our half-siblings. I believe you are the oldest."

"I am impressed. You have the family tree memorized?" He asked.

Qbaris told him, "Actually, I have gone through the list enough that, yes, I do remember a lot of the names and the order."

"I assume that you have a journal of all the siblings?" Rhixon questioned.

"You are correct. No one wants to read this journal. It was very detailed. I found it reassuring, because it showed me that I was not the only one. He had no love for any of them, except for the oldest, and he didn't really like him either. He wanted his own kingdom that was populated with all his own children, and he was willing to impregnate every witch on the island if need be."

"Oh, that sounds like torture. I will take your word for it. I am glad that you did read it because you know about all the half-siblings."

Shortly Drozan, Zolya, Avras, Arietta, Staedan, Shelyn, Xodius, and Zabine walked through the entryway to the courtyard. "We are here to continue the celebration!" They all announced.

"Welcome back!" Amaranth smiled and said to them. "Hey every-one, this is Rhixon. He is the oldest of my half-siblings."

They all went up to Rhixon, shook his hand and said, "Welcome to the family."

"These witches and wizards are not family, like you and I or Qbaris and I. They are all friends that are close like family," she informed them.

Within a few short minutes, the mystical creatures of the forest and grasslands came into the courtyard. Once again, it was filled with laughter, dancing, and celebration. A band of trolls came in playing drums and stringed instruments. They kept the music going for hours.

Odulore and Amaranth went into Trodus' room for a bit of quiet and privacy. "I know this is my father's room. I am thinking that we should clear it out and make it a baby room. It's right here between our rooms. I will put all of his stuff into my room. I have enough space for it all. Plus, it will help me go through his books and journals. What do you think?"

"I agree with you. I can't wait to fill that room with a baby," she smiles and hugs him tight.

They walked back out and joined in the celebration. The celebration went on until after the sunset through the trees. All of the creatures, witches and wizards exited the castle for the evening. Odulore and Amaranth went to their room for the second evening as a married couple.

Chapter 31

A few months passed in the Dark Underworld, Ozrig instructed Annamaaz, "You need to go to the Permeated Flame Island. The triplets should be coming shortly. I want to make sure that they have as much evil influence as possible when they enter the Dark Underworld. They will be ours."

She zoomed out through the portal and to the island. When Annamaaz arrived at Rose's hut, Zaleria was there with her. She could hear more commotion going on and went to find out what it was. When she arrived at Ember's hut, she too was getting ready to give birth and Crumazz was in her hut with her. Still there was more commotion and when she arrived at Piper's hut Qrizor was with her, because she was giving birth as well. Echo was also giving birth to her set of twins and Moira was with her. All the multiple births were happening at once.

Within a few hours there were multiple cries of babies. She was so pleased to see that all of the children were born. In total today they saw nine more added to their number. Each witch had the cribs in their own huts.

Annamaaz called for Qrizor, Crumazz, and Zaleria to join her and the rest of the witches out by the bonfire. "I want to make sure that all of these children are evil. Bring all of them here along with their mothers. I will do an evil curse on them all, plus you all, and the island itself."

They went and brought all the children and the witches to the bonfire as commanded by Annamaaz.

Annamaaz placed her hands on them, and repeated, "Silenenta Serpulus, Levitaeseo Infeceum, Invocim Intimiducto," as she went from witch to witch and child to child. "Now all of you will be evil from this moment forward. You now belong to the Dark Underworld."

This will assure that all are evil. While I am here, I am going to cast a spell on the three witches that have not given birth yet. This will induce their children to come. She walked over to Moira, laid her hands on her belly, and repeated "Extiulsis Personentus" three times. She did the same thing to Starla and then to Nissa. These three witches were immediately induced and their children were born within minutes, on the beach by the bonfire. Zaleria assisted Moira, while Crumazz was with Starla, and Qrizor with Nissa.

Once the children were born Annamaaz went to each of them, placed her hands on them, and repeated, "Silenenta Serpulus, Levitaeseo Infeceum, Invocim Intimiducto."

"I am done here, for now. Congratulations on all the evil children. I am pleased and Ozrig will be pleased as well. Remember I had said a few months ago that we would keep all of you pregnant. You are all expected to be pregnant within two weeks. All eight of you. I will be checking in on a daily basis between now and when you are all pregnant. It would be wonderful if you could all get pregnant on the same day. Having you all give birth on the same day is very convenient for everyone. Timing is everything. See you soon!" Annamaaz disappeared from the island.

Zaleria sat down by the bonfire, *WOW! What a day! She didn't mix words. She wants these witches all pregnant within two weeks. They just gave birth. They don't want anyone touching them. That's just insane. She said it would not be a picnic.*

Qrizor walked over to her, "You look like you are thinking. What's on your mind?"

"Nothing, just admiring all the witches and babies."

"Yes and they are all guaranteed to be evil. ALL of them, not just one of them. They have all accomplished something that you couldn't do. I can't wait to get back with all of them. It was SO much fun the first time," he told her.

Seriously, I did not need to know that. Zaleria thought to herself.

Crumazz joined them and asked, "Well, when do we get back to work with these witches? I loved the threesomes. Hey, maybe you can join us." He looked at Zaleria.

"No thanks, I have enough to do with these witches. Now I have a dozen babies to look after. This is not going to be easy. Hopefully I get help from the witches. I know I will be making all the meals for the remainder of today." She got up and went to the babies.

Qrizor and Crumazz went to the witches and massaged them while in their chairs by the bonfire.

Meanwhile, back at the Dark Underworld, Annamaaz arrived to Ozrig. "You are going to be so proud. We now have a dozen evil children. I put the spell on them so that they are all evil."

"Very good. Did you remind them about getting pregnant?"

"Yes I did. I told them within two weeks."

"That's my demon. Wait, you said a dozen. Did you induce all of them?" Ozrig questioned.

Annamaaz smiled, "Yes I did. All of the ones with twins and the one with triplets were already in the process. I only had to induce the last three witches. I told them that they needed to all get pregnant on the same day for the next one."

Ozrig let out a loud evil laugh, and he informed her, "We will get some new wizards and even a father/son combination. So, we will send them to the island. We need Zaleria to get pregnant with the other witches. There are also some witches. They will also go with the wizards. The wizards will get them pregnant as well.

Qrizor and Crumazz get the eight witches that they already have. They will continue getting them pregnant until these girls are ready to get pregnant. You will also have them teach those two boys to get the witches pregnant when they are able to. Qrizor will continue as long as he is able to. When we are done with him he will be put with Zaleria, who will be wore out around the same time. They will help the witches forever."

"I love this island. This is so evil. You are brilliant," Annamaaz told him.

A group of eight witches with two wizards appeared in the Dark Underworld. Ozrig gave an evil smile, "You all are early. This is perfect! You are going to an island. There is one purpose to this island. It is the Permeated Flame Island. Permeated because every witch that goes to this island is continually pregnant by the wizards. If your pregnancy takes too long, you will be induced. What is too long? You will all get pregnant at the same time and you will all give birth at the same time. So, if one starts to give birth, the rest will be induced because they are taking too long. Annamaaz, you get to take them to their new home."

"Everyone, let's go! Follow me!" She ordered them. They streaked over the water from the portal and landed on the beach of the island. The other witches were there with their children. Crumazz and Qrizor were massaging them while Zaleria was tending to the newborns.

"Hi everyone! I am back! This time I brought some friends and they are staying. They will be around to a different part of the island, but I wanted to make introductions. Zaleria, pay attention because you are going with them. We are moving you.

I will go around to our witches that gave birth today. We have Moira with Adonia, Starla with Melusina, Nissa with Nimue, Echo has Fawn and Feba, Piper has Peony and Paige, Ember has Crenorim and Qrornas, and finally we have Rose who has Lilac, Lilura, and Lydia. The wizards with these witches are Qrizor and Crumazz. They are father and son. Zaleria is married to Qrizor and their son is Crumazz. However, she will be joining your group.

Now for the new witches, we have Myra, Mistya, Alecto, Kalliope, Orchid, Lavinia, and Storm. The wizards are Rugast and Vumonar. Zaleria, you will be in this group. So, eight witches to two wizards. I expect that within a couple of days that all you witches will be pregnant. We prefer it if there are some multiple births. To make sure that we have you all evil enough. I will be casting the spell on you all. So, gather close, and get on your knees."

Annamaaz repeated this over each witch and wizard, "Silenenta Serpulus, Levitaeseo Infeceum, Invocim Intimiducto."

She flew them over to the opposite side of the island, "Here is where you will now live. I will be back in a couple of days to make sure that all you witches are pregnant. Remember that I will be checking on you, and you never know when." Annamaaz was gone with a black streak across the water.

Ozrig yelled, "Annamaaz, are you back?"

"Yes sir! Everyone is all set on the island."

"YES!" He screamed and laughed. "Let's go to our cave." He instructed her.

Chapter 32

Amaranth was standing on the dock at Bredenrath Pond. She watched the fish jumping and fireflies flying. *What an exciting time in Maerith Kingdom. Our child will come into this beautiful creation. The grasslands, forest, lakes, rivers, and wonderful creatures. It is time to announce that we will have a daughter. We will both raise her. She will have the life that I didn't. Not that I don't appreciate that Trodus and Tatiana raised me, but I always felt disconnected. This witch will be loved by many.* She thought to herself as she leaned over the railing and looked at her reflection in the water.

Odulore walked up behind her and put his arms around her with his hands on her belly. "It is time to announce to the kingdom and the whole island that we will have a daughter," he whispered into her ear.

She turned around, and looked into his eyes, "I completely agree. Let's send out the owls to request everyone to the castle this evening. I want to announce it just as the sun is setting. We can have fireworks or the pixies, fairies, and fireflies can create a beautiful display."

"Agreed," he smiled back at her. They walked hand in hand back to the castle.

"Ash! Oldirrim!" She shouted for the owls.

They landed in the courtyard by Amaranth and Odulore. "We need you to go out to all the castles, woodlands, and forest to announce to all that we request their presence at the castle courtyard this evening right before sun set," he instructed them.

The owls flew out of the castle and around the island to all the castles, forest, and woodlands. They stopped at the Langdale Castle where Avras and Arietta sat by their water garden.

“Odulore and Amaranth are requesting your presence in the Rissingshire Castle courtyard prior to sunset,” Ash announced.

Arietta stood up and shouted, “YES! I bet I know what they are announcing.”

“You think you know, but do you really? What do you think it is?” Avras asked her.

“I bet that she is pregnant. I hope I am right.”

Avras shook his head and smiled, “You are a hopeless romantic.”

“Yes I am!”

Ash and Oldirrim flew off into the forest where they made more and more announcements to the mystical forest creatures.

Avras and Arietta got Artimas and Axe out of the room. They flew together to the Rissingshire Castle. When they landed in the courtyard Odulore and Amaranth were there to greet them, “Hello!”

“We had to come immediately. I am excited for you two,” Arietta ran up and hugged her.

“What are you excited about?” Amaranth asked her.

“Your announcement, of course.”

“What do you think our announcement is about? We haven’t said anything to anyone about what it is.”

“I think you are announcing that you are pregnant. I know that you want children,” Arietta told her.

“Such a great guess. I will tell you when I announce it everyone today at sunset.”

“Oh come on Amaranth, I need to know.”

Odulore spoke up, “She said that you will find out with everyone else. It will be worth the wait.”

Qbaris appeared in the courtyard entry, “I hear that there is going to be an announcement this evening. Do I get to know about it ahead of time?”

“Dear brother, everyone waits until sunset. You are no different,” Amaranth explained to him.

They all laughed and then walked to the dining hall. Zizor came out from the kitchen, “Are we ready for dinner? Your last meal before your great announcement. Will you give me a hint about what it’s about?”

She laughed at him, “No, I haven’t told Arietta. I haven’t told Qbaris. I am not going to tell you. All of you get to find out when we announce it at sunset.”

“Ok,” he turned and yelled towards the kitchen, “Goblins, bring the dinner trays!” Goblins exited the kitchen with the trays. They placed them in front of everyone and quickly returned to the kitchen.

The dining hall became quiet as everyone was eating. That is until Zyrsit flew in and announced. “There is a dark cloud coming in over the water!”

Odulore asked him, “Which direction?”

"It's coming from the Dark Underworld portal. It isn't moving very fast, but it's coming."

"What? It's coming here? It shouldn't be able to get through the force field," Amaranth stated.

Odulore placed his hand on her shoulder, "I want to assure you that we have the hedge of protection around us with the Power of the Holy Dimension. That hedge of protection is powerful. It can defeat the Dark Underworld. No worries."

Amaranth placed her hand on top of his and closed her eyes, *I am so lucky to have him and the great protection of the Holy Dimension. I have a great family and great friends.* She opened her eyes, looked around the table, and smiled.

"What?" Arietta asked her.

"I am just so lucky to have you all and the protection of the Holy Dimension. For the first in my life I feel complete. I feel like everything is going to turn out right."

She smiled at her and said, "We are glad to have you as a friend. Both of you. We love you and even though you have not announced it, if you are pregnant, we will love him or her just as much." Arietta stood up, walked around the table, and gave Amaranth a hug.

The goblins returned and cleared the empty trays. Everyone else left the dining hall for the courtyard. As the evening wore on more and more witches, wizards, and creatures arrived in the courtyard. The sun kept getting lower in the sky to where it was just a sliver over the wall of the castle. The fairies, pixies, and fireflies flew into the courtyard and then danced up into the clear sky, and all around.

They flew down and around Amaranth. The glow and positive energy surrounded her. Odulore announced, "We would like your attention. It's not just for the great light display by also for the fairies, pixies, and fireflies. I will let Amaranth make the official announcement."

"I want to thank everyone for coming here this great evening. Yes, we have an announcement to make. We are very excited to announce that we are going to have a baby! We are going to have a girl!"

The courtyard erupted in cheers and the fairies, pixies, and fireflies flew up into the sky and danced. As they watched, the sky grew even darker. There were dark clouds that filled the sky above the force field.

Odulore shouted three times in a row, "With the Power of the Holy Dimension - Incenecto Vexenus for all of Parrcaster Island above and below, Flarello Viralerous for all of Parrcaster Island above and below, Proticum Banio for all of Parrcaster Island above and below, Immolortia Feliatis send your holy protection to Parrcaster Island above and below. Ignitim Serpite the dark and evil clouds to the portal of the Dark Underworld."

The dark clouds quickly left and the sky was once again filled with bright stars. Fireflies, pixies, and fairies danced in the sky once again.

"It's all good! The evil from the Dark Underworld was sent back to their portal. We have the extra hedge of protection over us. We want to thank everyone for coming out and celebrating with us. We know that everyone will love this baby girl almost as much as we will. Feel free to come by anytime if you'd like to help out," he chuckled, "Seriously though, we are so excited to share this news with you. It's been hard to not say anything, but we wanted to make sure things were going smoothly. Plus, we wanted to know whether it was a boy or a girl before announcing the news to all of you. Amaranth is already three months along. So, in just six quick months she will arrive. We will have a formal naming ceremony after she is born. You will all be invited to that as well. Have a great night."

Everyone walked up, gave Amaranth a hug, and congratulated them. There were many well- wishers from the kingdom that wanted to express their pleasure in the couples' news. A few hours passed before all had given their blessings and gone home. Odulore and Amaranth walked hand in hand to their room for the night.

Chapter 33

Crumazz walked the beach by himself. Everyone was still in their huts. The water was eerily still and the sky was clear. Annamaaz appeared in front of him, "How is everything going? Do we have pregnant witches yet? It has been a week."

"You can go check," he jeered at her.

"I wouldn't be so snarky if you know what's good for you. You get a pretty cushy life compared to others. Yes, you have to wait on these witches, but you get to have sex with them as often as you like. Come on, that's a pretty great deal."

"Yes, it is great. Plus, the children are really cute."

Annamaaz yells, "Witches! Come out here!"

The witches appeared from their huts with their children and walked to the beach. They sat down in their chairs after placing their children in their beach bassinets.

"When I left here a week ago, I told you that all of you needed to get pregnant within two weeks and that it had to be all in the same day. So, I am going to feel each of your bellies."

She went up to Rose and put her hands on her belly, "Ah, yes. I can feel the pregnant energy and lots of it. I predict that you will once again give use multiple children. At this time, I cannot tell if it will be two or three. I will check back in a week."

After Rose she went to Ember and put her hands on her belly, "I am very pleased to feel your pregnant energy. You also have a lot going on in your belly. You will have multiple children again."

She moved on to Piper and put her hands on her belly, "Your pregnant energy is harder to feel. You may have only one, but I think that you did not get pregnant with the others. Even if that is so, you will all give birth on the same day, no matter what."

Next she placed her hands on Echo's belly, "Oh, witch, you have so much pregnant energy going on in your belly. You are having multiple children and I would bet it is going to be triplets. You have done a great job."

Annamaaz looked at Moira, Starla, and Nissa, "You three only gave us single births last time. I hope that you have done better this time. We need many more evil children."

Moira walked up to her, and she placed her hands on Moira's belly, "You have done well. I feel a lot of pregnant energy. I would say that you will have at least two, hopefully, three children."

Starla sat in her chair with her belly covered up. "You need to uncover that belly so that I can feel if you are pregnant. Remove your arms!" She slowly removed her arms, and Annamaaz put her hands on her belly, "I do not feel anything. You do not have any pregnant energy here." She turned and yelled at Crumazz and Qrizor, "Why is she not pregnant? The others are."

Qrizor spoke up, "She was stubborn and did not want to have sex. We made her, but I think she made it so that she would not get pregnant."

"I will give you one chance to go and have sex with them and let them get you pregnant. You will do it right now, while I am here, otherwise, I will take you back to the Dark Underworld and I can't control what Ozrig will do to you there. He may get you pregnant or he may send you off to a torture cave."

Starla got up and went with Crumazz and Qrizor to her hut. While they were there Annamaaz went to Nissa and put her hands on her belly, "Another good one. You are full of a lot of pregnant energy as well. Overall, I am very pleased with you all. All except Piper are having multiples. When Crumazz and Qrizor get back, Piper, you will go have sex with them again. You need to make sure that you have multiple children. I want you all to have at least sixteen children born this time."

Annamaaz laid her hands on all the children and repeated over each one, "Silenenta Serpulus, Levitaeseo Infeceum, Invocim Intimiducto."

Starla, Qrizor, and Crumazz came back to the beach. Annamaaz place her hands on Starla's belly, "I am sending you pregnant energy so that you will get pregnant and with multiple children."

She looked at Piper, "Ok, now for you to go make sure you have multiples. Qrizor, Crumazz, you have to take her to her hut."

"Why don't you just send me pregnant energy like you did Starla?" Piper questioned her.

"Don't question me. Plus, Starla did just go have sex with them. So, it's not like she is relying on the energy I gave her. Now go with them, have sex with them and make sure you get pregnant with multiples."

They went off to Piper's hut. Annamaaz then went around to each witch and gave them all a heavy dose of pregnancy energy. "You all need to make sure to have twins. We would prefer triplets and if we could get quadruplets. Ozrig would be ecstatic."

A while later Piper, Crumazz, and Qrizor returned to the beach. Annamaaz walked up to Piper, placed her hands on her belly, and gave her pregnancy energy. "You will definitely have at least twins."

Annamaaz stood in front of them and announced, "Now that you all are pregnant, be warned, you will stay this way and carry them for a period of time that Ozrig feels is needed. We will send you goblins to take care of the children that were just born. I will return later, maybe tomorrow, maybe next week, who knows. Only Ozrig knows." She disappeared from them.

Zaleria sat in her chair by the bonfire on the beach that was at the opposite end of the island. Annamaaz appeared in front of her, "Hi Zaleria, are you pregnant? I will touch your belly." She sat there as she touched her belly. "I am so glad to feel your pregnant energy. I sent you more to make sure that it is at least twins. You have a history of single births."

Annamaaz stood back and shouted, "Myra! Mistya! Alecto! Kalliope! Orchid! Lavinia! Storm! Come to the beach now!"

The witches exited their huts and went to the beach. They all stood in a line, side by side. "Thank you for coming so quickly. I am going to feel your bellies to make sure that you are pregnant. If you are not or if the energy does not feel strong enough, you will return to your hut with Rugast and Vumonar to have sex with them."

She walked up and started with placing her hands on Myra, "Very nice, lots of pregnant energy, and I am sending you more. You must get pregnant with at least twins. Good job."

She continued on to Mistya, then Alecto, and Kalliope, "Very good, everyone so far is pregnant and has been given even more energy to make sure you all have at least twins."

When she got to Orchid there was no energy at all, "What! NO energy! You will get pregnant by Rugast and Vumonar or you will be sent back to the Dark Underworld where you will get pregnant from Ozrig or whatever he chooses to do with you." She shouted, "Rugast! Vumonar! Come quickly!"

They ran out of their huts to be in front of Annamaaz as quickly as possible, "Why is Orchid NOT pregnant?"

"She told us that no matter what we did to her, she would not become pregnant. She said that she is refusing to be a breeding witch," Rugast informed her.

"Very good, Orchid, you will return to the Dark Underworld with me. Ozrig will do as he sees fit with you. In the meantime, you will massage and pleasure all these witches as often as they want it and even when they don't. This is not an easy island for any of you."

Annamaaz continued on to Lavinia and Storm, "I am glad to feel more pregnant energy and I gave you even more. You two will have at least twins. I am leaving to return to the Dark Underworld with Orchid. Ozrig will do with her as he pleases. I will return periodically to check on all of you pregnant witches. You will all give birth on the same day. Whoever goes into labor first will determine the day you all give birth. I will return and all will be induced. The only reason I tell you is because this is your first pregnancy on the island." She and Orchid disappeared.

Zaleria looked at the other witches, "Trust me, it won't be easy. I was on the other side of the island before this. Annamaaz had me massaging and pleasuring the witches as well. The only thing is, I had to listen to these witches have sex with my husband and son. Yes, they too had threesomes. When it came time for the witches to give birth, she was there, and she induced the ones that weren't in labor. After they gave birth, she told them that they had two weeks to get pregnant again. That was only a week ago. I bet she went over there before here and made sure they were all pregnant as well. That means that if they go into labor before us, when she is done with them, she will come over here and induce all of us."

"I don't understand, why?" Mistya questioned.

"They are trying to populate this island with evil children. My guess is so that they can attack Parrcaster Island and all the other islands. The other side of the island has a dozen newborns and seven witches. So, if she told them the same thing she told us about multiple births and wanting at least twins. The other side will have at least fourteen next time. We also have seven, which means at least fourteen for us. There will be at least twenty-eight children born. The last time she had them all at the end of six months. I don't know if they will wait that long or if they will induce all of us early. If we give birth early, then we will get pregnant again quicker," Zaleria explained.

Vumonar asked, "So, we are here to get you witches pregnant and pleasure you?"

"Exactly. Trust me, when you can no longer do that, they will send you back to the Dark Underworld. I cannot imagine what they are going to do to Orchid."

Annamaaz and Orchid appeared before Ozrig in the cave of the Dark Underworld. "Why do you have a witch with you?" He asked.

"This one refused to get pregnant."

"Kezrin!" He yelled and it echoed in all the caves, caverns, and tunnels.

"Yes sir!" Kezrin appeared in front of them.

"What should I do with this witch? She refuses to get pregnant."

"Oh really? I can fix that. I will take her to my cave."

Ozrig let out an evil laugh, "Yes! She is all yours!"

Orchid and Kezrin went to his cave.

"How are the other witches?" Ozrig inquired.

"Oh, they are wonderful and all are pregnant with at least twins. It's going to be a wonderful thing. In just five or six months we will have at least twenty-eight more evil children. I gave them all evil pregnant energy. I only told them that it was pregnant energy."

Ozrig nodded and smiled, he grabbed Annamaaz, and they retired to his cave.

Chapter 34

Irreineot flew into the courtyard and walked into Odulore's room, "I have seen evil activity out over the water. It's in the southeast corner of the Kiniriden Sea toward the portal hole to the Dark Underworld. There's dark clouds coming out from the portal."

Odulore looked up from the journal his was writing. "Good to know. I will have to get the other wizards together. Can you let them know?"

He nodded, walked out of Odulore's room, and flew off to the other castles.

Amaranth glided into Odulore's room. She smiled at him from the doorway. He looked up at her, smiled, and said, "Irreineot was in here this morning. It looks like the Dark Underworld is going to try to cause some trouble. I sent him off to get the other wizards."

"Interesting, but with the protective hedge and force field over us, do we really have anything to worry about?" She asked him.

Odulore stood up from his table, walked over to her, put his arms around her, and whispered into her ear, "Everything will be ok, don't worry about it. I love you. You and our baby girl will be fine."

She looked up into his eyes, and smiled from ear to ear. Amaranth had a glow about her. Odulore thought to himself, *I love her glow and how she looks being pregnant. I can't wait to see her with more babies.*

Oizu and Zyrsit flew into the courtyard. Odulore and Amaranth went out to greet them, "Hi dragons!"

"The Dark Underworld is definitely up to something. The dark clouds are getting closer and closer to the island. We talked to Irreineot, and he should be back shortly along with the wizards," Oizu told them.

Amaranth sat down by the fireplace. *I am loving you baby girl, but, I am having a hard time doing much of anything. I am so tired. I will have to stay back while they deal with the Dark Underworld.* "Odulore, I will stay back. I am tired. Baby girl is zapping all my energy."

"No worries. You get your rest. We'll take care of this."

The wizards started to appear in the courtyard, Avras, Drozan, Staedan, and Xodius. Odulore told them, "We need to go out to the Kiniriden Sea the Dark Underworld is stirring up trouble and coming out of the portal. We need to block it so that they can only go between the portal and that new island."

"Why let them go to the island?" Avras asked.

"We know they are using those witches. They can have that island. The witches would not be on our side of things anyway. They thought Qrizor and Crumazz were awesome. I have the spell that we need to use, but we will need to go further out into the water. We'll take the Pegasuses out there. Avras, can you bring the winged lions?"

"Yes I can," Avras answered.

Azohr appeared, "I heard that you could use some help. I am here along with my griffins and gargoyles. We are ready to go after the Dark Underworld."

"Ok wizards, let's go!" He gave Amaranth a kiss, and they were all off on their creatures for the beach on the Kiniriden Sea.

Witches arrived from around the island. Arietta sat down next to Amaranth. "Witch, you glow so well even when you are tired."

"Thanks, I am more tired, but can't wait to meet her," Amaranth told her.

Zizor brought out some orange & pineapple juice for everyone. "Hey, there's no green tea in here," she told him.

"Yes, I know. No caffeine for you until after the little one is here," he answered her.

She laughed at him and took a drink.

"Are you guys ready for the little girl? What do you need?" Zabine asked her.

"One moment it seems like we have it all together and the next it's like we have so much to do and no time. I can't wait to meet her, but I am also scared and have great anxiety."

"Witch, you got this! You and Odulore are going to be awesome parents. I know it," she reassured her.

Puggaald and Glurx walked up to Amaranth, "Do you need us to do anything?"

"I am good. You can relax out here with us," she told them.

Dax and Darca walked into the courtyard. They both curled up by Amaranth's feet. Narella and Valora curled up next to the canines. A few minutes later there were hares and felines from around the island. They all went into protector mode and were at her feet.

The wizards arrived at the beach and continued out over the water. As they got closer to the edge of the force field they could see a demon figure approaching. It turned out to be Orzak, one of Ozrig's demon sons. He shouted, "Invocim Intimiducto" over and over. Streaks of lightning bounced off the force field.

Odulore and the wizards repeatedly shouted, "With the Power of the Holy Dimension - Incenecto Vexenus for all of Parrcaster Island above and below, Flarello Viralerous for all of Parrcaster Island above and below, Proticum Banio for all of Parrcaster Island above and below, Immolortia Feliatis send your protection to Parrcaster Island above and below. Ignitim Serpite the dark and evil clouds to the portal of the Dark Underworld."

They edged closer and closer to the force field. The lightning streaks stayed further and further away. Ozrig turned back into the portal.

A few minutes went by, and they waited to see if any darkness came through the portal. Slowly a dark cloud appeared and it zipped across above the water straight for the new island. Another few minutes and another dark cloud appeared out of the portal. This one also zipped directly over to the new island. They waited patiently and about thirty minutes later both dark clouds zipped back to the portal and disappeared.

"What do you wizards think? Should we wait to see if any more come out?" Odulore asked.

Avras responded, "It looks like it's only going to the new island. Do we know the name for the island?"

"No, we do not know the new island's name and have no verbal communication with anyone on the island. We have no idea what they are calling it."

"I say we go back to our lovely witches. I think this is all set for now," Drozan suggested.

Odulore agreed, "Let's go back." They turned and flew back to the castle.

When they entered the courtyard they found all their witches relaxing by the fireplace along with quite a few hares, felines, and canines. Dax sat up when Qbaris got close. He patted him on the head.

Amaranth's eyes were closed, Odulore carefully walked through the animals, and kissed her on the forehead. She opened her eyes and looked at him. "Get up, let's go to bed. You need more rest," he suggested to her and held out his hand. She took it and stood up. Odulore held her hand all the way to the bed, where he assisted in getting her settled in.

Odulore went back out into the courtyard, "She is resting now. I encourage everyone to come back in a day or two. She's been getting tired easily. This pregnancy is taking a lot out of her."

The witches, wizards, and animals all left, except Narella and Valora who went in and laid with Amaranth.

Chapter 35

Amaranth sat in her new lounge chair by the fireplace. She had her journal rested on her belly with a pen in hand as she began to write.

I am writing this journal for my little witch. You are my first child, my first little witch. My heart has been so full ever since I found out I am carrying you.

I get to be a mother. I have never been so excited and scared in my life.

The day I married your father, it was absolutely magic. We got married by the waterfall and his father married us. There were fairies and pixies that danced. Oh, I remember it so clearly. I will always remember that day.

Little witch you need to find you a wizard of a lifetime. I have found mine and he is your father.

That evening we were married was beyond words. I had never been with a wizard up until this point. Yes, I saved myself for your father. Our wedding night was filled with wonder, and we knew we were each other's one and only love. You my little witch are the magical miracle of our first night together.

I wanted to write this journal to you so that you knew how much you are loved and have been since you were conceived.

We did not tell anyone when we first found out I was pregnant with you. We wanted to make sure that we got past the first term.

It was so hard not to tell anyone. I wanted to shout it from the highest heights. We waited and waited. You continued to grow in my belly. My joy kept growing with you.

I have sung to you. I have read to you. Your father has also talked to you while you are in my belly. He is just as excited as I am to see you.

The day that we announced you to all on the island, there was great joy. Everyone rejoiced and celebrated. Ever since that day I have had an almost endless line of visiting witches here to help me.

Each day I have loved you more than the day before.

Each day I get closer to meeting you in person.

Each day I grow more and more excited.

Each day I get more and more tired.

You are taking my energy, but it is worth it.

You are my shining light.

You are my baby witch.

You are so loved and so wanted.

Your father takes care of me, like I am his queen.

He makes sure that I have enough to eat, to drink, and most importantly that I get enough rest.

He wants to make sure that you get the energy you need to grow.

We are growing closer and closer to meeting you.

I feel like it was just yesterday that I found out about you.

I keep getting these feelings and it is way too early for you to come join us.

You are an impatient little witch and will be coming very, very shortly.

Why did I write you a journal?

My mother did, but hers was not a loving journal. I want you to have a loving journal from your mother.

I want you to hear all the loving thoughts that I have had throughout this pregnancy.

Although right now, you are giving me some super strong pains. It feels as if you are on your way.

I am going to close this journal, because you are definitely on your way. I have to get my witches' help to bring you into this world.

I love you my little witch.

Amaranth closed her journal, put her pen down, and yelled loudly, "Arietta! It's time!"

She raced to her side, and yelled, "Odulore! It's time! The baby is coming!"

He raced to be with them and assisted with holding her hand.

Within a few hours, there was a little cry and the little witch was born. Arietta wiped her clean, and placed her in Amaranth's arms. "Congratulations on the birth of your little witch," she told them.

Amaranth kissed her on the forehead as she cradled her closely in her arms. Odulore leaned over and kissed them both on their foreheads.

Ash and Oldirrim flew into the courtyard. Odulore instructed them, "Go fly around the island announcing that the little witch has been born. Let the whole island know about our wonderful arrival." The owls flew away to make their announcement.

Arietta cleaned up the area while Amaranth held her little witch tightly in her arms. Odulore ran to the kitchen to let Zizor and the goblins know about the great news.

There was a bright light in the sky above the castle. Trodus and Tatiana appeared in front of Amaranth. "We are here to celebrate with you and to officiate her naming ceremony," Trodus informed her.

Odulore ran back into the courtyard, "I love it! I have my mother, my father, my wife and now my daughter. I cannot ask for anything more. This makes my life complete."

"Have you decided on a name?" Tatiana asked them.

"Yes!"

"Good, don't tell us. Wait until we ask for it during the naming ceremony," Trodus told them.

Within the next hour the courtyard filled with witches, wizards, and creatures.

Trodus began, "Please gather around. We are here for the naming ceremony of the little witch of Odulore and Amaranth. What a joyous occasion we are gathered for. These two were blessed on their wedding day with the hedge of protection from the Power of the Holy Dimension. This hedge of protection is now extended to their little witch upon this rejoiceful day of her birth and naming. Would her parents please share with us what her name is to be?"

"Her name is Amaryllis!" They both announced.

Odulore added, "This is because she is our star flower."

"We welcome Amaryllis to this community. We bless her with the hedge of protection from the Power of the Holy Dimension. May she grow strong in mind, body, and soul," Tatiana spoke upon her.

"Congratulations on the birth and blessing of Amaryllis," Trodus said to them. "We cannot stay. Unfortunately, we only came for the naming ceremony. Know that we are watching from the Holy Dimension and that your island does have a hedge of protection over it because of you Odulore. We will see you soon."

The bright light returned and as it disappeared, so did Trodus and Tatiana.

Amaranth held Amaryllis to her breast, who immediately latched on. She looked up at Odulore with an ear to ear smile on face, "This is the second best day of my life. The first is when I married you."

"I completely agree with you."

Witch after witch after wizard after wizard came up and shook Odulore's hand or gave him a hug and said, "Congratulations." They all told Amaranth congratulations from a distance, as she was still in her lounge chair feeding Amaryllis. After which all the guests left them alone.

Amaranth, Odulore, and Amaryllis were finally alone. The three of them were by the fireplace. The heat kept them warm, as the temperature was a bit cool after the sun had set.

"Now for you two to get up off that chair. Would you like my assistance?"

"Yes, you can hold Amaryllis, your daughter, your little witch. Enjoy!" She pulled her from her breast and handed her up to him. Not a noise did she make. The little witch snuggled right up to her father.

Ever so slowly Amaranth got up off her chair. She had not been out of it since earlier in the afternoon when she sat down to write in her journal. Now the sun had set, her legs were a bit weary.

They all walked to their room and laid Amaryllis in the middle of their bed. Amaranth laid down next to her, and Odulore laid down on the opposite side of her.

"I am so happy right now. My heart is full. I have you, my dear sweet and amazing wife. Now I have our daughter in between us in our bed. She came a bit early and is oh so tiny. We will need to put her in her bassinet when we sleep. I don't want to squish her accidently. For now, I just want to enjoy the three of us. Our little family just sends joy throughout my body from my toes to the tip of my head."

"I have to agree with you. This day has been so amazing and a miracle. I wrote her a journal telling her how much she is loved. Then while I am writing I could feel her getting into place to make her entrance. She did not take too long to come out. I was very thankful to have you and Arietta to help her make her fabulous entrance. Next, your parents showed up, what a great miracle. I did not know they were coming, but they made her naming ceremony super special. You two fill my heart and make me complete. I love our family. I look forward to expanding our family. I don't want them as close together as what my father did, but I would like one, once a year. How about four children?"

"I like your way of thinking. We can do that. What if we end up with a multiple birth?"

"Then we end up with multiples."

Odulore sat up, picked up Amaryllis, Amaranth gave her a kiss, and then he placed her in her bassinet. "Do you want something to drink? I am going to get me something," Odulore asked her.

"Yes, please."

He left for the kitchen. She sat up and looked over into Amaryllis' bassinet to watch her sleep.

Chapter 36

The witches laid in their chairs around the bonfire. Crumazz and Qrizor sat by whichever witch yelled for them. They jumped from witch to witch as they all yelled for them, one after the other, and back and forth.

Annamaaz appeared on the beach, "All right, we are all right here. Are we ready to have some children? It is time, whether you are ready or not. However, from the yelling, I would say that these children are coming right now."

First child to appear was Piper's, she had Pepper. Annamaaz placed her hands on Piper's belly and then the next one appeared followed very quickly by the third one. These were named Ulva and Ursula.

She moved on to Moira and laid her hands on her belly. Instantly the first came out into Crumazz's hands. He barely caught that one and the next one came out. Their names were Alaric and Angelic.

Next up was Echo. Annamaaz laid her hands on her belly as well. Qrizor was in position to catch both of the witches, Ebras and Enior.

Crumazz moved on to Ember and Qrizor joined him. Within moments of her hands on Ember's belly the first one came out, with the next two right in a row. She named the baby wizards Qonaxx, Crequam, and Cruqriv.

The only thing you could hear was babies crying as they came into the world. It was like a production line. Annamaaz laid her hands on the witch's belly and the children came out instantly or within seconds. Qrizor and Crumazz had to be there to catch them, they came out so quickly. Everything was going so quickly that the witch had to clean herself and the children, because they just laid them on the chair between their legs.

Next up was Starla. She had Maescia and Malise. Followed by Nissa who Norea, Nina, and Nicholas. The final one to give birth was Rose, who once again had triplets, and she named them Lavina, Lux, and Lilith.

Annamaaz stood before them and announced, "Wonderful work witches. You have done a great job. We now have eighteen more evil children. Congratulations! You are all helping us to populate this island. Ozrig will be pleased. You got pregnant within a week last time. We will go with that timing again. This time you had them a month earlier than last time. We will see how it goes if we will go five months or six months for you all to give birth. This means that your three births will all take place within a year. You will be expected to have a multiple childbirth again. No less than two children per birth. I told you that this would not a picnic. All of you will have a minimum of five children under a year old and some of you could have up to nine. Rose, if you give us three again, you will have nine under a year old. We may give you a longer break after that birth if you give us three. Anyway, I am off to the other side of the island. It's time for them to also have their children as well. This way I make one trip."

She disappeared and left them with their eighteen newborns and the previous dozen that are only five months old.

Crumazz hollered above all the crying babies, "YES! I have a total of thirty children! I am so awesome! Now, to get them all pregnant again. This is awesome! How many can I have? Oh, if I can get you all to have triplets, what an awesome day that will be. We will add twenty-one children to our numbers. I can't wait to have fifty-one children. Fifty-one evil children that I helped to create! So many in one year. What an achievement! I am so proud of myself!"

On the other side of the Permeated Flame Island Annamaaz appeared amongst the witches on their beach. They all looked comfortable sitting in their chairs with Rugast and Vumonar going from one witch to another massaging and pleasuring them.

Annamaaz announced, "I am here to induce all of you to give birth to your children. I am hoping to see multiple children. Just FYI, the other side of the island gave birth to eighteen children. Will you witches give me more? I hope so. Let's see, who to start with? Let's start with Myra and then I will go around the circle. Rugast and Vumonar, you will want to be ready. As soon as I lay hands on their belly, their first child will come out and it will be quickly followed by the next and if there is a third one it will follow quickly as well. You will not have time in between witches either. I don't have a lot of time here, so it will go fast."

Myra laid back as Annamaaz laid hands on her belly. Rugast was in place to help catch the newborn, which took just seconds. The first one was Maev and the second followed was Mina.

Next she moved on to Mistya. Once her hands were on her belly the babies came right out. Myrtle was first, then Marie, and Myrilee. Vumonar caught them all.

Keeping the pace, she moved to Alecto with Rugast. Aileen and Alexandra came right out after her hands were on Alecto's belly.

She wasted no time and went to Kalliope. Vumonar was right there for her and caught Karin, Kestrel, and Kamila.

Lavinia went next and had just two, Vrofaris and Vrasorin, both wizards and the first one to not have witches.

Annamaaz laid her hands on Storm. Her three wizards came right out in a row: Sipan, Shumorith, and Shodelis.

"Now we are at the one that I had to take back to the Dark Underworld. These are actually from Kezrin. Rugast and Vumonar, you both need to be here to catch them," Annamaaz instructed them.

She laid her hands on Orchid's belly. Instantly the first one came out, then the next three followed right in a row. Their names were Olazaleus, Osior, Ozenilorh, and Othall–all males, part witch and part demon.

"YES! We got our first quads! Of course it took a demon to do it. Great job Orchid. We may have Kezrin come here and get you pregnant again."

Finally, she went on to Zaleria. "You have done this before, in fact, three times before, but it was only one at a time and nine months a part. I can't wait to see how many come out of you this time. Plus, this time they will all be evil. No goodies here. That's not allowed on this island." Annamaaz laid her hands on her belly and the children came out instantly. Rugast caught them, Aphovae, Atahith, and Aweahl.

"Yes, you had triplet witches. I like it. You did much better over here and with Rugast and Vumonar. I am pleased and so will Ozrig."

She stood smiling at them all and announced, "I just want to remind everyone that the whole reason you are here on this island is to populate it. Your job is to get pregnant and have evil children. You witches did great. We now have twenty-two evil children. I will be checking back, but you will all be pregnant within a week. I told this to the other side. You will then give birth in five or six months. Being that they are one set of births ahead of you, it will most likely be five, you will have a week to get pregnant and then give birth in another five months. We want three births within a year. So, you have twenty-two now, we expect at least twenty-two next time and the following time. This will give us sixty-six evil children within a year. The other side has thirty evil children at this time. They are expected to add at least two for each witch next time. You will have more over here than they will. I have to leave."

Annamaaz disappeared in a black puff of smoke. Zaleria looked around and said, "This is absolutely ridiculous. We have twenty-two newborns, and they expect us to get pregnant within a week to have even more. I am over thirty-eight years old and haven't had any children in eighteen years and now I am having triplets. She wants me pregnant again in a week and with multiples? This is seriously the most evil place."

Rugast responded, "Well if you like, we can get you pregnant right away. We can work on it every day until Annamaaz comes back. This way you'll definitely be pregnant and have a better chance of multiples."

She looked at him and shook her head.

"You are complaining! I have never given birth before. The first time I get pregnant is by a demon and I end up with quadruplets. Plus, she is going to send him back here to get me pregnant again! So, quit your complaining. Be a team player," Orchid yelled at her.

Back in the Dark Underworld, Annamaaz appeared before Ozrig, "Well, what is your report? It better be good, or we are going to leave you on the island to get pregnant over and over."

"Oh yes, it is a great evil report. The witches with Qrizor and Cru-mazz birthed eighteen and the witches with Rugast and Vumonar, they birthed eighteen as well. Then Orchid, who got pregnant by Kezrin, she had quadruplets! They were all males too. We have a lot of witches, but we need more wizards and male demons. I need you to send me with powers to make them all have males," she reported.

"Yes, yes, yes. I love it! You will go back in a couple of days to make sure they all get pregnant. I will give you the power to make sure they are all males too. We need to keep this island populating with evil children. Although, we may need to add the size of the island." He laughed loud enough to fill all the caves, caverns, and tunnels.

Kezrin appeared before his mother and father, "What did Orchid have? How many? Can I do that again?"

Annamaaz smiled and told him, "She had quadruplets of all male demons. Great job!"

"Yes, you can do it again. Annamaaz will be returning to the island in a couple of days. You will go with her. I want you to impregnate Orchid and also Zaleria. I heard she was also complaining about being pregnant with triplets. We'll show her. This time it will be quadruplet males," Ozrig informed him.

They all disappeared to their caves.

Chapter 37

The sun rose over the castle wall. Amaranth sat in the courtyard with Amaryllis up to her breast. Arietta walked in and sat down on the chair next to them, "Are you ready for some company? I heard that your half-siblings are on their way. You have mothers and children coming to see you and little Amaryllis."

"I guess," she sighed, "I am still tired. Plus, the youngest ones are almost a year old. So, we are talking about a huge age gap and those children are going to want to run around. Can you make sure that they are entertained out in the grasslands after I meet them?"

She placed her hand on her shoulder, "I can most certainly do that for you. I can't blame you. How many people?"

"It's going to be sixty-six people if everyone comes. I am getting overwhelmed just thinking of this many people coming through here to meet her and I. Although, it's going to be the first time ever that we all get to meet one another."

"Witch, that is the coolest thing. I love that all these children and mothers turned out good. Qrizor wanted it for evil and it turned out to be the opposite. Does it make you wonder what's going on out on the island? How many more are there?"

Amaranth shook her head, "No, I try to keep him out of my mind. Plus, just the thought that he brought my brother into his sick plan. I realize Crumazz was evil, but he made no mention that he went with him on that escapade. I know that Qrizor was already banished at that point, but still. He could have said something," She sighed, "I am so glad that they are both gone. Plus, my mother. I am glad that her negative energy will never be around

Amaryllis. If any of these half-siblings or their mothers bring any negative energy, they will no longer be welcome in the Maerith Kingdom. They can stay in their own kingdom."

Arietta smiled, "I am in agreement. We do not need that here. Can we get them banished to that island?"

"Oh that would be great. They can all exchange stories of Qrizor. I mean, these mothers all had sex with him. You know when you think about it, it is strange that Qrizor waited until he went to the coven to bring in Crumazz. He was eighteen or close enough, for the youngest two before that."

"I bet he just didn't think about it, or he wanted them all for himself."

Rhixon and Antha walked in with Azalea. Arietta brought them over to them, "This is Amaranth and Amaryllis. Here we have Rhixon, who you already met, and then Antha and their mother Azalea."

They all nodded. "Sorry, my hands are full at the moment. Please sit. There will be beverages and snacks shortly," Amaranth said to them.

"No problem, Rhixon came back and told us about you. How wonderful that you have a little witch of your own. I don't know what to say. I didn't realize that he was married and had children. The first one only got to four months, and then we lost her. I am happy that I have these two. They are great. He just disappeared after Antha was born. I mean, like he was there when she was born. He gave them their names and then poof," Azalea explained.

Antha spoke up, "I had no idea until Rhixon said something."

More witches and wizards walked in that were mothers and half-siblings. Qbaris walked in amongst them.

"Hey Amaranth, how is little Amaryllis? She is so adorable. On another note, would you like me to do the speaking and inform them of some of the things we have learned?" he asked her.

"Yes, that would be great. I am not standing up at this point. She went from feeding to sleeping, and I am comfortable."

Qbaris stood up on the fireplace hearth and shouted, "Everyone, please come in and come closer. I am Qbaris and I am Qrizor's oldest son on this island and Amaranth's brother. Yes, we share the same mother and father. I want to share with you all what we learned from Qrizor's journal and then what we have done most recently."

He waited and they moved closer. "I want you all to know that we have no way of verifying Qrizor's journal, except through all of you. We had no idea until after he was banished that this journal existed. Let me tell you, none of you will want to read it. Parts of it made me want to scrub my brain and eyes. He was a crude and graphic evil wizard. I spared them from Amaranth and gave her the abbreviated version. First, no one should be treated the way he treated all of you. I lived with him and no idea this was going on. He did tell us that at most there were nine months between children. He wanted us all to be evil, and he was greatly disappointed in everyone because no one was evil. He made a point to write about wanting to create an island dedicated to himself. He was very proud that he had so many children. Every time he had sex with a witch she became pregnant. The most disturbing part is now coming. When he was in Xoba Kingdom he went to a witch's coven with his oldest son, Crumazz. They had sex together with each of the eight witches that were there. He was super proud of that. In total, he had fifty-four children before that coven. We have stopped counting his children at this point. This is because after they got pregnant he was banished. The witches were on Crumazz and Qrizor's side and were willing to get pregnant by both of them again if they could. With that, we severed their coven from this island to create their own island. At this point, we have no idea what has happened on that island, and we do not want to know. Does anyone have any questions?"

Raina stood up and said, "I am not surprised at any of this. Mine are the youngest, along with Xantha's. She had singles and I had three sets of twins. Yes, I have three sets of twins that are under two years old. It is crazy. I had no idea what I did wrong. I thought he was going to stick around. We live in Xoba Kingdom. I know which coven he went to. This is just so upsetting." She started crying.

Astrid looked her, "I feel your pain. I have triplets that are almost two. I think your first set of twins are only a month younger than my triplets."

"Witches, you are correct. Within a year and a month he got three of you pregnant with a total of a dozen children. Qrizor was very proud to be going around the island and getting witches pregnant, but not stick around. You are definitely not alone. We can only imagine what happened, but have no idea how you feel because we are his oldest children with the only witch that he married. I am not sure what good that did. Even for us, the three of us were only eighteen months a part. He started his pattern very early. As time went by he got more and more angry," Qbaris sympathized.

Rhixon stood up, "As the oldest of the siblings that were not part of his marriage, I was in shock when I first heard about the stories. I must say, I am really glad that he did not stick around. One story that Qbaris left off was how Crumazz was conceived.
Qrizor and his father got Zaleria, Qrizor's wife pregnant. So, on their wedding night, it was a threesome. If that's not bad enough, evidently, that was the same way Qrizor was conceived as well, and Qrizor's father. It was family tradition. It is one that I am glad is gone. I want nothing of that."

"I am glad that tradition is gone as well. I have three boys," Cyrena commented.

"Yes, we can all be thankful. With how much Qrizor wanted his island of evil children, I don't know if he would have tried it with the witches that were his own children or not. I have a feeling that he would have wanted that for everyone's wedding night," Qbaris responded.

He continued, "I must say that we just wanted everyone to know that Qrizor and Crumazz have both been banished. Our mother, Zaleria was also banished. They went to the Dark Underworld. Odulore and all of us wizards work on a regular basis with the Holy Dimension to make sure that the Dark Underworld has no power here. Also, anyone that wishes to go be and with them, that can be arranged. Their way of life and thinking will not be accepted here."

Coral stood up and glared at him, "So, if we don't think the way you do, we will be banished? My twin, Calla, and I have two sets of twins between two and three. Would you banish all of us if we don't think you? If only me and Calla, then good luck with the children. They are a handful."

"Honestly, we hadn't thought far ahead. We didn't think anyone would even consider wanting to be banished. We do not know what they are doing in the Dark Underworld. However, on first thought, I would say you and your children. I would not put that on another witch, but if there's one that wants your children, then I guess they stay here. By the way, what are you, not even twenty-one? You have so many years ahead of you, why would you want to go to the Dark Underworld?" Qbaris questioned her.

"Seriously, because I don't want to be judged for something that I was basically coerced into. What wizard is going to want me now with two sets of twins?" She broke out in tears.

Calla gave her hug and assured her, "We will get through this. We now know that we have a huge support system. Look around you. You have all the other witches that he took advantage of.

He was such a smooth talker and coerced, I would say, all of us that had his children. Thankfully, we have some older ones - both mothers and children that we may get some help from. We did not know this before."

Amaranth looked around at the courtyard and said, "I want to say that I am glad that you all came here. There is a support system here now that we all know about each other. There is support for the children as well as the mothers.

I was abandoned by both my mother and father. I was raised by Odulore's family. I knew I was abandoned my whole life. I only knew my mother's name. I did not find out my father's name until after they were both banished, along with my oldest brother. I knew nothing about them.

Having all of you here is overwhelming and reassuring all at the same time. I am glad that Amaryllis has such a large family."

Azalea walked up to the front of the group and stood next to Qbaris, "As the oldest mother here, I want to tell you that you can move forward and have a wonderful life on this island. I do not regret having my children with Qrizor. My children were raised by me, and they have turned out to be a wonderful wizard and witch. I have not married nor have I had any other children. I also do not plan on any more. These two are great. I am looking forward to them getting married and having children of their own."

"Thank you for that, Azalea. Now everyone can chat, and enjoy the beverages and snacks," Qbaris told them.

A couple of hours later, they all left, and Amaranth was able to relax again. "Thank you for all of your help, both of you!" She thanked Qbaris and Arietta.

"We'll leave you alone, well, with Amaryllis to enjoy the evening. Odulore is coming back shortly," Qbaris told her. Then he and Arietta left the castle for their respective homes.

Chapter 38

Down in the Dark Underworld Ozrig yelled, “Annamaaz! I have an evil idea. Get over here!”

She appears in front of him, “Yes, what is your idea?”

“I want you to go to the Permeated Flame Island and take Kezrin with you. I have a few things for you to do. You will have him impregnate Orchid again, plus, while you are there, he can impregnate Zaleria. I want them both with quadruplets. I also want to have all of the rest of the witches to have triplets. Make it happen. I will give you the power, and they will also all have males. No females for a while, we have enough of those.

You will also have the power to draw a rectangle in the sand, and in the middle you will show Zaleria, Qrizor, and Crumazz what a wonderful life that Amaranth is having. This will be make them all jealous and miserable.”

“I love your idea. It is perfectly evil.”

“Kezrin! Come here!” He appeared immediately in front of Ozrig and Annamaaz. “You will go with her, and you will impregnate both Orchid and Zaleria. They are to have quadruplet males.”

They left through the portal and arrived on the beach of the island where Zaleria and the other witches were relaxing in their chairs. Annamaaz announced, “I am here to make sure that all of you are pregnant. Plus to bring you great news! Every one of you will have triplet males. Well, almost, Orchid and Zaleria, you two get the pleasure of getting pregnant by Kezrin. He will make sure you both have quadruplet males. Now, Kezrin, take them both to a hut.”

Zaleria and Orchid walked off with Kezrin to Zaleria's hut. *This is beyond evil. I cannot believe this. I am almost 38, and I am going to have quadruplets!*

Kezrin looked at her, "Yes! You get to go first because of your complaining. Then when you are pregnant, you can go out and see what your next surprise is."

Meanwhile, Annamaaz went to each witch, laid her hands on their bellies, and pushed her magical energy into them. "You will be pregnant with triplet males. They will all come to term in five months time." Then she yelled, "Rugast! Vumonar! Come here!"

The wizards walked out of their huts and stood in front of her. "You should have been out here making sure these witches were massaged and pleasured. You are to do that from the time they wake up until they go to sleep. If they take a nap during the day, you are to continue what you were doing, anyway. If I find out that you are not doing this, we will take you back to the Dark Underworld."

They both nodded at her and then Zaleria walked out of the hut. She sat down in her chair. Annamaaz smiled, "I see that you are not happy. This means that Kezrin did his job. I know that you are not happy with being pregnant again after so many years off. That's what you get for coming to the Dark Underworld. Now, I will make your day even more miserable." She drew a rectangle in the sand, and pointed at it. A picture appeared. It was Amaranth having a picnic lunch with Odulore and Amaryllis.

"Recognize everyone? Let me remind you. This is your daughter. The one that you gave up for Qrizor. She is with her husband and newborn daughter. They are having a great picnic lunch. You ruined your life, but she is living a fabulous one." Annamaaz erased the rectangle.

Zaleria glared at her, "I had no idea that my life would be this miserable. I wasn't given a choice, but to give her up. I was locked away in a crypt for her entire life. Then I came to the Dark Underworld. None of this was planned by me, but for me. I dread being pregnant with quadruplets. I dread being pregnant. It is not enjoyable for me. I have not enjoyed any of my life."

Annamaaz laughed evilly. Kezrin and Orchid walked back to the beach. "I have done my job. Both of them are now pregnant with quadruplets. Did you show her what she is missing?" He asked.

"Yes, I did. It made her even more miserable. Ozrig will be pleased. The only thing that she and Orchid don't know is that they will have these quadruplets in five months. It's a beautiful day." She grinned, "We are done here. Have a great five months when we will be back to deliver all these children."

They disappeared from them. Zaleria shook her head, "Can you believe this? We are going to add twenty-six wizards in just five months time. This is insane. How much more can our bodies handle this? How many more times will they try?"

"Here you are complaining again. This is my second round of quadruplets. What are you complaining about? I have never had a normal pregnancy. Both of mine have been with a demon," Orchid snapped back.

Myra piped up, "I think this is a great life. I dreamed all my life to have lots of children. I love all these children. Plus, these two are here to massage and pleasure us all day and night. I can't wait to have these triplets and get pregnant again. They can use my body however many times they want."

On the other side of the island, Annamaaz and Kezrin appeared on the beach with the witches in their chairs. The wizards are doing their jobs with Rose and Ember.

Annamaaz announced, "I am back! I know that you are all happy to see me. This will be a quick visit. I am going to make sure that all of you are pregnant with triplet males. Then I will show Qrizor and Crumazz something that will make them miserable. I will start with Moira and work my way around, ending with Rose."

She went up to Moira, laid her hands on her belly, and pushed her energy into her. Then she moved on to Starla, and then Nissa. Echo smiled ear to ear when Annamaaz laid her hands on her belly. She moved onto Piper, then Ember, and she got to the last one, Rose. "The energy that you received will make sure that you are pregnant with triplets and that they are all males. I will also be back in five months for you all to give birth. Ozrig is also considering the possibility of giving you all a rest from pregnancy. You will have given birth three times within a year. He is deciding and when I come back in five months you will know the answer." She looked at Qrizor and Crumazz, "Now, the treat for the two of you." She drew a rectangle in the sand and a picture appeared. "Do you know who these are? Well, let me tell you. They are Amaranth and Odulore, with their newborn daughter, Amaryllis. They are having a great life. You two thought you would ruin her. You did not. You are here and she is not."

They both shook their heads and looked at each other.

"I can tell by your faces that you are not happy. This is why we are showing you this. I also want to share with you that Zaleria is now providing us with evil children, no thanks to you Qrizor."

"What?! I don't understand," he responded.

"We had her have sex with a father/son wizard combination, and she gave us triplet wizards. This second pregnancy is thanks to Kezrin here, and this time it will be quadruplet male demons. So, there's nothing wrong with her. It is you. The only reason you are still here on the island is that Crumazz needs an assistant with massaging and pleasuring these witches," Annamaaz and Kezrin let out loud evil laughs.

“Well, this is all we wanted to do for now. We will see you back in a short five months. Make sure these witches are massaged and pleasured all day and as much of the night as possible. That is your job. They will be miserable as these triplets grow to nine month size, but only in five months.” The disappeared.

Crumazz looked at Qrizor, “Seriously? You are only here as an assistant for massaging and pleasuring! You are not helping impregnate them? If that’s the case, then I do not want you in there with me when I have sex with them. You are done. You stay here by the bonfire only.”

Qrizor rolled his eyes and went over to Piper to massage and pleasure her. He said nothing to any of them. Piper put her hand on his chin and had him look right at her, “You better make it good because I didn’t get pregnant by you. I want you to make sure I get lots of pleasuring and only a little bit of massaging. I am going to be getting super miserable. I have three babies inside me, they are going to grow to their nine-month size in only five months time. So, almost twice as fast as normal. Pleasure me!” She put his head back down.

Crumazz went to Rose, laid his hands on her legs, moved them up her legs, and said, “You are my favorite. You have given me six evil witches. I look forward to three evil wizards from you. I will pleasure you the most.”

Chapter 39

Odulore, Amaranth, and Amaryllis were in Demack Grassland where they waited for the other wizards to show up. Avras and Arietta were the first to show up, then Xodius and Zabine, next were Staedan and Shelyn. Finally Drozan and Zolya appeared.

"Thank you all for coming. We are excited that you have all decided to take your relationships to the next level. We are even more excited that you all wanted to do it at the same time. You four couples are great friends to us. Our wish for you all was that you would come to want the blessing and protective hedge from the Holy Dimension. Today that wish is coming true for us. Is there anything that any of you would like to say? We'll start with Avras and work our way around to Zolya," Odulore began.

Avras took Arietta's hands, "I have never been happier than I am today. Today we are taking our love and making it truly forever."

"I love you and always will. We will be together forever," Arietta smiled at him.

Xodius looked into Zabine's eyes, "You are the love of my life, and now our love will go from this island to the Holy Dimension."

"Our love is multidimensional. It started as kids, and will go on forever," Zabine finished his thought.

Staedan gave Shelyn a hug, and whispered in her ear, "You are the love of my life. You are my forever. You and I will live together now and into the Holy Dimension."

"Our future children will be blessed as well," Shelyn said to him.

Drozan took Zolya's hands, and said, "Who would have thought that we would be standing here like this? You have made me a better wizard, and we will have this protective hedge around us and the children that we will have. I love you!"

"I love you too! I cannot wait to have those children with you. I look forward to spending the rest of my life with, both on this island and in the Holy Dimension," Zolya shared.

Odulore smiled from ear to ear when he heard what they all shared with each other. "The Power given to me from the Holy Dimension now spreads an extra hedge of protection over the two of you from now until the day you enter the Holy Dimension. What the Holy Dimension has blessed, no evil will ever be able to separate. The two of you now have everlasting life either in this world or in the Holy Dimension. No evil will be able to touch either of you. The Holy Dimension will protect you. Your children will also be protected by your hedge of protection until they are of age to marry. Are you all ready for the last step?"

"YES!" They all shouted.

"I now pronounce you, husbands and wives: Avras and Arietta, Xodius and Zabine, Staedan and Shelyn, and Drozan and Zolya. Wizards, kiss your witch," Odulore instructed them.

The couples all kissed, including Odulore and Amaranth. Amaryllis smiled as she was in between her parents.

Odulore looked around at the couples, "Ok, who here is ready for some fun wizard games? You witches get to watch."

"YEAH!" They replied. The wizards gave their witches one more kiss, and gathered together in the middle of the grasslands.

Qbaris walked into the grasslands, "Can I join you all?"

"Yes, come on over," Odulore responded. "We are going to play Littage first. This is where you will throw a lightning bolt and tag a rock. You will then use your energy to lift the rock and drop it right in front of you. The rock must be around the edge of the grassland and you cannot hurt any creature while doing this."

They all lined up side by side, and yelled, "Levitaiatis Demoucio." The lightning bolts went from them to the rocks at the edge of the grassland. They moved the rocks with their energy, motioning with their hands as if they are pulling the rock back to them. Avras' rock landed in front of him first, then Odulore, Qbaris, Drozan, Xodius, and Staedan.

"Great game everyone. Let's move on to Strauxor. Just a reminder for everyone. This is the one where we are flying over the grassland, encircling the perimeter, and the first one back wins. Only use your flying ability," Odulore explained.

"Mufflego Rasculus Protenim Annoactum," they all shouted. Instantly they all levitated and sped off. Around the outer limits of the Demack Grassland, they all flew. Odulore took the lead and was first. He was followed by Qbaris, Avras, Drozan, Xodius, and Staedan.

Odulore said, "Great job wizards! Let's go rejoin our witches. Plus, I want to get some snuggles from my little Amaryllis."

The wizards walked over to their witches, and they all went back to Rissingshire Castle to celebrate.

Zizor greets them as they entered the castle, "We have the trays all ready for your meal." They followed him to the dining hall.

Amaranth and Odulore stopped by Amaryllis' room, and laid her in her bed. Kissed her on her forehead, and walked to the dining hall to join everyone. "She was really tired, so we laid her down. We are so happy to be celebrating with all of you today," said Odulore.

The room was quiet, except for them eating. Then Qbaris spoke up, “I have met a witch. She lives over in Zodel Kingdom.”

“What’s her name?” Amaranth inquired.

“Armina, she’s so sweet. You’d like her. She has a couple of younger siblings. I’ll bring her over for you to meet her.”

“Oh, I can’t wait to meet her. When are you bringing her by?” she asked.

“I don’t know. I’ll see if she wants to come by tomorrow.”

Odulore sarcastically remarked, “So, we all will be gathering here tomorrow to meet her.” He chuckled.

Zizor and the goblins walked in and picked up all the empty trays. The group went to the fireplace. Evatius galloped into the courtyard, “I’ve been to Zallesian Kingdom. It appears a couple of the witches may be looking to work with the Dark Underworld.”

“What makes you say that? What did you see?” Odulore asked.

“I was walking around with Chrysonia, and we found ourselves in Zallesian Kingdom. We heard Coral and Calla talking about whether they should stay in Zallesian Kingdom or if they should figure out how to get out to the new island.”

Amaranth shook her head, “I am not surprised at all. The other day when they were here, Coral was questioning about being banished if she didn’t believe the same way we do. She wanted to know if her children would be banished as well or what would happen to them.”

“I am just saying that she and her sister Calla are talking about going to the Dark Underworld. They don’t know how to get to the island, but they want to. Do you think we should go talk to them?" Evatius questioned.

Odulore looked at the wizards, "I think we should go over there tomorrow and see what their concerns are. If they want to go to the island, that can be arranged. I would say that if Calla wants to stay here and take care of Coral's children, that's fine. If they both want to go, then all their kids go with them. They have eight kids between the two of them. I wouldn't want to put that on another witch. We'll meet here and then go over to see them after breakfast."

Amaryllis started crying. "I have to go get her. She's probably hungry again. Good night everyone," Amaranth left and went to her.

"Little witch, you are so sweet," she picked her up, and sat down in her rocking chair next to her crib. Amaryllis latched on to her breast while she cradled her in her arms rocking back and forth. Amaranth ran her fingers through her little one's hair, "You have the most beautiful black hair, and it is so long for your age. I love being your mother. Your father loves you too."

Odulore walked into her room, "Everyone left, so I wanted to come see my favorite witches. I love to see the two of you together like this. It warms my heart." He walked over and kissed each of them, Amaryllis on her forehead and Amaranth on her lips.

"This gives me so much joy. Today was a great day. Our friends were all officially married in front of the Holy Dimension. We get to spend time together as family. You and this little one are my world. I can't wait for our friends to have littles of their own," she told him.

They sat in a peaceful quietness, rocking back and forth, and Amaryllis went off to sleep. Amaranth slowly and quietly got up and laid her in her crib. They stood over her, and watched her sleep for a few minutes.

“Come on, let’s go to bed,” Odulore whispered and tugged at Amaranth’s arm to leave. “She will be fine. Plus, you need your sleep.” They tiptoed out of her room.

Chapter 40

Qbaris and Avras entered the courtyard of Rissingshire Castle. Odulore walked out from Amaryllis' room. "Are you ready? Are we taking the horses or the Pegasuses?" Avras questioned.

"We will take the Pegasuses. This will get us there quicker. Plus, we will be met by Tizohr. He's already over in Zallesian Kingdom. I told him what we know."

The three go over to the livery and take out the Pegasuses. Within a few minutes they flew out of the castle. The Zallesian Kingdom was on the far west of the island.

When they flew over the Demack Grassland, Evatius joined them. Tizohr greeted them at the edge of the Zallesian Kingdom. "I am ready to help you with these two witches. I have also heard about their talking right here at home. It's the same as what you told me. We do not want them here if they really want to be on that other island."

They arrived at the home of Coral and Calla. The twins live together with their four sets of twins. Coral came out, "What do you all want?"

"We are here to talk to you about what you brought up at the Rissingshire Castle. It sounded like you would prefer to go live on the new island. Is this correct?" Odulore asked her.

"Actually, after talking to Calla, this is what we want. We don't share the same opinion of Qrizor and Crumazz as the rest of you."

Calla came outside, "Yes, you all made it very clear that if there is a difference of opinion that those will go away. After we came home and talked more about the new island and this one. We decided that if we got the opportunity that we would go to the new one."

"Plus, we do not feel like we get support here in this kingdom or on this island. With the witches that are on the new island, most of them were twins. Our children will fit in better. They will have more that children that will understand them," Coral added.

Tizohr stepped forward, "You both want to take your children to the new island to be with the witches' coven? Are you sure? Once you make this choice, you cannot come back. There is no undoing it."

The twins looked at each other, then they looked back at their home where you could hear their twins running around inside, and they nodded, "Yes, yes, this is what we want. It certainly can't be any worse than what we have going on here. Here we have eight children that are basically running us ragged. There are no wizards that want that many children that are not their own. Plus, the witches here look down on us."

"I don't think you know how we have felt. It's been so hard with these twins and no help. So, we do not want to stay here any longer. Is this something that you can help us with?" Coral asked.

Odulore looked from one twin to the other and back, "Yes, we can help you with that. It's a simple command and you will be transported to the new island. You need to bring all the children out here and all of you will need to be holding hands or at least touching each other. The energy will go through all of you and transport you all at once. You also won't be able to take anything with you. You will be leaving everything behind."

Coral and Calla looked at each other, and then they both went inside to get their children. They were running around the home. As soon as they got two of them in hand, the others would run. It was pure craziness. Coral and Calla kept yelling at the children.

Qbaris asked, “Can we modify the spell to cover the home and take all the wizards and witches? I really don’t think they are going to get all eight of those children to hold their hands or each other’s hands. It is pure chaos in there.”

“Yes, I think we do need to go ahead and do this. First we will say Mystifotis Deminius and then we will add Coral, Calla, and all their children to the new island. Are you all ready?” Odulore explained.

“Yes!” They all agreed.

The four repeated three times, “Mystifotis Deminius Coral, Calla, and all eight of their children to the new Island!”

All was quiet, there was no sound coming from their home. Tizohr walked up to the entry and went inside. A few moments later he walked back out, “They are all gone! I hope they like their new life on their new island.”

They rode off. Tizohr went off to his castle, Evatius split off when they got near the forest, and the remaining three continued to Rissingshire Castle.

Avras, Qbaris, and Odulore entered the courtyard. Amaranth and Amaryllis sat by the fireplace. Amaranth wrote in her journal with one hand while Amaryllis was feeding. She looked up as they entered, smiled, and asked, “What did they say?”

Glurx came out and led the Pegasuses back to the livery. The wizards sat down by Amaranth.

"Well, they were definitely not happy with their life as it was going. They had no control over those four sets of twins. We made sure that they knew that it would only work once to get them to the island and there was no return. They were both good with it. We told them to go get their children. They could not round them all up to bring them outside. So, we transported them from inside their home to the new island. Tizohr verified that they were gone. We are assuming that they made it to the island," Odulore informed her.

Amaranth frowned, "I am sad that they left us. However, if that is what they wanted, then I hope they like their choice."

Over on Permeated Flame Island Coral, Calla, and their eight children appeared on the beach near Qrizor, Crumazz, and the witches.

"Woah! What are you all doing here? Where did you come from?" Crumazz asked them.

Coral spoke up, "We were not happy over in Zallesian Kingdom. None of the witches would help us and no wizards wanted us. Word got back to Odulore and the top wizards. They came out to us and asked if we wanted to stay or not. We told them no. We attempted to round these children and then poof, we are here."

He looked at them, and the children were off and running around the island. "Ok, let me inform you of what happens on this island. Basically, these witches here are pregnant for the third time in a year. These children are born every five or six months. Also, they are now only having triplets. So, things are not going to be easy, but we are all in this together."

Annamaaz appeared on the beach, "What do we have here? We have two more witches? They arrived willingly? This is different. Are you currently pregnant?"

"No," they both shook their heads.

"Ok, we will fix that very quickly. Both will have sex with Crumazz immediately. In fact, Coral, you go right now. Crumazz, show her to an empty hut. Now for Calla, you will be next. Did he let you know what happens on this island?"

Calla looked at her, "Yes, he did. We don't care about that. We just did not want to remain on Parrcaster Island."

"Interesting, you think you are going to like it better here?"

"Yes, we already had two sets of twins, and they are only six months apart. We also got pregnant on the same days, and had them on the same days. So, this is nothing new or different for us."

A few minutes later, Coral and Crumazz returned. He took Calla, showed her to her hut, and had sex with her. Then they returned to the beach.

Annamaaz looked at them, "Now for my favorite part. I place my hands on your bellies. The energy that I will give you will make sure that you have triplet males. All nine of you will give birth on the same day, even if I have to induce you." She placed her hands on Coral's belly, and then Calla's belly. "Oh, Ozrig is going to be so pleased. We love to have witches that think they know what they are getting into. We shall see how well you like it. Ah, yes, I must add that one thing that will happen between now and then is Crumazz and Qrizor will be massaging and pleasuring you and all the other witches all day and as much of the night as possible. Enjoy!" She disappeared as quickly as she appeared.

Qrizor brought two more chairs for them. They sat down, and he immediately started massaging Coral.

Chapter 41

Odulore, Amaranth, and Amaryllis flew over to Miserth Castle with the Pegasuses and carriage. It was a favorite of both witches to go this way.

They arrived at the castle, and were greeted by Dax and Darca, the Great Danes. Odulore and Amaranth walked to the courtyard with Amaryllis.

Qbaris hugged them all, "I am so excited that you are here. I have someone that you need to meet." They all went over to the fireplace where Armina is seated.

She stood up, and Qbaris said, "Odulore, Amaranth, and little Amaryllis, this is Armina. She is a wonderful witch that I am now dating. Things are getting more serious, so I wanted you all to meet."

"I am so glad to meet you. Amaryllis is only a few weeks old. She pretty much just eats and sleeps," Amaranth chuckled.

"It is so nice to meet you. Someone has to keep this guy in line. Good luck with that," Odulore laughed, "Seriously though, I am happy that he has found someone."

"I am happy to meet the three of you. Qbaris told me that I had to meet his sister and her family. He thinks Amaryllis is absolutely adorable. I hear all about what she can do. I think he melts every time she smiles at him."

"Hey now, don't tell everything," He laughed. "This just makes my day. Armina is a great cook, so we have a fabulous lunch for you. I know Amaryllis won't partake, but she will when she's older. Let's go to the dining hall."

The five walk over to the dining hall, and sit down. "I have made venison steaks, scalloped potatoes, and carrots cooked in brown sugar, cinnamon, and maple syrup. I hope you all enjoy lunch."

The room was quiet while everyone ate, well everyone except for Amaryllis, who slept while they ate. She was in a travel bassinet.

"This is great!" Amaranth spoke up with a mouth full.

"I agree!"

Once they were done, they all went back to the courtyard, and sat by the fireplace.

"What a great meal. Great job my witch."

Qbaris took Armina's hand, looked into her eyes, and got down on one knee. "Armina, I know that we have been together for a short time, compared to these two, but I do not want to live another day without you. I want us to be one. Will you marry me?"

She cried, and said, "YES! Yes, I will marry you!"

They all hugged as a group. Odulore interrupted the hug, and asked, "Are you going to want to be married by the Power of the Holy Dimension? If so, I volunteer to perform the ceremony."

"Yes, we do want you to do the ceremony. The Power of the Holy Dimension is important to us both. Plus, we want lots of children. A large family is in our future," Qbaris replied.

"I am so glad to hear that. Now Armina and Amaranth can plan your wedding. Amaranth did a great job with ours."

The group sat by the fireplace, and talked about wedding plans. Amaryllis slept for quite a while, but then she woke up. As her eyes opened, she cried, because she was hungry. Amaranth took her in her arms to feed the little witch.

After she was done feeding, Odulore suggested, “Why don’t we go home? We’ll leave these two, for now.”

“I agree. We’ll see you two later.” They walked out to the carriage and flew back to their own castle.

Qbaris took Armina into his arms, and hugged her tight. Then he kissed her on her cheek. Fairies and pixies flew into the courtyard, and encircled them. They all danced around.

Back at Rissingshire Castle, the trio land in the courtyard. Amaranth took Amaryllis into her room. She sat down in the rocking chair with her. Next to them was a bookshelf, Amaranth took a book off the shelf.

Odulore walked in and sat down by them, “Would you like me to read to her?”

She handed him the book. He opened it to the first page and read while he turned the pages and showed her the pictures, “There was an elf named Katar. He went for a walk in the forest. She met a hare named Nutmeg. The two of them played in the forest. They ran around the trees, up onto logs, and to the water’s edge. Katar and Nutmeg grew tired. They laid down and went to sleep.”

Amaryllis smiled when he read to her. Her feet kicked, and she giggled. Her favorite was the hare.

Amaranth laid Amaryllis down in her bassinet, and kissed her on her forehead. Odulore also gave her a kiss. They left the room quietly, and went back to the courtyard.

"Is that not the best news, Qbaris is now engaged? I love it. This is becoming the best island ever! Plus, they want a Power of the Holy Dimension ceremony. This makes me so happy," she said.

"Yes, plus, she can cook!"

"Hey, I can cook! I just don't have to. Why should I when Zizor does such an awesome job?"

"You do have a valid point."

They laid back on their chairs, held hands, and stared up into the starry sky. It was so peaceful.

Back at Miserth Castle, Armina and Qbaris sat by the fireplace with their journals out, "Let's write out everything we want to do for the wedding."

"I like that idea, what do we want? I mean, aside from the Power of the Holy Dimension ceremony with Odulore performing it, what is there?" she replied.

"They had their wedding at the waterfall. Do you want it by water? Where do you want the reception? What do you want served for the wedding feast? Who do you want to attend?"

"Wow! Lots of things to think about. To me the most important thing is the two of us getting married. I don't care where. So, you surprise me with a location. Then as far as what to eat, as long as someone else is making it, I am good. I want it to be small. Can we have just the four wizards and their witches, plus Odulore and Amaranth with little Amaryllis," Armina told him.

Qbaris hugged her tight, "This is what I love about you. It's going to be great. We will have a small and intimate ceremony. One thing I want to do is to write a journal for our future children. I want to make sure that it is an inspiring and encouraging journal.

In it I want to share love with them. It will be completely different from the journal that I received from my father."

"Yes, the journal you got from your father was not one to be repeated. I agree. I love that you want to write one with so much love," Armina kissed him on the cheek. "I need to go. We will be married soon and I will stay at that point. Until then, I will stay at my parents' castle. I will be back tomorrow or will you come by?"

"I will come see you tomorrow." They kissed, and she flew out of the castle on her white Pegasus.

Qbaris watched until she was out of sight, smiled, and thought to himself, *That witch is going to be my wife. I can't wait to start a family with her. Plus, I have a sister who has a great family. What a wonderful life since my father and brother were banished.*

Chapter 42

The black swirling smoke of the Dark Underworld swirled around the portal. Ozrig sat on his throne in the middle of the meeting area. He yelled, "Annamaaz! Come here!"

She appeared in front of him, "Yes?"

"You went out to the island. Why?"

"There were two new witches that appeared on the island. Turned out that Odulore transported them because they did not like being on Parrcaster Island. They did not get any assistance with their eight children."

"Witches with eight children, very good. How old are they?"

"The witches are twins, and they had two sets of twins from Qrizor."

Ozrig let out a loud, evil laugh that filled all the caves, caverns, and tunnels. "This is awesome! I love it! Someone doesn't agree with them, and they kick them off the island. This is the best!"

Kezrin and Korzath appeared before Ozrig and Annamaaz. "You two need to keep an eye on Parrcaster Island. Don't go on the island, but just watch it. Report back to me, especially if you see any signs of witches that want off the island," Ozrig told them.

The two demons left through the portal. They only got a couple feet from the portal and bounced off the force field. "What?!" Kezrin questioned. They slid along the force field and found that it led to the Permeated Flame Island. They kept going around the outside of the island. Korzath looked at Kezrin, "This is weird.

We can get to the island, around the whole outside, and back to the portal. However, that's it. We have a very narrow area that we can go. We can't see what's going on over on the Parrcaster Island."

"Yes, father is not going to be happy."

"I'm not telling him. You can tell him," Korzath replied.

"Why me? He likes you better."

"Exactly! I'm staying on his good side."

They went back down the portal and stood in front of Ozrig and Annamaaz. "Well, what did you find out? That was quick," Ozrig questioned them.

"We found that we have a narrow path to the Permeated Flame Island. We cannot get to the Parrcaster Island," Kezrin replied.

"How is that possible? Can we get around the entire island of the Permeated Flame?"

"Yes, we can go around the entire island. It's just Parrcaster that we cannot get to."

Annamaaz commented, "That is crazy! I know it's all the fault of them using the Power of the Holy Dimension."

"I know, and if that is the case, then we won't be able to get through it. We are powerless compared to the Holy Dimension," Ozrig admitted.

Korzath shook his head, crinkled his nose, and glared, "What? We can take that out. We just need to put all of our powers together. I know we can."

"Sorry, that is one thing we can't do. It is too powerful," Ozrig told them. "Why do you think we are all here? We used to be on the Parrcaster Island. I did not like how things were going. It was just too much good. So, they banished me here. Then they sent your mother to me. Anyone else that disagrees with them gets sent here. Although, now it looks like they have a choice of going to the Permeated Flame Island. I find that interesting."

Annamaaz responded, "From what I am told, they do not know the name of the island. Also, the reason that they sent them to the island was because the witches' coven was on the island. They wanted to be with the other witches. What they don't know is that they are sending them to a life of forever being pregnant, which actually helps us."

"Yes, it does help us, but there's a hiccup in our plan now. I don't know if that island will continue to grow. There will be too many witches and wizards on the island," He thought about that for a moment, "That will make them even more miserable. All these children, and less and less space for them. What they don't know is that the witches that are children now, when they get of age, they will also be getting pregnant, over and over and over again. Who will be the fathers? Of course, the wizards on the island."

"Yes, I have them all pregnant with males right now. So, there will be some available for the females that come after them. I love that the number of witches far exceed those of the wizards."

"The two of you are absolutely evil. My question is, will I get more witches? Right now I have two that are pregnant."

"Yes, Kezrin, we will let you have more witches. In fact, next time the two that just arrived are set to get pregnant, it will be by you," Ozrig informed him. "I want to make sure that everyone on that island is miserable. Is that currently happening?"

Annamaaz responded, "Yes, the wizards thought it would be fun getting the witches pregnant. However, now they are massaging and pleasuring the witches all the time, which is exhausting work. So much for fun. The witches are all pregnant. They all physically go to full term, but within half the amount of time. So, they are also miserable. I am sure the new witches are figuring it out. They have a few days of fun and then their life's quality goes downhill."

"You my evil love are the most evil around. I love it! You need to go check on those new witches. Make sure they are figuring out how miserable life is going to be from now on."

She took off out of the portal and over to the island. When she arrived on the island, she found all the witches in their chairs. "Oh, my witches, how is everyone doing? Getting miserable?" She inquired.

"So far, so good. We are feeling the little ones already. I didn't feel them this early with the other two pregnancies," Coral answered.

"Calla, what about you?"

"I am becoming miserable. My other pregnancies were not like this. I feel different. Although, it does help having the massaging and pleasuring."

"Yes, you will feel differently. This is nothing like you have ever felt. Next time you get pregnant will be from Kezrin. Then it will be even more different. Both of you, that is, will get pregnant from Kezrin next time," She said with an evil grin.

Poof, Annamaaz returned to the Dark Underworld. Calla looked at Coral and asked, "What have we done? Will we get pregnant from a demon next time? That's insane! I don't know if I really want to be here. Can we go back?"

"No, we cannot go back. You know that. Odulore told us that this is a one time thing. We could only come here, but not return. So, we're stuck with our decision."

Back in front of Ozrig stood Annamaaz, "Yes! They are miserable. I just heard Calla doubting their decision. That is the best. They know that they cannot return."

"My evilness, you are perfect!" Ozrig complimented her.

Chapter 43

Amaranth sat at her table, Amaryllis laid in her bassinet playing with her toes. She opened her journal and began to write.

My little witch, I have been having the best time of my life being your mother and your father's wife. These five months there have been so many changes in you, in me, in your father.

You rolled over on your own at four months old. You are currently playing with your toes. You smile, you coo, you make me happy with your giggle.

I am writing this journal for you so that one day you will be able to read all about how much you are loved and cared for. Now I will tell you about the day that I met your father for the first time.

I honestly don't remember the first time. He was always there. I will tell you what I was told. My mother dropped me in a basket on the front porch of a wonderful couple. The couple was Trodus and Tatiana, your father's parents. I was younger than you are now.

I always knew that I was dropped off and that they loved having me in their family. However, I always felt like I was missing something. I thought it was because I only knew who my mother was, but did not really know her. I knew the rumors around the kingdom and the island, but that was it.

Let me return to telling you about your father. Growing up, he was such a gentleman. He always treated me so well. I always felt like a queen. We were not raised as siblings. When we got into our teen years we would go on mini dates. We weren't allowed to date too much. His father worked with him to become a great wizard.

I remember his mother, Tatiana, died after a long bout with some illness. I don't remember what illness she had, but that she was in bed for quite a while, and then she was gone.

Odulore and I would sit on her bed, and she would tell us stories about dragons and fairies. Oh, she was always so creative. The stories that she would tell were so great. I wish she had written them down.

There were stories about dragons of all colors and sizes. The bright colors were good dragons, and the dark colors were evil dragons. The good dragons always won against the evil ones.

The stories of fairies, they were always good, and they took good care of anyone they came near. The fairy dust that they would sprinkle over everyone to give them good energy.

Oh yes, there were the wood elves. They lived in the forest. Their homes were in the trees. The elves protected the forest from anything evil.

There were evil trolls that would come up from a river that would try to cut down the trees where the elves lived. The trolls and elves would fight it out by throwing stones at each other. The elves were the ones that would win. The trolls would go back under the bridges by the river.

She was so creative with her stories. I almost forgot, but she made some stuffed animals of dragons, fairies, elves, and trolls. She would let us play with them when she told us the stories. It was magical.

I remember one time just before she died that both his mother and father told the stories. One would play off the other. It was so much fun.

There was another time where she had a couple of elves that got married and had a baby elf. They were so happy together, no matter what the trolls did, they were always happy. I think she was foretelling about our family.

Your father helped a family relocate to another island because they weren't happy here. He also called on the Holy Dimension for help with protecting our island.

Speaking of the Holy Dimension. This is one aspect of our life that we are making a priority. Odulore's father, Trodus,
performed our marriage ceremony, which included a protective hedge that is through the power of the Holy Dimension. This means that no one can touch us.

Also, that protective hedge extends to you and any siblings that you will have. Yes, you will have siblings. We do not know how many at this point.

You were blessed by Trodus with the protective hedge of Power of the Holy Dimension. I look forward to the day that you will understand what that means.

Your father performed the marriage ceremonies for those within our kingdom and called on the Power of the Holy Dimension to put the protective hedge around them and their future children.

The Holy Dimension will protect us here on this island, and then when it's your time, you will go to live in the Holy Dimension for all eternity

It's a beautiful thing when you get to be with your husband for all eternity in the beautiful Holy Dimension. I wish this for you in the future.

Right now you are my beautiful baby witch. You are so little at this time. Just five months old. You are growing every day. I look forward to watching all that you do through the years. You, my sweet witch, will grow to be a beautiful witch. You will one day have a sweet little witch just like yourself.

She put her pen down, and watched Amaryllis play with her feet. She smiled and giggled when she touched her toes. Amaranth smiled and giggled with her.

Odulore walked into her room, “What are you doing?”

“Watching our little Amaryllis. She is giggling when she touches her toes. It’s making me giggle. I was writing in my journal for her. I was telling her all about your mother and the stories that she would tell.”

“Those were great stories. I wish they would have been written down. Do we still have the stuffed animals?”

“I think we do. They are probably in her room. The animals stayed in there.”

Odulore left and went to Tatiana’s room. He found the trunk, and opened it. There were a couple of dozen animals: elves, fairies, trolls, and dragons. He took a couple of the dragons out, and went back to Amaranth’s room with them.

“I found them,” he told her, “I brought a couple of the dragons. They are all there. We can bring them all in here or all into her room. Which would you like?”

“Oh, I think we’ll put them in her room, and then we’ll just take out what she’s playing with when I bring her in here.”

Odulore lays a purple dragon next to Amaryllis. She looks at it, and holds its wing in her little fingers. “Is that not the most adorable thing you’ve ever seen?”

Amaranth smiled. Odulore put his arm around her, "You know that the two of you always make my day a good day? You make me smile all the time. I don't have any bad days with you. I wish this kind of happiness for everyone."

"This is why we bless marriages. Everyone should have this kind of life. Speaking of which, do we know when Qbaris and Armina are getting married?"

"I will go find out. You stay here with this little cutie. I am sure she's getting hungry or will be soon." He kissed her on the lips, and then kissed Amaryllis on the forehead. "I'll be back soon."

Odulore rode off on Magnus to Miserth Castle. It was a quick ride through the grasslands and forest. He arrived at the castle, and went into the courtyard. Qbaris and Armina were sitting by the fireplace with Dax and Darca.

"Hi! How are you two doing?"

"We are great. What's up?" Qbaris asked him.

He replied, "Amaranth and I were wondering if you two had decided on when to get married."

"Yes, yes we did decide on when. We were going to come over and let you know today. So, good timing. We are thinking in a few days. We'd like to be married here in the castle. Can you do that?"

"Of course I can. We had ours in just a short time also. It was quick, short, and sweet. We did have a lot of people over for the party afterwards. Do you want them over for the ceremony or just the party?"

Armina answered, "We would prefer them just for the party. The ceremony should be small and intimate."

"We can definitely do that. I will let Amaranth know. What are you doing about a dress? I know that while Trodus and Tatiana were here, that Tatiana worked on Amaranth's dress."

"I don't have anyone to help me with a dress. My mother died a long time ago and I have no witch siblings."

"No worries. Amaranth can help you with it. The other witches in the kingdom can help also. I am going to go back and let her know the details. She'll be over to help you later on today."

Odulore got back on Magnus and rode back to Rissingshire. He entered the courtyard and Magnus went back to the livery. Then he walked into Amaranth's room, "I found out that they want to be married in a couple of days. She will also need help with her dress. She has no witch siblings, and her mother died a long time ago."

"Ok, you can watch Amaryllis and I'll go over and help Armina. When should I leave?"

"After we all eat," he told her. Amaranth picked up Amaryllis, and they walked over to the dining hall.

Zizor and the Puggaald walked out of the kitchen with the food trays. They sat down, Amaranth held Amaryllis up to her breast to eat, while she ate.

"I love when they fix us goulash with venison. This is always made perfectly today. Some days it tastes better than others. Today is one of the tasty days. Amaryllis is going to love this stuff when she's able to eat real food."

"Yes, today is extra good," Odulore commented.

Zizor smiled, "I am glad you both like it. We played a bit with the seasonings. It will be great when Amaryllis can eat what we make."

"She is such a cutie and so good. We hardly ever hear her cry," Puggaald added.

After they had eaten, Odulore took Amaryllis, and Amaranth rode off to Miserth Castle on Raithy. It only took minutes and she was at the castle.

"Hi!" She said to them as she entered the courtyard.

"Hi! I am so glad that you came over. I really need help with my dress. I heard that your dress was beautiful."

"I am here to help!" Amaranth smiled at her.

Qbaris got up and walked off to his room. The witches were left in the courtyard by the fireplace. "Where do I start?"

"Do you have any dresses?"

"Yes, we can start with this one over here," she pointed to a dress that was hung over a chair.

The witches went to work on the dress. It took them a few hours to complete it. "Now, try it on, and I'll make final adjustments."

Armina put the dress on. This was a red gown with black lace trim. The top was form fitting and the bottom flared out at the waist. The front of the dress was a plunging neck line that went clear down to her belly button. The back was also a v-shape that went down to her waist. There was black lace that lightly covered the front and back. It was a large lace pattern, so it revealed a lot of skin.

"Witch, this is beautiful, he is going to want to tear that dress off of you. You are so sexy in it," Amaranth encouraged her.

She blushed. After the dress was fitted, she changed back to her normal clothes. “I hope he likes it. I want to have children, and would love to get started right away,” she smiled.

“Well, I need to get back to my little one and husband. I am happy you like your dress. See you later.”

Amaranth left the castle on Raithy and went back to Rissingshire Castle.

Chapter 44

Annamaaz left the Dark Underworld through the portal. She went to the Permeated Flame Island. When she got there, she was on the back part of the island. "Hello Witches! You all are looking so fabulously pregnant. Great job Rugast and Vumonar. I am glad that you are massaging and pleasuring these wonderfully wicked witches. It is time for all of you to have your children. This is going to be quick. Rugast and Vumonar, you will need to be on your game. We have triplet males coming from every witch here. I will start with Myra."

She walked up to Myra, put her hands on her belly, and she instantly went into labor. Rugast got the first one, then Vumonar got the second one, and the Rugast got the third one as well. Annamaaz walked over to Mistya right away. She laid her hands on her belly, and she went into labor immediately. This time Vumonar caught the first one, then Rugast caught the next one, finally the last one came out and Vumonar caught him. The induced labors continued. Following Mistya Alecto was next, then to Kalliope, on to Lavinia, and then Storm. She got to Orchid, "Oh my Orchid, your children will be slightly different from the others, as you know. You are having quadruplets and they are all demons." She put her hands on her belly, and the first one came out so quickly that Rugast barely caught him. Then the second, the third, and the fourth. "What evil looking demons! I am so proud of you. I can't wait until the next set."

Annamaaz went to Zaleria, "How are you doing?"

"I'm miserable. I can't wait until these children are born."

"You do realize that within a few days you will be pregnant again?"

"Yes, so you have told me. I will be forever constantly pregnant or giving birth. I am thirty-eight years old, how long do you think I am going to be able to give birth to quadruplet demons?"

"Oh you stupid witch, I can make you pregnant forever! There is no end. If your body gets too worn out, I will just have Ozrig cast a spell on you to heal your body, and we will start over. Now, lay back, it's time for you birth these demons." She laid her hands on Zaleria's belly, the demons came out one right after the other. All four of them were out. Zaleria laid there, exhausted.

"Don't forget, you are breastfeeding all of these children until we decide they are old enough for food. It matters not, what you think." She let out a loud evil laugh and disappeared.

Seconds later Annamaaz appeared on the other side of the island. Qrizor and Crumazz were massaging and pleasuring the witches on their chairs on the beach. "Hi witches! Your day has come. It's time to give birth to all of these triplets. It's your evil day!"

She walked up to Moira, laid her hands on her belly, and she immediately went into labor. Qrizor was right there to catch her three children. Then she went on to Starla, where she placed her hands on her belly. She went into labor, and Crumazz caught her three children. Annamaaz continued on to Nissa, and Piper, then Echo, then Ember, and Rose.

Finally she went over to Coral and Calla, "Now, you all thought it would be fun to be here. It's time for your children to be born. Oh yes, to make sure you have fun here, you will be pregnant in a couple of days, and it will be Kezrin, they will be demon children. Now, I will lay my hands on your bellies, and you will go into labor instantly with the three of them coming out immediately one after the other. I don't have all day for this."

Calla looked at her, she put her hands on her belly, and she said, "This is crazy! How," her body pushed one out, "Can," another one came out, "You," then the last one. "Do this?" Calla took a few breaths, "What just happened? The energy you pushed through me, pushed them right out. This is insane!"

Annamaaz went on to Coral, place her hands on her belly, and Coral said, "What? Wait!" The energy pushed out the first one, then the next, and the last one. "Holy smokes! That is crazy! Is this how it is every time?"

"Yes, it is, with the wizard/witch children. However, it will be much more fun when you get pregnant by the demon. Oh yeah, I forgot to mention to the other side, the next pregnancy will only be between three and four months. This five months waiting is just too much. We want this island populated and populated quickly. Have a great day!" She disappeared in a poof of black smoke.

She appeared back in the Dark Underworld. Kezrin went up to her, "My children were born today?"

"Yes, they were."

"I want to go and name them. I have eight, correct?"

"Yes, eight male demons. Go have fun naming them!"

Kezrin took off for the island. He appeared on the beach in a few seconds. "Hi my witches! Orchid and Zaleria. You two are MINE! Your children are MINE! I will name them. You get no choice. Oh yes, you two need to be pregnant as soon as possible. I will be back in a day or two, depending on my schedule." He laughed an evil laugh at them.

"Oh joy! What names do you have in mind?" Zaleria questioned.

“Well for you, my Zaleria, we have Rizzakin, Algroth, Arzan, and Vinnozeth,” he said as he pointed to each one.

“Now for you, my Orchid, we have Sakur, Garzirith, Molvoz, and Drazgen,” he told her as he pointed to each demon.

“I like these names, and this is what you will call each of them. Now, you will get pregnant again in a couple of days with four more demons. These will all be females. You have been warned.”

He disappeared in a poof of black smoke. Zaleria looked at Orchid, “I guess, the names could be worse. Although, I would have preferred to name them myself.”

“It didn’t make a difference to me. The part that worries me is the next pregnancy. Only a couple of days until we start this cycle all over again. Yikes. I already have eight within five months and now four more coming will be coming within the next three to four. That’s twelve within nine months. These two wizards better be massaging and pleasuring to make me feel better. My breasts are already sore from the first four. Now I have eight! Shortly I will have twelve. I will constantly have a child up to my breast.”

“Yeah, you have only one more child than I do. So, I definitely feel your pain. Plus, she was so mean with telling me that I will forever be having more and more children. Then if I physically get wore out, she’ll have Ozrig heal me to start over. I see no end to this and no way off this island,” Zaleria told her.

Myra walked over to Zaleria, “You know, things were better before you got here. Before you, I only had twins. Now, she has us having triplets and closer together. It’s all your fault! I don’t know where you came from, but you need to go back there. I want to go back to having twins, and not so close together. My breasts and crotch are going to be worn out way before I get to your age. Is she going to have Ozrig heal us all? Or is she just going to throw us away when they are done with us?”

"I don't know what her plans are for you witches. She only told me what she's doing to me. You are complaining to me!? I had three children that are now your age, and now she has me back making babies. Plus, it's not singles or twins, but triplets and quadruplets! She has poor Orchid only having quadruplets. So, don't come to us and complain. We have more children than you do. I have two more children and Orchid has three more children that you do. Go sit down, and feed your children." Zaleria glared and yelled at her.

Annamaaz and Ozrig were in the center of the Dark Underworld when Kezrin returned. "How did it go?"

"Well, that Zaleria has a mouth on her. I almost made her get pregnant today. She needs to be taught a lesson, so I will go back tomorrow for her. Do we want to stop with quads? Maybe we could make her extra, extra miserable with quints?" He asked.

Ozrig gave an evil smile, "I like the way you think. Yes, I knew she had a mouth on her. She needs to be super miserable. Keep her in line. I heard her complaining after you left."

They all let out an evil laugh so loud that it went up through the portal and made it to the island 'for all of the witches and wizards to hear.

Chapter 45

Amaranth put on her fancy dress, and then she put a beautiful dress on Amaryllis. Odulore put on his official suit. They got into the carriage, and the Pegasuses flew them to Miserth Castle. The other witches and wizards from the Maerith Kingdom joined them in the courtyard.

Odulore stood in front of the fireplace. Qbaris was on his left. Amaranth was seated with Amaryllis right in front on his right.

Armina was dressed in her red and black wedding dress. She stood at the back of the courtyard, and walked up to the front next to Qbaris.

Qbaris took Armina's hands, and looked into her eyes. Odulore said, "Today we are gathered here in the eyes of the Holy Dimension to join Qbaris and Armina in holy matrimony. I heard that the two of you have written your own vows. Qbaris, you can go first."

"Armina, you are my love. You are my whole world. I promise to be with you forever both on this island and the Holy Dimension. I will be with you in sickness and in health, for richer and for poorer, and forever more."

"Qbaris, my wonderful wizard. I have never been so happy since I have met you. You made my world complete when you asked me to marry you. I will be with you in sickness and in health, for richer and for poorer, both on this island and in the Holy Dimension forever."

He looked at each of them, and said, "Are you ready for the best part?"

"Yes," they both responded.

"Qbaris, do you take Armina to be your wife?"

"Yes!"

"Armina, do you take Qbaris to be your husband?"

"Yes!"

"The Power given to me from the Holy Dimension now spreads an extra hedge of protection over the two of you from now until the day you enter the Holy Dimension. What the Holy Dimension has blessed, no evil will ever be able to separate. The two of you now have everlasting life either in this world or in the Holy Dimension. No evil will be able to touch either of you. The Holy Dimension will protect you. Your children will also be protected by your hedge of protection until they are of age to marry. I now pronounce you husband and wife. You may kiss the witch."

Qbaris took Armina into his arms, and gave her a passionate kiss.

They turned toward the witches and wizards, "I give you Qbaris and Armina, husband and wife."

He took her hand, and they walked to the dining hall, followed by their guests. Zizor and the goblins walked out of the kitchen, "Congratulations!" They carried trays to their table first, and then to the rest of the guests.

"Thank you all for coming to celebrate our wedding. This is the most important day for us. This is the start of our wonderful future together. Enjoy your meal. Thank you also to Zizor and the goblins for making our wonderful meal. Normally Armina does all the cooking. Thank you. Enjoy!"

Odulore stood up, "We ask for the blessing from the Holy Dimension upon this meal, these people, and this marriage."

The trays were cleaned by all, so the goblins came and took them to the kitchen. Everyone walked out of the dining hall, and went to the courtyard. In the courtyard there was a band of trolls that played while the witches and wizards danced.

Amaranth had laid Amaryllis in a bassinet, while she danced. The little witch went off to sleep, even with the loud band that played, and everyone celebrated.

All the mystical creatures of the forest and the woodlands joined in the celebration. It was a happy evening for all of them.

The sun set over the castle wall, and the celebration continued on. Amaranth told Odulore, "We really should get going. Little one has been asleep, but I have a feeling that she will be waking up, just as we get home."

"Yes, we can leave," He told her, then he picked up Amaryllis and her bassinet, and put her in the carriage. They hugged Qbaris and Armina, and flew back home.

The celebration continued on for a few more hours, when finally everyone left. Qbaris looked at Armina, took her by the hand, and said, "My loving witch, it is time for us to go to bed. I have looked forward to this night for a while now. Let's go enjoy our first night together."

Armina smiled at him, and replied, "You are my love, and I am excited to be with you. Let's go!"

Back at Rissingshire Castle, Odulore, Amaranth, and Amaryllis arrived in the courtyard. They took her bassinet out, and walked her into her room. Odulore and Amaranth tried to quietly walk out of her room.

Amaryllis cried as her parents tried to leave her room. Amaranth went back to her bassinet, picked her up, and sat down in her rocking chair. Odulore kissed them both and went off to put away the carriage and Pegasuses.

Amaranth rocked Amaryllis while she fed her. She thought to herself, *What a great day. We have another couple that will spend eternity in the Holy Dimension with us. Plus, it's my brother. Now, I am back home to relax with my awesome little family. I love being Amaryllis' mom. I wish she could remain little forever. This is so great to rock her, have her feed, and spend some bonding time with her. I have a fabulous husband. I thought that I wanted to wait until Amaryllis was a year old before having a sibling for her. However, I am getting that yearning to have another one. I enjoyed being pregnant with her. Plus, it's not like I will have it instantly. Amaryllis will be almost a year old. It depends on if this one comes as quickly as she did. She was in a big hurry to get here.*

Odulore walked back into the room, "You are rocking, feeding, and smiling. I love watching you do that. You look so happy. That makes me happy."

"What do you think about starting to try for another one? She's already five months old. Even if the next one comes as early as her, she'll almost be a year old."

"Well, if it comes as early as she did, she will only be ten months old. So, hopefully, it will come later or at least more towards full term. This little was super early. I will say though, I am ready when you are. It's entirely up to you. You are the one that carries the baby, and has to go through the labor. I am here to support your decision."

Amaryllis finished with her feeding, Amaranth picked her up, and laid her in her bassinet. She closed her little blue eyes, and went off to sleep.

Odulore and Amaranth quietly walked out of her room, and went off to their room.

Chapter 46

The sun rose over the wall of the castle. Odulore woke up, and Amaranth was already out of bed. He got out of bed, and went to Amaryllis' room. "Good morning, my beautiful witches!" He smiled at them.

"Good morning, the little one woke up a couple of minutes ago and was hungry. So, here I rock her and feed her. How did you sleep?"

"I slept so well, because you were by my side. How about you?"

"It was a wonderful night, my love."

"Are you ready for breakfast? I think I could smell it coming from the dining room."

"I am ready, but she is in charge of when I get up. I am sure she'll be done in a few. You can go ahead and start eating. I will be there shortly."

Odulore sat down next to her, and he lightly laid his hand on Amaryllis' head.

"You are such a gentle father. She is so lucky. I can't wait for a second witch or wizard. Hopefully we will find out that I am pregnant again."

"I hope you are too. Oh, if there is a little wizard, how much fun I will have showing him how to be a wizard. Although, I will be just as happy if it's a little witch. How many do you want?"

"I don't know yet. I figure when I no longer have that feeling of wanting to be pregnant. I am leaving it up in the air. However many we have are good with me."

Amaryllis looked up at her, she took her breast out of her mouth, and coo'd at her. Amaranth and Odulore looked at her, and they both sighed a happy sigh.

"We are ready to go eat. I smelled French toast and bacon," Odulore told them. He helped her up off the rocking chair. The three of them went to the dining hall.

They sat down at the table, and this time Amaryllis was placed into a high chair between them. Zizor brought her some crackers for her to gum on and play with. The goblins brought out the trays with the French toast and bacon on them.

"I love this breakfast!" Amaranth shouted.

"Me too. Now after breakfast we have a meeting with the wizards of Maerith Kingdom. After we meet with them, then the other kingdoms will be sending their wizards. The meeting is to create one big kingdom. We will be the head wizard and witch over all of them."

"Over all of them? Wow! That's crazy. How do you think they will react to it?"

"They will work with it. Some have approached the wizards in our kingdom. They like how we run things."

The goblins came out from the kitchen, and took away their empty trays. A few minutes later Qbaris, Xodius, Staedan, Avras, and Drozan came into the dining hall, and sat down at the table. Amaranth got up and took Amaryllis out to the courtyard.

Odulore stood up at the end of the table, "Welcome wizards! We are meeting today to talk about bringing in the other kingdoms on the island. They are Zallesian, Xoba, Zodel, and Dravocia. These would enable us to have control over the whole island. We will have the whole island be more consistently run. Any thoughts?"

Avras opened his journal, and commented, "I wrote down a few things when I had talked to Azohr. He's in Zodel Kingdom. The one thing that he wanted most was for everyone to be on the same page. He thinks that there has been a lot that we have that his kingdom does not have."

All the wizards wrote down in their journals. Drozan spoke up, "The first thing that needs to happen is we need to arrange the hierarchy of the kingdom. We have all pretty much just gone along with whatever someone else suggested. There was no method. This meeting is my first. I would like to suggest that we put Odulore into the official position of Grand Master Wizard of Maerith Kingdom. This will be over our kingdom now and then when we merge all the kingdoms into one. If you agree, say Aye."

The rest of the wizards replied, "Aye!"

"I am honored to be the Grand Master Wizard of the Maerith Kingdom. I will serve you all to the best of my ability with the guidance of the Holy Dimension."

They clapped and cheered for a minute. Odulore interrupted them, "Thank you very much. Let's move on to more items on our agenda, albeit, not a formally written one. I will go around the table and let me know what you have heard, if anything. Avras, anything more?"

"Nothing more from Zodel Kingdom."

Drozan was next, "We are nearest to Dravocia Kingdom. They are pretty quiet."

"Unfortunately or fortunately we are nearest to the Zallesian Kingdom. This where Coral and Calla used to live. They were the problem of the kingdom. So, all is quiet," Staedan mentioned.

Seated next to him was Xodius, "We are located in the corner near Zallesian Kingdom and Dravocia Kingdom. Those have already been covered and I have not heard anything differently."

Avras added, "I also have talked to Xoba Kingdom. They are very thankful that the witches' coven was broken off."

"Ok, we will be joined very shortly by Tizohr of the Zallesian Kingdom, Azohr of the Zodel Kingdom, Dhenaxx of the Dravocia Kingdom, and Zaveus of the Xoba Kingdom. I am looking forward to having a great discussion with them," Odulore stated.

Zizor entered the dining hall with beverages for the wizards. He left a few pitchers on the table. The ogre left them to finish their meeting.

A few minutes passed and the wizards entered the dining hall, "Welcome to Rissingshire Castle and the meeting of wizards." Odulore and the wizards stood up and shook hands as they all entered and sat down.

"The reason for our meeting is to establish an official government on this island. For so long there has been nothing official. My father, Trodus, was an official Grand Master Wizard of the Maerith Kingdom and the island. Prior to your entering today it was voted that I would be the official Grand Master Wizard of the Maerith Kingdom. Now we will decide if you all want your kingdoms to be merged into Maerith Kingdom.

Qbaris was the unofficial Master Wizard. I am appointing him the official Master Wizard of Maerith Kingdom. He will serve in my capacity if I am unable to.

Next we have Avras who will now be appointed the official Record Keeper.

With knowing this, do you all have any questions before being admitted into Maerith Kingdom?"

Azohr spoke, "I am excited for Zodel Kingdom to be a part of Maerith Kingdom. My only question is, what part do each of us play in this government?"

"That would be my same question," Tizohr agreed.

"Same here," both Dhenaxx and Zaveus responded.

Odulore smiled, "I am glad to hear that question. I would like to have you all as advisors of what is going on in your area of the kingdom. I want your input, especially for your area. We will change all the kingdoms, except for Maerith Kingdom to regions. The island will now be called Maerith Kingdom. The area of what was Maerith Kingdom will now be Maerith Province. I will have Xodius create a map for everyone to reference. Your official titles will be Advisor Wizard of your region. Thoughts?"

"I like the change to region and the title of Advisor Wizard," Zaveus commented.

The wizards went back and forth over the next couple of hours where the details were discussed.

Zizor entered the dining hall, "Are you ready for lunch?"

"Yes we are. Thank you," Odulore answered.

Zizor returned the kitchen, then came back out with the goblins and the trays of lunch. "Today we have chopped steak with bacon, mushrooms, and white cheese with fried potatoes. I hope that you all enjoy it." Trays were placed in front of the wizards.

Amaranth walked into the dining hall, "Can I join you for lunch?"

"Of course you can, here have a seat next to Odulore," Qbaris place a chair for her. "Where is our wonderful little witch?"

"Oh, she's down for a nap. Time for me to eat."

Zizor placed a tray in front of her. She smiled at him, "Thank you."

The room was pretty quiet for the next minutes while everyone ate. The goblins came back into the dining hall with Zizor, picked up the empty trays, and returned to the kitchen.

"I will leave you wizards to get back to business," Amaranth told them. She got up and left the dining hall.

Odulore pounded on the table, "I guess I need to get a gavel. I think my father had one." He laughed and continued, "So, we have four official regions, plus the Maerith Province within the Maerith Kingdom. We no longer have the Parrcaster Island name, nor the other kingdoms. I am the Grand Master Wizard of Maerith Kingdom. Qbaris is the Master Wizard with Avras as the Record Keeper. We have Azohr, Tizohr, Dhenaxx, and Zaveus as the Advisor Wizards of their regions. Do we have any further questions?"

"I am happy this happened. It's been a long time coming. No questions from me," Zaveus responded.

Azohr said, "I have to agree with Zaveus. This has been a long time coming. I am not sure why it didn't happen, except for all of our fathers just went with whatever was happening. Thankfully Ozrig was banished. I have noticed that there's been no Dark Underworld activity above us."

"I have seen streaks of black smoke going from the portal to the island and back. Oh yeah, do we have a name for the island?" Zaveus inquired.

"That's a good point. We don't have a name for it. Although, it was the Coven of the Sacred Flame. How about Sacred Flame Island?" Odulore asked.

"Yes!" The rest of the wizards agreed.

"All right, it's decided. The island where the Coven of the Sacred Flame went to is now named Sacred Flame Island. Anything else we need to discuss?"

Tizohr added, "Are we going to give titles to our spouses?"

"Good question, Tizohr, I think it would be good for them all to have titles. How about whatever our title is, we add that to them? So, Amaranth will be the Grand Master Witch. Armina will be Master Witch, and then the rest are Advisor Witch." Odulore answered.

Amaranth had overheard what he suggested, and walked into the dining hall. "Excuse me, but how about asking a witch what title would be good?"

"Ok, what is your suggestion?"

"High Priestess for myself, then Priestess for Armina and Arietta, and Advisor Witch for the regions is better."

"Then it is so assigned. Thank you, Amaranth the High Priestess of Maerith Kingdom." She smiled, and walked out of the dining hall.

“Any further business?” Odulore inquired.

“No,” they all replied.

“Great, let’s go out to the courtyard, and enjoy some time together.”

All the wizards left the dining hall and walked to the courtyard.

Chapter 47

Amaranth put on a full-length form-fitting gown. It was a deep, dark purple with black and silver sparkles all over it. The top had a plunging neckline, and the back was fully covered. She put Amaryllis into a light purple frilly dress. They were all ready for the official ceremony of the kingdoms.

Odulore walked into Amaryllis' room, "My witches look beautiful! I am very proud to have the two of you by my side. This ceremony is going to be a great start to the future of the island. Let's go!"

They walked out into the courtyard. The chairs were all arranged by Zizor and the goblins. Within a few minutes they were all filled with witches and wizards. Odulore and Amaranth took the front chairs that were facing the rest of them.

"Welcome everyone! I am so happy to see everyone here. Today is a most historic day for this island. We are having a ceremony to officially rename the island, rename the kingdoms, and also pronounce official titles.

First, let us start by calling on the Holy Dimension to grant us its power and hedge of protection.

Next we are proud to announce that the island itself will now be name Maerith Kingdom. Amaranth and I are over Maerith Kingdom. Her title is High Priestess Amaranth, and my title is Grand Master Wizard Odulore. Amaryllis will grow into her title of the Priestess. The area that was formerly Maerith Kingdom is now Maerith Province.

Now for the other kingdoms. These will now be called regions. We have Dravocia Region, Xoba Region, Zodel Region, and Zallesian Region.

These regions will be under the overall rule of Maerith Kingdom. However, the former rulers of those kingdoms will now have titles of Advisors. I am proud to introduce you to Dhenaxx the Advisor Wizard of Dravocia Region, Zaveus the Advisor Wizard of Xoba Region, Azohr the Advisor Wizard of Zodel Region, and Tizohr the Advisor Wizard of Zallesian Region.

Their spouses will be referred to as Advisor Witches. We have Aruzith the Advisor Witch of Zodel Region, Phaopra the Advisor Witch of Zallesian Region, Litrixi the Advisor Witch of Dravocia Region, and Zudarina the Advisor Witch of Xoba Region.

Finally, I want to introduce Master Wizard Qbaris with Priestess Armina, and Avras Official Record Keeper of Maerith Kingdom with Priestess Arietta.

Oh yes, one more thing, we have officially named the new island that broke off as Sacred Flame Island.

We are all now official. Congratulations to everyone!"

The courtyard erupted in cheers and clapping. Zizor announced, "We have a nice buffet dinner for all of you that includes venison, elk, boar, potatoes prepared in a couple of ways: scalloped and mashed with garlic, a couple of salads, and a variety of desserts. It is ready, if you all will get in line. The trolls will have the tables and chairs while you are in line. Enjoy!"

Everyone filed into line starting with Amaranth and Odulore. They were followed by Qbaris and Armina, Avras and Arietta, then the advisors with spouses, and everyone else.

The buffet line went smoothly. Amaranth and Odulore made their way to their table, which was at the front of the courtyard with room for Qbaris, Armina, Avras, and Arietta, faced the rest of the tables.

Zizor and the goblins kept the buffet trays filled. After all the witches and wizards were seated with their food, the goblins cleaned up everything on the buffet except for the desserts. They spread those out across the tables.

Above Rissingshire Castle a white cloud appeared, and then descended into the courtyard. The cloud cleared away revealing Trodus and Tatiana. "Congratulations everyone!" Trodus began. "I am so proud of this day. You have all come together to form one kingdom. Why was this not done before? Honestly, we couldn't agree on anything except to leave each other alone. So, you all have done something that we never could do previously. Congratulations to all!"

"This is wonderful to see you and mother. I did not know that you wizards couldn't agree on anything. That makes this even better. It was easy for us to agree. Of course, some of our problems were already gone. This is more of a preventative measure. This will help for generations to come."

Tatiana smiled, gave out hugs, and said, "I am so proud of all of you. Congratulations!"

The white cloud reappeared, enveloped Trodus and Tatiana, and went away into the clear sky.

Off to the side in the courtyard, the trolls sat, picked up their instruments, and played music for all to dance to.

Armina pulled Amaranth aside, "I want to give you some good news. I am pregnant!"

"What? That is awesome! I am so happy for you and Qbaris. Amaryllis will have a little cousin to play with. She will love it. Let's announce it. Can we?"

"Yes, you can announce it."

Amaranth stood on the hearth of the fireplace, "Excuse me everyone! Attention everyone! We have an announcement to make! We are very happy to announce that Master Wizard Qbaris and Priestess Armina are having a baby!"

The courtyard erupted in cheering and clapping. Everyone walked up to Armina and Qbaris to congratulate them.

"Congratulations brother, fatherhood is the best thing. You are going to love it," Odulore said to Qbaris.

"Thanks. I am excited about it. Amaryllis is so adorable and such a good baby. We don't know yet whether we will have a witch or wizard. That should be known in a few weeks."

Zizor walked up to them, "We have added a congratulatory cake to the dessert table."

"You guys are awesome. Thank you so much," Qbaris replied.

The music returned and everyone resumed dancing. This went on for a few hours. The sun started to set over the castle wall. All the witches and wizards exited the castle, which left Amaranth and Odulore in the courtyard with little Amaryllis. She started to cry. "I must go change and feed her for the night."

Amaranth sat down on the rocking chair with Amaryllis. The little witch fed while Amaranth thought to herself, *It's been a busy day. I am so tired. I think I will have to start walking with this little one during the day. I need to get my energy up if I want to have another one. I do want another one. Now Armina is pregnant. I hope she has a little witch for Amaryllis to play with. We should wait a bit to make sure that this little one is a year old by the time we get the next one. I don't want it to come too early. Shoot, this one should only have been born a few days ago instead of five months ago. It is amazing how well she has done for being so early.*

Amaryllis looked up at her, and smiled while her breast was still in her mouth and a bit of milk ran down from her mouth. She couldn't help but smile and giggle, "You silly girl. I love being your mom. You make me smile so much. Do you want a sibling? A little witch or wizard to play with? I am sure you do."

Odulore walked in and sat down next to them, "How are we doing?"

"We are going wonderfully. She is just being silly and making me giggle. I do want another one. I am torn whether to wait or not. Want to throw caution to the wind and just go for it? That way, whenever it happens, it will be a welcome surprise?"

"I told you before, it's up to you. I will agree to whatever you want."

Amaranth stood up and laid Amaranth down to sleep. She and Odulore walked out of the room, hand in hand. They went out into the courtyard and looked up at the stars.

Chapter 48

Qbaris and Armina flew in their black carriage that was pulled by black Pegasuses to edge of the Demack Grassland right outside of the Rissingshire Castle. He helped her out of the carriage, and sat by the carriage.

Odulore and Amaranth carrying Amaryllis on her back, walked up to them. "How are you doing Armina?" Amaranth asked.

"This little witch is going to make her appearance at any moment. However, we did not want miss Amaryllis' birthday party with the dragon games."

She put Amaryllis down on the ground, Amaryllis walked over to Armina and gently patted her belly, "We are waiting for you. Come out soon. I want to play with you."

They all laughed. Qbaris and Amaranth sat down. Amaryllis walked around them all repeatedly.

Wizards and witches outlined the Demack Grassland. Within a few minutes, the first dragon took to the sky. It was a bright green dragon and was joined by a bright red dragon. They flew up, down, all around, and then floating in the air about a few large dragon lengths apart, they blew fire at each other.

There were various dragons that flew in and out. They were all colors: blue, purple, yellow, orange, white, and pink. Amaryllis' favorite one was the purple one.

Next up were the mini-dragons. Zyrsit was the first one that flew around the grassland. He flew above the witches and wizards, and even in between them.

Amaryllis yelled, “Zyrsit!” He came and landed next to her. She petted his scaly back, and he flew off into the grasslands.

“Yikes!” Armina yelped.

Amaranth looked at her, “What? Are you ok?”

“I don’t think so. This little one is coming right now. Amaryllis, I think your little cousin is going to share your birthday.” She squirmed as the labor pains hit.

“Ok, good thing you are already in the right chair. Odulore, can you get some towels?” Amaranth asked.

A few minutes later the labor pains shot through Armina, she raised her back off her chair, and winced. That subsided and then another one, this one made her push.

“One more push like that, and your little one will be here,” she told her.

“Ouch,” Qbaris said as Armina squeezed his hand. She gave it one more push, and the little one was born and cried.

“Congratulations, your little witch is born,” Amaranth took one of the towels and wiped her off before handing her to Armina.

Amaryllis jumped up and down, “Yeah! I have a little cousin!”

Armina relaxed on the chair with the little witch on her chest. Qbaris sat next to her, and gently smoothed the little one’s hair. He smiled at Armina, she smiled back at him.

Odulore inquired, “Do we have a name for her or do you want to do an official naming ceremony?”

“Official naming ceremony,” they said together.

"Wonderful, I can do that now or we can wait a day or two."

"We are all here now, let's do it now."

Odulore announced, "Please gather around. We are here for the naming ceremony of the little witch of Qbaris and Armina. What a joyous occasion we are gathered for. These two were blessed on their wedding day with the hedge of protection from the Power of the Holy Dimension. This hedge of protection is now extended to their little witch upon this rejoiceful day of her birth and naming. Would her parents please share with us what her name is to be?"

"Her name is Keeva!" They both announced.

"We welcome Keeva to this community. We bless her with the hedge of protection from the Power of the Holy Dimension. May she grow strong in mind, body, and soul," Amaranth spoke upon her.

The witches and wizards came up and congratulated them. They also wished Amaryllis a happy birthday.

Little Amaryllis walked up to Keeva, and gave her a kiss on the head. Then she put her hand on her shoulder, "I am glad you are here Keeva. We are going to have so much fun playing when you are bigger."

Amaranth smiled, and picked up Amaryllis, "It's time for you to eat. We'll let Armina and Keeva rest."

Zizor announced, "Lunch is ready for all. We have macaroni and cheese topped with venison. This is Amaryllis' favorite. At least the macaroni and cheese part is. The venison was added for all the adults. I hope you all enjoy."

Amaranth and Odulore placed Amaryllis at their table in her high chair. She had a bowl of the macaroni and cheese sat down in front of her. The little witch ate with her fingers, grabbing up fist fulls of macaroni.

"You cute little witch. I am glad that you like your first birthday meal."

"She also liked the dragons, especially when Zyrsit landed next to her. Zizor will be bringing out a little cake for her," Odulore smiled at them.

Everyone enjoyed their lunch. Then the goblins came out of the kitchen and cleaned up the courtyard. They were followed by Zizor. He brought out a chocolate cake with chocolate frosting on it and placed it in front of Amaryllis.

She squealed, raised her arms, and then planted both hands into the cake. Amaranth, Odulore, Zizor, and everyone around them clapped, cheered, and yelled, "Happy Birthday Amaryllis!" The little witch squealed some more, and then smeared the cake on her own face.

Puggaald walked out with a towel to wipe off the little one. He handed it to Amaranth. After Amaryllis was done, she wiped her down. Then took her out of the high chair. Puggaald cleaned up the high chair and anywhere the cake was.

Zizor and the rest of the goblins had the rest of the courtyard all cleaned up and back in order.

Qbaris walked up to Odulore, "This has been a great day. Thank you so much, and Amaranth too. She did so great with delivering Keeva. We are going to fly home and get some rest. My witches are really tired."

"You're welcome. I know they are. You guys go rest. We'll see you later on."

Amaranth and Amaryllis gave him a big hug, and said, "See you later," to Armina and Keeva.

Off they flew back to Miserth Castle. Qbaris helped them out of the carriage. Armina carried Keeva into her room, sat down in her rocking chair, held her to her breast, and fed her.

Qbaris came in and sat with them. Keeva fell asleep. Armina handed her to Qbaris, who laid her in her bassinet. The two walked out to the courtyard and relaxed for a couple of hours, when little Keeva woke up and cried. Qbaris picked her up, and brought her to Armina.

Back at Rissingshire Castle, Amaranth walked little Amaryllis to her room, picked her up, and placed her in her crib for a nap. She watched her lay there, *I am the most blessed witch on this island. Now I am an aunt. Not only that, I got to deliver my niece.*

Odulore sat in the courtyard with Avras, "How do you think things are going across the kingdom?"

"I think it is going well. It's been a great six months. I don't see where anything on a day-to-day basis has really changed. Everyone is getting along. I think when it will help the most is when we have to worry about anyone attacking us."

"That's good. I like when everyone gets along. I don't think we have to worry about the Dark Underworld at this point. They are pretty much trapped in their underground area and the Sacred Flame Island. There are other islands in the area, but we've never seen anyone from them."

Zaveus walked up, "I must say, this has been great. We are a bit smaller since the witches' coven broke off, but the overall energy in Xoba Region is lighter. We have happier witches and wizards. In fact, I have three witches that want to give their lives over to the Holy Dimension. They have three wizards that want to marry them."

"Ok, which witches are these?" Odulore questioned.

"Astrid, Xantha, and Raina."

"Great! These are victims of Qrizor. I am glad they are moving forward with their lives. Who are the lucky wizards?"

"Hakonn, Xupan, and Zitrix. Great wizards. They are already helping them with their children. Which says a lot. Raina has six boys. They have their hands full. All of them want to be married with the Power of the Holy Dimension."

"I can do that. We'll set something up. This is just awesome. Yes, Raina and Zitrix do have their hands full. Aren't they three sets of twin boys that are all under two?"

"Yes, they are. I will let them know. Thanks," Zaveus walked off.

Odulore and Avras sat at the table for a few minutes more. "I am going to head off for home with Arietta. See you later," Avras said.

Odulore walked into Amaryllis' room, Amaranth was still watching her sleep. He walked up, and put his arm around Amaranth. "I think you should let her sleep, and you should come out to the courtyard," he whispered to her. She smiled at him, and they walked out of her room.

Chapter 49

Two weeks later, Odulore, Amaranth, Amaryllis, Qbaris, Armina, Keeva, Avras, Arietta, and the wizards and witches from all the other regions flew into Xoba Region. They were greeted by Zaveus the Advisor Wizard and Zudarina the Advisor Witch of Xoba Region.

Odulore walked to the edge of the Kiniriden Sea. Everyone else was seated. Hakonn, Xupan, and Zitrix stood to Odulore's left. Astrid, Xantha, and Raina walked down the aisle, and stood to Odulore's right.

"Thank you all for coming. We are excited that you have all decided to get married in the eyes of the Holy Dimension. We are even more excited that you all wanted to do it at the same time. Is there anything that you all would like to say? We'll start with Hakonn and work our way around to Raina."

Hakonn took Astrid's hand, looked her in the eyes, and said, "I am so in love with you. The day you said yes, it made me the happiest wizard alive. Now for the two of us to be married before the Holy Dimension, is perfect. I love you and your boys, Odius, Odaprix, and Odileus."

"You have made me so happy. The day you walked into my life, into our lives, it has been happiness ever since then. I can't wait to be married to you in the sight of the Holy Dimension," Astrid told him.

Xupan put Xantha's hands in his, he stared into her eyes, "You and the boys are the light of my life. I am so happy we will be a family with the protective hedge of the Holy Dimension."

"You are the one that I have always dreamed of. You are the one that I love. You and my boys are my whole world. I am looking forward to marrying you and receive the protective hedge of the Holy Dimension." Xantha told him.

Zitrix pulled Raina close, "You my witch are my forever witch. You, me, those great boys. We will be together forever within the protective hedge of the Holy Dimension."

"I love you Zitrix! You and my boys are my complete world. Now we will be a loving family together under the hedge of the Holy Dimension," Raina said.

Odulore smiled and looked at each of them, "The Power given to me from the Holy Dimension now covers you all with an extra hedge of protection over the two of you from now until the day you enter the Holy Dimension. What the Holy Dimension has blessed, no evil will ever be able to separate. The two of you now have everlasting life either in this world or in the Holy Dimension. No evil will be able to touch either of you. The Holy Dimension will protect you. Your children will also be protected by your hedge of protection until they are of age to marry. Are you all ready for the last step?"

"YES!" They all shouted.

"I now pronounce you, husbands and wives: Hakonn and Astrid, Xupan and Xantha, and Zitrix and Raina. You may kiss your brand new spouse!"

They all took their spouse into their arms, and kissed them. The crowd clapped. Then the couples walked down the aisle back away from the sea.

The newly married couples all walked from the ceremony spot to another place on the beach where there were tables, chairs, and a buffet of food. A band of trolls played music, before, during, and after they ate.

Zitrix stood up on a boulder, “We want to thank everyone for coming. It’s a special day for the six of us and our twelve children collectively. The sun is shining, You all are here. We are so happy that Odulore performed the ceremony, and we are all under the protective hedge of the Holy Dimension. There is a wonderful buffet that was prepared by the goblins, led by Moruk the ogre. Enjoy!”

The couples and their children lined up for the buffet, and everyone else lined up behind them. Their trays were piled high with venison made in three different ways: ground into meatballs and covered with barbecue sauce, shredded into a pot roast with potatoes and carrots, and bacon-wrapped venison tenderloin steaks.

After the trays were emptied, everyone got up and danced to the music of the trolls.

A couple of hours later, Odulore, Amaranth, Amaryllis, Qbaris, Armina, Keeva, Avras, and Arietta all flew back to Rissingshire Castle.

Amaranth, Armina, and Arietta sat in the courtyard with Amaryllis and Keeva. Armina held Keeva up to her breast to feed her. They all chatted while Amaryllis played on the ground.

“Ok, when are you and Avras having children?” Amaranth asked.

“I am not sure. When is your second one coming along?”

“We have been talking about it and trying for the next one. I am hoping for very soon.”

Armina added, “Yeah, she’s a year old now. Time for another one.”

"I am all for another one. I can't wait for another one. I would love for her to have another little witch to play with. Odulore wants a little wizard, even though this little witch is wrapped right around his little finger."

Amaryllis toddled around the courtyard. She went up to Keeva and gave her kiss on the head.

"She is always doing that to her. I love how she loves her little cousin. With how gentle she is, it gives me great hope for how she will treat a sibling."

Arietta asked, "Ok, I have a question. Do you think we are going to have any problems with all the children of Qrizor getting older? Do you think any of them will turn evil? Right now they are not, according to his journal."

"That's a good question. I don't know. We've got siblings between the ages of eighteen and almost two. So, some of them we will be finding out pretty quickly. Others, we have quite a bit of time to find out. What will happen? Who knows. I hope that they all stay good and no one goes evil," Amaranth answered.

Amaryllis went up to Amaranth, "Mama, I am hungry."

"I know sweetie. Come on up here." She picked her up, put her on her lap, pulled out her breast, and had her feed while she continued to talk. "The interesting part of this family tree is that Qbaris is going to be twenty soon, and Raina, Xantha, and Astrid, who are the youngest mothers of the half-siblings, are going to be twenty-one. Thankfully they all just got married and are living under the protective hedge of the Holy Dimension. Those half-siblings could have more half-siblings coming. I'm not sure if those three are planning on any more children. I would think the ones that wouldn't be having any more are the ones with children over the age of ten."

Arietta replied, "Yes, I wouldn't want to start over after a ten-year gap."

"You have to have children first," Armina laughed. Amaranth and Arietta also laughed.

Odulore, Qbaris, and Avras all went into Odulore's room where they sat around the table. He said, "We haven't heard anything from the Dark Underworld. This is really weird. The last time that they left us alone we had evil on this island. However, now we have slowly been turning to the Holy Dimension. At what point do they try to come after us?"

"That's a good question," Qbaris said.

Avras commented, "I have a feeling that they are going to come back to us, and it's not going to be pretty. I am sure that they will be looking for revenge. We took away their ability to recruit more."

"I think you are correct, but with the hedge around the island, and their narrow area they can move, how are they going to get revenge?" Odulore questioned.

Qbaris asked, "I know the witches are probably talking about it, but what about all the children that Qrizor had? Do we think we are going to have any more that will turn evil? Do we think any of the mothers will decide that they want to leave?"

"I don't know how the Dark Underworld will get revenge. I also don't know if any of the children will turn evil. With the mothers, I think everyone is pretty much happy with where they are. I wish I could see into the future and know about the children because there are children all the way down to almost two years old. So, that's a large age gap to be able to predict," Avras answered.

Amaryllis finished feeding, then jumped down, and toddled into Odulore's room. She went right to him. "Hey sweetie, how are you doing?" He picked her up, put her on his lap, and bounced her up and down while she giggled.

"Ok, I don't see where the Dark Underworld will be able to get revenge successfully. However, I can see where some of these children may become evil. It's not out of the realm of possibilities. I just hope that it doesn't happen," Odulore added.

Qbaris suggested, "I would have the ones that live in Xoba Region keep an eye on the portal. We have three more wizards plus Zaveus. They will be able to give us reports."

"I think you are right. Can you let them know? Actually, let me get the owls to deliver that. Ash! Oldirrim!" The owls flew in and landed on the table. "You two need to go to Xoba Region. Give Zaveus, Hakonn, Xupan, and Zitrix a message. Tell them to keep an eye on the Dark Underworld portal, and report back on a daily basis what they see." The owls flew off with the message.

"That is taken care of. We can then prepare for whatever they are planning, and hopefully get ahead of it."

Qbaris smiled and looked at Avras, "Ok, with all this talk about children, when are you two having one? You've been married for over a year now."

"We are not sure. It'll happen when it does. Honestly, I have been enjoying it being the two of us. I do like children and want some of my own."

Amaryllis started to cry, Amaranth walked in, and picked her up. "I think she is getting tired. I am going to take her and lay her down." They walked out of the room.

"Well guys, I think it's time to call it a night. We'll get back together in a couple of days," Odulore said.

They all stood up and walked out into the courtyard. Everyone hugged, and then Avras and Arietta left first, and then Qbaris, Armina, and Keeva left.

Odulore went into Amaryllis' room where Amaranth was rocking her. He sat down next to them. Little Amaryllis went off to sleep. Odulore whispered to Amaranth, "You need to lay her down, and we can go to bed. How would you like to try for another one?"

Chapter 50

Meanwhile, in the Dark Underworld, Ozrig looked at Annamaaz, "It's time for more children to be born on Permeated Flame Island. You need to go make sure that happens quickly."

"You are nine days earlier this time. Are you sure?"

"Yes, get those children born. I want more evil children! From now on Kezrin and Korzath will take care of getting those witches pregnant. This way, I can have new evil demon children every ninety days. These witches need to be beyond miserable. These wizards need to be miserable because they will no longer be having children of their own. They will ALL be mine! They will ALL be demons! Now go! Take Kezrin with you to name those quads of the four witches. You can let the wizards know that they are all going to only massage and pleasure the witches. They are not to have sex with the witches. They can only pleasure them with their hands. I have spoken. You go now!"

Annamaaz went with Kezrin to the Permeated Flame Island. They appeared on the beach where Crumazz and Qrizor were massaging and pleasuring the witches. "Hi everyone! It's time to give birth to some children! I know you are all excited for this, especially Calla and Coral. Let me see, who do I want to go first? Let's go with Rose first. Qrizor and Crumazz, get ready because this is going to be fast as I go around the circle. Then I have some fabulous news for you all at the end."

She walked up to Rose, put her hands on her belly, and she instantly pushed the first one out. Crumazz almost missed her. The second one came out right after the first and then the third one.

Before the second one came out, Annamaaz was at Ember. She placed her hands on her belly, and the first one came out within seconds. Qrizor was right there for it. Then the second and the third.

Piper was next to Ember, she placed her hands over her belly, and the first one was pushed out onto the chair before Crumazz could get there. The second one pushed the first one out of the way, then Crumazz got there for number three to come out.

She moved on to Echo, placed her hands on her belly, and the first one pushed out onto the chair. Qrizor quickly went to her, and was able to get the second and third ones that were right after the first one.

Annamaaz moved on to Nissa before Crumazz was done with Piper. She laid her hands on her, within moments the first one was out with the second one close behind. Crumazz was there for the last one.

Starla was next, her first one was pushed out, then the second and third before Qrizor could make it over to. Annamaaz moved quickly.

"Alright, Moira, you are the last one of Crumazz's children," She laid her hands on her and the first one pushed out immediately. The second and third quickly followed and Crumazz got there in time to get number three.

"Now we are moving over to Coral and Calla. These two are pregnant with Kezrin's quadruplet females. Kezrin is here to assist them, but Crumazz and Qrizor are to assist as well."

She walked up to Coral, laid her hands on her belly, and the first one came out. Coral opened her mouth, but no sound came out. The next one, then the next one, and finally the fourth one came out. "You wanted to say something Coral?" Annamaaz asked.

"I was going to say that I wasn't ready. That was crazy fast! I don't get to name them?"

"No! That is Kezrin's job. He gets to name them. You just get to carry them. Now for Calla, it's time for the final four. Well, at least on this side of the island. You all give birth at the same time. It's more efficient for us."

She laid her hands on Calla's belly, within moments the first one came out, following quickly by the second, then the third, and finally the fourth.

"YES! We have them all born now. Kezrin, what do you want to name your eight children? Remember, you have eight more on the other side of the island. Oh yes, I have a message to give you all from Ozrig. He is not happy that it takes so long for you to give birth when getting pregnant from the wizards. Tomorrow, Kezrin will be back to get all the witches on the island pregnant. The best part about this, you will give birth in ninety days with quads. The day after you give birth, you will get pregnant. Every time you will have quads. We need this island populated, and it's taking too long. From now on, you will each have sixteen evil demon children per year. Oh yeah, Crumazz and Qrizor, no more sex with the witches. That is only Kezrin's job. You are only to massage and pleasure the witches by hand."

Kezrin looked at Coral, "The demons you had for me will be named Gorkir, Ruzalak, Iggomid, and Thagruth." He turned to Calla, and said, "The demons that you had for me will be named Dokalos, Egmeman, Urraren, and Brerkes."

The two disappeared in a black cloud. They appeared on the other side of the island by Rugast and Vumonar. "Hi witches and wizards! Today is a great day. You are all giving birth today. Aren't you all just so happy?"

Zaleria thought to herself, *Nope, not happy. I haven't been happy at all on this island. This is my fourth pregnancy on this island. I am almost thirty-nine. How can this get any worse?*

"Oh dear, you are complaining about your fourth pregnancy and being almost thirty-nine. Well, let me make my announcement early. I was going to save it for after she gave birth, but good news for you all. Everyone on the island will now get pregnant by Kezrin. Not only that, but he will back tomorrow to do this. The best part of this news is that you only have to be pregnant for ninety days. Yes, get pregnant tomorrow by Kezrin, then in ninety days, you will give birth to four demon children. ALL of you! Rugast, Vumonar, you are NOT to have sex with any more with any of these witches. You will be only pleasuring and massaging by hand. No more sex for you. So, now that we have the good news out the way, thanks to the complainer, we will move on to birthing some children and then the demons."

Annamaaz walked up to Mistya, then Myra, Storm, Alecto, Kalliope, and Lavinia. She laid hands on their bellies, all the witches instantly pushed out the first of their triplets. Then the second, and the third. Rugast and Vumonar scrambled around trying to help with all of the newborns.

"Now, it's time for those demon children to be born. We will do Orchid first because Zaleria is such a complainer. She will wait until Orchid's are born and Kezrin has named them." Annamaaz laid her hands on Orchid, the demons came out instantly, one after another, until all four were out.

Kezrin smiled, "Now for the names. They will be called Balvon, Ograth, Ulgras, and Kurnoth."

"Finally, we are here at Zaleria. Do you know what I have the power to do?"

"No!"

“I have the power to control how fast or slow these demons come out of you. We will do them one at a time and Kezrin will name each after they are out. I am also going to give you labor pains that you have never felt before.”

She laid her hands on Zaleria’s belly and held them there. She felt great pains in her belly. Zaleria cringed and sat up a bit. Annamaaz pushed her back down. After about fifteen minutes of pain, the first demon came out.

“I name this one Dezen.”

Annamaaz continued to hold her hands on Zaleria. The great pains continued and the second one took thirty minutes to come out.

“I name this one Dolraun.”

This next one took forty-five minutes to come out, and was more painful than the previous two. Zaleria laid there in pain and sweating.

“I name this one Digmeth.”

Finally the fourth demon child was born. Annamaaz never lifted her hands off of Zaleria’s belly. This was even more painful. She had never had any pain like this. It took ninety minutes for this to come out.

“I name this one Dokan.”

Zaleria laid there, flat on her back, her pain was still there, but slowly subsided. She did not look at Kezrin nor Annamaaz. She closed her eyes. She did not even want to look at the children.

“Kezrin will be back tomorrow to get you all pregnant. Have a great day!” They disappeared in a poof of black smoke.

"Can you believe this? We are now only having demon quads!" Zaleria said to the other witches.

Starla glared at her, "You need to quit your complaining. It is your fault that we are in this situation. Every time you complain it affects all of us. She punishes us too. We do not want demon children, but thanks to you, we are. Plus, every ninety days! That's sixteen children within a year! You need to find your way off this island. We are tired of your complaining."

"I don't think it's my fault. She did all of your labors instantly and quick. Mine took two hours, and she gave me this unbearable pain. So, you have it easy!"

The rest of the witches all got up and went to their huts. Rugast and Vumonar carried all of the children to the children's hut. This is where all of the children were at. The witches would take shifts of breastfeeding all the children. There was now one hundred and eight children in that hut. The two wizards helped to take care of the children, when they weren't busy massaging and pleasuring a witch.

Annamaaz and Kezrin returned to the Dark Underworld. "I hope you got all those children born. When do we get them pregnant again?"

"Yes, they are all born, and tomorrow Kezrin will make sure they all get pregnant with quads. You currently have two hundred and seven children on that island that are under a year and a half old."

"You have made me so evilly happy. That island needs more witches and wizards to take care of the children. Lets send some there. These are not allowed to have sex with anyone. They are only there to allowed to take care of the children." His evil laugh filled the Dark Underworld.

Chapter 51

Evatius and Chrysonia stood at the entrance to Calegan Forest. They were joined by a group of woodland trolls. Ripshider, the head troll told them, “I was over by the Crystal Crypt. There was black smoke coming from the entrance. I also saw Frally and Gairrulit in the entrance. They didn’t look like they could get out, but still. It made me nervous seeing them there.”

“That’s interesting. I wonder if they are working on getting out of there? We should go over there and check it out,” Evatius responded.

They all walked over to the side of the Calegan Forest closest to the Crystal Crypt. There was black smoke coming up from the entrance. The centaurs stood with the trolls, and they watched the crypt.

“Hey, did you see that?” Chrysonia whispered.

“What?”

“I thought I saw something fluttering in the entrance, but it’s gone now.”

“Do you think we should let Odulore know about this?” Ripshider questioned.

Evatius answered, “Yes, I think we should. So far, nothing major is going on, but we never know what’s going to happen.”

The group walked through the forest and to the entrance of the castle. When they arrived, they found Amaranth in the courtyard with Amaryllis. “Where’s Odulore?” Evatius questioned.

"He's in his room. You can go in."

Evatius and Ripshider walked into Odulore's room. "Hey guys! What's up?" He asked them.

"We were over by the Crystal Crypt, and there is black smoke coming from it. While we were there Chrysonia thought that she saw something fluttering in the entrance," Evatius said.

Ripshider added, "I was there earlier and thought that I saw Frally and Gairrulit in the entrance. They have not come outside."

"Ok, so there's movement there, but they have not left the crypt. That's both good and bad. Good that they haven't left, but maybe bad. It depends on if they can get out of the crypt. I will have to meet with Qbaris, Avras, and my advisors."

Ash and Oldirrim flew in and landed on his table. "Yes."

"You two need to send out messages to all of my advisors, Qbaris, and Avras. They need to come meet me here to talk about the Crystal Crypt." The two owls flew off to deliver the messages.

"Thank you guys. I am glad that you brought it to my attention. We need to know when there is any movement around the crypt. I do believe that the Dark Underworld still has access to it."

Evatius commented, "I am glad that Ripshider brought it to my attention. I would not have known about it otherwise. We were on the other side of the forest."

"Good job Ripshider! Thank you for paying attention. We need everyone to keep an eye out for anything that looks like the Dark Underworld may be up to something."

Ripshider responded, “Us trolls are always looking out for the forest and it’s surroundings. We will keep a close eye on the crypt.”

“Thank you, again.”

“We’ll leave you to what you were doing,” Evatius said. He and Ripshider left the room, and walked into the courtyard where Chrysonia waited for them. The trio left the castle.

A couple of hours later, Avras, Qbaris, and the advisor wizards from all of the regions gathered in the dining hall at Rissingshire Castle.

“Thank you all for coming on such short notice. Today I had a visit from Evatius and Ripshider. They had been over by the Crystal Crypt. There was black smoke coming from the entrance. Also, Ripshider saw Frally and Gairrulit in the entrance. Then when Ripshider, Evatius, and Chrysonia were over by the crypt Chrysonia thought that she saw some fluttering in the entrance. Has anyone seen anything else going on?” Odulore asked them.

Azohr spoke up, “I have seen the smoke, but it didn’t go anywhere. I have not seen any dragons–large or mini. Do we think that they have access to the Dark Underworld or do we think that they may be trapped inside the Crypt with nowhere to go?”

“Honestly, I don’t know. Either is a possibility. The thing is, how would we figure that one out? We can’t let them out without the risk of the Dark Underworld being able to come out,” Odulore mentioned.

Qbaris responded, “Is there a spell where we can specifically make them appear outside the crypt without opening the crypt?”

“Let me go grab the spell book my father left me. That would be awesome if there’s something in there for us to get them out of the crypt without opening it up to the Dark Underworld.” Odulore walked out of the dining hall and to his father's room. He picked up the book of spells, and returned to the dining hall.

Odulore opened the book on the table, "Let's see. Yes! We can use the same spell that we used on the witches to transport them to the island. We should be able to use that one. The thing is, we need to put together a cage to put them in. We do not want them to be out and free to roam."

"I can build that. I just need the dimensions, and I'll have it over there," Azohr informed him.

"Thank you Azohr. That will be really helpful. I suggest that we all go over there. Anyone not able to?" They all shook their heads no.

"Great! Let's head over there right away," Everyone walked out of the dining hall. Their animals were all ready to ride over to Eagleview Castle.

They got to Eagleview Castle all of them worked on the cages to hold the dragons. This took them about thirty minutes. After the cages were completed, they took them over to the edge of the Calegan Forest near the Crystal Crypt.

The cages were set up inside the Calegan Forest. The wizards lined up, and repeated the phrase twice, "Mystifotis Deminius Frally the mini-dragon to the mini-dragon cage."

Frally appeared in the mini-dragon cage, "What is going on? Hey! What? Where am I?"

The wizards lined up, and repeated the phrase twice, "Mystifotis Deminius Gairrulit to the dragon cage."

Gairrulit appeared in the dragon cage, "Hey! Oh, it's you guys. What do you want?"

“We want to know what’s going on in the Crystal Crypt,” Odulore told him.

“Why would Frally and I tell you that?”

“Because we can set you free or send you back,” Qbaris told him.

“I don’t think so. I think you guys are clueless. Do you really think your little force field will block off the Dark Underworld forever? Well, it won’t. Ozrig will fix the crypt. He will make it so that we can go anywhere,” Frally answered.

Odulore smiled at them, “So, right now, you can go anywhere?”

“No, we have free rein of the crypt though. It’s a nice large crypt with lots of tunnels. We can get to the entrance,” the mini-dragon informed them.

Avras asked, “There is no way for you two to go from the Crystal Crypt to the Dark Underworld? Does anyone from the Dark Underworld come to see you in the Crystal Crypt?”

“No and no. Once YOU put the spell on the Crystal Crypt, we have had no contact with the Dark Underworld. No messages, no visits, nothing. It’s just been the two of us trapped in there. Thanks!” Gairrulit sneered at Odulore.

“Sorry that it isn’t very comfortable. We do not want the Dark Underworld on this island. What are your plans?”

“We don’t have any plans. That is aside from trying to figure out how to get out of the Crystal Crypt. We did not have this in mind though. Going from the nice big crypt to these small cages.”

“Gairrulit, we have no idea whether you are siding with us or with them. Yes, this is an us versus them situation. There is no middle ground. Although, we can always send you back to the crypt.

That will be your only choice. Which do you want? The crypt and the Dark Underworld or freedom and living here, but evil is NOT allowed," Odulore told him.

The wizards encircled the dragon cages, while they listened to the conversation. Azohr spoke up, "Can we trust these dragons? Will they influence others on the island to side with the Dark Underworld? Who wants to trust them?"

"I am thinking that we need to leave them in some sort of cage. Maybe, make it bigger? I don't think they should have freedom to go around the island. I think it'll be too dangerous," Dhenaxx commented.

The wizards all shook their heads in agreement.

"I think we will get some trolls to guard the cages until something else can be arranged. Ripshider!" Odulore yelled.

"Yes!" He appeared before them.

Odulore instructed them, "Can you please have your trolls watch over these dragon cages? They are not allowed out of them for any reason."

"Not a problem. We will gladly guard them."

"Wizards, let's return to the castle dining hall and talk further," Odulore told them.

They all flew back to Rissingshire Castle, and went to the dining hall. "What do we have for ideas to keep those dragons under control, but not in such a small cage?" Odulore inquired.

Qbaris suggested, "How about creating a large area that will give them room to move, but it will also have a roof, and a floor. Once they are in this cage, we can put a protective hedge around them. What do you think?"

"We can definitely do that. It's a pretty easy build. I can get started on it in the morning," Avras answered.

"Perfect! We will do that, and we can help you. We're all set for now. Have a great evening with your families."

All the wizards left the dining hall, and went to their families.

Chapter 52

It was early in the morning, the sun was not up yet. Avras was outside of Eagleview Castle hammering and sawing. Dhenaxx and Zaveus joined him to help build the larger dragon cage. A few minutes later Azohr, Qbaris, Tizohr, and Odulore showed up to help them put it together. The cage was together within an hour. It had a solid steel floor with bars of iron, wrapped from one side, high on the side, across the top, and back down to the floor.

Odulore and the wizards spoke twice, "Mystifotis Deminius Frally the mini-dragon and Gairrulit the dragon to this new dragon cage." The two dragons appeared in the new cage.

"Perfect! This will be your new home. I hope you like it," Odulore told the dragons.

Gairrulit looked at him, "At least this place is bigger than the other cage. Although, I did like the Crystal Crypt. This will do."

"You think you have a choice in the matter? I don't think so. You were Crumazz's dragon. We cannot trust you. None of us trust you. None of us," Qbaris told him.

Frally commented, "I like it. It's kinda nice. They made this just for us."

"You are an idiot! I cannot believe that you like this. You are not very faithful to Crumazz."

"Why would I be faithful to someone that abandoned us?"

"Because they are going to take over the world!"

Odulore laughed, "You really think that Crumazz and the Dark Underworld are going to be able to take over the world? You are crazy! That's not going to happen. This is also why we will never let you out of this cage. You are stuck there."

"Ripshider, are the trolls ready to guard this cage?" Odulore asked.

"Yes, yes, we are. These two are going nowhere."

"Excellent! Wizards, time to go back to Rissingshire Castle. There is some fun to be had now."

They all left and went to Rissingshire Castle. Amaranth was seated in the courtyard with the witches. Some little witches and wizards were crawling, toddling, and walking all around the courtyard.

Amaranth whispered to Odulore, "Do we get to make the announcement now?" He smiled at her and nodded yes.

She stood up on the hearth of the fireplace, "Attention everyone! Please gather closer. Don't worry about the little ones. They can continue playing." She waited for them to walk in closer, "I am so happy to have all of you here. We have the best news. We are expecting a little witch! Yes! Amaryllis is going to have a little witch to play with." The courtyard erupted in cheers. The witches came up and gave her hugs.

"There is cake available over on the table," Odulore let them know. Zizor and the goblins placed the pieces of cake on the table in the courtyard. Everyone rushed to the table for cake, and then found a spot to eat.

Odulore announced, "While everyone is enjoying the cake, I want to let everyone know that we have captured two dragons. One regular size, his name is Gairrulit and the other is a mini-dragon, and his name is Frally. They are both in a cage over by

Eagleview Castle. The cage is being guarded by trolls. As much as possible, stay away from the cage. These two dragons are faithful to Crumazz and the Dark Underworld."

Odulore sat down next to Amaranth. She smiled as he took her hand. Avras and Arietta approached them and sat down. "We have an announcement and would like to tell everyone. Would it be ok to announce it now?" Avras inquired.

"Yes, especially if it's what I think it is. Please do so," Amaranth smiled.

Avras and Arietta stood up on the hearth of the fireplace. "Attention everyone! There is another announcement to be made." Avras waited a moment while everyone looked over. "I am pregnant with our first child! We are going to have a witch. Yes a little witch is coming to Eagleview Castle." The courtyard erupted in cheers. Amaranth jumped up and hugged Arietta.

"Yeah! This is awesome! We are expecting together. It's going to be so great." Amaranth jumped up and down.

Amaryllis ran out to Amaranth and hugged her legs, "What mommy?"

"You get a new baby witch here and Arietta is having a baby witch too."

She cheered, and jumped up and down, "YEAH!!" Moments later she ran back to play with the other children.

A band of trolls came into the courtyard and played. The witches and wizards danced for a few hours. After which they all left the castle.

Amaranth picked up Amaryllis, and took her to her room. She changed her into her night clothes, sat down in her rocking chair with Amaryllis on her lap, and laid her against her breast to let her feed for the night.

Odulore sat down next to her, pulled out a book, and began to read to her. “Baby bear did not want to go to bed. He sat in his chair by the window.

Mama bear asked him to go to bed. He sat there with his paws crossed. Mama bear asked him again to go to bed.

Papa bear asked him to go to bed. He sat there still with his paws crossed.

Mama bear went up, gave him a big hug, and asked him again to go to bed.

Baby bear gave Mama bear a big hug. Baby bear got up and went to his bed.

Mama bear and Papa bear kissed him good night.

Good night.”

Amaryllis was fast asleep. Odulore picked her up and put her in her bed. Amaranth and Odulore walked over to the livery, and went for an evening ride on their horses.

Chapter 53

It's just after sunrise on the beach of Permeated Flame Island. Crumazz and Qrizor massaged the witches, although they were asleep on their chairs. Annamaaz and Kezrin appeared in the middle of the circle.

Annamaaz shouted, "We are here to assist you all in giving birth to all these evil demon children. I hope that you all have been miserable. The great thing for us, is that these are all full term but in a third of the time. You all know the routine. I place my hand on your belly and the demons will come out of you. The longer I lay my hand, the more pain, and the longer that it takes for them to come out. How long it takes is entirely up to me. Oh yes, this time instead of waiting a day. Kezrin will make sure that you are pregnant with a new demon right after we go around the circle. He will go around the circle. No need to go off to a hut either. Let's get started. Moira, you get to go first."

She walked up to Moira, placed her hand on her belly. She held her hand there, the pains started immediately, and grew greater and greater. The first demon came out in five minutes and the second took ten minutes. Her third one took twenty minutes. Finally, it was her fourth one and it was out after thirty minutes. She laid there, breathed heavily, and closed her eyes. She did not want to even look at the children. Crumazz helped with the demon children. He cleaned them up, and put them in the bassinets that were waiting for them.

"Very good. Now let's go on to Starla. I think, I will let you get off easy." She laid her hand on her belly. She was only there long enough to get her to push the first demon out, and the rest came one after another, very quickly. Qrizor was there to help her with them.

Annamaaz stood between Nissa and Echo. She placed a hand on each one's belly. They both pushed immediately to have the demons come out one after the other. Both Crumazz and Qrizor helped with all the demons.

She moved on to Piper, then Ember, and Rose. All of them went into labor and the demons came out one right after the other until all four were out for each of them.

"Thank you witches. You are oh so cooperative. Now Kezrin will make you all pregnant with four more and you'll have them in ninety days. Aren't you all so lucky?" Annamaaz said.

Kezrin went to Moira first, then he moved around the circle impregnating each of the witches with more demons.

Moira glared at her, "This is beyond evil. Why did you make mine so painful and none of theirs? What did I do? This isn't fair."

"You are too whiny, I felt like making it painful. It's my prerogative. Don't complain and it won't be painful. You do realize that everything I am doing is just because I can. These demon children could come out at any point. They are all spiritual. The bodies are irrelevant. See you in ninety days."

They disappeared in a black cloud, and then appeared on the other side of the island in the middle of the circle where Rugast and Vumonar were massaging the witches.

Annamaaz shouted and startled them, "Hi witches! It's your lucky day! These demon children are coming to be with you. Then Kezrin is going to make sure you get pregnant again today. Myra, you get to go first."

She went to Myra, laid her hands on her, and the demons came out, one right after another until all four were out.

She went around the circle to Mistya, Alecto, Kalliope, Lavinia, and Storm. Their labors were all quick with the demons on their chairs. Rugast and Vumonar took care of them as quickly as they could get from one to another.

Kezrin went around to each of the witches right on the beach and impregnated them all with more demon children.

"Time for me to go up to the special hut where we have the problem witches. Kezrin, let's go."

In the special hut, Annamaaz and Kezrin appeared before the four witches, "You lucky witches get to have demon children today. Then Kezrin will impregnate you all right away. I will start with Orchid."

Orchid laid there while Annamaaz laid her hands on her belly. The first demon took fifteen minutes to come out. The second one was thirty minutes. The third one was forty-five minutes and the fourth one was an hour. Orchid was still breathing heavy afterwards. She laid there not moving while Annamaaz moved on to the next one.

"Oh, let me lay my hands on Zaleria. This one will definitely take awhile. You deserve the most pain and time. We'll make your labor long, hard, and painful." She laid her hands on her belly. Zaleria partially sat up in pain. The labor pains persisted over and over for an hour. Finally, she started to push and the first demon came out. The second one also took an hour. The third and fourth ones took an hour and a half each.

"Now it's time for Coral and Calla to provide demon children. I will have you both give birth simultaneously. After all, you are twins. Let's do this all together."

She laid her hands on both of them. Their labors both started and took only fifteen minutes for each of the four demon children. Kezrin went to each of them and impregnated them with more.

"Yes! I love this. I get lots and lots of demon children to fill this island and I don't have to go through any of the pain. This is great," Annamaaz celebrated.

They disappeared in a poof of black smoke.

"I hope we have a whole tribe of evil demon children," Ozrig told them.

"Yes, there is now sixty-four more, just for you. Do you know when there is going to be enough?" Annamaaz asked.

"I don't know yet. I am really enjoying the fact that we can make these witches and wizards miserable. Those witches can go through so much pain during labor. Then they have to deal with all those children that are just plain evil. I am enjoying this."

Kezrin said, "It is nice having all of these evil children to call my own. Plus, I get all the fun. None of them enjoy it, but I do."

"You are so evil. I love it! You really are my son," Ozrig gave an evil grin.

Ozrig shouts, "Korzath! Come here!"

"Yes!" He appeared in front of him.

"How is the tarantula cave doing?"

"Well, we could use some more witches and wizards. There are never enough of those. Do you have any?"

"I will work on that," he told him. Ozrig let out an evil laugh.

Annamaaz questioned, "Are you thinking of taking the witches and wizards from the island and putting them into the tarantula cave?"

“I could do that for a bit. Maybe after this set of demon children. It’s not like those demon children need the witches and wizards. This is all just to make them miserable. Let’s do a new form of torture. Demons are demons and don’t need to grow like a witch or wizard. They can come out at any time. It’s all just a show of who is in control of them.”

“I like it. I like it. We can change up the game at any point,” Annamaaz smiled.

Chapter 54

Amaryllis laid in her crib. She opened her blue eyes and sat up. It was dark and quiet. A few minutes later she laid back down, and closed her eyes. Off to sleep she went.

A unicorn looked over the side of her crib. She nudged her with her horn. Amaryllis smiled at the unicorn. "What's your name?" She asked the unicorn.

"My name is Stardust. Would you like to go for a ride?"

Amaryllis nodded her head yes, grabbed Stardust's horn, and she placed her on her back. Stardust walked out of her room. Another unicorn joined them.

"What's your name?" Amaryllis asked the new unicorn.

"My name is Starburst. Can we get your friend Keeva to ride with us?"

"Yes, that would be fun!"

After they got out of the castle, Stardust and Starburst ran, and took off flying toward Miserth Castle. They went over the Demack Grassland, and through the Calegan Forest. The three of them landed just outside the castle.

They walked into the castle, and into Keeva's room. She slept in her crib. Starburst looked over the side, and nudged her with her horn.

Keeva opened her eyes, "What?"

Stardust walked Amaryllis closer, "Come ride with us. You get Starburst."

"Ok," Keeva grabbed a hold of Starburst's horn, and was hoisted up on her back.

The four of them walked out of the castle. The unicorns ran and took off flying. They flew around the Maerith Province. Next they flew into Zodel Region where they went over the beach, and encircled all of Maerith Kingdom.

They flew into Xoba Region, then into Zallesian Region, and finally, Dravocia Region. The unicorns flew through the Calegan Forest in Maerith Province and the Delorvern Forest in Zodel Region.

Stardust and Starburst flew through the Lavalbourg Gorge, then over to the Glassy Lagoon. They were just above the water. Amaryllis and Keeva laughed and giggled the whole time.

They went over Bordshall Cove, Tortoise Lake, and Bredenrath Pond. The four of them landed in the Demack Grassland. The pixies came out and played with them.

Amaranth stood over Amaryllis as she slept with a smile on her face. *I hate to wake her up when she looks happy sleeping. I wonder what she is dreaming about.* Amaranth said to herself. She walked away, and let her sleep for a while longer.

In her room, Amaranth sat down at her table with her journal. *I am going to write some more to my little witch.* She wrote

My little witch, you are sixteen months old now. I love how you lay in your crib and sleep so well. I just looked in on you, and you were smiling while sleeping. I would love to know what you were dreaming about. It must have been happy stuff with the big smile on your cute little face.

You are running around this castle, no more crawling, no more toddling. In just a few months you will have a little witch to play with. It could be earlier because you came way early. In fact, you were here in four and a half months. So, she has been inside me longer than you were. Will she be here in a few months, weeks, or days?

You will make a great big sister witch. You play so well with Keeva. The three of you will be such good friends, cousins, and playmates.

I wish that I would have had a sister witch growing up. Don't get me wrong, I loved growing up with your father, but it's just not the same. You share things with a sister witch that you don't share with a wizard.

I want to share with you my life. I was born at Miserth Castle to Qrizor and Zaleria. I am the youngest of their three children. My older brothers are Crumazz and Qbaris. The four of them live in Miserth Castle. I do not have details, but I do know that Qrizor made Zaleria give me up. She took me to Rissingshire Castle and dropped me off. I was raised by Trodus and Tatiana, who are your father's parents. Growing up, I knew who my mother was, but that was it. I did not know my father and brothers.

Tatiana died and went to the Holy Dimension when I was young. So, it was myself, Trodus, and Odulore that lived in the castle. That is until Trodus died and went to the Holy Dimension. Thankfully, that was only a few months before things went really strange.

One day, we were enjoying Rissingshire Castle, some dragons came and took me away to the Crystal Crypt. I was told I was being taken because my mother was dead and I needed to continue her work. This was told to me by the dragons, and then by

Crumazz. Yes, my brother kidnapped me, but I did not know he was my brother at this point.

I read a journal that my mother left for me. She told me not to trust Crumazz, but did not tell me that he was my brother. Instead, she gave me potions to kill him. I was told that he was evil and I would never escape the Crystal Crypt if I did not get rid of him. So, I did.

Once I was back at Rissingshire Castle, your father proposed to me by the Bredenrath Pond. It was so romantic. I, of course, said yes. We were married just nine days later. The best part was that our wedding was blessed by the Holy Dimension. Trodus and Tatiana came back and performed our wedding ceremony.

You came along just four and a half months later. My life has been filled with so much joy ever since you came into our lives.

Your favorite things are being rocked to sleep, having your father read to you, and spending time with friends and family.

Amaryllis woke up from her nap, she yelled, "MAMA!" Odulore walked by Amaranth's room, and walked into Amaryllis'. "Hey sweetie, I know you yelled for your mother, but here I am. Do you want to get out of that crib?" He asked her.

She lifted her arms up for him to pick her up, which he did. He carried her to Amaranth's room, "Someone yelled for you. I thought I'd bring her to you."

Amaryllis reached out for Amaranth. She took her, and stood her on her lap, "Are you ready to play?" Amaryllis squirmed to get down. When she got on the ground, she ran around the room, and then out into the courtyard.

Odulore ran after her. Amaranth sat there with a smile on her face as she could see him running after her. Amaryllis kept on running around the courtyard. Odulore sat down and watched her. He caught Amaranth's eyes and smiled at her. She got up off her chair, walked out to her chair by the fireplace, and slowly sat down. She winced when she sat down.

"Hey, you winced, are you ok?" He asked.

"Yeah," she winced again, "I just have been having a few pains here and there."

"Ok, how close together is here and there? You have made it longer than you did with Amaryllis. Well, by five days anyway," he chuckled.

"They are getting closer, but the last ones I had were a few hours ago. Yes, I know. It'd be nice if I carried them to full-term, but this one is doing so well."

"I am going to get some towels from Zizor, and send Ash to let Arietta know that this little one is on its way."

Great, but she is also pregnant. We announced the same day. She didn't say how far along she was, but that she knew it was going to be a witch."

"I will still send him. I will be right back." He walked off to the kitchen.

Ash flew up next to him. "You need me?"

"Yes, I do. Can you let Arietta know that Amaranth is getting ready to have our second little witch?"

"I can do that. I am off." He flew away.

Odulore walked into the kitchen, "Zizor! We need towels."

"Ok? Why?" He asked.

"We are going to have another witch today. Amaranth is getting labor pains."

Zizor handed him some towels, and he went back to Amaranth, who was now laying on the chair.

Arietta flew in on Artimas. "Hello High Priestess Amaranth! How are you doing?" She asked her.

Amaranth winced, "I was doing better earlier, but these pains are coming quicker. I think she is going to be here in a few minutes."

"I have towels ready," Odulore told them.

She knelt down next to her, "This one is not as easy as the first one. It's harder for me to get down here. Let me know when you are going to push."

Odulore handed Arietta the towels, and took Amaranth's hand.

A pain hit, and she curled up a bit. "Ok, pushing is going to start," She winced and yelled, "Now!" A couple of pushes later and the little witch appeared.

Arietta smiled, handed her the baby, and said, "Here's your little witch."

They both had smiles on their faces, and Odulore called Amaryllis over, "Come on Amaryllis, come meet your little sister witch."

"She is so tiny," Amaryllis commented.

Amaranth chuckled, "You were this tiny too."

"Will you do a naming ceremony later today or tomorrow?" Arietta inquired.

Odulore responded, "I think we will wait until tomorrow. It was too much for her to have so many people around last time."

"Wait, how many days is this one and how many was Amaryllis?"

"This one is one hundred and forty-five and Amaryllis was one hundred and forty. Maybe next time it will take longer," Amaranth laughed.

"So, you made it less than five months with both of them. I haven't had any pains, yet. I wonder if I will make it to the full nine or not."

"I think part of my issue with having them come so early is because my parents were also siblings, their parents were also siblings, and it went back at least one more generation like that."

"That's crazy! I am glad you broke that family tradition."

"Me too. These little witches are adorable, and I love their father."

Odulore gave both of them a kiss on the forehead, "I love all of my witches."

Arietta cleaned up the courtyard, and went to the kitchen, "Zizor, where do you want these dirty towels?"

"Just put them in the basket over there. Those need to be washed. Thanks!" Zizor told her.

She returned to the courtyard, "I am going to head for home. Have a great evening all of you!" Arietta flew out of the castle on the back of Artimas.

Chapter 55

Rissingshire Castle was filled with witches, wizards, pixies, fairies, trolls, goblins, dragons, centaurs, and more. It was a day of great celebration.

Odulore stood up on the hearth of the fireplace. Amaranth was next to him holding the new little witch. Little Amaranth ran around the castle with other little witches and wizards.

"Thank you for coming today. We are all gathered here for the naming ceremony of the newest witch daughter of Amaranth and I. It is a joyous day as we bless her with the protective hedge through the power of the Holy Dimension that we received through our marriage. This now extended to her as we name her. Amaranth, what name have we given her?"

"Alyssum"

"We welcome Alyssum into the protective hedge of the Holy Dimension. We welcome Alyssum into the Maerith Kingdom. We present to you Alyssum!" Odulore announced.

They all clapped and cheered. Amaryllis jumped up and down and yelled, "YEAH!"

Zizor walked out from the kitchen, "Food is in the dining hall. For those that can't fit in there, there is some available in the corner of the courtyard."

Odulore, Amaranth carrying Alyssum, and Amaryllis walked into the dining hall. Their seats were at the head table, and the goblins brought their trays to them.

Avras and Arietta walked up to their table. "This is a great day. I cannot wait to have our little witch here. You will be doing our naming ceremony. We just want our little one to stay put a bit longer," Avras told them.

"I will gladly perform the little witch's naming ceremony. Just let me know when."

Qbaris and Armina, holding Keeva, walked up to the group. "Are we having a separate little party here?" Qbaris inquired.

"No, they want me to do the naming ceremony for their little witch. That is when she decides to make her appearance. They are hoping for a bit of time right now."

Armina smiled, "Good luck with that. They appear when they are good and ready. This little one made it to about six and a half months. Amaranth's little witches appeared in less than five months."

"Oh wow, so I am less than five months at this point. I wonder when she'll decide she's waited long enough?"

"This one waited a whole five days longer than Amaryllis." The witches all laughed.

"Let's go dance in the courtyard!" Odulore yelled. The dining hall cleared out within minutes.

Music from the trolls filled the courtyard. The pixies, fairies, and fireflies danced in the sky above the courtyard.

Outside the castle in the Demack Grassland there were a great many animals that gathered, winged lions, owls, hares, tigers, canines, griffins, gargoyles, centaurs, and more. Those with wings flew overhead and those without wings sat scanning the Maerith Province for anything that looked out of place.

The evening wore on and everyone left. Amaranth took the witches into their room. She fed Alyssum while she rocked her, and Amaryllis was in her crib.

Odulore was in his room at his table. He had a journal out and wrote in it.

To my sweet witches,

I am writing this journal to tell you about me, your father. I want you to also know that I love you more than anything. At this time we have just two sweet little witches. I have no idea how many we will have, but I do know that they will all be very much loved.

I want you all to know that we have covered you with the hedge of protection that is through the power of the Holy Dimension that your mother and I accepted the day we got married. This protection will cover you until you get married, then you and your husband will need to accept the hedge of protection through the power of the Holy Dimension.

Although you are little at this point, some of you are not even born yet, you need to know what to look for in a husband. This is the wizard that will rule your castle. He will need to know how to protect you from evil. He will need to be faithful to only you. This is the wizard that will help you to raise your little witches and wizards. He will need to protect them as well.

You will know when you meet the right one. Your heart will pound. Your stomach will flutter. The one thing you need to make sure of is that you are married to that wizard BEFORE you have sex with him. If he is the right one, he will voluntarily wait until your wedding night.

You, my sweet witches, are the most precious thing that I have, aside from your mother. You must be precious to a wizard before he takes your hand in marriage.

My father is Trodus, and my mother is Tatiana. They were great examples of true love. My mother took in your mother when she was an infant. She was raised in our castle, but my mother and father made sure that she knew that her mother was Zaleria.

My father left me a journal that told me of her family. I will let her tell you about her family.

My mother died and went to the Holy Dimension when I was little. My father did not find another witch. He raised Amaranth and I. I believe he did a great job. However, he hasn't been gone too long.

One thing we did learn is that the ones that go to the Holy Dimension can come back. You just don't know when. We have had visits from them. The most important one is the one that set us on the right track for our marriage. They came and Trodus performed our wedding ceremony.

Oh, I wish you would have gotten to know them. They were great. They made sure that we knew about the Holy Dimension.

Sleep well my sweet witches. Sleep well. I love you.

Zyrsit flew in and landed on his table, "What are you writing?"

"I am writing a journal for them to read when they are older."

"Witches and wizards always write in journals," he replied.

"Yes we do. It's our way of talking to the next generation. For those reading, we get to peek into what the previous generation went through and what they thought. We also add in family history to make sure that it gets passed on to the next generation."

Odulore shut his journal. Zyrsit flew out of the room alongside of him.

Chapter 56

The Permeated Flame Island had children crawling and walking around that were evil and demon. The witches were always pregnant. The wizards grew more and more angry because they were always massaging the ever pregnant witches. This island was nothing more than a breeding ground of evil for the Dark Underworld.

Ozrig said to Annamaaz, "This is getting old. These witches are miserable, but it's no longer fun. I need something different. What do I do with this island?"

"The most evil thing of all. You can make the island disappear and condemn all of them to the Dark Underworld caves. Make all of the witches and wizards now have to take care of all of those children."

"I like that idea. Stand back while I command these witches and wizards to come to me." He raised his arms and yelled, "Echulso Arachniulso all mother witches and slave wizards to me!"

Instantly the seventeen witches and four wizards were in front of them. "Welcome to the Dark Underworld. This is where you will be living from now on. All you pregnant witches are pregnant with demon children. I call all the demons to exit the witches and go to the demon cave." There was instantly a dark cloud all around the feet of the witches. It moved along the floor and exited the room towards the demon cave. The witches then fell to the ground.

"What in the world? I feel like my insides left," Zaleria stated.

Annamaaz replied, "Yes, your insides did leave you. The demon inside you left. That was the easiest you've ever had it. Don't get used to it."

"Now that none of you are pregnant. Let me tell you what your life will now be like. You will take care of all those children that you had that were not demons. Only the evil children will be on the island. Everyone is going to live here. I am destroying that island. We no longer need it.

These evil children still need to be breast fed. So, you will all breastfeed all of the children. It does not matter if the child is yours or not.

Annamaaz, how many children do we have that need to be breastfeeding?"

"That would be one hundred and sixty-eight evil children under the age of two years old. Calla and Coral have eight children that are almost four years old and a few months over four years old. Those do not need to breastfed, but Calla and Coral will help breastfeed the other children. There are plenty of them that still need it."

"Perfect! All you witches can go to the caves where I will be sending the children. Oh yeah, you wizards, you will also be helping with the children. I am now commanding that none of you will be able to get pregnant, but will still breastfeed. I am also commanding that none of you will be able to have sex with each other. Now go to the children's cave."

The witches and wizards walked away to the children's cave. Zaleria thought to herself, *About time I don't have to go through labor. However, now I have to have a child up to my breast almost all day long with many children needing to be fed. These breasts are going to be sore.*

Ozrig raised his arms, “Echulso Arachniulso all evil children to the children’s cave and all demons to the demon cave!”

There was a black streak of smoke that appeared between the island and the portal to the Dark Underworld while everyone returned.

One more time Ozrig raised his arms, “Expuliatis Felem the Permeated Flame Island!” The island burst into flames, then into black smoke, and disappeared.

Zyrsit, Ash, and Oldirrim sat on a boulder on the edge of the beach. They watched as the island burst into flames, then into black smoke, and disappeared.

“Did you see that?” Ash questioned.

Zyrsit replied, “I think so. Did you see an island disappear?”

“Yes I did. We have to go tell Odulore. He’s not going to believe this,” Oldirrim added.

The owls and mini-dragon flew to Rissingshire Castle, and landed on the hearth of the fireplace. Odulore and Amaranth sat in their chairs reading. “You will never believe what we saw!” They all told them.

“What?” Odulore asked.

Ash answered, “The island disappeared. The Sacred Flame Island, it disappeared right in front of us.”

What do you mean it disappeared?

“It burst into flames, then turned into black smoke, and finally poof–gone. It disappeared. There is no more island.” Oldirrim explained.

"You need to let Qbaris, Avras and my advisor wizards know. Then ask them to come here. We will all go check it out."

The three of them flew out of the castle to let everyone know. Odulore got up and went into his room. He put a map of the area on his table, and put a question mark next to the island.

About an hour later, the owls and mini-dragon flew in and landed on his table. "Did you get to everyone?"

"Yes we did," Ash answered.

Fifteen minutes later Qbaris and Avras entered his room followed by his Advisor Wizards. "Thanks for coming on such short notice. These three have told you what they saw. We all need to go out by the water and see what's going on. Let's go."

The wizards left on their flying animals to the beach area in Xoba Region. It took only minutes to get there. They landed on the beach and looked out at the Kiniriden Sea.

"Does anyone see the island?" Odulore inquired.

Qbaris replied, "No. It is not there. How is this possible?"

"I do not see it and I have no idea," Avras answered.

Azohr asked, "Can Ozrig make the island disappear?"

"Evidently he can," Tizohr replied.

They all flew back to the Rissingshire Castle and gathered around the fireplace.

"So, if Ozrig no longer has the island, will he be coming after this island? Will he be coming for the Crystal Crypt? It does not appear that they can come up into the Crystal Crypt. They have completely abandoned the dragons. What to do?

Number one, are they coming after this island?

Number two, will they want the Crystal Crypt?

Number three, do we transport the dragons from their cage to the Dark Underworld?

Number four, do we put a seal on that portal?" Odulore asked them.

Azohr answered, "I vote for sealing all of the portal after we transport the dragons to the Dark Underworld."

"I agree with him," Dhenaxx agreed.

Zaveus also agreed, "Yes, let's do that."

"I also agree," Tizohr added.

Qbaris and Avras both said, "I agree."

"So, it is unanimous, we will seal the portal after sending the dragons to it. Let's go out to the dragon cage."

All of the wizards left on their flying animal, and landed next to the dragon cage. Odulore raised his arms and chanted twice, "Mystifotis Deminius these dragons to the Dark Underworld!" Instantly they were transported.

"Ok, let's go to the beach again and I'll cast the spell for closing off the portal." The wizards all flew to the beach.

Odulore raised his arms and chanted twice, "Incenecto Vexenus all portals to the Dark Underworld." A violent, intertwining duo of streams of energy went out from Odulore to the portals. He then lowered his arms and sat down on the sandy beach.

"Are you ok?" Qbaris asked.

"Yeah, that one took a lot of energy, especially right transporting the dragons."

They waited a few minutes, "Ok, I am ready to go back. You all can go back to your castles, as well. I will see you later." The wizards flew off in many directions.

Chapter 57

Rhixon rode through the Delorvern Forest on Kaspa, his black Percheron stallion. He arrived at Corlach Castle. Azohr was in his room. “Azohr! Azohr!” He yelled into the castle.

Azohr came out of his room, “What do you need?”

“I want to be a part of the wizards, like you. What can I do?”

“You are a half-sibling of Amaranth, aren’t you?”

“Yes, yes, I am. So, I do have some powers. I just don’t know how to use them. My mother has some witch powers, but knows nothing about wizards.”

“Come on into my room. I can show you some books.”

The two of them walked to Azohr’s room. “Have a seat.” He told him, and grabbed a book off his shelf.

“The first thing that you need to know about is your family history. If you don’t know your family history, then you need to start with what you do know and create your own journal for future generations. We’ll read from my family history.”

“What does this have to do with wizard powers?”

“If you don’t know where you came from and how you came to be, how are you going to move forward? You have to start somewhere. Now, I know that part of your family history you can get from Qbaris and Amaranth. The other part you will have to get from your mother.”

"Ok, I am not sure I want to know everything there. Amaranth did give me some of the basic information. So, I can start from there. Once I get my family history, what do I do from there?"

"From there you will need to look to the Power of the Holy Dimension. This is where all of our powers come from. If you power does not come from there, this island is not for you. Although, from what I heard, you don't have to worry about any of that. Let's look at the book I have regarding the Power of the Holy Dimension." Azohr opened a book he had on his table.

The book was about 3 inches thick with a dark blue cover, and it was bound with brown leather straps. The paper inside it was a yellow parchment. The gold lettering on the cover read, "The Power of the Holy Dimension."

Azohr opened the front cover and started to read.

This book will give you the Power of the Holy Dimension, which is meant for good. All that comes from here will help in your daily life and in the forever life.

The Holy Dimension will be where you go after your life in this world has ended. Do not be afraid of anything in this life nor of going into the Holy Dimension.

When you accept the Protective Hedge of the Holy Dimension, you will go from this life to the next when it is your time. Only the Power of the Holy Dimension knows when that time will be. Do not let anyone tell you otherwise.

The first and most important order of the Power of the Holy Dimension commands of you is that you treat one another with kindness and love.

"Do you understand everything so far?" Azohr asked Rhixon.

"Yes, it seems pretty simple. However, what powers do I get out of this?"

"It will take reading the whole book to understand all of the powers that you have. What else will help is if you go to wizard games. The wizard games will help you understand how to use your powers and what they can do. Also, if you want to come along whenever the wizards need to do something. You can observe what is going on."

"That makes sense. When will that be?" Rhixon inquired.

"I'm not sure when the wizard games will take place. However, I can let you know about the wizard gatherings. In fact, where do you live right now?"

"I live in a small place with my mother and sister. Why?"

"How would you like to live here with Aruzith and I? This would make it easier for you to know when wizard gatherings are going to happen. You can read this book too."

"Let me go to my mother and sister and let them know." Rhixon told him.

"Yes, please go. I will let Aruzith know and when you get back, we'll show you to your room."

Rhixon got on Kaspa, and he rode back to his mother's home. When he arrived, she was out front with Antha gardening. "Hi mother! Hi Antha!"

"Hi Rhixon! Where have you been?" Azalea asked.

"I have been at Corlach Castle with Azohr. He is going to show me how to be a wizard. He also told me that I can live there with him and Aruzith."

Antha laughed, "Rhixon, you are crazy. He is too important to help you."

"She does have a point, even if she could have worded it nicer." Azalea looked at her and then back at Rhixon. "What do you think you will accomplish living there? What are you going to do, be just a wizard?"

"Yes! I want to be a wizard and one of the Advisor Wizards. This will be great. I will have a room to myself."

Azalea shook her head, "If you think this is what you want. Yes, you can go live there. If it does not work out, we will be here, and you can come back here."

They had a family group hug. Rhixon got his things, and rode back to Corlach Castle as fast as he could.

Meanwhile, Azohr walked into Aruzith's room. "Do you trust me?" He asked.

"Yes, what have you done now?"

"I have offered to help Rhixon learn how to be a wizard. I also offered to have him live here. We have plenty of room for him and his horse."

She looked at him, smiled, and said, "Why am I not surprised? You are such a helpful wizard. I am sure that you will teach him well. Of course, he may live here. It's always great to have one more."

A few minutes later Rhixon arrived on his horse with all of his belongings. Azohr and Aruzith walked out to greet him. "You can leave your horse here, and we'll show you to your room," Aruzith said.

They walked him to his room, "Here you are. I hope you like it. Dinner will be soon in the dining hall. Ogrok the ogre will let us know when it is ready."

"Come with me to my room and you can take the book we were reading and read it in your room." Azohr and Rhixon walked over to his room. He handed him the book. Rhixon went to his room to read.

Aruzith walked into Azohr's room, "You are such a kind-hearted wizard. I love having another wizard in the castle. I can't wait to see how he grows. My only concern is who his father is, although, he had no contribution to his upbringing."

"I don't think you need to worry about that. The reason he did not stick around was because the children were not evil. Rhixon and Antha are both good. I know this because Azalea is my sibling. She has a lot of good history in her."

"Do you think we should invite them all to live here? We have so many rooms and it's just the two of us. I can't have children, so no worries about them taking up rooms we will need. We never know how long Antha will live here anyway. She will get married and move in with her wizard. Your sister is always welcome here." Azalea informed him.

Azohr nodded his head, "I agree with you. I will ride out and see her. Hopefully, they will come back with me." He left his room, and flew off on Zudoz, his favorite gargoyle.

Azalea and Antha were out tending to the vegetable garden when Azohr landed on the side of the garden. "Well hello Azohr!" Azalea greeted him.

"Hello! How are you witches doing?"

"We are doing well. What can we do for you?"

"Aruzith and I would like to invite the two of you to come live with us at Corlach Castle. Each of you will have your own rooms. We have so many rooms that are sitting empty. You are family. Plus, you will be close to Rhixon. What do you think?" Azohr asked.

Azalea stood up, looked at Antha, who nodded, and looked at Azohr, "Great idea. We accept. The goblins can bring all of our things. We will ride our horses, Fran and Fizzy. I will come back to the garden. It's so relaxing."

The three of them rode back to Corlach Castle, Aruzith was in the courtyard when they arrived. "Welcome Azalea and Antha! We are glad to have you here. Please leave your horses, and I will show you to your rooms."

They dismounted and followed her. "This is your room Antha. I hope that you like it." Azalea and Aruzith walked on to the next room. "This is your room. I hope it is to your liking. I am really excited to have you both here. It will be great to have more witches here than wizards."

"Thank you, yes, I love this room. It's actually much roomier than what I had at my little home. I will be going back to my garden periodically. I can bring back the vegetables to help provide for the meals. If you like, I can do a garden right here in the castle."

Aruzith said, "We will talk to Azohr about a garden right here. Ogrok will let you know when dinner is, and I will leave you to get settled."

Back in the courtyard, Azohr sat by the fireplace and wrote in his journal. Aruzith walked up to him, "We have a full castle now. I love it." She gave him a hug.

Chapter 58

There was a rainbow that arched over Maerith Kingdom. Arietta sat in her chair by the fireplace in the courtyard of Eagleview Castle and admired it.

Avras sat at the table in his room. He saw the rainbow out his window. There were eagles that flew over the castle.

Aslan and Raja sat outside the castle and watched the eagles. Amaranth flew in on Ranios the black Pegasus. She walked up to Arietta, "How are you feeling?" I do believe it is almost time for your little witch to make her appearance."

"Oh, I think she's going to stay a bit longer. No pains so far. We will be able to have a nice visit. I heard that Azohr and Aruzith took in Azalea, Rhixon, and Antha." Arietta mentioned.

"I had not heard that yet. That will be a nice arrangement. I am sure that Azohr is going to help Rhixon become a great wizard."

"That would be nice of him to do that. Do you know why he would take them all in?" Arietta questioned.

Amaranth smiled, "Yes, I do. Azalea and Azohr are siblings."

The two of them continued to talk about various topics such as the children, the weather, and more. Avras sat at his table and wrote in his journal.

Dear little witch,

You are the first of many children that your mother and I will have. We are hoping for a great many. As many as the Power of the Holy Dimension will grant us.

As is tradition, I will give you some family history. My father and mother kept to themselves. My father, Zuxon, is from a long line of good wizards. My mother, Saffron, is from a long line of good witches. They grew up together on another island, Toltara Enclave. It's not too far from Maerith Kingdom. When they lived here it was called Parrcaster Island.

Why did they come to Parrcaster Island? They were told that this new island would afford them a great place to live and raise a family. I am happy that they did. I met your mother on this island. She was in a neighboring region. I would sneak over to Xoba and visit her. We would go to the beach, and ride horses.

I look forward to you making me a father. I can't wait to see you in person. You are so special. I will see you soon, little witch. I will write to you again.

Avras looked out his window to the courtyard where Arietta was in her chair. It made him smile to see her so pregnant.

Arietta winced. Amaranth noticed, "Hey, was that a wince? Are you feeling pain?"

"Yes and yes. It is all of a sudden and it's coming quickly again and again. Yikes, again."

"Ok, I will go get some towels from the kitchen. I think this little one is coming right now." She walked off to the kitchen, "Hi Treizig, can I have some towels? The little witch is arriving."

He handed her some towels, "When you are done with them, just place them in the bin."

Amaranth returned to the courtyard next to Arietta, "How are the pains?"

"Coming closer and closer together. How do you know when to push? You did such a great job delivering Amaryllis and Alyssum."

"You will get a pain so great that you can't help but to push."

"That is right now." She pushed, took a breath, and then pushed some more. The next push, the little witch came out, and cried.

Amaranth took the little witch, cleaned her up, and handed her to Arietta. "Congratulations for having such a beautiful little witch."

Ash landed on the hearth of the fireplace, "Is there news?"

"Yes, Ash, there is news. Go back to Rissingshire and bring back Odulore, Amaryllis, and Alyssum. He needs to do the naming ceremony." He flew off over the Demack Grassland.

"Odulore! Odulore! Your presence is requested at Eagleview Castle. The little witch has been born and needs to have the naming ceremony."

"Very well, I will get the little witches together, and we will be there. Thank you."

Odulore gathered Amaryllis and Alyssum together. They got into a carriage and flew off to Eagleview Castle.

Back at Eagleview Castle, Avras came out of his office when he heard the cry of the little witch. He kneeled down by Arietta and the little witch. "Oh, such a beautiful little one. She looks like her mother."

Arietta smiled at him as she held the little witch on her chest. She found her breast and latched on quickly. Arietta thought to herself, *Oh what a wonderful feeling. My wizard, my little witch, and friends. My heart is full.*

The carriage landed outside the castle. Odulore helped the little witches out and into the castle. "I hear we have a new little witch. How is everyone doing?"

"They are doing well. I assume you are here to do the naming ceremony. We want to keep it simple and with a small group of friends and family. Basically, just us," Avras said.

"I understand. We can do the simple ceremony. Are you ready? Do you have a name?"

"Yes, we do have a name for her, and we are ready."

"Ok, we'll start. We are gathered here for the naming ceremony of the little witch of Avras and Arietta. We are here to bring the hedge of protection through the Power of the Holy Dimension to this little witch. This hedge of protection will be with her until she marries. Do you have a name for her?"

"Yes," they both answered.

"What is the name of this little witch?"

"Her name is Azula."

"Welcome Azula to the hedge of protection through the Power of the Holy Dimension. We welcome Azula to Maerith Kingdom."

They all hugged. Amaryllis jumped up and down and yelled, "YEAH! Another witch!"

"It's meal time," Treizig announced from the dining hall. They all went into the dining hall to eat. However, Amaryllis fell asleep in her high chair. Her mind drifted off into dreamland.

Stardust galloped through the grassland and over to the river. She jumped into the sky and over the rainbow. A trail of sparkles followed her everywhere she went.

She was joined by Starburst, and they ran together with sparkles flying everywhere.

Stardust was a white unicorn with purple sparkles throughout her coat and mane. Her horn was white and purple spiral striped.

Starburst was a white unicorn with multi-color sparkles throughout her coat and mane. Even Her horn was multiple colors that spiraled together.

The unicorns flew to the beach and out over the water. They went so far that they disappeared, and then they flew back. They took turns jumping over the rainbow.

Amaryllis watched from her crib. Stardust walked up to her and let her climb onto her back. Starburst had Keeva on her back. They galloped through the Calegan Forest and the Demack Grassland.

They stopped by Tortoise Lake where the unicorns proceed through the water. The little witches giggled on their backs. The witches got down and played in the water. The unicorns stayed next to the little witches. They picked them up by their horn, put the on their backs, and galloped off.

The unicorns dropped them off in their cribs.

Amaryllis woke up in her high chair. “Dream, dream, unicorns,” She said.

“What about unicorns?”, asked her mother.

“I dreamed of unicorns.”

“I am happy for you. Unicorns are good luck.”

Chapter 59

A white cloud covered Maerith Kingdom, Odulore was out in the castle courtyard with Qbaris, Avras, Azohr, Rhixon, Tizohr, Dhenaxx, and Zaveus. Bright lights and streaks of lights came from the clouds. They watched to see what else would happen.

"The clouds are white, so that's better than dark. I would say that these are coming from the Holy Dimension, but I do not know why," Odulore stated.

It was about 30 minutes later, Xodius arrived at Rissingshire Castle. "What's going on?"

"We have no idea yet. Wait with us."

In a short time Staedan and Drozan arrived. "No, we do not know what's going yet. Do you two have any ideas?" Qbaris asked them.

"No, we were wondering if you guys did."

"It started out as a single small cloud, and it expanded to cover the entire sky. Slowly the bright lights and streaks of lights started coming in also," Odulore told them.

The streaks of lights came closer together. The clouds began to swirl around the castle. They got faster and faster. Soon there was thunder along with the lightning above the castle.

The wizards watched the sky. Odulore called out, "Who is in the clouds? Is there anyone in the clouds? If there is, please show yourself."

A bright light blinded them all for a moment, and when the light went away, Trodus and Tatiana appeared before the wizards.

"Wizards! We are here to help you. There is coming a day very soon where the Dark Underworld is going to rise up and you are going to have to be prepared for it. They are going to bring all their evil powers to try to take over the island. Although it's been quiet, it is brewing. Are you ready?"

"Yes, we are ready," Odulore replied.

"We are going to need Amaranth as well. Plus Qbaris, you will also play a vital role. They are going to use Qrizor, Zaleria, and Crumazz to lead the charge. Amaranth and Qbaris' powers will work stronger against them than anyone else. We will need to practice pooling our powers together. This is not going to be easy," Trodus informed.

Tatiana spoke up, "I will help with Amaranth. She's going to have to really pull from all of her strength. Her defenses that she wants to use to protect her witches. That's going to have come through, even though her mother, father, and brother will be right in front of her."

"How many witches and wizards are we going to need?" Azohr questioned.

Trodus nodded, "That's a very good question. I would say that we want as many as possible. We will really need any that are children of Qrizor. Their powers will help. They do need to be the older ones. The younger ones will be too impressionable."

"We do have Rhixon, here, that is a child of Qrizor. He is here to learn how to be a wizard. He can help," Azohr mentioned.

"Oh good. Are there any other witches and wizards that are his children that are over the age of twelve?" Odulore asked.

Qbaris spoke up, “Yes, in fact, there are fifteen: ten witches and five wizards.”

“We need to bring them here. All of them need to learn how to use their powers. Tatiana will work with the witches. I will work with all of you wizards. Go get them right away.”

The wizards took off to Zodel Region. Azohr and Rhixon went to Corlach Castle to bring back Antha. Tizohr went to Onyx’s little home to bring back Jade, Rhodonite, and Sapphire. Dhenaxx went to bring back Okius, Thaxeor, and Zinaxx. Zaveus went to the Dravocia Region for Tia, Cedonia, Artemis, Samara, Shyla, Raven, Topaz, and Arabella.

Within the hour they all returned to Rissingshire Castle. They stood before Odulore and Tatiana. Amaranth and her witches council all joined them. Odulore started, “I will take the wizards, and we will go through how to use your powers and Tatiana will take all the witches and do the same. This is going to take the remainder of the day. We will work on it until the power of the Dark Underworld returns.”

“Witches, come with me. We will be working in the courtyard over by the livery,” Tatiana informed them. They all followed her to the other courtyard.

The wizards remained in the courtyard with Trodus. “First thing we need to get straight is that our power comes from the Holy Dimension. Without this, you have no powers that will be of good. We are going to start with calling upon the Holy Dimension.

Holy Dimension, please be with us. Please give us the good powers to defeat the evil powers of the Dark Underworld. Put an extra protective hedge around the wizards and witches of this island. We dedicate this fight with evil to your glory.

Next up, we will work on throwing our good energy to combine energy that will go against evil energy.

Let's line up side by side. I am going to give you an order to line up in. This will assist you in maximizing your powers. Odulore, Qbaris, Avras, Xodius, Staedan, Azohr, Rhixon, Okius, Thaxeor, Zinaxx, Drozan, Tizohr, Dhenaxx, and Zaveus." They all line up in order.

"Next you will all raise your arms with your hands pointing out front. Keep your arms straight and hands pointed at where the evil energy is coming from. You will either go directly against the evil energy or the evil being. Understood?"

They all nodded and shouted, "Understood!"

"Ok, on the count of three you will shout, Morinius Annoenis, and then you'll see the bright white energy go out from your fingers and it will fight against the evil energy. Their energy will be in a red or orange color. Ready? Here we go. Three, Two, One."

"Morinius Annoenis!" They all shouted. White energy shot from their fingers and made a barrier, being that there was no evil energy for it to fight against.

Trodus commented, "Great. We will continue to do this a few more times. Then we will take a break. This energy will take a lot out of you. We will need to make sure that you eat very well with lots of meat and potatoes. Let's do it again. Three, two, one."

"Morinius Annoenis!" They shouted again.

This went on for thirty minutes, and then they sat around the fireplace for a bit to regain their energy. They snacked on venison jerky.

Meanwhile, Tatiana had the witches also practicing. "Witches, we need to work on casting a spell. Our spell uses crystals. Part of our strength comes through the crystals. All of our strength comes from the Holy Dimension. Before we get started, we will call on the Holy Dimension.

Holy Dimension, come to us, be with us. We ask that you provide us with your strength and power. We ask that you extend an extra hedge of protection around the wizards and witches. We dedicate this fight against evil to your glory.

Let's get started. First thing we need is the crystals. We will use the Amethyst for protection, Jade for abundance, Peridot for positivity, Citrine will dissipate negative energy, Blue Howlite will absorb anger, Sodalite for endurance, Agate for strength, Ematite to guard against negative energy, Smoky Quartz will prevent fatigue, Black Obsidian is a spiritual protector, Cherry Quartz for peace, and Quartz will magnify the other crystals. Each witch will grab a crystal. When we line up, we will either be in front of, alongside or behind the wizards. This all depends on where the evil energy is coming from. We want to make sure that we are working with the wizards. Now line up in this order: Amaranth, Arietta, Zolya, Shelyn, Antha, Jade, Rhodonite, Sapphire, Tia, Cedonia, Artemis, Samara, Shyla, Raven, Topaz, Arabella, Armina, Phaopra, Litrixi, and Zudarina.

After you are all lined up with your crystals, we will then shout Morinius Annoenis on the count of three. When you are with the wizards, you will all shout together. Ready witches?"

"Ready!" They all shouted.

"Three, two, one."

"Morinius Annoenis!"

"Let's do that again. Three, two, one."

"Morinius Annoenis!"

They kept working on it for the next thirty minutes. Then they took a break to enjoy a snack of venison jerky.

Trodus walked over, "Tatiana, let's get them all together and practice some more after their snack." She nodded. He went back to the wizards. After their break, the witches walked over to join the wizards.

"Ok, now we are going to all practice together. The first practice is going to be with the witches in front of the wizards. Then the second practice we will have the witches alongside the wizards, and then they move to make a "V" with the witches facing away. Finally, we will do one practice with the witches back to back with the wizards. First practice lineup, now."

All the witches and wizards lineup in the order they practiced. The witches had the crystals in their hands. Trodus shouted, "Three, two, one."

"Morinius Annoenis!" All the witches and wizards shouted.

"Great! Next, let's do the "V."" The witches moved.

"Three, two, one."

"Morinius Annoenis!" They all shouted.

"Perfect, now back to back."

"Morinius Annoenis!" They all shouted.

"Great! Let's take a break."

The witches and wizards sat down and had more venison jerky. Zizor brought out water for them.

This continued until late into the evening. Trodus told them, "We will resume this tomorrow." The witches and wizards departed the castle.

Trodus and Tatiana sat down with Odulore and Amaranth. "You know this is going to take a lot of positive energy. This is going to be an exhausting time. This is serious business. You two will need to do more than your best. The results of this encounter will be for the island. Also, if we put enough positive energy behind this we could destroy the Dark Underworld." Trodus informed them.

Odulore inquired, "So, if we do this right than we could destroy the Dark Underworld?"

"Yes, yes, that is correct."

"We will get this to work. We will destroy them!"

The wizards and witches waited for the Dark Underworld to appear.

Chapter 60

Ozrig called out, “Qrizor! Zaleria! Crumazz!” They appeared before him.

“Yes!” They answered him.

Ozrig announced, “We are going to Parrcaster Island. You three are coming with me. We are going to take over the island. You are going to help me. We are going to destroy everyone on the island!”

“What! We are going to do what?” Zaleria questioned.

“You heard me. We are going to take over the island and destroy everyone on it! This island has always been in my sights. I want to destroy all those good witches and wizards. They are so good it’s sickening. I want the island to be mine! All mine!”

“You want to destroy everyone?” Qrizor asked.

“Yes! What is it with you three? Did you not hear me when I told you what I wanted to do? Why the questions? I want to destroy the island. The witches, the wizards, the animals, the mystical forest creatures, ALL of them! Now, are you with me or not?”

Zaleria said, “I can’t do it. I still have two children on the island. I cannot and will not destroy them. I don’t care how good they are!”

“Why does that not surprise me? You are too soft. You can go back to the children’s cave. What about you two? Qrizor? Crumazz? Are you two too soft?” Ozrig sneered at them.

"I will go with you. I abandoned all those children for a reason. They are all too good. I will gladly destroy the whole island with you," Qrizor stated.

"Crumazz, you are quiet. You haven't said anything."

"Yes, I will go with you. My own sister banished me. She wanted me dead. So, I will gladly go back and destroy that island. I did not have anyone that came to my defense," Crumazz told him.

"We will be heading out just before sun down. I prefer it to be dark. I like the darkness. It will be the three of us. Now, go back to the cave and I will call you when you are needed. That's all."

Meanwhile, back at Rissingshire Castle, the witches and wizards gathered together in the courtyard. Trodus and Tatiana stood in front of them. "We are going to work on making sure that we have all our possible power. First we will draw on the hedge of protective power from the Holy Dimension. Then we will eat a hearty meal that Zizor has prepared for us. After we eat, we will keep an eye on the sky, especially as it gets close to sun down. Ozrig prefers it dark.

We call on you Holy Dimension. Please extend your protective hedge to this island. Extend your holy hand around each witch, wizard, and creature. We dedicate this island, these witches, wizards, creatures, and this fight with evil to you. Thank you for your protection.

Ok, everyone. Let's eat!" Trodus instructed.

They all got up and walked into the dining hall. Zizor and the goblins brought out the trays of food. Odulore spoke up, "I am happy to have all of you here. I wish it was under different circumstances. Enjoy the meal that Zizor has prepared for us a hearty venison, potato, and root vegetable stew. Eat up!"

The goblins brought out extra bowls of stew and set them along the table. Then they set out pitchers of water.

After they ate, the wizards and witches went back out to the courtyard. It was silent as they watched for the sun to start to set.

Slowly the sky started to grow dark. The wizards and witches lined up in a "V" to keep an eye on the sky. The witches had their crystals in their hands.

A dark cloud started across the sky and moved in the direction of the castle. It moved closer and closer. Trodus shouted, "Ready! We are going to start repeating the phrase over and over. We are not waiting for them to get too close. On the count of three, two, one!"

"Morinius Annoenis! Morinius Annoenis! Morinius Annoenis! Morinius Annoenis! Morinius Annoenis! Morinius Annoenis!"

A bright light went through the crystals of the witches and emanated from their hands. When the light hit the dark cloud, it started to separate.

Trodus instructed, "Let's keep chanting and keep moving to the edge of the water."

"Morinius Annoenis! Morinius Annoenis! Morinius Annoenis! Morinius Annoenis! Morinius Annoenis! Morinius Annoenis!"

The witches and wizards levitated and chanted all the way to the water's edge. The bright light got stronger and brighter.

Ozrig, Qrizor, and Crumazz raised their arms and sent their evil orange energy straight for the bright light energy that was being sent their way.

Both energies were strong and stood their ground for a couple of hours. Then the orange energy would make headway and then the bright light energy would make headway.

The orange energy started to separate again. Qrizor and Crumazz broke off from Ozrig. The witches followed the direction that they went.

The witches and wizards kept chanting "Morinius Annoenis! Morinius Annoenis! Morinius Annoenis! Morinius Annoenis! Morinius Annoenis! Morinius Annoenis!"

Trodus could see that the witches and wizards were going to get tired soon from the strained look on their faces. So, he called out, "Almighty Power of Holy Dimension, please bring down your holy hand and take this fight from us. Please take away the Dark Underworld. Take them from this island. Take them from this world."

The bright light energy expanded in size and brightness to the point it temporarily blinded the witches and wizards, and then there was a loud boom, and the orange energy vaporized instantly. Ozrig, Qrizor, and Crumazz were gone. The sky cleared and there was no trace of the Dark Underworld.

Trodus announced, "They are gone. With that loud boom, they were destroyed. They were not banished. You will no longer have to worry about the Dark Underworld. Let's go back to the castle to celebrate."

The witches and wizards returned to the castle. They all sat down in the courtyard. Tatiana stood up on the hearth of the fireplace and said, "I am so proud of all of you. I realize that took a lot of energy out of you also. Zizor will be bringing out water and the goblins will have venison jerky."

After a half an hour, Odulore stood up, and announced, "I want to thank everyone for all of their hard work. I want to especially thank my father and mother, Trodus and Tatiana, for coming back here and bringing us the extra protection from the Holy Dimension. With all of your help and theirs we have defeated the Dark Underworld. They are gone. I am so relieved. I know you had the venison jerky for a snack, but the goblins have made more venison stew with potatoes and root vegetables. Shortly there will be a band of trolls coming to play music along. Plus, the rest of the island witches, wizards, and creatures will join us for this great celebration. Thank you again and enjoy the day!"

"It's been our pleasure to come back. The first time for splitting off the witches' coven, the next for the wedding of Odulore and Amaranth, for Amaryllis' naming ceremony, and now to eliminate the Dark Underworld. We would like to stay to celebrate with you, but unfortunately we cannot stay. I do not know when we will be back," Trodus stated. He took Tatiana's hand, and they were whisked away in white clouds.

Chapter 61

Amaranth sat in the courtyard while Amaryllis and Alyssum played on the ground. She turned to the entry to the castle. A wizard and a witch walked through that she had never seen.

"Welcome to Rissingshire Castle! I am Amaranth. Who are you?"

"I am Zuxon and this is Saffron. We have come here from Toltara Enclave across the Kiniriden Sea to the east." He told her.

Odulore walked out from his room, "Welcome! What brings you here? We are not the closest to the water?"

Zuxon went to him, "Our wizard son, Avras lives on this island. We know that he lives in Maerith Kingdom. We came to see him. Do you know which castle he lives in?"

"They live in the castle that is just northwest of us across the Demack Grassland. It's called Eagleview Castle. They will have tigers by the entry." Odulore explained.

Saffron said, "Thank you. We will take our dragons over there."

They turned, walked out of the castle to their dragons, and flew over to Eagleview Castle. The dragons landed on the ground in front of Aslan and Raja, the tigers that guard the castle.

"State your business," Aslan told them.

"We are Zuxon and Saffron. We are here to see Avras."

Aslan walked into the castle courtyard, "Avras, You have visitors. Their names are Zuxon and Saffron. Shall we show them in?"

"Yes, please do. They are my parents and I haven't seen them since I have been here," Avras excitedly told him. He stood up and waited for them to be shown in.

"Mother! Father! It is so good to see you both. What brings you here?" Avras hugged them both. "Arietta! Come quick! Bring Azula!"

She ran out of her room with Azula in her arms. "What?"

"I want to introduce you to my parents. They are here from Toltara Enclave." Avras took Arietta and Azula, and walked up to his mother and father, "I would like to introduce you to my wife, Arietta, and our daughter, Azula. This is my father, Zuxon, and my mother, Saffron."

"Pleased to meet you," they all said.

Avras said, "Come, sit, we'll talk in the courtyard." They all sat in the courtyard.

"What brings you here?" Arietta asked.

Zuxon responded, "We wanted to see you. Plus, we wanted to find out who we talk to about having Toltara Enclave added to Maerith Kingdom."

"I am glad that you came. To be a part of Maerith Kingdom, you will need to go before the Grand Master Wizard Odulore and his council. I am his Official Record Keeper."

"Oh how wonderful, do I go to him directly or is there a regular time that they get together?" Zuxon inquired.

"I will send Artimas over to Rissingshire Castle to let him know your request." He shouted out, "Artimas!"

He came right away. "Please fly over to Rissingshire Castle and let Odulore know that Zuxon is over here. He has come to ask for Toltara Enclave to become a part of the Maerith Kingdom." Artimas flew out of the castle.

Odulore sat at his table in his room. Artimas walked in, "I bring you a message from Avras. Zuxon is over at Eagleview Castle. He is asking for Toltara Enclave to become a part of Maerith Kingdom."

"Please send word back for them to come to Rissingshire Castle in a couple of hours. I'll send word out to the rest of the council. Thanks." Artimas left and went back to Eagleview Castle.

"Ash! Oldirrim!" Odulore shouted. They flew in and landed on his table. "I need you to go around the council and let them all know to meet here in a couple of hours. We have an island that wants to join in Maerith Kingdom." The owls flew off.

Back at Eagleview Castle, Saffron asked, "How old is Azula?"

"She is a month old," Arietta responded.

"She is so adorable. Can I hold her?"

"Yes," she handed her to Saffron.

Artimas landed in the courtyard, "Come to Rissingshire Castle in a couple of hours. He is sending the word out to the rest of the council."

"Perfect, we have time to sit here and enjoy the sunshine. When we go over, it'll be just the two of us."

Zuxon and Avras flew off to Rissingshire Castle after a couple of hours. They landed outside the castle, and walked into the dining hall.

All of the council was in the dining. Odulore was at the head of the table. "Welcome Zuxon! I am glad to have you here. I have heard that you want to have your island, which is called Toltara Enclave, included in Maerith Kingdom. Is that correct?"

"Thank you. Yes, that is what we'd like. What is the process that we need to go through to do this?"

"It's pretty simple. You are the head wizard of Toltara Enclave, correct?"

"Yes, we don't have much of a government or anything. I am the oldest on the island, so they ask me questions on what to do."

"Ok, we will need to vote on whether or not we want the island to join us. Wizards, any questions?"

Azohr asked, "My question is, what kind of people and creatures do you have? Are they good? Do you have any problems with evil?"

"We don't have any problems on the island. Everyone just does their own thing and leaves everyone else alone," Zuxon replied.

Odulore questioned, "All right, that's a good thing. We just got rid of the Dark Underworld, so we are not looking for anything evil. We've had our fair share for a bit. Let's take a vote. Avras, make sure to write down who votes which way. We'll go around the table and then I will cast the final vote. Give your name and your vote."

"Qbaris, I vote yes."

"Azohr, I vote yes."

"Tizohr, I vote yes."

"Zaveus, I vote yes."

"Dhenaxx, I vote yes."

"Avras, I vote yes."

"Odulore, I vote yes."

"That was a unanimous vote for yes," Avras reported.

"I am happy to report that Toltara Enclave is admitted into the Maerith Kingdom. With you being the head wizard of the island, we will make you the Advisor Wizard of Toltara Enclave. We welcome you to Maerith Kingdom!" Odulore announced.

Zuxon smiled, "Thank you! I can't wait to let them all know."

"We are done here for now. Have a great day!"

The wizards all departed the castle. Avras and Zuxon arrived at Eagleview Castle. They joined Saffron, Arietta, and Azula in the courtyard. "How did it go?" Arietta inquired.

Zuxon replied, "It went great! We are now a part of the Maerith Kingdom, and I am the Advisor Wizard of Toltara Enclave."

"That means that you, Saffron, are the Advisor Witch of Toltara Enclave. It really is a great position. Amaranth is a great witch to work with."

They continued to talk by the fireplace for a couple of hours. "I am going to go lay Azula down. She's getting sleepy. I'll be back."

Avras inquired, "Why do you all of a sudden want to be a part of Maerith Kingdom? I know what you told them, but really, what's up? I've been over here a while and you have not visited."

"We knew that you wanted to be on your own. You have this great castle that was your great uncle's, and now you have your own family. As far as why become part of the Maerith Kingdom, why not? We have heard great things about Odulore, especially with him defeating the Dark Underworld. That is the best," Zuxon responded.

"I know this was his castle. I love that we live here. It doesn't answer why you have never been over. You did not come to our wedding, nor did you come for Azula's naming ceremony."

Saffron looked at him, "You did not give us enough notice to come for the naming ceremony. As for the wedding, your father was not doing well. Thankfully, he is better now."

"Ok, well, now that you are a part of the kingdom, you will have to be able to come when Odulore requests for meetings, like we did today. You only get a couple of hours notice," Avras said, shook his head, and rolled his eyes.

Arietta sat down next to him, "What did I miss?"

"I'll tell you later."

"Well, I think we should be going. We will return soon," Zuxon said and put his hand on Saffron's shoulder.

They had a group family hug. Zuxon and Saffron took off on their dragons. Arietta asked Avras again, "So, what did I miss?"

"Just my parents giving excuses of why they didn't come to our wedding and Azula's naming ceremony."

"Oh, give them a break. It's not like they live on this island."

"I know, but they flew over here to be a part of the kingdom."

They laid back in their chairs to watch the stars up in the sky.

Chapter 62

Amaranth went for a walk with Amaryllis and Alyssum in the Demack Grassland. As they walked, they found themselves by Bredenrath Pond. The three witches looked into the water. They saw red and blue fish swimming.

The blue fish swam to them, popped his head out of the water, and said, "Hello sweet witches, are you having a good day?"

"Yes, we are," Amaryllis replied. "What's your name?"

"My name is Dewdrop. What's yours?"

"I am Amaryllis. This is my mother, Amaranth, and my sister witch Alyssum."

A red fish came up beside Dewdrop, and popped her head out of the water, "Hi everyone!"

"I am Amaryllis. What's your name?"

"My name is Garnet. Today is as beautiful as the three of you."

The fireflies came up and danced above the fish. The little witches giggled. Amaranth smiled and said, "Thank you. Today is a beautiful day. We are spending the day walking around the province."

After the fireflies flew away and the fish went back into the water, the three witches walked around the edge of the pond and walked into the Calegan Forest. Alyssum started to get excited. She was kicking her feet and reaching out her arms.

Amaranth winced and said, “Hey watch it little witch, you are kicking me.” She thought to herself, *This little one is so lucky to be carried, but man, she has a kick.*

“I saw it!” Amaryllis yelled.

“What did you see?”

“I saw the purple and white horn!”

“What are you talking about?”

“The unicorn, Stardust. I her purple and white horn.”

“Where?”

“Way up there.”

They walked in the direction that Amaryllis pointed. The little witch was determined to find Stardust. She marched quickly through the forest. A troll came up and walked beside them. “Where are you going?”

“We are going to find Stardust,” Amaryllis told him.

“Oh really? Who is Stardust?”

“She’s a unicorn. I saw her up ahead.”

The four of them continued on a worn path through the forest. Another troll came up and walked beside them.

“Where are you going? Can I come too?”

Amaryllis looked at the troll and told him, “We are going to find Stardust. Yes, you can come along.”

“Who is Stardust?”

"My unicorn friend."

The troll nodded his head and walked alongside them. Shortly there were fairies that flew by them as they walked. Amaranth turned, while she walked, and looked at all the creatures that joined them as they walked. There were pixies, rabbits, and squirrels along with the fairies and trolls.

They arrived at the edge of the Calegan Forest, which was right by the Lavalbourg Gorge. At the far edge of the river there was a waterfall. The witches were excited to see a family of unicorns drinking by it. They slowly walked in their direction. The unicorns raised their heads to watch them.

Amaranth, Amaryllis, Alyssum, and all the creatures stood close by the unicorns as they all looked at each other. There was a long silence. Amaryllis broke it, "I am looking for Stardust and Starburst. I thought I saw Stardust in the Calegan Forest."

"My name is Sparkles. Stardust and Starburst should be around here somewhere. We all live behind the waterfall. We call this place Rainbow Falls."

"I am Amaranth. This is Amaryllis and Alyssum. These are our creature friends."

"Can we see Stardust and Starburst? They have been in my dreams." Amaryllis asked.

"Yes, we do come to those that have a creative imagination. Some will see us in their dreams only and others will be able to see us in person. You three are lucky. Not all of the witches and wizards will see us."

Two unicorns came flying out through the waterfall and landed on the shore next to the witches. Alyssum squealed, kicked and waved her arms when she saw them.

"Stardust! Starburst!" Amaryllis shouted.

The two unicorns went up and nuzzled the little witches. "How did you find us?" Stardust asked.

Amaryllis answered, "We saw you from a distance in the forest. So, we followed what direction you went."

"You must be very observant. Normally, no one sees us in the forest," Starburst told her.

"I was hoping we would see you while we went for a walk. I have seen you both in my dreams."

"Yes, that is where most children see us. There are a few lucky ones, such as yourselves that get to see us in person. Did you meet Sparkles? We have a couple of dozen unicorns that live behind the waterfall. If you'd like, we can take you there."

Amaranth inquired, "Does that include me or is this for the little ones?"

"Yes, you may come as well. You are able to see us, which tells me that you are a believer in unicorns. Those that do not believe, cannot see us," Starburst answered. "You will need to ride on our backs and hold onto our manes."

The witches got on their backs, Amaryllis got on Stardust and Amaranth with Alyssum on Stardust. The unicorns took off, and they went through the waterfall without getting wet. Behind the waterfall was a cave that sparkled from all different colored crystals. There were pink, purple, blue, green, red, yellow, orange, and white crystals. The unicorns were the same colors. Some were multi-colors. It was bright for being in a cave. There were rainbows all over the place.

"Welcome to Rainbow Falls. I am the king unicorn, my name is Solstice. This is my queen, Aurora. What are your names?"

"I am Amaryllis. This is my mother, Amaranth, and my sister witch, Alyssum."

"Pleased to meet you all. We are going to have a celebration meal. Would you like to join us?"

"Yes, that would be wonderful," Amaranth replied.

"Great, let's go to the celebration cave. Follow us." The unicorns led them to another cave that was decorated with clouds made of cotton candy, mini cakes of all colors, and tables of candy.

"We will be bringing out the food, don't worry, we have more than just candy. I hope that like carrots, beets, celery, corn, and other vegetables."

"Yes, the little witches and I like them very much."

"One thing to let you know before it comes out. The vegetables will be of a variety of colors. We have carrots that are purple, beets that are blue, celery in pink, corn is multi-color, and we also have lettuce that is lavender in color. They all taste the same as what you are used to."

"Adventures in food!" Amaryllis shouted.

"Yes, that is a great way to look at it. Adventures in food. I hope you like your adventure."

The gnomes brought out the food and placed the trays on the tables. "Please enjoy!" One of them told the witches.

"I want a purple carrot," Amaryllis announced.

"You can have one. You have more than one if you like it."

They ate the vegetables, and sat back to enjoy looking at the decorations. "Ok, now that you have had the vegetables, you can eat the cakes and candies," Solstice told them.

Amaryllis took a bite of a yellow cake, "I love lemon! This is yummy!"

"I agree with you, and so does Alyssum. She is loving all this food," Amaranth added.

After their goodies, they stood up, "What else is in these caves?"

"Let's go to our crystal room. I am sure you will like that," Aurora motioned for them to follow her.

When they entered the crystal cave, it was beautiful, and bright. There were crystals of shapes, sizes, and colors all over the walls and ceiling.

"You were so right. These are beautiful. I can't imagine anything more beautiful. There are so many colors."

The witches inched closer to the crystals so that they could see all the details on them. "Is this how you make the rainbows?" Amaryllis questioned.

"Yes, we do make the rainbows and we use the crystals to do so, along with the waterfall. Thus, why we call it Rainbow Falls."

"We should be getting back. We were only going for a walk. I am sure their father is worried about where we have been for so long," Amaranth said.

Aurora smiled, "Yes, we don't want him to worry. Starburst and Stardust will take you back on the other side. You can come visit us any time you like. We love visitors."

The witches got on the backs of the unicorns, and in a few short minutes they flew back through the waterfall and were on the shore of the river.

“Bye!” They all said to the unicorns as they flew back through the waterfall.

“Well witches, it is time to walk back to the castle. How was that for an afternoon?”

“I love it! I got to meet the unicorns from my dreams,” Amaryllis said with excitement.

The three witches walked back into the forest where the forest creatures followed them. A troll looked up at Amaranth, “Did you like your trip behind the waterfall?”

“Yes we did.”

“They don’t let us trolls back there. The unicorns told us that they trust trolls.”

“Interesting.”

They continued their walk, and came upon Ash and Oldirrim. They were flying around the forest. “Hey, what are you two up to?” Amaranth inquired.

“We are looking for you. Where have you been? You three have been gone for quite a few hours,” Ash blinked his big eyes at them.

“We went to the Rainbow Falls and saw the unicorns,” Amaryllis told them.

"You saw unicorns? Ok, well, Odulore was looking for you three. Something is going on and he needs you Amaranth," Oldirrim told her.

The owls flew next to the witches as they walked out of the forest and through the grassland. They were greeted by Puggaald and Glurx when they entered the castle.

"Odulore needs you Amaranth. He is in his room. We'll take the little witches to their rooms," Glurx told her.

"Thank you."

She gave Alyssum to Glurx and walked into Odulore's room. "I heard you were looking for me."

"Yes, we need to go through these journals. Something is odd about Toltara Enclave. We will need to go there," He told her.

"Ok, when are we going?"

"As soon as the wizards and witches get here. The goblins and ogres will take care of the children while we are gone."

GLOSSARY

Creatures

Annamaaz–female demon in the Dark Underworld that is the companion to Ozrig.

Artimas–winged lion companion of Avras

Ash–brown barn owl

Aslan–Tiger at the entrance to Eagleview Castle

Aurora–queen unicorn

Axe–winged lion companion of Avras

Chrono–owl that lives at Glottenham Castle

Chrysonia– female centaur in the Calegan Forest

Darca–Great Dane that lives at Miserth Castle

Dax–Great Dane that lives at Miserth Castle

Dewdrop–blue fish that lives in Bredenrath Pond.

Evatius–centaur

Fenian–head elf at Langdale Castle

Flickwe–gnome that lives in The Crystal Rose Witches Coven in Xoba Kingdom

Fraevie–bright green dragon, guards Rissingshire Castle

Frally–black, mini evil dragon that lives in the Crystal Crypt

Gairrulit–evil black dragon that lives in the Crystal Crypt

Garnet–red fish that lives in Bredenrath Pond

Glurx–goblin, lives in the Rissingshire Castle and does janitorial work

Irreineot–evil dark red dragon that lives in the Crystal Crypt

Jaril–head angel in the Holy Dimension

Kaspa–black Percheron stallion horse, owned by Rhixon

Kezrin–demon from the Dark Underworld

Korzath–demon from the Dark Underworld that is in charge of the tarantulas.

Magnus–black Percheron stallion horse–19 hands high, owned by Odulore

Moruk–Ogre in Xoba Region

Mystical Forest Creatures–centaurs, barn owls, gnomes, rabbits, pixies, birds and unicorns.

Narella–Gray Selkirk Rex cat

Nesquix–Rabbit

Ogrok–Ogre at Corlach Castle

Oizu–evil black dragon that lives in the Crystal Crypt

Oldirrim–white barn owl that lives in Rissingshire Castle and Calegan Forest.

Ozrig–head demon of the Dark Underworld

Periwinkle–rabbit

Puggaald–goblin that lives in the Crystal Crypt that is silent because of having been in a fight with a wizard when he was young and the wizard took his voice away from him.

Pymmut–evil dark green dragon that lives in Crystal Crypt

Raithy–black Pegasus that lives at Rissingshire Castle

Raja–tiger at the entrance to Eagleview Castle

Ranios–black Pegasus that lives at Rissingshire Castle

Ripshider–head troll of the woodland trolls that live in Calegan Forest

Solstice–King unicorn

Sparkles–unicorn

Starburst–unicorn

Stardust–unicorn

Tamon–pixie that lives in the forest

Treizig–Ogre at Eagleview Castle

Turmodoir–bright green dragon that guards Rissingshire Castle

Valora–black cat that belongs to Amaranth

Zezerm–goblin at Rissingshire Castle

Zizor–Ogre that works in the kitchen at Rissingshire Castle

Zudoz–gargoyle that lives in Zodel Region

Zyrsit–miniature green dragon, he's a good dragon that lives in the Calegan Forest.

Places

Alacana Falls–located in the Lavalbourg Gorge

Bordshall Cove–Glottenham Castle overlooks it and Staedan and Shelyn live there. This is at the far west of Maerith Kingdom.

Bredenrath Pond–pond on the west side of the Calegan Forest

Calegan Forest– the forest across the grassland from Rissingshire Castle. Lots of mystical creatures live there.

Cardminster Fields–located in Dravocia Kingdom

Corlach Castle–where Azohr lives that is in the next kingdom over

Coven of the Sacred Flame–a group of witches that Qrizor and Crumazz got pregnant, turned into an island, formerly of Xoba Kingdom

Crystal Crypt–where the evil wizard lives along with other evil creatures including witches–Amaranth's mother lived here.

Dark Underworld–where all the evil is banished to when they die

Delorvern Forest - located in Zodel Kingdom

Demack Grassland–between Calegan Forest and Rissingshire Castle.

Dravocia Kingdom - to the north of Maerith Region

Dravocia Region–formerly known as Dravocia Kingdom

Eagleview Castle–overlooks Tortoise Lake, Avras and Arietta live there in Maerith Kingdom

Glassy Lagoon–Grimtol Castle is in the middle of it. It is also at the far end of the Maerith Kingdom.

Glottenham Castle–overlooks Bordshall Cove. Staedan and Shelyn live there

Grimtol Castle–in the middle of Glassy Lagoon, where Xodius and Zabine live

Holy Dimension–where all the good go when they die

Kiniriden Sea–the water all around the Maerith Kingdom island

Langdale Castle–sits atop the Lavalbourg Gorge; Drozan and Zolya live there

Lavalbourg Gorge–in Maerith Kingdom near the Langdale Castle

Maerith Kingdom–the kingdom that Odulore is head of. At the beginning of the story it includes the Calegan Forest, Demack Grassland and the Rissingshire Castle. Part way through Maerith Kingdom is now the entire island.

Maerith Province–the region formerly known as Maerith Kingdom

Miserth Castle–where Zaleria and Qrizor are taking over

Parrcaster Island–the island where Maerith Kingdom, Dravocia Kingdom, Zallesian Kingdom, Xoba Kingdom, and Zodel Kingdom are located. The name changes to Maerith Kingdom part way through the story.

Permeated Flame Island–what the Dark Underworld calls the island of the witches from the Coven of the Sacred Flame.

Petrobiens Reef–another island that is partially evil, but mainly good

Rainbow Falls–the waterfall in Lavalbourg Gorge

Rissingshire Castle–where Odulore lives and is the head of the Maerith Kingdom.

Sacred Flame Island–what Odulore named the island that was previously the Coven of the Sacred Flame.

Toltara Enclave–the island that Zuxon and Saffron live on

Tortoise Lake–sits near Eagleview Castle

Wargon Forest–located in Xoba Kingdom

Xoba Kingdom–south of Maerith Kingdom, the Coven of the Sacred Flame was here prior to being their own island

Xoba Region–formerly Xoba Kingdom

Zallesian Kingdom–kingdom to the west of Maerith Kingdom

Zallesian Region - formerly Zallesian Kingdom

Zodel Kingdom–the kingdom to the east and just over the mountain

Zodel Region–formerly Zodel Kingdom

Witches & Wizards

Acacia–witch partner of Qrizor, lives in Dravocia Region

Akiye–witch partner of Qrizor, had one set of twin girls plus a girl, lives in Zallesian Kingdom

Alecto– witch partner of Rugast and Vumonar, lives on the Permeated Flame Island

Alyssum–witch daughter of Amaranth and Odulore

Amaranth–witch that came from a long line of evil witches.

Amaryllis–the first witch daughter of Amaranth and Odulore

Arietta–witch that lives at Eagleview Castle with Avras

Armina–witch that lives in Zodel Region

Aruzith–witch wife of Azohr, lives in Zodel Region

Astrid–witch partner of Qrizor in Zodel Kingdom

Avras–Wizard that lives in Eagleview Castle with Arietta

Azalea–witch partner of Qrizor, lives in Zodel Kingdom

Azohr–wizard in the Zodel Kingdom over that can help Odulore with griffins and gargoyles, lives in the Corlach Castle

Azula–witch daughter of Avras and Arietta

Blossom–witch partner of Qrizor, lives in Zallesian Kingdom

Calla–twin to Coral, witch partner of Qrizor, had two sets of twins, one set girls & one set boys, lives in Zallesian Kingdom

Circe–twin to Cordelia, partner of Qrizor, had two sets of twin girls, lives in Dravocia Kingdom

Coral–twin to Calla, witch partner to Qrizor, had two sets of twin girls, lives in Zallesian Kingdom

Cordelia–twin to Circe, witch partner of Qrizor, had two sets of twin girls, lives in Dravocia Kingdom

Crumazz–evil wizard that lives in Crystal Crypt

Cyrena–witch partner of Qrizor, lives in Zodel Kingdom

Dhenaxx–wizard that lives in Dravocia Kingdom

Drozan–wizard that lives at Langdale Castle with Zolya

Echo– witch partner of Qrizor & Crumazz, lives at the Permeated Flame Island in the Xoba Kingdom, had twin girls

Ember– witch partner of Qrizor & Crumazz, lives at the Permeated Flame Island in the Xoba Kingdom, had twin boys

Hakonn–wizard partner of Astrid

Kalliope– witch partner of Rugast and Vumonar, lives on the Permeated Flame Island

Keeva–witch daughter of Qbaris and Armina

Lavinia– witch partner of Rugast and Vumonar, lives on the Permeated Flame Island

Lia–witch partner of Qrizor, lives in Zallesian Kingdom, had 2 boys and a set of twin boys

Litrixi–witch partner of Zaveus, lives in Xoba Region

Mistya– witch partner of Rugast and Vumonar, lives on the Permeated Flame Island

Moira–witch partner of Qrizor & Crumazz, lives at the Permeated Flame Island in the Xoba Kingdom

Myra- witch partner of Rugast and Vumonar, lives on the Permeated Flame Island

Nissa– witch partner of Qrizor & Crumazz, lives at the Permeated Flame Island in the Xoba Kingdom

Odulore–good wizard that lives at Rissingshire Castle, in charge of the castle and the kingdom

Onyx–witch partner of Qrizor, lives in Zodel Kingdom

Orchid– witch partner of Rugast and Vumonar, lives on the Permeated Flame Island

Phaopra–witch partner of Tizohr, lives in Zallesian Region

Phoenix–witch partner of Qrizor, lives in Dravocia Kingdom

Piper–witch partner of Qrizor & Crumazz, lives at the Permeated Flame Island in the Xoba Kingdom, had twin girls

Qbaris–wizard that lives at Miserth Castle and is Qrizor's son

Qrizor–Crumazz's father, evil wizard

Raina–witch partner of Qrizor, lives in Xoba Kingdom, had three sets of twin boys

Rose– witch partner of Qrizor & Crumazz, lives at the Permeated Flame Island in the Xoba Kingdom, had triplet girls

Rugast–father of Vumonar, wizard on the Permeated Flame Island

Saffron–witch, mother of Azohr

Shelyn–witch partner of Staedan, lives at Glottenham Castle

Staedan–wizard partner of Shelyn, lives at Glottenham Castle

Starla– witch partner of Qrizor & Crumazz, lives at the Permeated Flame Island in the Xoba Kingdom

Storm– witch partner of Rugast and Vumonar, lives on the Permeated Flame Island

Tatiana–Odulore's mother and Trodus' wife

Tizohr–wizard that live in Zallesian Kingdom

Trodus–Odulore's father, good wizard

Vumonar- son of Rugast, wizard on the Permeated Flame Island

Xantha–witch partner of Qrizor, lives in Xoba Kingdom, had three boys

Xodius–Wizard that lives at Grimtol Castle with Zabine

Xupan–wizard partner of Xantha

Zabine–Witch that lives at Grimtol Castle with Xodius

Zaleria–witch wife of Qrizor, mother of Amaranth, Crumazz and Qbaris

Zaras–father of Zaleria, Qrizor, and Crumazz

Zaveus–wizard that lives in Xoba Kingdom

Zitrix–wizard partner of Raina

Zolya–witch that lives at Langdale Castle with Drozan

Zudarina–witch partner of Dhenaxx, lives in Dravocia Region

Zuxon–wizard, father of Azohr

Qrizor's Children

Acacia & Qrizor

Mardella–daughter

Serafine–daughter

Akiye & Qrizor

Electra–daughter

Euphenia–twin to Evanora, daughter

Evanora–twin to Euphenia, daughter

Astrid & Qrizor

Odaprix–triplet to Odius & Odileus, son

Odileus–triplet to Odius & Odaprix, son

Odius–triplet to Odaprix & Odileus, son

Azalea & Qrizor

Antha–daughter

Rhixon–son

Blossom & Qrizor

Mystia–daughter

Venus–daughter

Willow–daughter

Calla & Qrizor

Agate–twin to Zena, daughter

Ezohr–twin to Odapix, son

Odapix–twin to Ezohr, son

Zena–twin to Agate, daughter

Circe & Qrizor

Arabella–twin to Topaz, daughter
Raven–twin to Shyla, daughter
Shyla–twin to Raven, daughter
Topaz–twin to Arabella, daughter

Coral & Qrizor
Clover–twin to Meadow, daughter
Meadow–twin to Clover, daughter
Oceana–twin to Opal, daughter
Opal–twin to Oceana, daughter

Cordelia & Qrizor
Artemis–twin to Samara, daughter
Cedonia–twin to Tia, daughter
Samara–twin to Artemis, daughter
Tia–twin to Cedonia, daughter

Cyrena & Qrizor
Okius–son
Thaxeor–son
Zinaxx–son

Echo & Qrizor or Crumazz
Ebras–twin to Enior, daughter
Enior–twin to Ebras, daughter
Fawn–twin to Feba, daughter
Feba–twin to Fawn, daughter

Ember & Qrizor or Crumazz
Crenorim–twin to Qrornas, son
Crequam–triplet to Qonaxx and Cruqriv, son
Cruqriv–triplet to Qonaxx and Crequam, son
Qonaxx–triplet to Crequam and Cruqriv, son
Qrornas–twin to Crenorim, son

Lia & Qrizor

Draxeor–son
Shabras–twin to Shudore, son
Shudore–twin to Shabras, son
Ubus–son

Moira & Qrizor or Crumazz
Adonia–daughter
Alaric–twin to Angelic, daughter
Angelic–twin to Alaric, daughter

Nissa & Qrizor or Crumazz
Nicholas–triplet to Nina and Norea, son
Nimue–daughter
Nina–triplet to Norea and Nicholas, daughter
Norea–triplet to Nina and Nicholas, daughter

Onyx & Qrizor
Jade–daughter
Rhodonite–daughter
Sapphire–daughter

Phoenix & Qrizor
Marigold–daughter
Serafina–daughter

Piper & Qrizor or Crumazz
Paige–twin to Peony, daughter
Peony–twin to Paige, daughter
Pepper–triplet to Ursula and Ulva, daughter
Ulva–triplet to Pepper and Ursula, daughter
Ursula–triplet to Pepper and Ulva, daughter

Raina & Qrizor
Azosior–twin to Azutora, son
Azutora–twin to Azosior, son

Elzaviar–twin to Enzatrix, son
Enzatrix–twin to Elzaviar, son
Rhaharis–twin to Rowix, son
Rowix–twin to Rhaharis, son

Rose & Qrizor
Lavina–triplet to Lux and Lilith, daughter

Rose & Qrizor or Crumazz
Lilac–triplet to Lilura & Lydia, daughter
Lilith–triplet to Lavina and Lux, daughter
Lilura–triplet to Lilac & Lydia, daughter
Lux–triplet to Lavina and Lilith, daughter
Lydia–triplet to Lilac & Lilura, daughter

Starla & Qrizor or Crumazz
Maescia–twin to Malise, daughter
Malise–twin to Maescia, daughter
Melusina–daughter

Xantha & Qrizor
Izalenor–son
Oruzohr–son
Zijamar–son

Rugast & Vumonar's Children

Alecto
  Aileen–twin to Alexandra, daughter
  Alexandra–twin to Aileen, daughter

Zaleria
  Aphovae–triplet to Atahith and Aweahl, daughter
  Atahith–triplet to Aphovae and Aweahl, daughter
  Aweahl–triplet to Aphovae and Atahith, daughter

Kalliope
  Kamila–Triplet to Karin and Kestrel, daughter
  Karin–triplet to Kestrel and Kamila, daughter
  Kestrel–triplet to Karin and Kamila, daughter

Mistya
  Marie–triplet to Myrilee and Myrtle, daughter
  Myrilee–triplet to Marie and Myrtle, daughter
  Myrtle–triplet to Marie and Myrilee, daughter

Myra
  Maev–twin to Mina, daughter
  Mina–twin to Maev, daughter

Storm
  Shodelis–triplet to Shumorith and Sipan, son
  Shumorith–triplet to Shodelis and Sipan, son
  Sipan–triplet to Shumorith and Shodelis, son

Lavinia
  Vrasorin–twin to Vrofaris, son
  Vrofaris–twin to Vrasorin, son

Demon Children

Calla & Kezrin

Brerkes–quadruplet to Dokalos, Egmeman, and Urraren, son
Dokalos–quadruplet to Brerkes, Egmeman, and Urraren, son
Egmeman–quadruplet to Brerkes, Dokalos, and Urraren, son
Urraren - quadruplet to Brerkes, Dokalos, and Egmeman, son

Coral & Kezrin

Gorkir–quadruplet to Iggomid, Ruzalek, and Thagruth, son
Iggomid–quadruplet to Gorkir, Ruzalek, and Thagruth, son
Ruzalek–quadruplet to Gorkir, Iggomid, and Thagruth, son
Thagruth–quadruplet to Gorkir, Iggomid, and Ruzalek, son

Orchid & Kezrin

Balvon–quadruplet to Ograth, Ulgrast, and Kurnoth, son
Drazgen–quadruplet to Garzirith, Molvoz, and Sakur, son
Garzirith–quadruplet to Drazgen, Molvoz, and Sakur, son
Kurnoth–quadruplet to Balvon, Ograth, and Ulgrast, son
Molvoz–quadruplet to Drazgen, Garzirith, and Sakur, son
Ograth–quadruplet to Balvon, Kurnoth, and Ulgras, son
Olazaleus–quadruplet to Osior, Othall, and Ozenilorh, son
Osior–quadruplet to Olazaleus, Othall, and Ozenilorh, son
Othall–quadruplet to Olazaleus, Osior, and Ozenilorh, son
Ozenilorh–quadruplet to Olazaleus, Osior, and Othall, son
Sakur–quadruplet to Garzirith, Molvoz, and Drazgen, son
Ulgras–quadruplet to Balvon, Kurnoth, and Ograth, son

Zaleria & Kezrin

Algroth–quadruplet to Arzan, Rizzakin, and Vinnozeth, son
Arzan–quadruplet to Algroth, Rizzakin, and Vinnozeth, son
Dezen–quadruplet to Dolraun, Digmeth, and Dokan, son
Digmeth–quadruplet to Dezen, Dolraun, and Dokan, son
Dokan - quadruplet to Dezen, Digmeth, and Dolraun, son
Dolraun–quadruplet to Dezen, Digmeth, and Dokan, son
Rizzakin–quadruplet to Algroth, Arzan and Vinnozeth, son
Vinnozeth–quadruplet to Algroth, Arzan, and Rizzakin, son

Spells & Potions

Spell name: Alterenim Serpenerous

Who uses the spell: Odulore

What does the spell do: made a dark cloud disappear

Any special effects: amber dust flew from his handing

Spell name: Flarello Viralerous

Who uses the spell: Trodus & Odulore

What does the spell do: creates a spell blocking barrier

Any special effects:

Spell name: Ignitim Serpite

Who uses the spell: Trodus

What does the spell do: Trap someone in an object such as a castle or crypt. This is to be used sparingly. This spell cannot be undone until those trapped die or the caster of the spell dies. There is no exit. There is no visible blockage that can be removed. This is an invisible wall that keeps those inside in and outside out.

You will need to be within 25 feet of the object. It will take effect immediately.

There is no way to dig under the force field either. As they dig down, the force field goes with it. If there is water, it will trap the water way in the trapped zone. At the edge of the force field, it will go to the bottom of the water.

Any special effects:

Spell name: Incenecto Vexenus

Who uses the spell: Odulore

What does the spell do: for all of Parrcaster Island above and below–to lock magic portals

Any special effects:

Spell name: Immolortia Feliatis

Who uses the spell: Odulore

What does the spell do: end your protection to Parrcaster Island above and below–magical guardian spirit

Any special effects:

Spell name: Proticum Banio

Who uses the spell: Odulore

What does the spell do: for all of Parrcaster Island above and below–to strength the magical barrier

Any special effects:

Spell name: Corentus Miserula

Who uses the spell: Ozrig

What does the spell do: dark water spout appeared with evil spirits, demons, witches, warlocks, and wizards pouring out of it and the sky became dark

Any special effects:

Spell name: Purifenis Dragate

Who uses the spell: Odulore

What does the spell do: create a deep gorge

Any special effects: cause the ground to shake and deep gorge will be made to where the coven will now be their own island.

Spell name: Silenenta Serpulus

Who uses the spell: Annamaaz

What does the spell do: Creates a pressure trap of demonic energy.

Any special effects:

Spell name: Levitaeseo Infeceum

Who uses the spell: Annamaaz

What does the spell do: Creates a barrier of demonic energy.

Any special effects:

Spell name: Invocim Intimiducto

Who uses the spell: Annamaaz

What does the spell do: Creates a shock wave of demonic energy from the caster.

Any special effects:

Spell name: Extiulsis Personentus

Who uses the spell: Annamaaz

What does the spell do: induces the pregnant witch to have their child immediately.

Any special effects:

Spell name: Mystifotis Deminius

Who uses the spell: Odulore

What does the spell do: transport the ones the caster says and a location to transport them to

Any special effects:

Spell name: pregnant energy

Who uses the spell: Annamaaz

What does the spell do: makes the witch pregnant with the right amount of evil children

Any special effects:

Spell name: inducing energy

Who uses the spell: Annamaaz

What does the spell do: makes the pregnant witch induced and controls the pain and length of delivery

Any special effects:

Spell name: Morinius Annoenis

Who uses the spell: Odulore

What does the spell do: fight against the evil energy

Any special effects: white energy from the fingers

Potion: Philter of Immobilizing

To brew, gather the following ingredients and follow the steps closely and with great attention to detail.

- 5 teaspoons of Sour Basil
- 3 teaspoons of Mountain Garlic
- 1 sprinkle of Fire Quassia
- 2 heaps of Water Petal
- 4 bits of Dream Parsley

Squeeze the Sour Basil by summoning Puggaald and having him do the work for you and put the result in a cup. Add some ice, let it melt to turn it into a smooth emulsion, then add the Mountain Garlic, a quarter first, then a half and then a third of it.

Fill a pan with unsalted seawater, add the mixture and let it steep while you make friends with the dragons, then come back and bring it to a boil. Let it simmer and steep while you take a power nap before adding the Fire Quassia and Water Petal, a half at a time, alternating between the two.

Bring everything back to a boil, turn off the heat, mix in the Dream Parsley and let everything rest over night.

Stir the mixture a final time, if it sticks you know it's right. Your potion is ready to be used.

Potion - death potion

- 1 teaspoon of Angel Galangal
- 4 tablespoons of Dream Blossom
- 2 heaps of Autumn Leaves
- 1 dash of Cave Oregano
- 6 bits of Devil Curry Leaf

Crunch the Angel Galangal and put the result in a container. Add some ice, let it melt to turn it into a lumpy cream, then add the Dream Blossom, first one tiny amount, then everything else.

Fill a pan with water and kill it, add the mixture and turn up the heat, then turn on the stove and bring the mixture to a boil. Let it steam for a short while before adding the Autumn Leaves and Cave Oregano, a quarter at a time of a mixture of both.

Gently warm the currently disgusting mixture, mix in the Devil Curry Leaf and let everything rest for a few minutes.

Whisk the mixture gently to break up any potential clumps. Your potion is ready to be used.

Map of Kiniriden Sea and islands

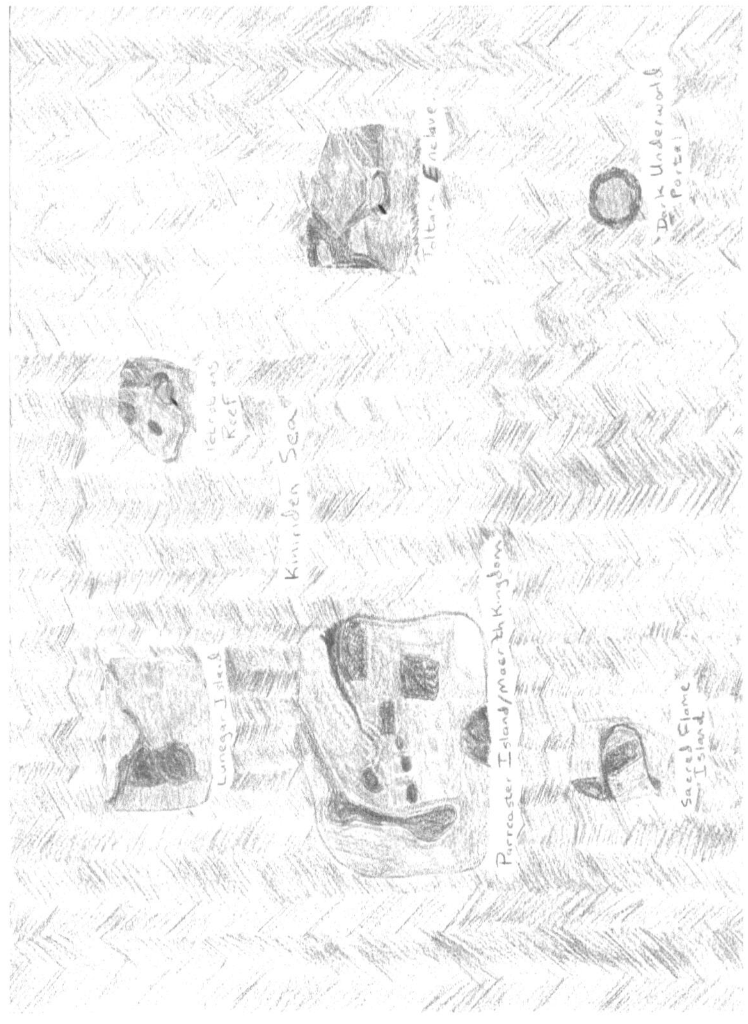

Map of Maerith Kingdom

Map of Parrcaster Island

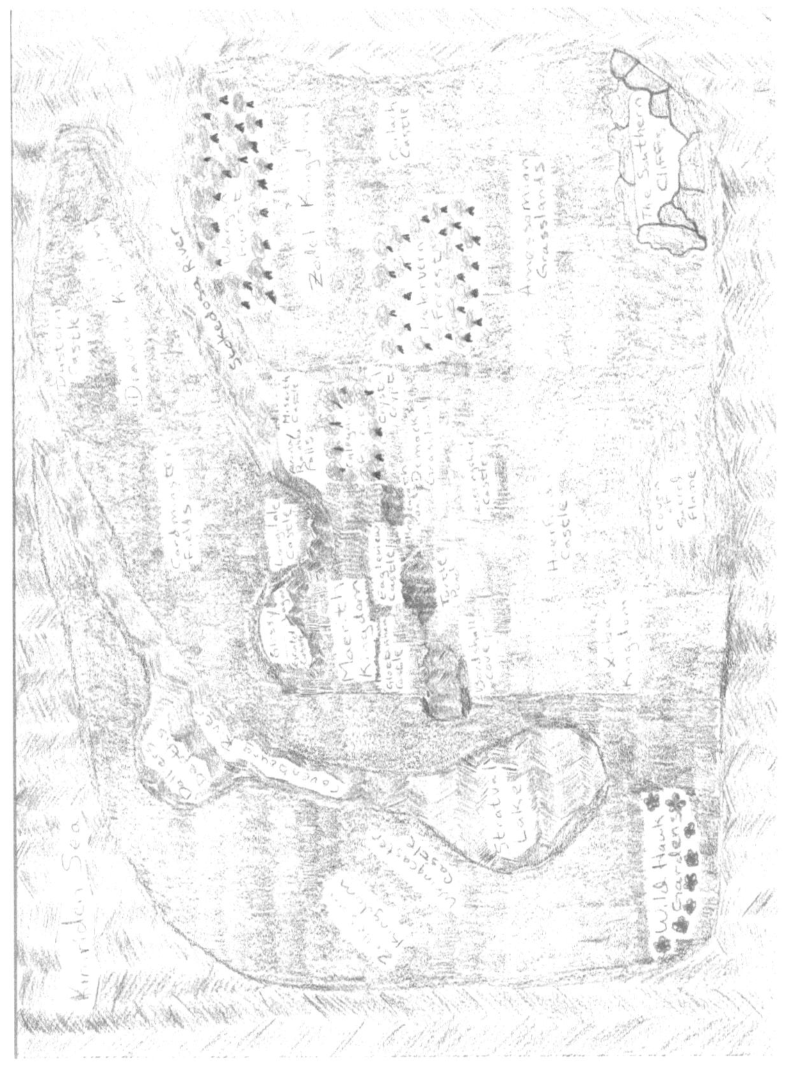

Map of Toltara Enclave

Map of Petrobiens Reef

Map of Sacred Flame Island

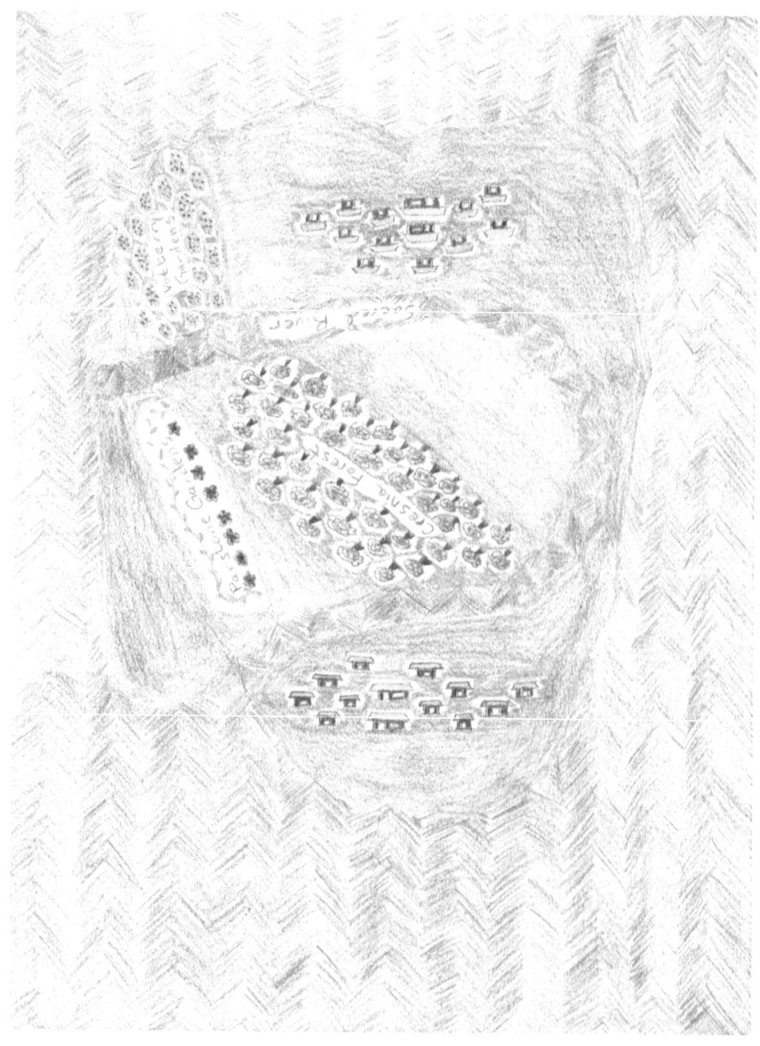

About the Author

Mandy Jo used to read fantasy many moons ago. She came across a writing contest that she only needed to include a barn owl somewhere in the story. At that same time she found the Harry Potter movies on an app and decided to watch them. While watching them Mandy Jo decided to write a fantasy piece for the contest. She started with a goal of 5,000 words and it turned into this novel. Plus, there will be more books coming in this series.

Website - mandyjo.live

Twitter - @mandyjo_author

Facebook - @mandyjoauthor

Instagram - @mandyjo_author

Volley - mandyjo.live/Volley-Writing